# SILENT SENTINELS

## The Sequel to the Mourning Doves

By

## Patricia Huff

authorHOUSE®

AuthorHouse™
1663 Liberty Drive
Bloomington, IN 47403
www.authorhouse.com
Phone: 1 (800) 839-8640

Published by AuthorHouse 01/25/2016

ISBN: 978-1-5049-7127-0 (sc)
ISBN: 978-1-5049-7117-1 (e)

Library of Congress Control Number: 2015921370

Print information available on the last page.

# Acknowledgement

**M**any thanks to my family and friends for their contributions to Silent Sentinels, with special appreciation to:

Joseph P. Hougnon, Jr. for his help with "About the Book," and assistance in meeting the specs for my photograph. Gina Marie Hougnon Schlageter - - photographer, proof reader and computer guru.

Liz Mueller, who read the Silent Sentinels' manuscript and gave me positive feedback. Liz is an inveterate reader; I knew I could trust her judgment.

# Readers Praise The Mourning Doves

**A murder. A kidnapping. A love that time cannot kill. And killers who try again and again to rip the lovers apart forever. This book is enthralling in its emotional aspects, brilliant in its love story, an extremely thrilling mystery. This novel is a whodunit that keeps you guessing until the very end. Great! Highly recommended. The Romance Studio's (5-hearts) review. By: Sarah Sawyer, Director**

To me, The Mourning Doves is a sensitive, informed, tender reflection of relationships between men in combat, children and children, and children and their parents. I worried about Jason's combat experience, his unresolved PTSD (Post Traumatic Stress Disorder), his delayed reaction. His initial interaction with Kathryn is so tender and moving. I also found myself feeling the loss of Ann (Jeffreys) as another tragedy when Jason returned to England after the tragedies he had (already) endured. His combat experience also confirmed my belief that combat, be it air, land, or sea has the same effect on the human beings involved, regardless of which war it is, at any time in human history, or which weapons of destruction are used. "On the eighth day, man created war." Your statement is genius. The Mourning Doves is an intense roller coaster ride throughout. A great story. Have you tried to get it to a screenwriter? It would be a great movie.

Bob Janes, Elk Grove, California

The Mourning Doves is wonderful! I saved the last few chapters for two days, until I couldn't stand it anymore, because I didn't want it to end. And what an ending, I would never have guessed. It's truly one of the best books I've ever read, and I've read a lot of books! I loved it!

Bev Taber, Stockton, CA

The Mourning Doves is what I call real "entertainment," a type of writing that Graham Green used to do when he wrote for pleasure. One of the pleasures of relationships is that it broadens us to pick up on others' characters, mindsets, mental "tones," feelings and emotions. Your characters reflect this. For example: Kathryn's: "I gave up the spiritual dimension of my life to put more energy into material things," expressed as: "I traded Him in for worldly pursuits," seems just right for a person her age. She doesn't realize the all-encompassing nature of the Divine yet. Writing the characters from the inside out makes the work come to life. Also, kudos for the even-handed presentations of Christianity and the Native American Religions.

Travers Huff, Hollywood, CA

I couldn't contain my enthusiasm until I'd finished your wonderful book, to tell you how much I'm enjoying it. At first glance, I thought, "My god, how could this chick have so much to say about one bird species?" The farther I get into it, I'm bound up by the story to the extent that I forget I'm reading a novel and find myself transported to the scene you're describing. This, to me, is the mark of true literary genius.

Bill Lamkin, Modesto, CA

I started The Mourning Doves last Friday. It's now Monday, and I'm on page 503, NOT wanting to get to the last page. I can't wait for your second book.

Sue Kelly, Maui, Hawaii

I am LOVING your novel!!!! Cannot put it down. It may be my excuse for not getting Christmas cards out this year. You paint beautiful pictures in my mind's eye.

Ellie Anderson, Moscow, Idaho

*Now, dear reader, the stage is set.*
*Turn the page to immerse yourself in*
*Trish Huff's latest Romance/*
*Suspense Novel . . .*

## The Silent Sentinels

*Confronted by what was too
horrifying to conceive,
Civilization has agonized for generations,
In private hells of its own design . . .*

*PH*

# Prologue

In the distance, the snow-capped mountains speared sharply into the brilliant blue sky. Puffy white clouds drifted by, momentarily softening the jagged peaks. An army of majestic trees marched up the steep terrain, stopping short of the sheer cliffs between forest and sky. Nearby, pine and incense cedar embraced a stream-fed lake. In the grassy meadows, wild flowers in gay shades of pink, purple, and gold lifted their faces to the sun. The heady fragrance wafted across the valley.

In the camp, the sweet scent warred with the stench of rotting flesh, urine and feces, expelled at the moment of violent death. The final humiliation.

An icy wind slapped the girl's thin sweater and seeped beneath to chill her body. The prisoners, with a few spoonfuls of thin gruel in their shrunken bellies, were bent over the never-ending task of digging mass graves. All too soon, their lifeless bodies would be entombed there.

When the chaos erupted, she was working at the far end of the trench, daydreaming about how it would feel to run barefoot through the sea of grass beyond the razor-sharp fencing, imagining what it would be like to pick a bouquet of the bright flowers.

It took a while for the disquieting hum to penetrate her thoughts. The sound, like that of bees swarming, quickly escalated into frantic screams. She circled around the other prisoners and slipped through the panic-stricken throng.

Colonel Berndt raised the spade and brought it down. Blood spattered his face and jacket and dripped off his sharply creased trousers. Body parts were strewn at his feet, a headless torso lay twitching on the ground.

Her hands flew to cover her eyes. "Monster, evil monster." She fell to her knees and rocked there.

Every shocked eye, prisoners and captors alike, stared at her. When she raised her head, the Major was looming over her, glaring down. He grabbed her by the scruff of her neck and yanked her to her feet.

Pitching the spade aside, the Colonel shrieked, "Shoot her!"

The Major unsnapped the holster at his side and retrieved his Lugar P-08. A contemptuous smile nudged the corners of his mouth, his piercing dark eyes intent upon the commanding officer's face.

"I'll take care of it," he said quietly.

The Colonel stepped back, shying away from the threat stamped on the officer's face. Every soldier in the camp feared the Major. Colonel Berndt was no exception. Headquarters had rejected the Colonel's numerous requests to transfer the Major. But scuttlebutt from Berlin hinted at the Fuehrer's increasing paranoia. Berndt was convinced that the Major was a Gestapo Agent sent by the Fuehrer to spy on him.

The Major grabbed the girl's wrist and dragged her along behind him. She stumbled, lost her balance and pitched forward. The Major ignored her plight, though she was sure he knew the gravel along the path was tearing the flesh on her arm and legs.

It wasn't the first time the Major had defied the camp Commandant. He had interceded on her behalf before. Even so, she thought she might be better off dead than alive. A bullet in the back of her head would put an end to the torture she had endured, for the most part at the hands of the Major.

Even when he scowled, as he was now, she wondered how anyone as brutal as he could be would have such a serenely handsome face. He was tall and lean and strong. His every move spoke to power. Large, luminous dark eyes, reminded her of a fallen angel painting she'd seen at the museum in Warsaw.

When the Major struck a match to light his cigarette, fear constricted her chest. She drew a ragged breath and held it, willing herself not to whimper or cry out. When the others screamed and begged for mercy, the Major had forced her to watch as he slaughtered them. If she closed her eyes or turned her head, he threatened her with the same fate. Over time, six young women had died. She hadn't known why they were expendable and she was not, until the Major said the women were gifts for her, to prove how much he cared.

She grasped the edges of the operating table, trying to get beyond herself, to spin her mind away from what he would do to her. She closed her eyes to shut out the madness that was consuming his face. He took great care in burning her, carefully aiming the light, studying, sometimes for many minutes, before he took a drag on the cigarette and flicked the ashes to the floor.

*Part One*

# Chapter One

*Summer, 1961*
*Phoenix, Arizona*

Jason Borseau, co-owner and CEO of KSOL-TV, slid a stack of documents to one side and flipped the switch on the intercom.

"Yes, Mr. Borseau," his secretary, Mary Robards, responded.

"Please give Tom Dixon a call. Tell him I'm ready to discuss the contracts he wanted me to review. See if seven-thirty Friday morning is acceptable. We'll have to meet in the legal department's conference room. Casey has reserved ours," he added, referring to his partner, Casey Matson.

"I'll check with Mr. Dixon right away."

"If that isn't convenient, ask him what will work for him, and let me know."

"Yes, sir."

The late afternoon sun slanted through the shutters behind his desk and scudded across the pale gray carpet. Jason leaned back in his plush leather chair, mentally checking off the tasks he'd set for himself that morning. He thought another hour should do it. Wonder of wonders, he might get home before dark.

Following a faint knock on the door, Christian Grayson opened it a crack, and peered in. "Hi, boss, can you spare a few minutes?"

"Of course, come in," Jason responded.

Christian paused to admire the flowers in cut-crystal vases—a potpourri of pink rosebuds, lilacs, and bridal wreath, noting the way they gave substance to the glass-topped tables. "Nice," he said, smiling at his boss.

"They're Kathyn's contribution to 'my sterile office'." Jason pointed to a chair in front of his desk.

Christian crossed the room and sank into a butter-soft leather chair. "How is the family?"

"Couldn't be better," Jason responded. "How about seeing for yourself? Have lunch with us this weekend." Jason flipped the pages of his calendar. "Make that next weekend."

"With bells on."

"Great, we'll expect you at eleven or so." Jason circled his desk, eased a hip on one corner, and leaned toward KSOL's investigative reporter. "What's up?"

Christian settled deeper into the down-filled chair. "The City Council assignment."

Jason grinned. "Sorry to have saddled you with that, but summer vacations put us in a bind. I know how you feel though. I did time in that ho-hum arena. Just keep in mind that it's temporary."

"Ho hum? Maybe not." Christian frowned. "The City has rules and regs above and beyond those of private enterprise. Right?"

"All public agencies do. Coffee?"

"Sure." Christian rose and followed Jason to the bar.

"Aside from the fact that I'm always glad to see you, I needed a break." Jason's hands swept across his black hair threaded with silver. The salt and pepper effect added a distinguished quality to his movie-star good looks, enhancing the strong angles and planes of his face. In addition to his sculpted features, Jason had a charismatic grin, sky blue eyes, and a trim, six-foot-three frame.

"I've spent the entire day analyzing one proposed contract. Anyone with an ounce of brains could've reduced the language to ten pages, max." He nodded at the documents on his desk. "We used to finalize agreements with a handshake. Now, it's all about covering the station's ass to avoid lawsuits. Have you noticed how the folks in our legal department look like they're sucking lemons."

Christian laughed. "Now that you mention it."

"Black, right?"

"Yes, thanks."

Jason handed the mug to his ace reporter, then stirred a generous dollop of cream into his coffee.

After settling himself in the chair again, Christian said, "Jace, I have questions about how the City does business."

"What kind of business and with whom?"

"Business in general. You know?"

"No, Christian, I don't know. I just hope this is idle curiosity."

Christian shrugged. "Pretty much."

Jason returned to his perch on the desk and sipped his coffee. "Pretty much?"

"Oh, you know how it is: When I get an itch I have to scratch it."

Jason's brows drew together. "What bit you this time?"

"Damned if I know, boss, it's a gut feeling."

"We're talking about the Phoenix hierarchy, so you need to be more explicit."

"If I knew what is bugging me, I'd tell you. I just want to nose around a little."

Several thoughts ran through Jason's mind as he studied this young, handsome Negro from Georgia. To get a college education and to compete in a white world, especially in the South, must have taken unbelievable commitment and perseverance. Jason admired Christian, his intelligence, his honesty and integrity. Unlike some of his colleagues, envy didn't play a part in Christian's character. As such, he'd earned the fellowship and respect of his peers—a singular feat in the broadcasting business, where narcissistic egos were the rule rather than the exception. Job-wise, Christian was like a hunter tracking his quarry. He burrowed beneath the surface of every story, instinctively separating fact from fiction—a talent that often eluded other reporters.

"You'd like me to leave it alone."

"No, I just don't want you stirring up a hornet's nest needlessly. I'll give you the go-ahead on one condition: You *will* tiptoe ever so lightly through the City's hallowed halls. Do *not* stir up the powers-that-be, unless it's absolutely necessary. With your reputation, if you show up asking questions, even if they're as innocent as newborn babes, the staff will sweat bullets, to say nothing of the angst you'll create among the politicians. When I asked you to cover the Council meetings, I wondered if the City fathers would begin looking over their shoulders."

"It boggles my mind to think I'm that intimidating."

"Christian, think about it. You were awarded the Pulitzer for exposing an arm of Carlo Gambino's crime syndicate. If it weren't for you, the mob would have taken over the electronics industry here. You're a celebrity, KSOL's super sleuth. However, in this instance, there's a down-side: your reputation precedes you."

Christian laughed. "Thanks for the compliment. I think."

Jason took a swallow of coffee and set the mug beside the files on his desk. "Anything else?"

"The Ladies of the Night Murders."

"Okay." Jason drew out the word.

"The cops are nowhere with the investigation. Five young women are dead, alleged prostitutes, all minorities so far—Mexicans, Negroes, Orientals. Last weekend another girl went missing, a white girl, according to the intel I've picked up on the street. Maybe she left the City of her own volition. Maybe not. If I'm lucky, my main snitch may've seen or heard something. It'll take a few bucks to grease her palm, but I'd like to give it a shot."

"The Chief's been quoted as saying 'there isn't a shred of physical evidence.' Surely he knows more than he's releasing to the media," Jason said, referring to Police Chief, Morton Salinger. He rose and circled his desk. "How long will you be in the field?"

"I'm not sure, a few days, more or less. I'll keep in touch."

"Every day."

"Like I always do." Christian set the mug on the bar.

"Okay, go get the bad guys. Christian, take care of yourself."

"Count on it, boss."

**C**hristian bolted into the elevator, nearly colliding with Jason's partner.

Casey Matson braced himself. "Whoa, big fella!"

"Jeeze, I'm sorry." Christian stepped aside to let him pass.

A grin split Casey's angular features. "You look like a man with a mission."

Christian nodded. "How about you? I hear you're running for the State Assembly."

"You heard right."

"Great. See y'a," Christian said as the door slid shut. When it opened, he hurried along the hallway to the accounting department. He glanced around, looking for KSOL's controller, Caroline Adams Keene. At last, by standing on tiptoe, he spotted her next to a filing cabinet that was taller than she was.

"Hi, Caroline. How about a cash advance?"

As she tipped her head from side to side, Caroline's blonde, corkscrew curls danced. "How much? A million, two?"

"A hundred should do it."

"And, *it* would be?"

"I may have to grease my snitch's palm."

"For a hundred bucks, you can grease both of my palms, the soles of my feet—"

"Caroline!" he said, prancing like a horse at the starting gate.

Chuckling at Christian's impatience, Caroline unlocked the petty cash drawer, grabbed two fifty-dollar-bills, and handed them to him. "Go, I'll sign the slip."

"Thanks, pal." He tucked the bills into the front pocket of his jeans and took off.

"A whirlwind just swept through my office," Caroline muttered to herself.

# *Chapter Two*

As he vaulted the concrete steps, Christian wondered why government buildings seemed to have so many steps. Maybe to elevate what Jason called "the powers-that-be" above the masses.

On the fly, Christian waved at Marcie Fairfield, the Arizona State University student that worked part-time at the City's information desk.

"No you don't, TV-man." Marcie wagged a finger at him. "You have to sign in like everyone else."

"Puleeze do it for me, Marcie." Running backwards to the elevator, he said, "I'll help you with your next speech."

Marcie flipped her long, blonde hair over her shoulders. "Okay, Christian, it's a deal. Wait, where are you going?"

"The City Manager's office."

"Paul Hewitt isn't in today," Marcie shouted at Christian's still moving figure.

"It's his secretary I need to see."

"Okay, but don't forget—"

Christian burst through the door into the City Manager's office. He smiled at Paul Hewitt's secretary. "Hi, Helen."

Helen Burgess glanced at the clock and back at Christian with a look that dared him to ask for anything at this hour. "What do you want?"

Christian grinned. "I'm sorry to bother you so late in the day." He drew a deep breath and closed the door. "I'll appreciate it, if you'll copy some agendas for me."

Helen grabbed a pencil and pulled a pad of forms from the top drawer of her desk. "Which ones?"

Christian shrugged an apology. "All of them, for the past year."

The pencil went airborne. "Do you know how much that will cost?"

The grin on Christian's face widened. He reached into his pocket and pulled out a fifty-dollar bill. "This should cover it. Oh, don't bother with the agendas for July or the first two meetings in August."

"Christian, Mr. Hewitt isn't in today, and I can't do this without his authorization."

"Actually, the agendas are a matter of public record. I guess I could call the station's legal eagles."

Helen pushed her thick, horn-rimmed glasses up on the bridge of her nose. "Never mind, but it'll take a lot of time. Why don't you pick them up on Thursday or Friday?"

"If you don't mind, I'd rather wait."

Helen began to fidget, eyes darting to the door.

Christian's smile froze. Jason was right. Hewitt's secretary looked as if she wanted to make break for it. "It's just research, Helen. I didn't mean to upset you."

She glowered at him. "I'm not upset." Rising from her chair, she hurried to the file cabinet behind her desk.

"My mistake," Christian said, as the hair on the back of his neck bristled.

# Chapter Three

Christian pushed away from his desk. Rising, he massaged his temples as he wandered aimlessly around his apartment. He paused to straighten the photo of his parents, recalling how he'd had to browbeat them into having it taken.

"Yes, Helen, you *were* upset, but why? What am I missing?" he muttered as he strode to the kitchen to pour another cup of coffee—sludge, his mind amended as he grimaced at what looked like mud and set the cup aside. He opened the refrigerator, snagged a bottle of Chardonnay, popped the cork, and made his way to the hutch in the dining room. He grabbed a crystal goblet and tipped it back and forth to let the light from the chandelier lance through its diamond-cut facets.

His best friend, Jaclyn Devereaux, had given him a six-piece set for his twenty-third birthday, now more than four years ago. Being a recluse, Christian hadn't used all of them, at least not at one time. Pouring as he walked, he smiled, recalling the first time they'd shared a bottle of wine at his place, a pricey *Chenin Blanc*. The label had hooked him. "A light, dry vintage with a delicate bouquet, and a subtle, piquant spirit to tantalize the most discriminating palette."

Who could pass that up? Without hesitating, he'd forked over the big bucks.

So much for impressing Jaclyn. "You can't be serious." She'd slanted a glance at him through eyes the color of aged whiskey. "It's profane to drink fine wine from a plastic glass. The *Vino* gods will punish us."

For whatever reason, the ornate packaging did seem to enhance the flavor, the ambiance as well. Aside from being elegant, and he felt sure, expensive, he valued the gift, because it was from Jaclyn. And Christian valued Jaclyn.

If it weren't so late, or so early, depending on one's point of view—three, in the am—he'd call her, invite her to join him. As tempted as he was to pick up the phone, it would be unkind to awaken her at this hour. Jaclyn was an investigator for State Attorney General, Alan Sheffield. Her days were often longer and more arduous than Christian's, and he seldom worked eight to five.

Christian had met Jaclyn poolside five years ago. Both had been new to the City, to Shady Creek Apartments, as well. She'd taken the chaise lounge next to his. After watching her wrestle with the cap on her suntan lotion, he'd offered to help. Once he'd popped the top, they'd chatted, and discovered they had something in common—their jobs. It had marked the beginning of a friendship that had flourished.

He'd known Jaclyn for three years before she told him scattered bits and pieces about her tragic past. She had survived the Holocaust in Europe. She had never talked about what she'd endured, only about the atrocities that had befallen other prisoners. As if she had been an observer. Christian felt sure there had been *no observers*, but he'd never questioned her.

In September, Jaclyn would celebrate her thirtieth birthday. It had become a tradition for them to spend their birthdays together. He'd take her to The Flame, a popular downtown restaurant, or the swanky Green Gables Inn. Her choice.

His brows drew as he thought about their outings. Whenever they entered a public place, Jaclyn always held back to scan the crowd. At first, he'd wondered if she felt uncomfortable being with him. Although the color of his skin was like coffee heavily laced with cream, he was nonetheless a Negro in a white world. However, bias wasn't in sync with Jaclyn's character, and Christian had mentally kicked himself for harboring that traitorous thought, no matter how fleeting it had been. Nor did he think it was due to her training as a cop. Maybe Jaclyn was looking for someone, but he didn't think so. Her expression was one of anxiety, not expectation. No, Jaclyn was on the lookout for someone. Maybe one day she'd tell him who she was afraid of, and why.

Christian sauntered into the living room, opened the drapes, and peered down at the flagstone patio, four floors below. He'd needed a break.

It had surprised him to see how many construction projects the City had authorized over the past year. Still, it made sense considering the rate at which Phoenix was growing—purportedly, a thousand new residents a month, with businesses springing up to provide services to the growing multitude.

As the first icy sip of wine slid down his throat, Christian sighed with pleasure. Back at his desk, he took another sip, then set the fragile stem to one side. Frowning at the typewritten pages, he picked up the top page for a closer look at the items he'd highlighted. If there were inconsistencies in the way the City was doing business, he hadn't spotted them. He qualified that thought with, *not yet*. Putting half a dozen pages side by side, he let his gaze move back and forth across them. The pulse in his throat began to jitter.

Grinning, Christian slammed his fist into the air. "Gotcha."

# Chapter Four

## Wednesday Morning

Christian glanced around, mentally focused on what he'd need. His tape recorder. He took it from the top drawer of his desk and slipped it, along with a couple of extra tapes, into his briefcase. As he drove from one place to another, it had become a habit for him to document information, his perceptions as well. He started for the door, then detoured to the bedroom, and stood in front of the full-length mirror. Where he was going, anything short of the tackiest garb would set off an alarm. The tom-toms would start beating. Only those seemingly forsaken by God and man could hear them—the miscreants living in the derelict buildings along a three-block strip, or those prowling the streets and alleys on the Westside. Within seconds, they'd scurry like rabbits into their holes.

As far as the City was concerned, he'd mark time until he could talk to Jason. His boss was tied up this weekend. Monday would be soon enough.

Christian added sunglasses and a bedraggled hat and pulled the narrow brim down to hide his forehead and brows. The two-day growth of beard would have to do. He wore faded blue jeans shredded at the knees and a short-sleeved

T-shirt, yellow with age. He'd bypassed the shower, knowing if anyone got a whiff of soap, he'd be made in a second. His scruffy brown boots were expensive when new. Where he was headed, there were those who'd kill for them. If things got dicey, he'd have to rely on the knife he'd tucked into the makeshift leather sheath inside his left boot. He'd spent hours practicing. If trouble arose, he felt confident he could have it in his hand in a second. Still, if his fears became reality, he wasn't sure what he'd do. He wouldn't like taking a knife to a gunfight.

He got into the elevator, smiling to himself when the man and woman already in the car backed away and huddled in a corner, clearly putting as much distance between themselves and this seedy-looking character as they could. He was ready for the mean streets.

Christian maneuvered his dark blue, two-door sedan into a horizontal parking space. He checked the time, six-twenty, then locked his watch and class ring in the glove compartment, his briefcase in the trunk.

He'd hoof it the last half-mile—head lolling, shambling along, humming tunelessly, or mumbling to himself. He'd spent considerable time studying the lost souls lurking in the shadows of the sordid world he was invading.

Even at this early hour, heat shimmered up from the streets and sidewalks. As the distance melted away, the stink of ripe garbage, vomit and sweat, the cloying stench of adulterated sex, emanated from the bowels of this hellhole, an eternity away from the posh neighborhoods and lofty lifestyles in Scottsdale and upscale Phoenix.

Christian staggered to a graffiti-emblazoned wall and leaned his back against it. Without moving his head, his gaze swept the street, searching for the face he knew. A few feet away, music, if one could call hard rock music, blasted like a rocket through the open barroom door. Heavy on the bass, the sound launched itself like a physical assault against him.

Promising nude dancers, massage parlors, and every tactile sensation known to humanity, red and blue neon lights flashed on and off, day and night, on this alien planet where no one seemed to sleep.

And yet, lined up on a second floor balcony, fluorescent colored pots held plants that had dared the odds and won. Not only were they surviving, they were thriving. The vivid array of blossoms, bright yellow to intense shades of red, peeped above the rims. It touched him to know that someone cared enough to bring a modicum of civility to his or her bleak existence.

Near the end of the block, an abandoned fire station listed precariously to one side. Boards in a crosshatched fashion had been nailed over the doors and windows. In the barren field beside it, an ethnic mix of children played kick the can. There were plenty of those lying around, Christian mused. Some of the kids looked barely school age, a handful of others a bit older. Their carefree laughter seemed as implausible to Christian as the cheerful pots of flowers. He thought about the ghetto where he'd spent most of his childhood and decided it had been Shangri-La compared to this.

Directly across the street, a group of young men, late teens or early twenties, circled one another. Knives, known on the street as pig stickers, glinted in the light. The air sizzled with a steady stream of the foulest language Christian had ever heard at one time, although he'd heard it all. The conflict, possibly drug or gang-related, would let blood, he felt sure.

With the exception of the impending brouhaha, the barrio was quiet this morning. Too quiet. He wondered if something he couldn't envision was about to go down? He studied everyone within his line of sight. They seemed to fit—the locals going about the business of surviving, sifting through garbage bins, probing the gutters, looking for anything that might make their lives, if only for the moment, bearable. A cigarette butt was a major find, a treasure. Sadly, Christian realized, they had become so inured to trouble, the impending knife fight didn't merit a glance.

Behind every face lay a tragic story, and Christian never forgot it for a moment.

He spotted her at the same moment she saw him. Chantelle. At least that's what she called herself. A leggy, light-skinned Negro, nearly six feet tall. The Afro hairdo added several more inches. Her full mouth, slicked with dark purple lipstick, curved in a seductive smile. As she strolled up to him, slender hips swaying from side to side, calculating eyes, black as coal, lingering on his face a moment, then sweeping down his body. Her tongue slid over her upper lip as she focused on his manhood.

"Uh, huh," she said, grinning. "What's up?"

"Lookin' for you," Christian responded.

A sensuous smile arched over her even white teeth. She rubbed her index and middle fingers with her thumb. "Twenty bucks'd give you the ride of your life, lover." She cocked her head, glanced down again. "I'd even throw in a—"

"Cut the crap, Chanty. I'm here on business," Christian said to cut her off before he could imagine what she might "throw in." He waved a twenty under her nose and jerked his head toward the alley. When she reached for it, he drew it away, took her elbow, pressed her around the corner, and nudged her along, until they dead-ended at the backdoor of a ramshackle building.

"How come you never want to get it on with Chantelle, baby?"

"This is business. Now get your mind off *my* business, and tell me if you knew any of the murdered women."

Chantelle lifted the silver chain around her slender neck, freeing the cross held captive by her abundant cleavage. Christian averted his eyes from the narrow strips of purple satin struggling to confine her jutting nipples. With a sidelong glance, she slipped the crucifix into her mouth, slurped noisily as she sucked it. "I knew 'em, a couple of 'em real well."

"I need names, Chanty," Christian said.

Shrugging, she let the crucifix fall from her fingers. "Only know what they called theirselves, like my real name ain't Chantelle. Bet you didn't know that."

"Keep talking." She began rattling off names. Christian snatched the tiny notebook and stub of a pencil from his back pocket and started scribbling. Sunshine and Desiree, Cactus Flower and Angel Eyes, Precious and Moonglow. How hopeless could it get? He finished jotting down the names. "Did you identify the bodies?"

"No, but I heard there wasn't much left. Word is, the cops figure they was killed in the same order they went missing."

"Five bodies have been found, another girl is missing. Who was the last to disappear?"

"Moonglow, a white girl. 'Guess they ain't found her yet."

"Any idea where these girls were from?"

"Get real. If you end up here, you ain't gonna tell nobody where you're from. Take Precious. Her old man'd been doing her since she was five. Think she wanted to get found?"

"No, I'm sure she didn't," Christian said softly as he tucked the twenty beneath the waistband of Chantelle's crimson mini skirt. "Did they walk the same beat as you?"

"Some of the time, not all."

"Weren't you upset when they set up shop in your territory?"

"Nah, they was just kids, hardly had tits, runaways mostly. Come on, they had nothin' like these sweet jugs of mine," she said, thrusting her ample breasts to within a breath of his chest.

"Nooo competition." Christian smothered a smile. "Who took 'em, Chanty? Who did those horrible things to them? Six girls don't disappear without someone seeing or hearing something. What's the word on the street?"

"Only that one of them block-long Caddies was seen cruising the neighborhood before a couple of 'em vanished."

Christian's brows drew. "A limo?"

"A shiny black one, with them windows you can't see through. Anyways, that's what I heard." She jangled the silver bracelets on her wrists. "'Don't know nothin' first hand, and don't want to."

He knew it was too much to expect, but gave it a shot anyway. "Did anyone get a license number?"

She threw back her head and laughed. "You're kidding, right?" Serious again, she said, "The rest of us are scared shitless. I mean, them girls got picked off one by one, four weeks apart, as if whoever done it was on some kind'a schedule."

"That's perceptive of you, Chanty."

"Whatever that means," she said. "You sure use big words, Chris. I like a man who uses big words. Sure I can't interest you in some of the local merchandise?"

"Sorry." He tucked another ten next to the twenty. "Thanks for your help, and be careful. I wouldn't like it if anything bad happened to you."

With a shy smile, she said, "You take care, too, hon."

He gave her a quick hug and walked away. "Later," he called back over his shoulder.

When he hit the main drag, Christian heard the sirens an instant before he spotted the body sprawled face up on the sidewalk, a predictable end to the fracas he'd seen earlier. He glanced around. There wasn't another soul in sight. The locals had vanished. The last place he wanted to be was at the scene of a murder when the cops arrived, and the sirens were getting louder by the second.

Abandoning his previous act, Christian raced around the corner, increased his speed on the straightaway, and ran full bore until he was several blocks away.

Concern for Chantelle nagged at him. He should've gone back for her. After mulling it over, he decided she'd stay where she was or find a hidey-hole. Christian had no idea how old she was, twenty-five maybe. She'd survived this long without his help, without anyone's help, he surmised.

# Chapter Five

Christian sidestepped into a café a few feet from his car. He slid into a booth next to the windows, the uneasy feeling continued to haunt him.

The middle-aged waitress with bright red hair sauntered over. After giving him the once over, she said, "What can I get'cha?"

"The coldest beer in the house, any brand, a cheeseburger with everything on it, and fries."

"Can you pay for it?"

"Yeah, I can pay." Christian took off his hat and sunglasses, reached into the front pocket of his jeans, and held up the last twenty he'd brought with him.

"Sorry, we get a lot of deadbeats in here."

"Washing dishes in exchange for food is a scenario I've managed to avoid."

"Scenario, huh?"

He nodded. "Yeah, you know, scenario, situation." She gave him a blank stare. "Terri," he said lifting her name from the tag pinned to her stiffly starched, apple green uniform, "my throat's dry as dust, so about that beer—"

"Sure, no problem." She hurried away, figuring she'd blown any chance for a tip.

Christian donned his sunglasses and turned to the window. It was after eight. Potential customers or folks on their way to work hurried by. He studied their faces for the few seconds it took their legs to propel them past the café.

"Burger'll be up in a minute," the waitress said as she set the frosty Pabst in front of him.

"Thanks." He tipped the bottle, started to take a swig, then set it down. Two men, one tall, one short, Mutt and Jeff personified, white, late thirties, or early forties, scanned the area, moved on, and came back. Christian grabbed the menu, and held it so that only his eyes and hat were exposed.

"Mutt" flattened his nose against the glass, peered through the window. He returned to his partner and hooked a thumb toward the café. Who the devil were they? If they were looking for him, they were doing it so blatantly he figured they weren't all that bright. Even so, the problem was how to get to his car? They probably had a ride nearby. Christian turned his back to the window, tipped his beer, and drank deeply.

"Here y'a go." The waitress set his burger down and slid the ketchup and mustard to him. "Anything else?"

"Yeah, let me pay you now." He handed her the twenty. "Assuming there's a back door, I'd like to leave that way."

She cocked her head. "You in some kind'a trouble?"

"See those men making love to the lamp post?"

"Yeah," she said, chuckling.

"I think they're following me, and I'd like to avoid a confrontation with them."

"Confrontation, huh?"

Laughing, Christian said, "A fight, if that's what they have in mind. Have you seen them before?"

"Huh, uh, not that I recall." She glanced at them again. "But, hey, it's okay if you go through the kitchen and out the back way. I'll get your change."

"No, keep it."

"Well, thanks. I thought sure you were gonna stiff me."

"Stiff you, huh?"

"You know—"

Smiling, Christian's tawny eyes twinkled. "Yeah, I know, and thanks, Terri."

She grinned. "Any time."

Christian took his time eating the cheeseburger and fries. When he finished the beer, he signaled the waitress. She hurried over. "I need another favor."

"Name it."

"I'm going to leave my hat on the table. If you'll point to the restrooms, I'll head that way, then duck into the kitchen. I'm hoping my *friends* will think I'm coming back."

She swiveled around and aimed her finger at the hallway.

"I owe you." Christian rose slowly, and took his time angling around the counter. Once he knew the two men couldn't see him, he dashed through the swinging doors into the kitchen, shot past the surprised cook, and out the backdoor. In the alley, he skirted around the garbage bins to within a foot of the sidewalk, and peered around the corner.

It was like watching a Keystone Kop movie. The men's noses were pressed against the café window. They drew back in surprise, looked at one another, arms akimbo, when they didn't see Christian. Then, they almost knocked one another down, trying to get through the door. It would have been hilarious, if Christian hadn't been the one they were targeting.

He had a feeling that Terri would stall them as long as she could. He raced to his car, hunkered down, unlocked the door, and crawled inside. He kept his head down, started the car, and whipped the wheel sharply to the left before he sat up and checked the traffic behind him. He gunned the engine, barely missing the rear fender of the car in front of his. Speeding to the corner, he hooked a left, turned right at the next light, and took another left two blocks down. Christian kept an eye on the rear and side-view mirrors until he was certain he wasn't being followed.

He reached into the glove box, grabbed his tape recorder, and pressed the button. "My snitch, Chantelle, said a limo was spotted before a couple of the girls, early to mid-teens, vanished." He described the two men he thought were after him. "I didn't spot them in the ghetto. Several possibilities—they weren't there, they were well hidden, or they followed me from Scottsdale." Mulling it over, he said, "I may be overreacting. My instincts've failed me a few times." Christian's fingers tightened around the steering wheel.

"In my opinion, something is going on with the City. Several high dollar construction projects were sublimated to the consent calendar. That means the agenda item simply got a pass from the Council, with little or no discussion, and limited backup. I don't know if that's a big deal or not."

Then it occurred to him that he'd recorded the information as though someone else would be listening to it.

"Stay on track," he muttered, even as he knew where he could stash the tape to keep it safe.

Tomorrow, he'd hit the *Arizona Republic's* morgue, comb through the newspaper articles about the murders. The reports had been sketchy. He drew on what he'd read at the time—hikers and spelunkers had discovered the bodies miles apart in the desert. The girls were kidnapped a month apart, Chantelle said, "as if the killer was on some kinda schedule." If she was right, it might be possible to predict when the killer would strike again.

# Chapter Six

## Late Friday Morning

Alan Sheffield gazed at South Mountain in the distance, before turning his attention to the busy streets and sidewalks ten floors below. He couldn't distinguish one person from another, but he'd made a commitment to protect and serve them. As the Attorney General for the State of Arizona, Sheffield took his job very seriously.

He'd never dreamed this was where he'd end up. After several years as the district attorney for Yuma County, Sheffield had become a special agent for the FBI. Subsequently, he'd solved the kidnapping of Jason Borseau's son. The story had hit the headlines in every major newspaper in the country. Naïvely, Sheffield had assumed that the furor would die down. Actually, it was just the beginning. Avariciously seeking a hero, the ravenous eyes of the media zoomed in on him and stayed there. The reporters kept Sheffield in sharp focus until the voters elected him by an overwhelming majority to the State's highest law enforcement office.

The reporters loved Sheffield. They were always looking for a good quote, and he never disappointed them. His blunt appraisal of any situation contrasted sharply with the hackneyed politicians who said what they wanted their constituents to hear, or what their constituents wanted to hear. An *Arizona Republic* reporter wrote, "With Alan Sheffield, what you see is what you get. Refreshing, ain't it?"

Using the former attorney general as a benchmark, Sheffield didn't fit the part. Cameron Malone had been a sixty-year-old, obsequious politician. Several years shy of fifty, Sheffield came across as a much younger man. He was tall and lean, with strong features, and an enigmatic smile. Blonde hair swept boyishly across his forehead, his eyes a hard-bitten emerald green. Years before, Jason Borseau had likened his friend to "a fair-haired Sioux warrior, only the war paint is missing."

Originally from Chicago, Sheffield, the only child of middle-class parents, had graduated from Harvard Law School. It was by virtue of a scholarship that he could afford to go there. After passing the Bar, he'd marked time as an assistant district attorney in the Windy City. In the late 1940's, he'd moved to Yuma, where he'd met Jason Borseau. Over time, they had become close friends. Jason's second wife, nee Kathryn Whittaker, had appeared on the scene in 1952.

Sheffield moved away from the windows, stood behind his desk, and eyed the stack of proposed legislation as he did so. The AG's comments were due next week. Sheffield didn't believe a new law should be enacted, unless two laws already on the books were repealed. He likened government to a ship careening dangerously close to a shallow reef, with political expediency and self-interest at the helm.

"Come in," he said in response to the rap on his office door.

"Why can't I get you on the intercom?" his secretary Moira Fleming said in a scolding voice.

"I turned it off."

"You should have told me," she fumed.

"Moira," Sheffield said softly, "just tell me what you want."

"Kathryn Borseau is here," she sniffed. "I told her she'd have to make an appointment, but she insisted on waiting."

"Great, send her in."

Marshaling her short, ample frame, Moira stomped out.

Sheffield's brows lifted. Moira had been bossing Attorney Generals around for twenty-odd-years. One of these days he'd have to tell her who was really in charge.

Kathryn glanced over her shoulder as she stepped into Sheffield's office. Her fingers flicked the ruffled collar on the sheer cerise blouse beneath a white silk shantung suit.

Years ago, Sheffield had decided Kathryn was the only truly beautiful woman he'd ever seen. Immense gray eyes dominated her features. Cherubic lips and an upturned nose gave her an impish look. Today, she'd drawn her curly, honey-colored hair into a chignon at the nape of her neck.

"Alan, I've upset your secretary. I apologized, but for a second, I thought she was going to smack me."

"Scary, huh?" Sheffield planted a kiss on Kathryn's cheek. "I'm delighted to see you."

"It's been far too long. I've missed you." She roamed around his office, pausing to straighten a frame above the credenza, studying Sheffield's law degree. "I like your office better than Jason's. Glass and chrome are so cold and impersonal."

"Yeah?" Sheffield glanced around. It was a comfortable room, with mahogany furniture, brown leather sofas, well past broken-in, and oriental rugs, threadbare enough to appear authentic. The AG's offices were located at Central Avenue and Van Buren Street.

"Moira hung my credentials. Otherwise, this is what my predecessor left behind."

Kathryn settled into one of the four sumptuous chairs in front of his desk. Sheffield sat beside her and leaned toward her. "Did you just drop by to chat with an old friend?"

"As glad as I am to see you, I'm here because I'm worried about Jason. I think he's up to something, maybe in cahoots with you."

Sheffield made a moue. "Why would you think that?" Seeing the expression on her face, he laughed. "Okay, make that: why do you think he's up to something?"

"Because, for the past several days, he's closeted himself in the library, and paced for hours. When I ask him what's wrong, he says, 'It's nothing for you to worry your pretty head about.'"

"Maybe he doesn't want to upset you in your delicate condition. You are with child, aren't you?"

"How can you tell? I'm only two months along."

"Pregnancy agrees with you, your skin takes on a special glow."

"Imagine that." Smiling, Kathryn patted her cheeks. "Alan and Jason, my *Hardy Boys*. But please, if you know what's bothering him, tell me."

"Something has him by the throat." Sheffield frowned. "He dropped by this morning, demanding to know—as only Jace can demand—if my office is working with the Phoenix Police on The Ladies of the Night Murders. I should have told him straight out that we weren't. But, he was so obnoxious about it, I razzle-dazzled him about conflict of interest just to jerk his chain, and—"

"He blew up."

"Did he ever. He called me a blankety-blank bureaucrat and stormed out of here. I called his office, but his secretary said he was in a meeting. He hasn't gotten back to me."

Kathryn sighed. "Alan, could you have dinner with us tonight? You're welcome to bring Sandra, referring to Sandra Parker, who worked at KSOL-TV, and dated Sheffield. "I think you're the only person who can find out what's going on."

Sheffield checked his calendar. "I'm free as a bird. I'll talk to Sandra and get back to you." He glanced at his watch. "Hey, what are you doing for lunch?"

"'Joining you, I hope. I know, let's go to The Flame."

"Great, give me a minute, and I'll have my car brought around."

"But it's an easy walk from here, four or five blocks."

Sheffield grabbed his suit jacket and shrugged into it. "Kathryn, I hate anything that smacks of exercise." He grinned. "So, after all these years, you still think of Jace and me as the *Hardy Boys*."

"Boys, in any case. Neither of you will ever grow up," she said, laughing. "Uh, Alan, is there a back door or do we have to face Moira?"

"Wouldn't she have made a great drill sergeant?" Sheffield squirreled his mouth to one side. "She's a super secretary. And she's been here so long, she knows where all the bodies are buried."

Kathryn rolled her eyes. "Big surprise there. Who do you think buried 'em?"

"I hadn't thought of that. Okay, heads up, shoulders back, eyes straight ahead. Ready, set, go." He opened the door to the outer office. "I'll be back at two," he said, as they marched past Moira's desk.

# Chapter Seven

## Friday Afternoon

Jason didn't know where to turn next. After Christian's phone call Wednesday morning, Jason had called his reporter's number dozens of times and gotten no answer. This morning, on his way to the station, he'd driven to Christian's apartment building. That had been a waste of time. The Super had said his job didn't include keeping tabs on the tenants.

Grasping at straws, Jason had stopped by Alan Sheffield's office, hoping his old friend, the State Attorney General might be working on The Ladies of the Night Murders. Sheffield had said it would be a conflict of interest to discuss an investigation with a civilian, friend or not. Jason had called the AG a bureaucrat and stormed out of his office.

Jason grabbed the phone and dialed Christian's number. After ten rings, he hung up and activated the intercom.

"Yes, Mr. Borseau," Mary Robards said.

"I apologize for pressing, but is it possible that Christian phoned again, and I didn't get the message?"

"Nooo, shall I check with the newsroom? Maybe they've heard from him."

"Please. I'm ready to call it a day, but I'll wait for you to get back to me."

"I'll do it right away."

"Thanks," he muttered. What could've happened to Christian? There had to be a logical explanation, but what? Where did he go after he left my office? Jason picked up the phone and dialed Caroline's extension.

"Mrs. Keene," she answered.

"Caroline, did Christian get a cash advance from you Tuesday afternoon?"

"A hundred bucks. Why?"

"Because I can't find him, and I'm concerned. No, I'm worried sick. Do you have any idea where he was headed when he left your office?"

"No, but he was in a hurry, said he needed to grease someone's palm."

"Yeah, and I'm beating myself up for not asking whose."

"Do you think something bad has happened to him?"

"I don't know."

"Anything I can do to help?"

"The only thing that'll help is if Christian calls or shows up."

"Where in the world could he be?"

"If I find out, I'll let you know." Rising, Jason went to the windows behind his desk. He'd encouraged Christian, all of KSOL's employees, to take the initiative, to stretch themselves—their minds, imaginations, talents. Jason didn't like being bound by rules, arbitrary or otherwise, and he'd never imposed them on anyone else. That would change. From now on, anyone going into the field would have to file itineraries with their respective bosses.

Hindsight. How he hated it.

When the intercom buzzed, he spun around, leaned over his desk, and flicked the switch. "Yes."

"No one in the newsroom has heard from Christian. Is there anything else I can—?"

"When you talked to him, was there anything unusual about your conversation?"

"Unusual? Unusual might not be the way to put it."

Jason's gut fisted. "How would you put it?"

"He was in a hurry. I asked him if I could give you a message, other than to tell you he'd called. He said he had to talk to you and asked where you could be reached."

"He needed to get in touch with me. Urgently?"

"Now that I think about it, I'm afraid so. I told him you were on your way home. The strange thing was, he hung up without telling me good-bye. Christian never does that. Why didn't I ask him where he could be reached?"

"Mary, you did everything you could. But if he calls again, find out where he is, let me know right away, and tell him to stay put." Jason flipped the key and grabbed his briefcase, wondering what to do next. Call the police? If Christian was okay, he'd be mortified if the cops put out an APB, and picked him up. If Jason didn't hear from him by tomorrow morning, he'd report him missing. Too bad if Christian's ego got a little bruised.

# Chapter Eight

## Friday Evening

When Christian came to, the last thing he remembered was stepping out of the elevator into the subterranean garage in his apartment building. He had no idea where he was, or how long he'd been there. How could this have happened? He'd been alert to danger all his life. What colored kid growing up in Georgia hadn't?

All the signs had been there. "Mutt" and "Jeff" had targeted him at the café. Was it because of his interest in the City, or because he'd talked to Chantelle about the murdered girls?

The following morning, after a very early breakfast at a café on Scottsdale Road, Christian headed back to his apartment. He'd driven several blocks, when he noticed that a faded blue van kept popping into his rearview mirror. As soon as he'd gotten home, he'd tried to reach Jason at the station, but had missed him. When he'd called Jason's home, the butler had said they were expecting him. Christian had decided to drive to the Borseau estate, but he'd made it no further than the garage.

His hands and feet were tied, a blindfold covered his eyes. If they were going to kill him, and he assumed that was the plan, what were they waiting for? What had he gotten himself into?

His stomach pitched as he drew in the putrid stench of decaying flesh. He tried not to think about what had died there. After holding on as long as he could, he'd soiled himself. The stink rising from his own body was ghastly and demeaning.

Lapsing in and out of consciousness, with the heat frying his brain, and pain numbing his senses, he hadn't thought about trying to escape. If he'd been kidnapped by the men he'd seen at the café, they couldn't let him live—he could describe them. In fact, he'd described them as Mutt and Jeff in the audio tape he'd made after leaving the ghetto. He hoped Jaclyn would find it in her apartment. If only he'd left her a note or called her. In hindsight, that's what he should have done, but he'd been in a hurry.

Christian leaned as far forward as he could. His fingers painstakingly snaked up to the knots. There were a lot of them, and they were tight. As he struggled to undo them, each time his hands cramped, he was forced to stop. He was making progress, but it was slow going, and his captors could be back at any moment.

When the last knot gave way, Christian jerked off the blindfold, blinking as the shadowy edges and angles of an abandoned warehouse came into focus. He rubbed his hands and stretched his fingers to get the circulation going, untied the ropes binding his ankles and pushed up out of the chair.

It was later than he'd imagined, twilight dimmed the sky. Pain spiked up his spine as he limped from window to window and peered through the steel bars covering them. He tried to figure out where he was. The only thing within sight was a row of dilapidated buildings. Clones of the one he was in, he felt sure.

Blood seeped from the wound above his right ear, his head pounded, even as his adrenaline began pumping. He went from truck door to truck door. All of them were chained and padlocked.

Too much time was passing. Slices of moonlight streamed through the barred windows. Edging along, Christian felt the building with his hands as if it were in Braille. At the far end of a long hall, he literally stumbled into a stairwell. Cautiously ascending the steps, choking on the dust his movements were sending airborne, he cringed as the ancient boards creaked beneath his weight.

When he got to the top of the stairs, he was confronted by stacks of empty pallets. He slipped quietly through the narrow aisles to the windows along the far wall, only to find them sealed. With a sinking feeling, Christian realized, if he broke a window and jumped, he'd drop two stories to the pavement below. So much for that option. He made one last round of the floor. Behind a stack of empty cardboard boxes, he found a door, but it was secured with a dead bolt.

Moving to an adjacent window, Christian pressed his cheek to the glass. A fire escape with a midlevel landing led to the street below. It would take a miracle for him to make the jump successfully, and if the kidnappers were nearby, the glass crashing to the street would bring them running.

# Chapter Nine

## Friday Evening

Sheffield flashed his credentials to the guard manning the gate. While the officer checked with the Borseaus' internal security, Sheffield gazed at Sandra. She was attractive, without being pretty in the traditional sense. Her hair was as bright as a new copper penny, set off by sky blue eyes. She had a trim figure. But her cynical view of the world and those inhabiting it was a bit much, even for Sheffield, who considered himself something of a cynic. They'd been seeing one another for three years, sleeping together occasionally, a relationship of convenience. Or habit.

Uninvited, a solemn smile and haunted dark eyes invaded his thoughts. He shook off the image and tapped the steering wheel in time with the jazzy tune on the radio.

The officer saluted him. "It's an honor, sir."

"Thank you." Sheffield drove toward the sprawling mansion along the park-like boulevard lined with Arizona Sycamores, Black Pines, and a variety of flowering shrubs.

"Charming little place," Sandra muttered.

Sheffield chuckled. "Your boss never does anything in a small way, but I don't have to tell you that."

"I seldom see him, never talk to him. Only Caroline interacts with him."

"Caroline's great, isn't she?"

Sandra shrugged. "If you're into dictators."

"Really? That's hard to believe, although I've never worked with her."

"Exactly. You've never worked with her."

"Since we're early, let's snoop around." Sheffield was relieved to forego the subject of Caroline. A take-charge person like Sandra resented playing second fiddle to anyone. If he let her, Sandra would take over his life. He was careful not to let her.

Sheffield swung onto a side road. "On our left, the last tee of their three-hole golf course. There are guest cottages behind the orchard. Beau Meredith's place is in a secluded corner of the property. He co-pilots when Jason and his DC-3 soar into the wild blue yonder. Have you ever seen so many trees and shrubs? I recognize the palms and that's about it.

"They have horses, but I don't know how to get to the stables. Probably that way," he said, pointing to a narrow lane paved with brick, shadowed by bowers of trees. "Jason and Kathryn both ride, but she was practically born on a horse." He laughed. "It was the only way to get on and off the mountain she grew up on."

"Good grief," Sandra said, "how many acres do they have?"

"Forty or so. Dead ahead, the landing strip, the hangar is behind it. That's where Jason's plane goes beddy-bye. It wouldn't surprise me if he tucks it in and kisses it good-night."

Sheffield made a U-turn and circled back to the mansion. "And, here we are," he said as he parked in front of the adobe brick two-story.

"I wasn't expecting a mansion," Sandra said.

Sheffield's hands lingered on the wheel. "Wait until you see the interior. Navajo wall coverings and rugs, fine art, artifacts from every period of Arizona history. And cactus—cacti, I guess, from the giant Saguaro to the barrel and pear varieties. There are Koi ponds and waterfalls and broad balconies along the suites upstairs."

"Your place isn't exactly shabby."

"Actually, it's far more elegant than I would've chosen for myself, one of the few compromises I was willing to make. The Attorney General is supposed to have a proper place to entertain, not that I do much of that, even though I should."

A burley, bespectacled officer placed his hands on the roof of the car, leaned down, and peered at them through the open window. "May I help you, sir?"

"We'll be going in shortly," Sheffield said.

The officer's eyes flared. "Mr. Sheffield." He drew back as if the car were on fire. "I'm sorry, sir."

Sheffield smiled at the gun-toting sentry. "No problem." As the guard strode away, Sheffield turned to Sandra. "It might be easier to break into Fort Knox."

"So it would seem."

An *esplanade* of crimson bougainvillea arched above the broad steps to the elaborately carved front doors. Sheffield pressed the bell. Moments later, the Borseau's English butler, Cyrus Tidwell—tall, austere, and perfectly correct—opened the door.

"Good evening, Mr. Sheffield, Miss Parker. This way, please." With a sweep of his hand, the butler struck out ahead of them.

"Awesome," Sandra whispered, as her high-heeled shoes clicked across the dark ceramic tile. On one side of the spacious foyer, waterfalls cascaded into ponds partially obscured by masses of fern, philodendron, and baby tears. A dazzling array of Azaleas provided color.

They rounded a corner to see Jason striding toward them. "Hey, buddy, Sandra, I was delighted when Kathryn told me you were joining us for dinner."

They walked along the broad hallway to the conservatory, where the last day's light, a burnt orange glow, spilled through two walls of windows. Other guests were milling about, cocktail glasses in hand. Sheffield wondered how he was going to get Jason alone for a chat.

It was a huge room, with sleek, modern furniture in contrast to the ambiance throughout the rest of the house, where beauty and comfort reigned. Two grand pianos angled keyboard to keyboard in a far corner. Tucked away behind dark plantation shutters, a state of the art audio/video system gave Jason the wherewithal to preview programs at home.

"Sandra, I don't think you've met my parents, Andre and Camille Borseau," Jason said. "Sandra Parker is the station's assistant controller."

Nodding and smiling, Camille, petite and refined, and Andre, tall and dignified, acknowledged Sandra.

"And you know Jon." Jason nodded toward Jonathan Fitzgerald, also a member of his staff. "Next to Jon are his wife, Ariel, and her father, Anthony Carlotti. Not to forget Garrett Donnelly, who produces and directs Kathryn's 'Good News' show. I'm sure you've met Valerie," he said, referring to his partner, Casey Matson's wife.

"Of course," Valerie said, with a toss of her dark shoulder-length bob.

"Hello, Val, Casey. Hi, Fitz, Garrett," Sandra said. "It's nice to meet you, Ariel, and you, Mr. Carlotti."

"Sandra, our son, Anthony, is spending the evening with friends," Kathryn said. "This is our younger son, Josh, and our little one, Lauren." She lifted their daughter into her arms.

"How do you do," Joshua said as he extended his hand to Sandra, then to Sheffield. "It's nice to see you again, Mr. Sheffield. You're the Attorney General, aren't you, sir?"

"Yes, son, I am." Sheffield gripped the small fingers, noting how the boy's wide gray eyes dwarfed his other features. With curly honey-colored hair and delicate features, he looked even more like his mother than he had the last time Sheffield had seen him. In contrast, their daughter looked every bit as much like Jason, with startling blue eyes, and curly dark hair. Though Jason's hair was strewn with silver, Sheffield always saw his friend with the black mane he'd had when they first met.

Lauren tucked her face into the curve of her mother's neck, occasionally peeking out shyly. Jason was already heading for the bar. "Shef, what are you and Sandra drinking?"

"A tall brandy and water for Sandra, Scotch-rocks for me."

It struck Sheffield how truly remarkable Jason was. He thoroughly admired his friend's brilliant mind and spirit—the resolute force that fueled Jason's dynamic personality.

Setting aside mental flashes of the harrowing experiences he'd *enjoyed* with Jason, Sheffield turned to Kathryn. "So, when do you expect the new baby?"

Jason spun around and stared at his wife. "The what?"

"Oops," Sheffield muttered.

With an impish grin, Kathryn said, "Surprise," as she handed Lauren off to her Grandfather Borseau.

Jason rushed across the room and swept her close. "Why didn't you tell me?" Without waiting for an answer, he glared at Sheffield. "And you know about it because?"

Sheffield laughed. "A lucky guess."

"Cute, Shef, very cute." Jason cupped Kathryn's chin in his hand and lifted her face to his. "We need to talk, Mrs. Borseau." He planted a kiss on her forehead and strode back to the bar.

"Sorry about that," Sheffield whispered to Kathryn.

**J**ason swirled three-fingers of Courvoisier in a cut-crystal snifter. He'd caught the conspiratorial look between Sheffield and Kathryn before she'd practically strong-armed Sandra to the nursery for a story-telling session. The senior Borseaus had retired to their suite after concert pianists, Kathryn and Jon Fitzgerald had played two of his parents' favorite Chopin Waltzes.

A cool breeze ruffled the green and white striped canopies over the *cabañas* at opposite ends of the flagstone deck. A waterfall cascaded between the olympic-size pool and the children's swimming hole, replete with pilings, a stationary raft, and a sandy beach, in keeping with a seashore. Seated next to the diving board at a round, glass-topped table, Sheffield and Jason drank in silence.

Jason took a sip of brandy and rolled the snifter between his fingers. "This isn't a social call is it, Shef? Did Kathryn call you?"

Hesitating, Sheffield stuck the meerschaum between his teeth, fished the lighter out of his jacket pocket, and took his time lighting it.

"Well?"

"No, she didn't call me." With a guileless smile, Sheffield puffed contentedly. "I ran into her downtown, and we had lunch. You know how much Kathryn likes The Flame, the aviary and all. One thing led to another, and she invited Sandra and me to dinner."

"Sort of bumped into her, did you?" Jason said. "Where?"

"What's this, an inquisition? Do you think we're having an affair?"

"Don't flatter yourself. Kathryn went to your office, and I want to know why. Surely you don't think I let her roam around without keeping an eye on her."

"She still has bodyguards?" Sheffield spat out.

Bewildered, Jason said, "Of course, I won't risk having her kidnapped, held for ransom, or my children. Shef, do you know how much I'm worth?"

Sheffield studied his friend's face. "Twenty or so million the last time we discussed it."

"Times two," said Jason in a despondent voice.

Sheffield jammed the pipe stem between his teeth. "Am I supposed to feel sorry for you because you're richer than Croesus?"

"I'm not asking for pity, you ass. Why did Kathryn come to see you?"

"Because she's worried about you," Sheffield snapped. "What's going on?"

The chair screeched as Jason pushed away from the table.

"Jace!"

"It's Christian Grayson. He's missing."

"The station's crime guy."

"Yes." Jason fingers raked through his hair.

"That's why you came to my office?"

Jason nodded. "I gave him permission to spend a couple of days in the field. Christian had two investigations in mind: I'd assigned him, temporarily, to cover the City Council meetings. At one or more of those meetings, he'd gotten a gut feeling that something was amiss. Also, he wanted to look up his 'main snitch' to see if he could get a line on The Ladies of the Night Murders. He said it'd take a few bucks to loosen 'her' tongue. Since the murdered women were prostitutes, I have a hunch Christian's snitch is, too. I checked with Caroline to see if Christian had gotten an advance. He had, a hundred bucks."

Scowling, Sheffield's emerald green eyes drew into feline slits. "When was that?"

Jason collapsed in the chair and tossed off the rest of his brandy. "Tuesday, late afternoon." He stood again, pacing back and forth like a lion trapped in a cage.

"The last thing Christian said was that he'd keep in touch, every day. He always has, until now. I've dialed his number so many times it's tattooed on my brain. This morning, before I came to see you, I went to his apartment and talked to the super. I thought Christian's phone might be out of order. It wasn't. Yesterday, shortly before eleven, Christian called my office. He called here, too, but I was between the two places. No one's heard from him since. I questioned my secretary again this morning, and she admitted that Christian indicated some urgency in getting hold of me. It's only been a few days, but I have a very bad feeling in my gut."

"Jace, why didn't you level with me this morning?"

"Because you always think I'm over-reacting."

Rising, Sheffield gazed into his friend's troubled eyes. "Are you?"

"No." Jason grasped Sheffield's shoulders. "Christian is in trouble, and I'm going to file a missing person's report."

Sheffield nodded. "You just did."

# Chapter Ten

## Friday, Late Evening

Christian found a tarp behind one of the pallets. Wrapping it around his right hand, he turned his head and plowed his fist into the window. The glass shattered and crashed to the pavement below. After knocking out the remaining shards, he hoisted himself to the ledge. He knew the odds of making the jump successfully were slim to none. Sweat coursed down his face. He took deep breaths to gather the strength he had left. Focusing on the fire escape, he leapt. The moment he was airborne, Christian thrust his arms into a horizontal position. The pavement was coming up fast, too fast. He stretched out to give himself forward thrust. To his amazement, he was able to grasp the edge of a stair. He launched his body up, grabbed the railing, and swung his legs onto the landing.

He rose on shaky legs and started down the stairs. The two men he'd seen at restaurant darted around the corner.

The taller one jabbed a toothpick between his front teeth. "Where d'ya think you're going, sport?" He reached into his back pocket, produced a black jack, and slapped it against his hand.

"What do you want with me?" Christian said.

"You stuck your nose into things that're none of your business," the shorter man said.

"Like what?" Trying to figure a way out, Christian glanced around. He spied a box of scrap lumber a foot or so behind him. Back stepping into the shadows, he hunkered down, and curled his fingers around a two by four. As weapons went, it wasn't much. If they hadn't found his knife, he might be able to get one of them, not both. If he went for it, and it wasn't there, it could be fatal.

"Let's get this over with, and get out of here, Lou."

"No names. Shut up."

"What difference does it make? He ain't gonna be around."

"Shut your trap!" He stabbed an index finger at Christian. "Don't make me come after y'a."

Diaphanous clouds drifted across the sky, only an occasional moonbeam severed the darkness. Christian's hands tightened around the board as he jumped to the pavement below. Pain spiked up his leg. Either he'd sprained or broken his ankle. Swinging the makeshift club with both hands, he kept the men at bay as he hip-hopped around the corner, and scooted beneath a truck ramp. The men were seconds behind him. Christian pressed his hands against his chest to still the wild thudding.

"Where'd he go?" Ben said.

"'Couldn't've gotten far," Lou responded.

Christian could see their boots on either side of the ramp.

"If he gets away, we're dead."

Christian's hand slid to his boot. His knife was there, and he eased it out of the sheath.

"Hear that?" Ben said.

Lou pointed at the ramp. "We know yer under there. Give it up."

"What am I supposed to've done?" Christian said as he poised the knife, prepared to strike.

"You butted into our boss's business," Lou said.

"What business would that be, Lou?"

"Come out'a there, and I'll tell you."

"I don't seem to have a choice," Christian said as he reached out and plunged the knife into the Lou's kneecap. With a vicious twist of the blade, he jerked it free, and crawled to the street. The tall kidnapper lay writhing on the ground, clutching his knee, screaming.

Before Christian could scramble to his feet, Ben shot around the ramp, swung the sap, and struck a crushing blow to Christian's head. With a grunt, he fell face down on the concrete. Ben kicked him viciously, until he was sure the black man was no longer a threat.

"I'm bleeding, my knee's ripped apart, I'm gonna be a cripple."

"He's dead," Ben said as he felt for a pulse. "I'll get the van."

"We're gonna give this bastard to Borseau," Lou sobbed, rocking back and forth. "If he doesn't back off, the same thing'll happen to his wife and kids."

"Forget that, I hafta get you to a hospital. We'll toss him in the City dump with the rest of the garbage."

"Don't argue with me!"

"You're not the boss, Lou."

"I'm not *the* boss, but I'm *your* boss, so get moving."

"I'm going, I'm going, don't get your bowels in an uproar."

# Chapter Eleven

## Saturday Morning, five am

"**M**arried?" Sheffield nearly dropped the glass of water he'd started to drink, hoping he could dilute the scotch he'd drunk at the Borseaus. "As in I do, you do?"

"The thought never crossed your mind?" Sandra said.

The pounding in his head was getting worse by the second. He went to the bathroom, grabbed a bottle of aspirin, popped three, chased them with water, and went back to the bedroom. He walked to the windows and drew the crimson moiré drapes aside.

"I still feel married to Gina."

"That's absurd. You've been divorced for years and years."

Sheffield gazed at the rugged cliffs rimming the gulch behind his house—the Attorney General's house. He wasn't the first to live there, nor would he be the last. The moon, a ghostly apparition, arced low in the western sky. In the east, a faint silver glow outlined the mountains that tumbled away to become faint in the distance. A boulder-strewn *arroyo*, dry at this time of year, snaked through the canyon at the foot of the cliffs. Unwilling to sacrifice the view, Sheffield had the wall around the estate replaced with a chain-link fence.

He turned to look at Sandra. "What's wrong with the way things are?"

"Apparently nothing, as far as you're concerned." She propped a pillow against the headboard and sank into it.

Sheffield took a pair of jeans from the closet and tugged them on. "Is this about having children?" He dropped into a chair to pull on his boots.

"Good lord, no." Sandra rose and slipped into a filmy white negligee. "Speaking of children, I didn't appreciate being dragged to the Borseaus' nursery for a story-telling session. What was that about?"

"Jace and I had things to discuss, in private." Sheffield went back to the windows, and spotted the Rottweilers—noses to the ground, searching for the bad guys, as if the Attorney General was in imminent danger. True, the estate was in a remote area—thirty or so miles northeast of Scottsdale, and several winding miles from the main highway. In addition to the pair of formidable Rotts, State police officers manned the security gate around the clock.

"Obviously, what you and Jason talk about is none of my business." Sandra put her wrists together. "If curiosity is a crime, cuff me and haul me off to the pokey, Mr. Attorney General."

"Now who's being absurd?" Sheffield said as he buttoned a blue plaid, western style shirt.

"Am I? It's one secret after another."

He shrugged. "The reporters think I'm refreshingly direct,"

"They aren't in love with you."

In love? They'd never talked about love. Love was what he'd felt for his wife, for their son Michael who'd been killed in Korea, by *friendly* fire. Gina had accepted their son's death. Sheffield hadn't. He'd emotionally distanced himself from her and from every other living soul. Oh, he'd gone to the office, taken care of business, but every time he'd looked at his wife, he'd grieved anew for Michael. Less than a year after their divorce, Gina had remarried and moved to the East Coast. He hadn't seen or heard from her since.

"You just think you're in love with me," he said at last. "You're wrong."

Studying her face in the dim light, Sheffield said, "I like you, Sandra, very much."

"If there was a *love* in there somewhere, I missed it."

"In my opinion, being *in love* is an over-rated emotion." He shook his head. "I was in love with Gina, but when she needed me most, I let her down. I loved my parents and they're gone. Michael's dead. I'll never stop loving or missing Michael."

Sandra flicked a tangle of hair away from her face. "That was eons ago. You should have gotten over it by now."

"What a callous thing to say." Sheffield's boots hit the floor. "If you were a parent, you'd understand how impossible that is."

"Nothing is going to bring your son back."

"No, nothing is." He bowed his head. "Sandra, no one has ever proposed to me before, and I'm flattered. But I need to think long and hard about this, so do you."

"I've done all the thinking I intend to do. And, I refuse to live in sin any longer. So, I'm going to plan our wedding—a formal affair, with a champagne reception and an orchestra and a honeymoon in the Bahamas." Pausing, she tapped her lips. "My father and I haven't spoken for years. Do you think Jason would give me away? If you'd ask him, he'd do it."

Sheffield was stunned. "Sandra, stop. You're going way too fast for me. My god, how long have you been planning this?"

"What? Oh, the wedding? Since I was barely out of my cradle, and if you think I'm unique among women, you're dead wrong. Again."

Smiling, Sandra said, "You don't eat right, but I'll fix that. I'll prepare nutritious meals, and develop an exercise program for you. Shef, you need me."

"What I need right now is coffee." He went to the door. "Shall I bring you a cup?"

Sandra blew a kiss in his direction. "Yes, please."

Sheffield shut the door and leaned against it. He felt like he'd been run over by a truck. "Now what, genius?" He flipped the light switch and ambled along the hall to the stairs. "Why didn't I see that coming?"

# Chapter Twelve

**A** nightlight glowed on the wall beside their bed. Years before, when Jason realized that Kathryn was afraid of the dark, he simply put one there. He glanced at the clock on the nightstand. It was a few minutes past five. He gazed at her, his beloved wife as he tucked the covers around her. The house was air conditioned to the point of being frigid. His mountain girl, transplanted from Idaho's Bitterroot Wilderness to the desert, couldn't abide the intense heat. Lying down again, Jason closed his eyes, and at last, exhaustion overcame his anxiety about Christian.

Minutes later, the shrill whine of the alarm system shattered the pre-dawn stillness. Jason leapt out of bed, raced across the room, and pressed the switch on the intercom. Kathryn grabbed her robe and hurried to the children's bedrooms. The system had never malfunctioned before. Jason hoped this was the first time.

"Officer Nichols, sir. It's Mr. Grayson. Someone dumped him in front of the gate. An ambulance is on the way, but in the meantime, we're afraid to touch him."

"I'll be right there. Call Alan Sheffield, tell him what's happened, and ask him to get here as fast as he can. And, Steve, send a couple of men to the house. My family is not to be left alone for a second." Jason slammed down the receiver.

Smothering a yawn, Kathryn shuffled back into the bedroom. "What's wrong with the alarm system?"

"Nothing. It's Christian, he's been hurt." Jason pulled on his boots and strode to the door. "A couple of our officers are on their way to the house."

Kathryn's hands flew to her cheeks. "Hurt? What happened?"

"I don't know."

"A car accident?"

"I don't think so."

"Oh, God, dear, sweet Christian."

"Kathryn, don't fall apart," Jason said, as he unlocked the nightstand drawer and retrieved his .38.

Her eyes flew open. "Why do you need that?"

"Maybe I won't," he said over his shoulder as he charged through the door.

Kathryn slumped down on the edge of the bed. "Be safe, my love."


**W**eapons drawn, Jason's guards had closed ranks around Christian. They stepped aside to let Jason through. Hunkering down, he touched his reporter's bloody face. "Christian, son, who did this to you?" Jason murmured, knowing no answer would be forthcoming. In the distance, he heard the siren warbling as it crossed the adjacent street.

"Hurry up, dammit."

The words were barely out of his mouth when the ambulance screeched to a stop beside them. Two paramedics flew out of the vehicle. One of them squatted beside Christian, lifted his eyelids, and checked his pulse. "Oxygen, leg and neck braces," he bellowed "Get the gurney, radio the ER at St. Vincent's. Tell 'em I need to consult with 'em," he shouted as he hooked the brace around Christian's neck. "And tell 'em to line up a neurosurgeon, stat, and have the OR ready when we get there, twenty minutes."

Jason walked with flagging steps to his officers. "What happened?" he said to his chief of security.

"The men heard a vehicle slam to a stop in front of the gate. They went out to see what was going on, and saw Christian lying next to the curb," Jacob Stein responded.

"License number?"

"The plate was covered with mud. Deliberately, I'm sure."

"Make, model?"

"A vintage blue van the officers described as a delivery truck. They called for an ambulance, buzzed me, alerted you." Jacob's dark eyes bored into Jason's. "Any idea who did this or why?"

"Not a clue." With a shake of his head, Jason turned away as Sheffield's car drew alongside the curb. "Shef and I will follow the ambulance to St. Vincent's. Jake, lock down the house. It's possible Christian is being used to blindside us. I'll ask Shef to contact the police."

Sheffield shook his head as he watched the paramedics slide the gurney into the ambulance.

"Follow the ambulance, Shef," Jason called out to him.

Sheffield reached into the car, grabbed the bubble light, and jammed it on the roof. When he slid behind the steering wheel, Jason was already in the passenger's seat, staring straight ahead. Sheffield started the engine and toggled the siren. He pushed a pale lock of hair from his forehead and muttered, "Christian was left on your doorstep. Someone's sending you a message."

Nodding slowly, Jason murmured, "Notify the police, will you?"

Sheffield snatched the mic from the dashboard and floored the accelerator.

# Chapter Thirteen

The hospital complex sprawled across two city blocks—a modern six-story structure, with an enclave of buildings that streamed like the tentacles of an octopus from the main building through glass-enclosed corridors. Much like the increasingly popular shopping malls, each corridor ended where a specialty began—X-ray and radiation facilities, the cancer diagnostic and treatment center, obstetrics and gynecology, physical therapy and psychiatry. The central building housed the ER facilities, outpatient services, maternity, surgery, ICU, and the recovery rooms.

Convenient to the hospital's dismal reality, Greenwood Memorial Cemetery was a short distance away.

Sheffield and Jason strode behind the paramedics into the frantic activity that pounded against the ER at St. Vincent's. The hospital staff zigzagged around one another and the patients-in-waiting to avoid the collisions that seemed destined to occur. After he'd called the Phoenix police, Sheffield had contacted his chief investigator. Sheffield spotted his people on one side of the lobby and the men in blue on the other, eyeing one another suspiciously.

Sheffield held back, while Jason kept pace with the gurney to the elevator. Chief of Police, Morton Salinger, leaned against the wall, drinking coffee from a plastic cup. He glanced up and scowled. "Shef, what're you doing here?"

Sheffield put a restraining hand on his chief investigator's arm. Already tensed for action, Sam Erikson spun around. "The Attorney General can be anywhere he damned well pleases."

"All right, Sam," Sheffield said quietly. Turning, he shook the Chief's hand. "As you probably know, Jason Borseau and I are close friends. Christian Grayson, the station's investigative reporter was thrown from a vehicle at Jace's estate. His security force found Christian unconscious, and from all appearances, savagely beaten." Sheffield shrugged. "I was the first law enforcement officer Jace thought to call."

The Chief's icy blue eyes narrowed. "Well, Borseau isn't a stranger to me either, but I hear you two go back a long ways."

"We do."

"Okay, Shef, this is police business, we'll take over now."

"I have no intention of abandoning this investigation." Sheffield's hard unwavering eyes met the Chief's. "It may be a racially motivated hate crime."

The Chief's face reddened. After years of abuse, blood vessels radiated along the cavernous lines of his face. His cheeks huffed in and out as he inhaled and exhaled.

"What makes you think so?"

"Call it a gut feeling. If I'm right, and I believe I am, that puts the crime within our jurisdiction."

"What?"

"If Christian was attacked because he's a Negro, it's a violation of his civil rights."

"'No way to prove that, is there?"

"No, but Jason can't come up with any other reason his reporter might've been targeted."

The Chief tucked his thumbs beneath the belt that split his considerable bulk in two. "I don't have a problem with your agency taking the lead, as long as you keep me advised."

"That goes without saying. Also, Chief, I've been wondering why the Feds haven't taken the lead on the Ladies of the Night Murders. Five women have been kidnapped and brutally murdered. Another girl has disappeared."

"Because the FBI is not going to muscle their way into my investigation and second-guess what I do."

"Still, they have the resources to—"

"Butt out, Shef, it's my case. It sounds like you think the police force is expendable. Folks are grumbling about the empire you've built for yourself—got an army working for you—dozens of agents and officers, most of 'em ex-military—guerilla fighters, a team of sharpshooters. Helicopters, for Christ's sake, the wherewithal to start a war."

"Or stop one," Sheffield said quietly. "Well, Chief, the killer is targeting minorities, and that's a violation of their civil rights. Whether you like it or not, that *is* within the State's jurisdiction."

Salinger's eyes narrowed. "If you push me too far, you'll be sorry, Shef."

"Is that a threat?" When the Chief didn't respond, Sheffield said, "Your officers are welcome to assist mine in securing the area. Sam Erikson's in charge. Have you met?"

Salinger drew himself up. "I've seen him with you is all."

"Give me a minute." Sheffield strode to Sam and guided him an earshot away.

"Police chief, my ass," Sam growled. "He's on the take—drugs, prostitution."

"Which we can't prove, so we deal with him."

Sam's dark eyes smoldered. "Who does he think he is anyway?"

"We can't spare the energy it takes to care." Sheffield gripped his investigator's arm. "Contact the FBI. See if they'll do our lab work," Sheffield added.

Nodding, Sam expelled a long breath. "I sent a couple of our agents to Grayson's apartment. When I hear something, I'll find you. Oh, I've assigned Jaclyn to cover your backside."

"I've been meaning to talk to you about her. Fearless is one thing, reckless is quite another. I'm afraid she's trying to prove something."

"She puts herself on the line, but I don't think she's reckless." Frowning, Sam said, "When Jaclyn came aboard, I checked her out for the AG. Do you know what I'm talking about?"

"Yes."

"I can't remember the name of the concentration camp."

"Trepskýa, in Poland," Sheffield said, adding, "Maybe, for Jaclyn, fear comes in different sizes and shapes than it does for the rest of us."

"'Could be."

"Does she have family in the States?" Sheffield asked.

"An aunt and some cousins in the Midwest. Her parents died at Treblinka."

"I know she isn't married, but is there someone special?"

"Not to my knowledge." Sam smiled. "Hey, Shef, she's available, same as you."

"That may be past tense for yours truly."

Sam's rugged features split in a grin. "You asked Sandra to marry you?"

"It was the other way around—she proposed to me. I felt like an idiot, said I'd have to think about it. I guess that piece of paper would mean a lot to her."

"Hey, boss, marriage is tough enough when there are *two* enthusiastic candidates. Anyway, if you change your mind . . ."

"It isn't *my* mind I'd have to change." Sheffield sent a curt nod in the Chief's direction and headed for the elevators.

Jaclyn Devereaux was a step behind the AG as he exited the elevator.

"Hey, buddy," Sheffield called out.

Jason stopped pacing and flopped into a chair. "Where'd you go?"

"Sorry, I had to get Salinger under control. I'd like to shoot him, but as you know, even if I fired at him point blank, I'd miss."

Jason chuckled. "Shef, you should've been a comedian."

"Oh, sure, I'm such a funny guy."

Jaclyn stood at a respectful distance. Sheffield thought about her chilling past. Who among his generation didn't know about the Holocaust? Still, he'd gotten it into his head that none of the prisoners had escaped Trepskýa—alive. Such a beautiful woman, he mused, with large, solemn, elfin-shaped eyes, a small straight nose, full lips, and dark hair that cascaded to the middle of her back.

"Shef, how am I going to live with this?"

"Hmmm?" It took Sheffield a moment to switch his focus to Jason. He jammed his hands into his jeans' pockets, and said, "The same way you live with everything else, by blaming yourself."

Hearing the elevator door open, Sheffield turned to see Sam striding toward him. He lifted a hand in acknowledgement. "Shall I contact Christian's parents?"

"No, Beau is flying to Georgia to get them. He should be back before nightfall."

"Shef, Jaclyn, let's talk," Sam said.

Sheffield gave Jason's shoulder a reassuring pat. "I'll just be a minute."

Jason nodded at Sheffield's retreating figure. Turning away, he drifted to the windows.

Sam unbuttoned his windbreaker and grabbed the pack of Old Golds from his shirt pocket. "Well, boss, Grayson's apartment is a mess. The chairs and sofas, mattress and box spring are shredded, pictures slashed. The file drawers in his office are empty, even his typewriter ribbon's missing. His car is in the same sort'a shape, the glove box was jimmied." Sam grabbed a cigarette and shoved it between his lips.

"Grayson's keys weren't on him, so why didn't they simply open the glove box?" Sam took the Zippo from his pocket, and torched his cigarette. "Does Borseau know what they might've been looking for?"

"Not specifically, only that for the past month or so, Christian has been covering the City Council meetings. He told Jason he was curious about how they were doing business. Nothing suspicious there, at least not on the surface. He also wanted to talk to his snitch to see if something fell out about The Ladies of the Night Murders. If that's what this is about, he may've uncovered something. And maybe that's what the calls were about. Shortly before eleven Thursday morning, Christian called Jason, but he missed him at the station, so he called his house, but Jason wasn't there, either."

Sheffield frowned and stared at the floor. At last, he lifted his head, gazed from Sam to Jaclyn, then he walked several steps away. They waited in silence.

Several minutes passed before he strode back to them. "Let's try to piece this together from Christian's point of view. He urgently needs to tell Jason something. When Christian called the estate, the butler said Jason was on his way home. What would Christian do? I think he'd decide to drive out there. Let's say the kidnappers nabbed him between eleven and eleven thirty, either in the elevator or the garage. His car was there, so it isn't likely he was nabbed elsewhere. Broad daylight in a public place, they'd hustle him out of there fast.

"His apartment must've been searched later, his car, too, probably in the wee hours of the following morning.

"The kidnappers wouldn't know Christian had asked for time off, probably figured he'd be missed almost immediately. They were in a hurry. They unlocked Christian's car, probably his trunk, but overlooked the glove box. Someone stays with the vehicle, another person takes Christian's keys to his apartment. Oops, the glove box is locked, and he, or she, doesn't have the key. A tire iron would make a handy prying device."

"Sounds logical, I'll check it out," Sam said, jamming the cigarette butt into a sand-filled receptacle.

Jaclyn stepped between them. "What time did Mr. Borseau try to call Christian back?"

"At about eleven-thirty. I think during that critical half-hour or so things fell apart for Grayson. All assumptions, of course.

"Only by the farthest stretch could it be a hate crime." Sheffield shook his head. "If the Chief figures that out, we're screwed. If the attack on Christian was racially motivated, why search his car or his apartment? Why not kill him right away, why hold him—to torture him? Maybe, but the kicker is: Christian was dumped on Jason's doorstep. Someone believes Christian was investigating something for the station. If that's the case, Jace and his family are at risk. I think Christian is the messenger, back off or else. If so, they've sorely misjudged Jason."

Frowning, Sheffield shrugged as he glanced from Sam to Jaclyn. "For the moment, that's enough surmising."

Sam rubbed the stubble on his chin. "Your theory about where they took Grayson is probably right. Our guys found bloodstains a few feet from the elevator in the garage. The Feds are willing to do the lab work for us, whatever else we need, too. They still think of you as Special Agent Alan Sheffield, said their expertise and facilities will continue to be available to us."

"Good, that may keep the Chief in line, but we'll need a court order to officially coordinate the investigation."

Jaclyn touched Sheffield's arm. "Why didn't they kill Christian?"

Sheffield glanced at Jason. "They had to believe they had," he said solemnly.

"It'll be a bitch to question everyone in that apartment building. It's an enormous place," Sam said.

Jaclyn turned to her partner. "About that, I—"

Cutting her off, Sam added, "We'll check with the phone company, see if Grayson's calls to Borseau were made from his apartment."

"We need to trace Christian's movements after he left Jason's office," Sheffield said.

Jaclyn's dark eyes gazed intently into Sheffield's. "I'll get on that right away."

Sam flipped page by page through his notebook. "We'll keep a man posted at Grayson's apartment."

Sheffield's brows shot up. "Once we've collected the evidence, let's throw that bone to Salinger."

A meaningful glance passed between his agents. "That won't keep the Chief happy," Sam said.

Sheffield looked from one of them to the other. "It's a start. We don't want them involved with lab work— fingerprints, blood pathology—" Drowning out his voice, a thunderous blast shook the hospital followed by two more explosions in quick succession.

"Get away from the windows," Sheffield yelled to Jason.

Sam shouted at Jaclyn as he sped to a public telephone booth. "Go to the lobby, see if you can find out what's going on. Take the stairs!" Jaclyn's dark hair sailed behind her as she raced to the lighted exit sign. Sheffield hurried to the window.

"It's City Hall," Jason said."

Stunned, the AG watched in silence as orange flames and black smoke licked the sky.

"City Hall blew," Sam shouted to Sheffield. "'On my way."

"Wait, I'm coming with you. Jace, stay here, or I'll have someone take you home." Sheffield was backing away, jabbing a forefinger at his friend. "Those are your options." Sam held the elevator door, and Sheffield raced through it.

# Chapter Fourteen

**M**aneuvering the State vehicle past the smoldering ruins, Sam parked well away from the fire engines and ambulances.

"You shouldn't be here," Sam said, frowning at Sheffield.

"You're worried about me."

"Hey, if something happened to you, I'd have to break in a new boss."

Sheffield smiled. "Yeah, yeah, you love me, admit it."

"Jeeze," Sam muttered.

They climbed out of the faded red Jeep and froze like statues, silently taking in the grisly spectacle. Intense heat radiated in waves from the burning rubble. Only one wall of the four-story building had survived the blasts, an ebony monolith, testifying to the devastation below.

Sam lit a cigarette. "There isn't a lot left to investigate."

"That wall is going topple any second," Sheffield said. "Sam, find the chief, or whoever's in charge from the PFD. Tell them I said to back off until it can be shored up."

"The Chief was standing by the fire engines a few minutes ago." Sam scanned the area. "He's not there now, but I'll find him."

Frowning, Jaclyn stared at the burning rubble. "Could people still be alive under there?"

"Not a chance." Sheffield shook his head. "No one could've survived." He nodded at the four body bags lying side by side between the two ambulances. "While you're at it, Sam, see if you can find out how many folks were in there."

"Gotcha," Sam said as he charged off.

A throng of bystanders rimmed the area cordoned off by Sheffield's agents and the Phoenix Police.

Taking Jaclyn's arm, Sheffield said, "How many agents do we have on-site?"

"Sam and I and the SWAT."

"Okay, Sam's in charge, you're his back up." Sheffield looked around. "There's nothing more I can do here. I'd appreciate a lift to the hospital. My car is there, and I'd like to see how Jace is holding up, and check on Christian."

Jaclyn's stricken eyes met his. "I pray Christian makes it."

"Do you know him?"

"We're friends," she said softly, then added, "best friends."

Sheffield gazed at the smoking ruins. "I'm sorry." He hesitated a moment. "Is he more than a friend?" The question seemed to puzzle her. "Are you romantically involved?"

Jaclyn shook her head. "No."

"Why don't you hang out with me at the hospital? At least until Christian is out of surgery."

"Thanks, but we're spread too thin as it is."

"First the attack on Christian, then this. Makes you wonder, doesn't it?"

Jaclyn stared at him. "Do you think they're connected?"

Sheffield shrugged. "It's too early to tell. Jaclyn, be straight with me. Can you work on Christian's case?"

"I'm a cop, Shef."

"Without question, but it's personal." Sparks flew from her eyes. "All right, we'll see how it goes."

"I won't let you down."

He smiled. "That possibility never entered my mind."

Sheffield spotted Sam striding away from the Fire Chief to his fellow agents. Sheffield was glad his chief investigator had called in Rip Vashay, and the State's Special Weapons Attack Team.

He gazed at Jaclyn. Tall and slim, her features were enhanced by rose-kissed, olive skin. Long, dark curly hair framed her oval face. Sheffield decided that amber was too tame a word to describe Jaclyn's golden eyes. Large and almond shaped, they seemed to mirror her soul.

Sheffield braced himself as a mob of reporters skirted the yellow tape and, like bees to honey, swarmed around him. Flashbulbs popped, television cameras rolled. He'd refrain from calling this a crime scene, although his gut told him that's what it was.

Ted Brown, one of Jason's newscasters, held a microphone inches from Sheffield's face. "Any insight as to what this is about, sir?"

"No." Death and destruction had pervaded the State Capital. Mere words couldn't describe the outrage he felt. But this was neither the time nor place to air his feelings, and he set them aside.

"We'll have to sift through the ashes before we'll know what caused the explosion—implosion, rather," Sheffield said, recognizing it for what it was. An amateur could blow a building to smithereens. It took an expert with the knowledge of structural engineering to place the explosives to do what had been done here. Three walls of The Tower, as it was called, had buckled and collapsed inward.

"Any idea how many people died in there?" Theodore Brown said.

"Four unidentified bodies have been recovered. We've asked the Fire Chief to back off until the remaining wall can be shored up."

"Shef, are you in charge of the investigation?"

"Officially, yes," Sheffield said, knowing his remark would enflame Mort Salinger.

A reporter from KTOP-TV shouted, "In cooperation with other law enforcement agencies?"

"Of course," the Attorney General replied. "The media can help by airing this message: If anyone saw or heard anything unusual or in any way suspicious, call my office or contact the Phoenix Police.

"That's it, we have work to do." As the questions hammered on, Sheffield held his hand up like a traffic cop at an intersection. As he strode away with Jaclyn at his side, he heard Ted Brown wrapping up the interview.

"That was State Attorney General Alan Sheffield. Witnesses reported hearing a blast, followed by two more, before The Tower collapsed."

# Chapter Fifteen

After dropping Sheffield off at the hospital, Jaclyn went to the office. When she left the elevator on the tenth floor, Moira was at her desk talking on the phone. Jaclyn smiled at Sheffield's secretary, mouthed "good morning," knowing it was anything but, and headed for the office she shared with Sam.

Sighing, Jaclyn dropped her shoulder bag on the brown leather sofa, instantly cognizant of the headache that thudded behind her eyes. Normally, she jump-started her system with mega-doses of caffeine, but there was nothing normal about this day. She strode to the mini bar next to the windows and poured a cup of coffee from the carafe, expecting it to be day-old and cold. To her surprise, it was a steaming hot and tantalizingly fragrant. No matter how serious a crisis might be, Moira never missed a beat.

Jaclyn sipped the potent brew as she wandered around the room, thinking about Christian, thinking about what had happened at City Hall. She wasn't a stranger to how a moment in time could devastate lives forever.

As if on cue, horrifying memories from her past overwhelmed her. No matter how many years had come and gone, she'd never get past that day when everything changed for her—that terrifying day when the Germans came and the men in uniform prodded her parents into a canvas-covered truck. As if it were happening at this very moment, she heard her mother screaming "Jaclyn, Jaclyn," until the butt of a rifle silenced her. It was the last time she'd seen her parents.

In the ghetto, pandemonium reigned—fear so palpable it tainted the air—men, women, children, fleeing in all directions, begging for mercy. Jaclyn tried to scoot under a hay wagon, but a soldier grabbed her and carried her through the gate into the town square. Within minutes, the invader's tanks thundered through the streets. After cranking the cannons into position, the order given, in a split second, the buildings behind the wall exploded. Nothing remained, but smoldering rubble.

"Let me go!" Jaclyn wailed, pounding her fists against the soldier's gray shirt. "I want my mother. I want to go home!"

Without a flicker of emotion, the young trooper pitched her, as if she were a sack of flour, over the tailgate into a truck. Less than an hour later, the soldiers herded Jaclyn, along with countless other children, into a rail car, and transported them to Trepskýa, a concentration camp near Poland's southern border.

There were two compounds. One camp, Jaclyn soon learned, was for the recovery of valuables the prisoners brought with them. The other, also with a single vocation, carried out Hitler's madness:

The Final Solution.

In the beginning, if it weren't for the old people, she would've forgotten her name. Day after day, the elders reminded her that she was Jaclyn Devereaux, and she was eleven years old.

Within days after her arrival at Trepskýa, the elders warned her that if the guard called the number tattooed beneath her forearm, she would disappear forever. Hundreds of prisoners already had—old men and women and children, even babes in their mother's arms. Their captors had murdered them. They were dead.

So, it came as no surprise when the guard shouted her number. She simply got in line with the others that would die that day.

But, as she trudged along destined for the "showers," an officer grabbed her arm and plucked her out of the line. The other prisoners shambled on. In a matter of minutes, their suffering and humiliation would be over. Jaclyn knew if she didn't die today, she'd die tomorrow, or the next day, or the day after that. This officer was trying to confuse her, a predator toying with its prey, a cruel, mind-wrenching game, devised to give her hope, then snatch it away.

That's what they did—ruse after ruse. A white armband meant you'd be spared. The next day, a green one would save you, then yellow or black or red. Prisoners bartered with one another for whatever current circle of cloth would keep them from the showers, or from the bottom of a pit with bullets in the backs of their heads. Desperate to survive, some resorted to stealing the coveted color of the day from family or friends. Somehow, she knew from the start that it was simply another way for their captors to demean them.

She walked behind the officer to the camouflaged building she'd come to know as the infirmary. Once inside, he said, "Take off your clothes." Staring at him with wide stricken eyes, Jaclyn retreated to the farthest corner of the room. "Take off your clothes and get on the table. Now!"

And, so it began. At night, in the underground bunker, beneath one of the filthy cots that marched along the walls, she'd curl up, like a snail retreating into its shell. Trembling, her heart beating wildly, then stopping, she'd hear his boots strike the concrete ramp. Thirty-three steps. Jaclyn always counted them. They grew louder and louder until he was in the maze of rooms, the fearful echoes ricocheting from wall to wall. It didn't matter where she hid, the Major always found her. At night, the operating room in the infirmary was deserted, and that was where he raped and tortured her. The Major had absolute power over her body. Although Jaclyn was helpless to stop the denigration of her flesh, she was determined not to let him destroy her mind.

Night after night, Jaclyn dreamed the dreams of the damned. If she could fly, she'd soar through the ravines to the top of the farthest mountain. If she were invisible, he couldn't find her. If she were dead, the torture would stop. Dying was the only way to escape, to end the inhumane experiments, the brutal, senseless torture, the hideous sights and sounds, the nightmares.

"Oh, God," she murmured as she struggled to force the memories away. Swiping at the tears sliding down her cheeks, she shook her head, as if to cleanse it. She gazed through the windows. Smoke continued to rise from the burning rubble. A few hours before, City Hall had lorded it over the smaller buildings nearby. For decades, the power brokers had done business there, although Jaclyn really didn't know exactly how long The Tower had reigned in downtown Phoenix.

As agonizing as she knew it would be, after having assured Sheffield that she could work Christian's case, she'd do it, hell or high water.

What did they know for sure? According to Jason Borseau, Christian had two things on his mind—getting up to speed on how the City did business or make that *funny business.* And The Ladies of the Night Murders.

The City! An almost forgotten memory nudged her mind. A month or so before, she'd dropped by Christian's apartment, hoping he'd join her for a swim. It would have to be later, he'd said. He was helping an ASU student practice a speech. When he'd introduced them, Christian had said the girl worked part-time at the City's reception desk.

It was a long shot, but if the girl had been on the job Tuesday afternoon, maybe she'd seen Christian, if that's where he'd gone. If not, Jaclyn could rule it out, and move in a different direction.

"What was her name?" Jaclyn murmured. "It started with an *M*. Margaret, Meggan? No. Melissa, Marsha? Margie, Marcie? "That's it, Marcie! Marcie Fairfield!" she said, triumphantly.

Jaclyn dropped into the chair behind her desk, and grabbed the phone book, hoping Miss Fairfield didn't live in a sorority house or dormitory. If that were the case, it'd be tricky to track her down, especially on the weekend. Jaclyn ran her index finger down the list of names beginning with an "F". "Ah, M. Fairfield. Surely, it won't be this easy," she murmured as she dialed the number.

"Hello," a lilting female voice answered.

"Is this *Marcie* Fairfield, who works at the City's reception desk?"

"Yes, who's this?"

"Marcie, this is Jaclyn Devereaux. I'm an investigator for State Attorney General, Alan Sheffield."

"O'm'gosh, is this about what happened at City Hall? I was watching a program on KTOP-TV, when—"

"No, I'm calling about a mutual friend, Christian Grayson. We met at his apartment."

"Sure, I remember."

"Marcie, did you work at City Hall Tuesday afternoon, and if so, did you see Christian?"

"Yesss," she stammered. "What's this about?"

"We're trying to track his movements between then and now."

"Why?"

"Christian has been injured."

"What happened? Was he in a car accident?"

"No, he was assaulted."

"Assaulted?"

"Christian was attacked, beaten."

"But, who'd do such an awful thing? He'll be okay, won't he?"

"We won't know until he's out of surgery." Jaclyn wound a lock of hair around her forefinger, the mindless habit having endured since she was a baby. Though her head had been shaved at the camp, the habit had survived. "Getting back to Tuesday, did Christian have an appointment with a City official?"

"I don't think so."

Nerves jangling, Jaclyn rose, and stretched the phone cord as far it would reach. Pacing back and forth between the windows and her desk, she asked, "Do you recall what time he got there?" Her gaze roamed around the room, focusing on objects, without seeing them—the antique clock between the windows, Sam's desk opposite hers, piled high with files, their respective degrees on the walls behind their desks, the mahogany conference table, four battered leather chairs.

"Three-thirty, give or take a few minutes. He was in such a hurry, he asked me to sign him in, said he'd help me practice my next speech. I asked where he was going, and he said to the City Manager's office. When I told him Paul Hewitt wasn't in, he said it was Hewitt's secretary he needed to see."

"The secretary's name?"

"Helen Burgess. It's Miss Burgess. She goes ballistic, if you call her Mrs."

Jaclyn went back to her desk and jotted down the name. "Were you still on duty when he left?"

"Yes."

Taking a quick sip of coffee, Jaclyn asked, "What time was that?"

"About an hour later, four-thirty or so."

"Did he mention why he needed to see Miss Burgess?"

"No. Like I said, he was in a hurry."

"Did he say anything when he left, or did he seem upset?"

71

"Not at all upset. I asked when he could help me with my speech. He said he'd be busy today, but he'd be free on Sunday, and to give him a call."

"Did you? Call him, I mean?"

"No, because I'll be busy tomorrow. I've made a date to go to the sock hop at the SUB—the Student Union Building—with friends."

"Did he mention what he'd be doing today?"

"No, and I didn't ask."

"Is there anything else you can tell me?" Jaclyn asked.

"Well, when he left The Tower, he was carrying a really thick stack of papers."

"Any idea what they might've been?"

"Not a clue."

"Marcie, you've been a big help. If you think of anything else that might be helpful, call me." Jaclyn recited the phone number at the office. "If I'm not in, leave a message, and I'll get back to you."

"Does what happened to Christian have something to do with that awful thing at City Hall?"

"Not as far as we know."

"The TV reporter said people died."

"Unfortunately, yes, but it's too early to know who." Jaclyn quickly scanned her notes. "Marcie, if you like, I'll keep you up to speed on how Christian is doing."

"If it wouldn't be too much trouble."

"No trouble at all."

"Thanks, Miss—"

"Devereaux—Jaclyn Devereaux."

"I'm sorry, I'm not thinking straight."

"I understand. Thanks, Marcie."

Jaclyn hung up, stuffed the notebook into her purse, and left the office. "Moira, if the AG calls, tell him I'll check in with him as often as I can."

"I'll make a note of it." Lowering her glasses, Moira peered over the rims. "Oh, Sam called while you were on the phone. He'd like you to meet him at Shady Creek Apartments." Moira cocked her head. "Isn't that where you live?"

Jaclyn nodded. "Yes, as does Christian Grayson. I'll be in touch."

"Will you come back here or—"

"Probably not."

"All right, dear. I'll be here if you need me," Sheffield's secretary added.

"You always are. We couldn't get along without you."

Moira blushed. "What a nice thing to say."

"And thank you so much for the coffee. Caffeine deprivation had me down for the count. Okay, 'call you later."

"Be safe," Moira said softly.

# Chapter Sixteen

"Thanks for lending a hand," Sam said to the FBI's crime scene investigators.

"No problem," Kirk Williams said. Of the four agents, he appeared to be the man in charge. "If you'll bring us up to date, we'll get started."

After apprising them of the situation, Sam said, "The Attorney General thinks Grayson was probably taken here." Pointing to a dark blue sedan, he said, "That's his car. The windows are intact, so either he didn't lock up, or the perps had the keys. Grayson is the crime investigator for KSOL-TV, which makes it doubly hard to believe he didn't lock his car. Still, if they had the key, why break into the glove box?"

"Sam," Jaclyn called out as she slammed the door of the Jeep, and strode to him.

"My partner, Jaclyn Devereaux," Sam told the Feds. They nodded in unison.

"No mistaking who you fellas are," Jaclyn said, admiring their black FLAK vests, with FBI printed in bright yellow letters. "What do you want me to do, Sam?"

"See if you can get a line on when Grayson was last seen. Talk to his neighbors, find out if they witnessed anything out of the ordinary."

"By the way, my apartment is directly below Christian's," Jaclyn interjected.

"You live here?" She nodded. "How handy is that? You can question yourself."

"Ha, ha, funny man. Oh, I thought you might be hungry, so I picked up a cheeseburger and fries for you. Catch," she said, as she tossed the brown paper bag to him.

"Thanks, Jaclyn, I appreciate it." Sam turned to Agent Williams. "How about one of your men processing Grayson's apartment?"

"I'll take it," Scott Lindsey said as he hefted a large, leather satchel, bulging with the equipment he'd need to do the job.

"Hey, Sam," Jaclyn yelled as she strode away. "Shef wants a meeting at his place tomorrow morning, at six in the am."

"Okay, I'll pick you up at five."

"No need for you to go out of your way, I'll just take my own car. See you later."

Agent Lindsey followed her into the elevator. "Jaclyn Devereaux. You're French."

"The majority of my ancestors were. In France, my name is pronounced Zhaclean," she said as she sized him up. He was impressive—six feet tall and fit, with broad shoulders tapering to a slender waist and hips, thirty-something, facial features an intriguing combination of angles and planes.

He grinned. "Do I measure up to your expectations?"

"Actually, you're exactly how I think an FBI agent should look," Jaclyn responded, with an impish tilt of her head.

"I'll take that as a compliment." He grinned and the sharp edges of his face softened. "I think you're pretty, too."

Jaclyn laughed. "How long have you been an investigator?"

"Seven years with the FBI. You?"

"Five, with the State Attorney General."

The elevator door opened. "This is it," Jaclyn said, as they approached Christian's door that had been secured with yellow crime scene tape. Her chest constricted, she dreaded what they might find inside.

"Should I break it in, or—"

After dangling the key in front of the agent's face, Jaclyn unlocked the door. They ducked under the tape, and went in. The entryway led directly to the living room.

Jaclyn spun around. Books and audiotapes were strewn about, the fabric on the couch and chairs in shreds, desk drawers empty, and pitched aside.

"If only we knew what they were searching for?" Twisting her fingers together, she murmured, "Christian is so neat—a place for everything, everything in its place. "Look, I'll get out of your way," Jaclyn stammered, as she backed toward the door.

"You and Grayson are friends?"

"Yes," Jaclyn said.

"Isn't your being involved in the investigation akin to a surgeon operating on a family member?"

"I can handle it," Jaclyn said stiffly, as she closed the door behind her. She slumped against the wall in the hallway. "Christian, what in God's name did you step into?"

"**S**ugar or cream?" Karen Maynard asked as she handed a delicate china cup and saucer to Jaclyn.

Jaclyn smiled. "Black is fine, Mrs. Maynard."

"Please call me Karen," she said, with a smile.

Jaclyn glanced around the living room. "Your apartment could be featured in *House Beautiful*."

"Thank you. As you see, my husband and I prefer a monochromatic setting."

Jaclyn guessed so. Stark white carpets, drapes, and furniture, only token color in the dusty-rose pillows on the couch and chairs, and three huge, matching floor pillows, nestled around a lake-sized glass-topped coffee table.

"The pillows come in handy for casual entertaining," Karen said, following Jaclyn's gaze. "Of course, if we decide to have a family, our apartment is not child-friendly."

"It puts my place to shame," Jaclyn said.

"Interior decorating is what I do." Karen tucked a strand of blonde, chin-length hair around one ear. "I'd be happy to re-decorate your apartment. My goal is to match my clients' décor to their personalities. I think of it as getting in touch with their inner hues."

Jaclyn wasn't sure she wanted to get in touch with her inner hues. "I, uh, don't—"

"No pressure, just think about it."

"I will." For a very long time, she thought. "As I said, we're trying to track Christian's movements from Tuesday afternoon on."

"Hmmm." Karen Maynard pursed her shimmering rose colored lips. "We saw him Wednesday morning."

"Do you recall what time that was?"

"About five-thirty. We always get an early start when we go spelunking."

Jaclyn had trouble picturing this elegant woman, attired in satin, dusty-rose lounging pajamas, rummaging about in caves. Her skin didn't look as if it had ever seen the sun, her long, manicured fingernails didn't seem cave-friendly, either.

"Ordinarily, we go on Saturday, camp out, and come home Sunday evening."

"This weekend being an exception?"

"My husband is an architect. He'd scheduled meetings with clients. We're going on vacation soon, and he had some issues to resolve before we leave."

"You're sure it was Christian you saw?"

"Not at first." Karen rolled her immense cornflower blue eyes. "We almost got off the elevator on the second floor. I mean, he was so scrungy-looking, like a homeless person."

"Headed for the mean streets," Jaclyn muttered to herself.

Karen leaned toward Jaclyn. "I'm sorry."

"Just talking to myself."

"Oh." Karen shrugged. "What is this about? Is Christian in trouble?"

"The worst kind." *At last, she thinks to ask.* "Between the time you saw him and today, someone nearly beat him to death. It's a miracle he's alive."

"That's horrible." Karen gaped at Jaclyn. "But surely no one in this building was involved."

"Until we know why Christian was targeted, everyone who came in contact with him is suspect." Jaclyn glanced at her notes. "How well do you and your husband know Christian?"

"Not well at all, only to say hello. He mostly kept to himself. Well, we often saw him with you, and on TV, of course. A crime reporter, wasn't he?"

"Past tense? Don't be too quick to put Christian in the ground. He's a fighter. He'll make it."

"Is, was. I didn't mean anything by my choice of words."

"I'm sure you didn't. Forgive me for snapping at you. As you pointed out, Christian and I are friends. Under the circumstances, I'm not as objective as I should be."

"Apology accepted," Karen said, icily.

"So, on the morning in question, the three of you got out of the elevator in the garage?"

"Yes."

"Did you see Christian leave or was he still there when you left?"

"It takes considerable time to load our gear, so he was long gone by the time we left."

"All right. I guess that's all I have. For now," she added. "Call me, if you think of anything else that might help, or if you hear other tenants who mention seeing or hearing something suspicious." Jaclyn handed a business card to Karen.

"Certainly."

"I'll need to talk to your husband before you leave for vacation. What is his first name?"

"Alexander, but everyone calls him Alex."

"If you'll give me your phone number, I'll ring you later to make an appointment with him." Jaclyn jotted down the number Karen dictated. "Also, I'll need a map, nothing elaborate, to pinpoint where you and your husband went spelunking. I'll pick it up later or you can slip it under my door, number 308. Thanks for the coffee." Jaclyn set the cup and saucer on the coffee table, tucked the notebook into her purse, and left the apartment.

She glanced at her watch, it was after three. It had taken four hours to interview the tenants on Christian's floor—the ones who had answered their doors. Unlike Karen Maynard, each of them had been quick to ask what had happened to Christian. Only her conversation with the elegant interior decorator had raised Jaclyn's hackles. She decided to take the stairs down to her apartment. Maybe she'd see something out of place along the way. Later, she'd try to contact Sheffield, and then check in with Sam.

"Fancy?" Jaclyn glanced around, wondering where her beloved Siamese was hiding. "Ah, there you are," she said, seeing the cat hunkered down on top of the China cabinet, peering over the decorative trim, her electric blue eyes squeezed into slits. With a loud, deep-throated growl, the cat flattened her ears, and scooted away from the edge.

Instantly on guard, Jaclyn reached inside her jacket and grabbed her .38. Clutching it with both hands, brandishing it from side to side, she crept in a crouched position from one room to another, checking behind the drapes, in the closets, under the beds, behind the shower curtain. Something had upset Fancy, but nothing seemed out of place.

She went back through the living room to the entryway, opened the coat closet, and glanced in. She checked the front door lock. It didn't appear to have been tampered with. Jaclyn spun full-circle one last time. After holstering her weapon, she picked up an audiotape on the floor and put it on the top shelf next to the hi-fi, one of Fancy's favorite roosts.

"You did a bit of flying today, didn't you? Come down now, all is well," Jaclyn cooed, in a reassuring voice, even though she still felt uneasy. "How I wish you could talk."

"Yeow!" the Siamese responded loudly.

Jaclyn heard a rustling sound behind her, but before she could react, something struck the side of her head. Dazed, she fell to her knees, then collapsed on the floor. A pair of boots flashed by her, the front door slammed shut a second later. It took several minutes before Jaclyn could sit up, several more minutes to struggle to her feet, and stagger to the couch.

The person who'd invaded her home and struck her down had been concealed in the closet behind her coats. If she told Sheffield, he'd connect the attack on her to the attack on Christian. He'd take her off the case. Jaclyn would not let that happen. She grabbed a tissue from the decorative dispenser on the coffee table and pressed it to her temple.

"How am I going to explain this?" she said, staring at the bloody tissue. "I'll probably have a black eye to boot."

Jaclyn looked up at Fancy. The Siamese was peering down at her mistress, with the superior expression, typical of her breed.

"Okay, if there's a next time, I won't doubt you for a second. 'Hope to God there isn't," Jaclyn added.

Why did someone invade my apartment? There's nothing of value here—costume jewelry, an old typewriter, ditto the stereo, and TV. Could it have something to do with

Christian? Whether it does or not, that's what Sheffield will assume. Jaclyn glanced around, searching for answers, as if they were somewhere in the room.

She rose from the couch, went down the hall to the bathroom, looked in the mirror, and studied the damage to the side of her face.

"Not too bad, so far," Jaclyn murmured. "God knows what it'll look like in the morning. If I dab on a little makeup, maybe Shef and Sam won't notice." Knowing there was little chance of that.

Jaclyn opened the medicine cabinet, grabbed the bottle of peroxide, poured a little on a cotton ball, cleansed the wound, and slapped on a Band-Aid. She swallowed a couple of aspirin, hoping to stave off another headache, and went back to the living room.

It was a few minutes past three. There was still time to make it to *The Arizona Republic* before they closed. The newspaper's morgue was one of Christian's choice haunts when he was investigating a crime. She wouldn't call Sheffield, until she was sure her voice wouldn't reflect the anxiety she was feeling.

"Fancy, I see your 'I told you so' expression. Gloat if you must, but please get it out of your system while I'm gone. See you later."

"Yow!"

"You always have to have the last word," Jaclyn said as she hooked the strap of her purse over her shoulder, and left the apartment, making sure the door was locked. As she walked to the elevator, she reminded herself to call a locksmith and arrange to have dead bolts installed on her apartment door.

# Chapter Seventeen

**J**ason guessed the neurosurgeon's age to be in the middle to late fifties. A skullcap, matching his green scrubs dangled from his hand. As he talked and gestured, the ties swept the tile floor.

Jason caught sight of Sheffield and waved him over. The AG acknowledged him with a nod, then stopped to talk to the agents he'd assigned to the surgical wing before joining Jason and who Sheffield assumed was Christian's surgeon.

"City Hall is a pile of ashes," he said. "When I stopped by the office, there was a slew of messages from George Pearson. Our esteemed Governor is in a panic about the City Hall *incident*. He's afraid it will adversely affect his image. As if I give a hoot about the politics in light of this human tragedy. Four people are dead. 'Fix it, Shef,' was his message to me."

"From what I saw on the tube, it isn't fixable," Jason said.

"All the king's horses and all the king's men—" Sheffield muttered.

"Shef, this is Dr. Marengo, Christian's neurosurgeon. Alan Sheffield," he said.

Dr. Marengo's eyes flared. "The Attorney General?"

Sheffield nodded. "How's Christian doing?"

"Well, as I was telling Mr. Borseau, he suffered a hairline fracture. I inserted a shunt to relieve the pressure. There were other injuries—a fracture of the right tibia, several broken ribs. Fortunately, his lungs weren't punctured." Dr. Marengo paused. "I'm confident there is no brain damage. The orthopedic surgeon that operated on his leg said, with therapy, there shouldn't be any residual problems in that area. Does he have relatives I should be talking to?"

"His parents are flying in from Georgia," Jason said. "May I see him?"

"He's still in the ICU." The doctor frowned at Sheffield. "This *was* a random attack on a person of color, wasn't it?"

Sheffield's emerald green eyes burned into the doctor's. "Probably not."

"I suppose it's too soon to know when Christian will be able to leave the hospital," Jason said.

Dr. Marengo pursed his lips. "I'll know more in a day or two, but right now I'd be guessing. The sooner the better, assuming Mr. Grayson was and still is a target. Would that be a correct assumption?"

"That's why I've posted guards," Sheffield responded.

"Still, if anything should go awry, the hospital staff and patients would be at risk."

"I can only assure you that every effort will be made to keep the patients and the hospital staff safe."

Dr. Marengo did not look convinced. He turned to Jason. "Out of curiosity, Mr. Borseau, what is this young man to you?"

"Christian is KSOL-TV's investigative reporter. He's also my dear friend."

"I see," Dr. Marengo murmured.

"Dr. Marengo, please don't take this as criticism. But, since Christian took a severe beating, and he hasn't regained consciousness, even though I'm convinced that you're eminently qualified, I guess I'd feel better if we got a second opinion."

"Did you have someone n mind?"

"Yes, have you heard of Andrew Kirk?" Jason said.

"Of course, he has a sterling reputation."

Jason nodded. "We go back a very long ways."

"Actually, I'd be willing to step aside and let him take over." He glanced at Sheffield. "I hope you don't think I'm, how do you say it? Copping out."

A sardonic smile nudged Sheffield's lips. "Now why would I think that?"

"Shef!"

"Yeah, yeah, forgive my bad manners."

"We are who we are, Mr. Sheffield. If we're talking about courage, try to imagine the guts it takes to slice into someone's brain," Dr. Marengo said.

"Touché." Sheffield saluted the neurosurgeon. "Are you ready to go, Jace?"

"As soon as we see Christian. Oh, before we hit the street, maybe you should wipe that egg off your face."

# Chapter Eighteen

Sooty, moisture-laden clouds roiled overhead. Ear-splitting thunder, streaks of lightning, and intermittent rain pelted the City. Jason's plane circled over the estate. Sheffield's Mercedes ground to a stop as Beau Meredith landed the DC-3. Kathryn was waiting for them on the tarmac. Jason hurried to his wife, and swept her into his arms. Sheffield leaned his elbows on the hood of the car.

"Christian?" she whispered, drawing away to search her husband's face.

"He's stable, the doctor says he'll make it. Erring on the side of caution, he didn't say Christian would be as good as new." Jason pressed his lips to her hair. "We saw him briefly. His head's swathed in bandages, right leg's in a cast. He's hooked up to an alarming assortment of tubes and bags."

"Was he conscious?"

Jason shook his head. "The anesthetic hadn't worn off."

As the steward rolled a ramp into place, Beau Meredith swung through the hatch and dropped to the runway. Jason lifted his thumb, aiming the familiar World War II salute at his copilot, who responded in kind. During the conflict, Jason had piloted a B-17 in Europe, Beau, a B-24 in the Pacific.

Jason and Kathryn strode to the plane, leaving Sheffield pacing along the strip with his hands stuffed into the back pockets of his jeans. Jason bolted up the ramp and disappeared through the hatch, reappearing a minute later with Christian's mother. Christian's father followed them down the ramp.

"Hello, I'm Kathryn," she said, smiling at the feminine version of Christian's face.

"Sarah Grayson. Our son never fails to mention how kind your family is to him."

"And he to us," Kathryn said, hugging the tiny woman.

Jason and Christian's father walked side-by-side to Sheffield.

"How's my son, Mr. Borseau?"

"He's doing very well."

Christian's father gazed into Jason's eyes. "Then he's going to make it?"

"Barring complications, which the doctor doesn't foresee," Jason assured him. "Mr. Grayson, this is Alan Sheffield, the State Attorney General. He's investigating the attack on Christian." Jason glanced at the thunder clouds racing across the sky. "Before it starts raining again, let's go to the house, get you settled, then go to the hospital."

"We plan to stay at a hotel near the hospital, if there's one that will accept us. We've put you out too much already."

Jason frowned. "We'd like you to stay with us."

Christian's father studied Jason's face. The fierce black eyes didn't waver, the deep timber of his voice resonated, "That would be hard for us to do."

"I'm sorry you feel that way," Jason said.

Hesitating, Carl Grayson glanced at Kathryn. "I don't mean to seem ungrateful to you and—"

"Kathryn." Jason turned to smile at her. "My wife's name is Kathryn."

# Chapter Nineteen

Sheffield draped his jacket over the back of a chair, unbuckled his shoulder holster, and shoved his .38 into the nightstand drawer. He went into the bathroom, splashed cold water on his face, and caught sight of himself in the mirror. The rotten day he'd had stared back at him with bloodshot eyes. He left the bedroom and went downstairs.

Carl Grayson had refused to stay in the Borseaus' home, but at his wife's urging, he'd agreed to spend the night in one of the guest cottages. It was an evening Sheffield wanted to forget. Christian's mother had collapsed in tears at her son's bedside. Before leaving the hospital, Sheffield had called Sandra to tell her he'd be busy with the two investigations. He'd try to keep in touch.

Sheffield had checked with Sam and Jaclyn every hour or so. He glanced at his watch. It was after midnight. He'd slept only a couple of hours the night before. *Tired* couldn't begin to describe how exhausted he felt. Even so, he was wired and doubted if he could sleep. He'd scheduled a meeting with Sam and Jaclyn for six the following morning.

His Japanese houseboy, Sejii Hayashi stood ramrod straight at the foot of the stairs. A head shorter than Sheffield's lean six two, the jujitsu expert's body was hard edged, and heavily muscled. Sejii was twenty-six, an orphan who'd worked his way to the States on a freighter. The cargo was off-loaded in Stockton, a seaport inland from the Golden Gate Bridge. As was pre-arranged with the Captain, Sejii had left the ship, and hitchhiked to Phoenix where he'd begin his new life in America.

Sheffield often frequented the Japanese restaurant where Sejii worked. No matter how stressful the AG's day had been, the young man's exuberance never failed to lift Sheffield's spirits. They'd become friends, and eventually, he'd offered Sejii room and board, in exchange for doing odd jobs around the house. In the beginning, Sejii had been out of control—cleaning, cooking, washing, ironing, and gardening, from dawn 'til dark. Finally, at Sheffield's insistence, they had struck a bargain. Sejii would put in a maximum of three hours a day doing tasks around the house. He'd go to school, and Sheffield would pay for his education.

The next fall, Sejii had enrolled at Arizona State University in Tempe. Next semester, he'd begin his junior year. With glowing eyes and an infectious grin, Sejii was quick to say, "Soon I will be an American citizen."

"Want dinner, boss?" Sejii said.

"Thanks, no, but I'd like breakfast for three people at six-thirty. Wake me up at five-thirty with a cup of strong coffee, please. Strong," he said, flexing his arm to bring up muscle.

"Boss make joke." Sejii grinned at Sheffield. "*Hai*?"

Smiling at his faithful companion, the AG patted Sejii's shoulder. "*Hai*, I'm joking. Go to bed, my friend. I have some thinking to do."

"You very tired. Miss Parker stay very late, boss have very bad day, better hit sack soon."

"I will." Sheffield chuckled at the skeptical expression on Sejii's face. "That's called nagging."

Sejii's hands flew into a prayer position. Crossing his right thumb over his left, he steepled his fingers. Stolidly aspiring to the culture of his ancestors, he bowed and backed away before turning to leave the room. After five years, Sheffield had given up trying to change his loyal companion.

Sheffield went to the den and sank into one of the chairs in front of his desk. Choosing a pipe from the rack on the table beside him, he lifted the humidor cover, filled the bowl, and tamped the tobacco with his thumb. Having left the house in a blur that morning, he'd neglected to take a pipe along. Sheffield sucked on the stem. He flipped the gold lighter Sandra had given him for Christmas, and read the inscription: *The light of my life. Forever, Sandra.* His chin dropped to his chest. Even though he hadn't meant to mislead her that's exactly what he'd done. Sheffield couldn't believe how dispirited he felt. Uninvited, Jaclyn's image crept into his mind. He blinked her away, rose, left the room, and went upstairs.

# Chapter Twenty

**O**vernight, the storm had dissipated. In its wake, the bright blue, rain-scrubbed sky sparkled overhead. In the distance, sunlight shimmered along the rugged slopes. Casually attired in short-sleeved shirts, jeans, and boots, Sheffield and his investigators sat at a round, wrought-iron table on the veranda.

"Let's see where we stand, starting with you, Sam," Sheffield said, pouring cream into his coffee. Sejii charged around the table waving a spoon.

Sheffield smiled. "Thank you, my friend, but I can stir my own coffee."

Leaning down, Sejii jerked his head toward Jaclyn. "Missy very pretty."

"It's not polite to whisper," Sheffield said softly.

"Okay, boss, Missy very pretty!" he shouted.

Jaclyn tucked her smile behind her napkin. "Thank you for the compliment, Sejii."

Sejii grinned, bowed, and hurried through the sliding glass doors.

Sheffield winked at Jaclyn.

Sam was all business, flipping page by page through his notes. "Let's start with the safe. It was partially intact, but the contents in it, like everything else, were reduced to ashes."

Sheffield leaned toward him. "Does the City keep a lot of cash on hand?"

"From what the Director of Finance . . ." Sam paused to flip back a few pages in his notebook. "Lee Crooks said there were a few thousand dollars, plus some checks they'd received too late on Friday to deposit in the bank."

"What else?" his boss said.

"Name it, that's where they kept it," Sam said. "All the microfilm, tape recordings of Council meetings, year-end audit reports, records of all their transactions, as-built drawings of every building, roadway, permits, licenses, deeds."

"As much as I hate Sunday morning quarter-backing, why would they put all their eggs in one basket? Jesus," Sheffield mumbled, mentally chastising himself for using two clichés in a single sentence.

"So much for the safe being fire-proof," his chief investigator said.

"The vault had to have been left open, and I don't think it was by accident. Remind me to tell Moira to duplicate our records and stash them off-site." Rising, Sheffield left his investigators and paced along the bluff. He gazed into the distance, rubbing the palm of one hand with the knuckles of the other. Turning back, he focused on Jaclyn, until her puzzled expression forced him to look away.

As Sam glanced from his boss to his partner, a smile tugged at the corners of his mouth.

Sheffield came back to the table. "Let's go out on a limb. Let's assume Christian came up with something damaging about the City."

"Wait a *minute*," Sam said. "There's nothing to tie Christian's kidnapping to City Hall."

"I said, let's go out on a limb," the Attorney General shot back.

"That's a shaky limb we're about to crawl out on."

"Call it a gut feeling—"

"May I interject a word or two?" Jaclyn said, with a facetious smile.

"Hey, Jaclyn, what's with the Band-aid, and what looks like the makings of a black eye," Sam said, tipping his head side to side, "Did someone take a poke at you?"

"I made a middle of the night trip to the bathroom without turning on the light, and smacked into the door. I'm fine. Now where was I? Oh, a while back, I met a young woman, Marcie Fairfield, at Christian's place. I'd dropped by to invite him for a swim, but he was helping her with a speech. Marcie's an ASU student, who works part-time at the City's reception desk, when there *was* a reception desk.

"I called her on the off-chance that she'd seen Christian Tuesday afternoon." She gazed at Sheffield, "You said, according to Mr. Borseau, something about the Council meetings had piqued Christian's interest. Whether it was at the meeting the night before, or earlier, we have no way of knowing. In addition to that, he wanted to investigate The Ladies of the Night Murders. He intended to tap one of his snitches, and needed money to loosen his or her tongue.

"Also, Mr. Borseau said Christian left the station on Tuesday at about three. I know how he operates. It was too late in the day for him to get ready for what he calls the mean streets. And I was right. He went to City Hall. Marcie said he was in such a hurry, he asked her to sign him in. When she asked him where he was going, he said the City Manager's office. She told him that Paul Hewitt wasn't in, and Christian said, 'It's his secretary I need to see.' Helen Burgess died in the blast yesterday. To Miss Fairfield's best recollection, Christian was there for about an hour. Marcie said when he left he was carrying a stack of papers or documents. I didn't see him Tuesday evening, so I don't know whether he was at home or not. We don't see one another every day.

"I've talked to most of the tenants on the fourth floor. Karen Maynard, Christian's next-door neighbor said she and her husband saw Christian in the elevator on Wednesday morning at about five-thirty. They were going spelunking. Normally, they go on Saturday, but her husband, an architect, had scheduled a meeting with a client. Mrs. Maynard said, at first they didn't recognize Christian. In fact, she said they almost got off of the elevator on the second floor, because he was so scrungy-looking, like a homeless person, and they were uncomfortable being in close proximity to him. When Christian goes *under*, he plays the part—tattered clothes, sunglasses. He doesn't shave or shower when he invades the mean streets." Jaclyn frowned as she sipped her coffee.

"What's bothering you?" Sheffield asked.

"Karen Maynard. The interview was almost over before she wondered why I was asking questions about Christian. What can I say, something about her seemed off. She's elegant, gorgeous, but she's also narcissistic. That may be why she comes across as insensitive. I still need to talk to her husband, so I'll get another crack at her. I asked her to draw a rudimentary map of where they went spelunking, suggested she could slip it under my door, hoping that would ignite a fire under her, and I'd get it ASAP. It wasn't there this morning, but I left too early to roust them out of bed. I'll drop by their apartment when I get home.

"I wasn't going to tell you this, but I guess I'd better. After I interviewed Karen Maynard, I went back to my apartment. Fancy, my Siamese, was on top of the China cabinet, ears pasted to her head, slits for eyes. She yowled— as only a Siamese can yowl—and I knew something had upset her. Nothing seemed out of place or missing, but—"

"That's rich!" Sam guffawed. "Jaclyn has a guard cat."

"Neanderthal! She's more intelligent than some people I know, present company included."

"See what Jaclyn thinks of us, Shef?"

"There's no *us* about it."

"Okay, I'm sure you have a highly intelligent feline. Truce?"

"Maybe. I'll think about it," Jaclyn grumbled.

"All joking aside," Sheffield said, "did you think someone had been in your apartment?"

"At first, with everything that's going on, I chalked it up to being edgy. Actually," Jaclyn said quietly, "someone *was* in my apartment. I can't believe you guys fell for that old, I ran into a door bit."

"Tell us what happened?"

"When I saw how Fancy was acting, I drew my gun, checked every room in the house, but I only gave the coat closet in the entryway a cursory glance. I'd just turned away, when the intruder coshed me, and I went down. As he raced past me to the door, I got a quick glimpse of his boots, and that was all I saw. Wait." Jaclyn frowned. "They weren't ordinary boots. They looked expensive, black with hand-tooled burgundy accents. I'd never seen anything like them.

"It took me a few minutes to pull myself together. By that time, it was too late to follow him. I say him, but I suppose it could have been a woman."

"You don't have a deadbolt on your door?" Sheffield asked.

"It's being installed today."

"Jaclyn, we need to talk about this."

"That's why I didn't want you to know how I got this." Jaclyn pointed at the Band-aid on her temple. "I was afraid you'd take me off the case."

"That's what we're going to discuss."

"Shef, I—"

"Later." He pressed the palm of his hand toward her. "Let's get back to this intruder. Was anything missing or out of place?"

"As far as I could tell, nothing was missing. If he was looking for anything of value, he was out of luck." Jaclyn hesitated. "And the only thing out of place was an audio tape on the floor near the door. Fancy likes high places, so I'm sure she knocked it off."

"Did you listen to it?"

"Nooo."

"Does Christian have a key to your place?"

"Yes. You're suggesting he might have left the tape in my apartment." Sheffield shrugged. "I'll play it when I get home."

Frowning, Jaclyn said, "After I got my wits about me, I went to the *Arizona Republic's* morgue. Christian does a lot of research there. Sure enough, he'd gone there Wednesday afternoon, and checked out a dozen or so reels of microfilm. When he'd finished with them, the Librarian, Mrs. Beckman, said she saw him drop them in the receptacle at the desk. At the end of the day, when she began re-filing the film, she discovered many were missing. It had been a heavy day, and she was frustrated, knowing she'd have to compare the remaining microfilm with the checkout list. Now get this, the list is kept in a top drawer under the counter, and—"

"It was gone," Sheffield said.

"Exactly," Jaclyn said. "Ms. Beckman said she didn't know if she'd ever figure out what is missing."

"Wow!" Sam exclaimed.

Jaclyn scooped a lock of hair away from her face. "Even so, I didn't turn up anything to connect Christian's kidnapping with what happened at City Hall."

"Not so, Jaclyn. Now, we know Christian went to see Hewitt's secretary. I wonder what she does that would interest him," Sheffield said.

"Well, obviously, she answers the phones, types and files, puts the weekly agendas together, sort of a blueprint that outlines projects the Council will consider," Jaclyn said.

"And Christian would have to pay for the copies," Sheffield added. "Jaclyn, try to locate Christian's informant, see if she found out anything about the murders. I think Jace said *her*."

"Christian's most reliable informant is a prostitute that hangs out on the Westside, but I can't recall her name. When we're through here, I'll see what I can stir up in that neighborhood."

"Good job. Is that it?" Sheffield asked. Jaclyn nodded. "Okay, Sam, other than the couple who saw Christian in the elevator, have any other witnesses turned up?"

"Not in the strictest sense," he replied. "An attorney, Joseph Anderson, said he'd returned to the building at ten-thirty Thursday morning. When I asked how he could be so sure of the time, he said as he'd started down the ramp into the garage, he'd glanced at the clock on the dash. Initially, he'd left the building at about seven-thirty, but when he got to the office he realized he'd forgotten some documents he needed for an eleven o'clock court appearance. Anderson said there was a van parked in his assigned space. Since it happened routinely, he simply slipped into a spot reserved for guests."

"Could he describe the vehicle?" Sheffield said.

"A van. Blue, faded to white in places. Also, he said the windows, except for the windshield, were blacked out. It has to be the same vehicle Borseau's officers described."

Jaclyn asked, "Did he get a look at the license plate?"

"Not that he could recall."

Sheffield frowned. "Where's his parking space in relation to the elevator?"

"The first one left of the lift," Sam responded.

"But he didn't see anyone who looked suspicious," Sheffield pressed, "or anything that seemed out of order?"

"He was in a hurry, but he said he'd think about it. If anything else comes to mind, he'd call us."

"Did you check *him* out?" Jaclyn said.

"The attorney?" She nodded. "No, I didn't single him out, if that's what you mean. We're running background checks on everyone who lives there. Imagine my surprise to learn my partner's a tenant."

Jaclyn rolled her eyes. "I tried to tell you at the hospital, but you cut me off."

"Sorry about that."

Sheffield lit his pipe, and between puffs, said, "Getting back to this attorney, Anderson, Jaclyn has a point. He could be playing us."

"It's not likely, but it's possible," Jaclyn said.

"If that's the case," Sam said, "why'd he come forward? We hadn't knocked on his door."

"Eventually, you would have. What if someone saw the van *and* the attorney at about the time Christian was kidnapped, and he hadn't been upfront about being there." Jaclyn shrugged. "If he's involved, coming forward was the smart thing to do. What if he knew the van would be parked in his space? And did he really have a case on the docket. I'll check that out," she added.

Sheffield turned to Sam. "What area of law does he practice?"

Sam rifled through his briefcase, and handed the attorney's business card to the AG.

"Corporate attorney. Okay, see if he'll give us a list of his clientele."

"No good deed shall go unpunished," Sam muttered.

"Christian was nearly beaten to death, and four people *are* dead," Sheffield fumed. "We're going to look under every rock, climb out on every limb, shaky or not. Until it's proven otherwise, we're going to treat Christian's abduction and the bombing at City Hall as two elements of a single crime."

"Your call," Sam said, closing his notebook. "That's all I have."

"I think we can assume that Christian was abducted Thursday morning, that he was held somewhere, until Friday night, or very early Saturday morning, and then dumped at Jason's estate."

Sejii set a large silver tray on the serving cart and placed a frosty compote of strawberries, bananas, and kiwi before each of them.

"Thank you, Sejii," Jaclyn said, smiling at him.

"Only first course," Sejii said as he scurried back into the house.

Sheffield leaned toward Sam. "Other than Paul Hewitt's secretary, who else lost their lives?"

Sam flipped through his notes again. "The head honcho's assistant in the project engineering department, the building inspector's assistant and the City Clerk."

"Why were they there on a Saturday, and so early?" Sheffield muttered. "Is that usual, or were they lured there, and then murdered?" A thought struck him. "Sam, where were they?"

"Where?" Sam said. "Oh, I see, you mean when the bombs went off?"

"Yes, had they gone their separate ways or were they together? The City Manager's office is on the third floor in the west wing. The Engineering Department is on fourth floor in the east wing. The building inspector's office, second floor west, the City Clerk's office, third floor east."

"I'll try to find out. I see where you're going. Did they go to their respective offices, or did they get together to discuss something pertinent to them all?"

"Exactly," Sheffield said. "Jaclyn, check the financial records of the victims and get copies of their income tax statements for the past five years. Check their travel records, destinations, hotels, where they ate and with whom, who they slept with, where they shopped, their families and friends. Check their personal holdings, real estate, stocks, bonds. You know the drill. Then, move on to the City's middle and upper management, especially those who managed to survive, including Paul Hewitt and Lee Crooks. Go clear to the top. By that, I mean the Council. That'll take in the

Mayor, who'll be furious, and down the ladder to the janitors, and maintenance people."

"I'm on it," Jaclyn said.

Sejii peered around the screen door. "Sejii listening," he said. "Boss very excited."

"Eavesdropping isn't polite either," he retorted.

"Next course coming up!"

"Bring it on, my friend," Sheffield said.

**A**fter walking Sam to his car, Sheffield returned through the side gate. The guard dogs Ansel and Baggo dashed to him, tails wagging, leaping around him like pups. "Yeah, what if I were a burglar?" he said, giving each of them a scratch behind an ear. "Okay, boys, back to work."

As he rounded a corner of the house, he smiled when he saw Jaclyn embracing the scenery, turning full circle to take it in.

"Awesome," she said, "I love the scent of mesquite."

"So do I. I never take any of this for granted," Sheffield said, gazing from the purple shadowed crevices to the gilded summits. "Jaclyn, how long have you been in Arizona?"

"Ummm, since 1956, five years."

"And you moved here from . . .?"

Jaclyn angled her head. "Ah, the Attorney General investigates his investigator."

Two bright spots appeared on Sheffield's cheeks. "It's the nature of the beast," he said, smiling.

"That's why you're good at what you do," Jaclyn said, returning his smile. "To fill you in on what was missing from my resume, which I'm sure you've read: my father, Paul Devereaux, was an American citizen, an investment counselor. He worked with an elite group of banking firms in Krâków, most were Jewish-owned. On a trip to Paris to visit relatives, he met my mother. They were married a year later. Then, shortly before I was born, they came to the States. When I was a few months old, we returned to Poland. Our arrest was a matter of wrong place, wrong time. We were attending a Bar mitzvah for the eldest son of one of my father's clients."

"Did you tell them you weren't Jewish?"

Shaking her head, Jaclyn said, "As someone once told me, they bury their mistakes. Anyway, after the war, the displaced persons agency in England contacted my father's sister in Broken Bow, Nebraska. I went to high school there. After missing more than three years of school, I had a lot of catching up to do. Of course, I was an oddity—the girl from a foreign country, who'd been in a concentration camp. I couldn't connect with the kids my age, nor they with me."

Sheffield took her hands in his. "I guess not. While you were in a death camp, the girls in the States were playing with dolls, the boys with tin soldiers."

With a sad smile, she said, "Oh, I understood the disparity between us. In spite of all that, it was thrilling to be free, to come and go as I pleased, to roam willy-nilly wherever I chose to go. I took long walks in the countryside, conjured up visions of the Plains Indians, like the Arapahos, astride their spotted ponies, lined up along the bluffs." Jaclyn turned to the mountains again. "Much like yours."

"How old were you when you left Poland?"

"Now you're ever so cleverly trying to find out how old I am."

"Subtlety is not my forte." Sheffield laughed as they walked side by side along the pool. "Let's go inside and have a glass of Sejii's exotic iced tea."

"Speaking of Sejii, how were you lucky enough to find him?"

"Spinning the spotlight from yourself to Sejii won't distract me. Sejii," Sheffield called out as he closed the sliding glass door.

"*Hai*," said the houseboy behind them.

Sheffield whipped around. "One of these days, you'll give me a heart attack."

"Iced tea coming right up, boss. Pretty lady want lemon?"

Jaclyn gazed helplessly at Sheffield.

"He wants to know if the pretty lady wants lemon in her tea," Sheffield said.

"Please, Sejii, and thank you."

"We'll be in the den," Sheffield said, taking Jaclyn's elbow.

"Sejii find you," he shot back exuberantly.

The Attorney General chuckled. "I know you will."

Sheffield led Jaclyn to a burgundy leather sofa. She glanced around, thinking that it was a serene room, for all of its pillared elegance. Mahogany furniture blended quietly with taupe walls and dark hardwood floors. The pattern in the rugs breathed only a little color—ivory, pale mauve, and subdued teal. The wrap-around windows provided a view of the distant peaks, indirect lighting kept faith with the mellow atmosphere.

Jaclyn snuggled into the corner of the sofa, tucked one leg under the other, and turned to face him. "Tell me something. Is this routine between you and Sejii off the cuff or an act you put together to entertain your guests?"

Sheffield gazed at her thoughtfully. "A friend of mine suggested that I should've been a comedian, that I missed my calling by becoming an attorney." Seeing the question in her eyes, he said, "Jason, tongue in cheek, of course."

Silent for a long moment, at last, with a rush of air, Jaclyn said, "I was fourteen when the war ended."

Sheffield's gaze swept from her face to her white-knuckled fists. "How did you escape?" He sensed, rather than saw her stiffen.

She glanced at him warily. "What makes you think I escaped?"

"Unless the intelligence got it wrong, none of the prisoners survived Trepskýa."

Her dark eyes blazed, then froze on his face. She sprang from the sofa, and fled to the windows.

Sejii tiptoed in and set the tray with two tall frosty glasses on the table in front of his boss.

"Thank you," Sheffield said softly. Sejii bowed and made a hasty retreat. Sheffield picked up one of the glasses and went to her. "Do you take sugar?" Jaclyn shook her head. Taking her chin in his hand, Sheffield turned her face to his. Tears swam in her eyes. "Forgive me for upsetting you."

"You're right, I escaped." Her lips curved in a haunting smile. "The Major who'd laid claim to me shortly after I arrived at the camp, smuggled me out."

Sheffield rocked back on his heels, too stunned to speak. In the camp for three years, fourteen when she escaped. He did the math.

She lifted her eyes to his. "At first, I had no idea why we were there. We were just numbers. How very hard they tried to reduce those numbers to zero." Her hands flew to cover her face. "Oh, Shef, the old people, the children!"

Sheffield reached out to her. She shook him off and backed away. "When the war was winding down, they were in such a hurry to kill us, they didn't bother to check these." She pushed up her sleeve and held out her arm.

Sheffield stared at the tattoo, a ghastly reminder of Hitler's madness. "I'm sorry, Jaclyn." He took her in his arms, and pressed her to his chest.

"You want me, don't you?" she said quietly.

His arms tightened around her. "I'm not unique among men, Jaclyn. I may be old, but I'm not dead. You're a beautiful, desirable woman."

She buried her face in the curve of his neck, head throbbing, legs trembling. The Major's voice invaded her mind. "You're mine, forever."

"I'm not free," she whispered.

Sheffield drew away. "Are you married?"

"No."

"Engaged?" Jaclyn shook her head. "Dating someone?" She shook her head again.

With a tender smile, Sheffield wiped the tears on her cheeks. "I spilled your tea."

She laughed and wept as if they were a single emotion. "Sejii will clean it up."

"Now you're getting it, simply replace the L's with R's. Sejii rill crean it up."

"He's wonderful, isn't he?"

"Yes, he's wise and kind. His devotion to me is humbling, and I'm forever grateful for his friendship."

Jaclyn gazed up at him. "You're wonderful, too."

"I'm glad you think so." Sheffield felt the tension begin to flow out of her.

At last, she said, "If things were different—"

"What has to change for us to be friends, to spend time together?"

Taking his face between her hands, she said, "This is a conflict of interest."

"No, *this* isn't, but—"

"There is a personal conflict. Miss Parker."

"Sandra," he said softly.

"Sam said you're getting married."

"He was wrong. Sandra would like me to marry her, but I don't love her," he said quietly.

"Still, I imagine you've been intimate."

"Yes."

"A relationship you could never have with me. You think I'm beautiful, desirable? Nothing could be farther from the truth. When I look in a mirror, I see a shaved head, and sunken eyes in a cadaverous skull. A silent scream stretches my mouth into a grotesque grimace. Dead people. I see dead people—men, women, children rotting in ditches. Shef, I didn't escape, I'm one of them."

The suffering etched on Jaclyn's face took Sheffield's breath away.

"I made a pact with the Devil, and I'll never be free." Jaclyn grabbed her purse and bolted to the front door. "Sooner or later, he'll find me, and he'll come for me."

"Jaclyn, wait!"

"No." She flung the door aside and raced through it.

# Chapter Twenty-one

It was after eight when the Borseaus returned from St. Vincent's hospital. Christian's vital signs had improved, but he still had not regained consciousness. Jason had phoned Andrew Kirk, in Yuma. The renowned neurosurgeon had readily agreed to review Christian's case. Time being of the essence, Kirk had agreed to catch a flight to Phoenix the following morning.

Ordinarily, Jason left the house no later than six-thirty. Kathryn had expected him to skip breakfast and blast off like a rocket to the station. To her surprise, he'd decided to take the day off.

Kathryn kept Lauren company while she bathed and dressed. Josh was able to fend for himself. Now a teenager, Anthony considered himself a man, and his parents respected his privacy.

"Josh and I are going for a swim, Mom," Anthony said.

"Okay, hon'." Kathryn smiled, musing about how handsome their eldest son was. One day, he'd be a heartbreaker. Her stepson, but he was *hers*—their souls as one from the moment they'd met. Anthony had been five years old. Now, he was a youthful copy of Jason—killer blue eyes, dark hair, tall and rangy, with a muscular body, the charismatic grin.

"Anthony, stick close to Josh. He gets too frisky."

"Gotcha," Anthony said.

"Josh, mind your brother."

"Okiedokie," he yelled.

"Get a move on, squirt," Anthony said as he charged down the stairs with his brother in tow.

As she came through the door of Lauren's room, Kathryn smiled at Jason's mother. "They sound like a herd of elephants." She lifted Lauren's chin. "Be good for nana. Thanks for minding her, Mother."

"Spending time with my granddaughter is pure pleasure," Camille responded. "We're going to have breakfast on the balcony."

"That sounds like fun." Kathryn kissed her daughter's cheek, hugged Camille, and left the bedroom.

To avoid the heat, Kathryn usually rode much earlier, but this morning, as she walked along the bridal path to the stables, a breeze kept the blazing sun at bay.

Christian. Anguish fisted in Kathryn's heart and mind. Her fingers caressed the crucifix she always wore around her neck. A silent litany moved her lips.

It wasn't easy for Kathryn to take people into her life. Once she had, it was equally hard to let them go. Jason was right. Not only were mountain folks clannish, they were suspicious of outsiders. Strange tales emanated from the remote areas in central Idaho. The Basque—invoking the language they'd brought with them from Europe— communicated by calling from peak to peak, echoes ricocheting eerily through the deep ravines. Strangers, who dared to invade their terrain, might find themselves challenged by grim-faced men on horseback, rifles slung over their shoulders. There were tales of people vanishing, never to be found. Kathryn didn't believe a word of it. She thought the legend was designed to keep people away.

Thoughts of *home* opened a floodgate of memories. After her parent's divorce, she'd lived with her paternal grandparents, Benjamin and Sarah Whittaker, on a mountaintop in Idaho's Bitterroot Wilderness. Due to the number of Eagles that nested there, her grandfather had dubbed it The Aerie.

Kathryn smiled, recalling the wild child she'd been— the forest her playground, the creatures her playmates. Once, she'd befriended a mountain lion and her cubs. Every day she'd sneak food from under Annabelle the cook's nose. Until one day, Bill Hazelton, her grandfather's foreman had spotted her mere feet away from the Cougars.

"I 'bout had a heart attack," Kathryn had overheard Bill telling her grandfather. "I were gonna shoot that old cat. 'Raised my rifle, sighted her in, but I couldn't pull the trigger. There Katie-girl were, jabbering away to that cat and her three youngins. Now you tell Katie-girl, either she keeps away from 'em, or I'll hafta shoot 'em. Them cubs are too young to make it on their own, so I'd hafta put them down, too."

That night, Kathryn had cried herself to sleep. A few weeks later, she'd ventured back to the Cougars' den, a cave deep inside the mountain. They were gone, and she'd never seen them again.

After Kathryn's grandparents died, Bill and Annabelle had stayed on at the Aerie. Then, five years ago, Annabelle had passed away. Reluctantly, Kathryn had mothballed the stone mansion her grandfather had built. They had brought Bill, kicking and screaming, back to Scottsdale. Since then, he'd overseen the stables.

She didn't know how old Bill was. He didn't know either, or so he said. He was crippled with arthritis and couldn't do hard, physical work anymore. Of course, none of the hired hands could do anything to please the crotchety old geezer.

Kathryn laughed out loud. "Lazy sons-a-bitches," he'd say, "don't know a damned thing 'bout horses, sets on they asses, lest I got my eye on 'em ever second."

As she came through the massive double doors into the stable, Kathryn was surprised to see Christian's father leaning against a stall. She hesitated a moment, then strode to him.

"I see you've discovered Pride. Beautiful, isn't he? Of course, he's black, so I imagine you think so," she called out defiantly.

Christian's father studied her a moment, then turned away, knowing all too well that he blamed the Borseaus as he blamed all white people for his father's death. A few days after Carl's twelfth birthday, a mob of local white gentry had lynched Jack Grayson. It was a capital offense for a Negro man to touch a white female. When a little girl had fallen from her bicycle, his father had helped her to her feet. Why he had touched her was of no consequence.

As if borne on the wings of an ill wind, word of the hanging had spread quickly to the ghetto fringe where the Graysons lived. Carl had raced to the village, stunned to see his father swinging from a light post, his features twisted in agony from the torture he'd endured. On either side of the tree-lined boulevard, people had fled into stores, peering through the windows at the boy. His screams could be heard blocks away. Impotent with rage, Carl had collapsed on the sidewalk and pounded the concrete until his fists were raw and bleeding. A while later, still shaking with sobs, he'd retrieved a fruit crate from the sidewalk in front of the mercantile, and climbed on it. By standing on his tiptoes, he'd been able to saw through the rope—ironically, with the pocketknife his father had given him for his birthday. Carl Grayson would never forget the sound of his father's body falling with a final, hollow thud to the street.

Forcing the vivid memory away, Carl glanced away from Kathryn. "Yes, I've worked with horses, and Pride is magnificent."

"His sire is an Arabian stallion. Satan. Only my grandfather, and later, Jason, could ride him. That old devil delighted in intimidating me. I swear he snickered every time I tried to mount him. This youngster," she said, patting Pride's withers, "was born in the Bitterroot Wilderness, in Idaho, to Seraphina, my Appaloosa dam. Jason named him Satan's Pride," Kathryn rambled on as if by doing so she could span the distance between them.

Pausing, her mercurial eyes held him captive. "I'm not prejudiced, Mr. Grayson. Well, that's not quite true. I find ignorance intolerable," she snapped. "I take exception to being judged by the color of my skin. Your son is my dear friend, and because my skin is lighter than his, you don't believe I could or should care about him. My husband loves Christian like a son. It was cruel to hurt Jason the way you did."

The black man's eyes narrowed. He studied her face, then with leaden steps, he began to walk away. Hesitating, shoulders hunching, he turned to her again. "Do you ride well?"

Startled by the question, Kathryn retreated a step. "Yes," she said at last, with an arrogant click of her chin. "Hill Billies ride very well, and that's what I am."

Carl nodded toward the stall next to Pride's. "Would it be all right if I saddled that filly and rode with you?"

Kathryn gaped at him. "You're our guest. Short of burning the place down, you can do anything you please."

With a sheepish grin, he said, "I haven't been told off like that since my mother passed."

"Oh, dear," Kathryn groaned as she sagged against the stall. "I have a temper, but my granddad swore it took a lot to rile me up."

"If you're riding Pride, I'd like to saddle him for you."

Kathryn smiled. "Maybe you'd rather ride the black stallion, instead of the white filly."

Christian's father threw back his head and laughed. "You're not going to give me any quarter, are you, Mrs. Borseau?"

"If we're starting over," she said, with an impish grin, "I'm Kathryn."

"And I'm Carl. I'd be pleased to ride the filly. What's her name?"

"Sizzle. If you'd saddle Pride for me, I'd appreciate it."

"What's goin' on, Katie-girl?" Bill leaned heavily on his cane as he limped toward them.

She spun around. "Oh, Bill, this is Christian's father. Carl, this is my oldest and dearest friend, Bill Hazelton. He's known me since—"

"She were a whippersnapper, and mule-stubborn, jest like her granddaddy, the finest man I ever knowed. Now Katie-girl's dragged me to this god-forsaken desert. 'Guess I'll be here 'til I croak." Bill extended his hand to Carl. "I were plumb sick about what happened to yer boy. I hear he's gonna be okay. Thet's right, ain't it?"

"If we can trust what the doctor tells us." Carl shook Bill's hand, then hefted the saddle to Pride's back. "His mother and I won't believe it until he can talk to us."

"I'm sure thet'll be real soon."

"Carl, Bill oversees the stables."

"Ain't no picnic with them lazy studs Jace hires."

"But you keep them in line. Right?" Kathryn kissed her old friend's cheek. "Why don't you go to the house and have breakfast with Jason and Andre?"

"Mebbe, I'll see how't goes here."

"We're going for a ride, so we'll catch up with you later."

"Katie-girl, take it slow'n easy on thet black devil's youngin."

"Compared to Satan, Pride's a pussy cat."

"Don't know why I'm beatin' my gums. Katie-girl don't listen to nobody anyways," he said to Carl.

"Then why do you keep nagging?"

"Waste a'time, thet's for danged sure," he muttered as he limped away, shaking his head.

"Carl, Bill would die for me. In fact, he almost did."

"I'd be interested in hearing about that."

Kathryn studied his face. "It's a long story."

"I have the time." Carl handed Pride's reins to her and picked up Sizzle's.

"When Jason's son, Anthony, was six years old, he was kidnapped. This ghastly attack on Christian is a grim reminder of how cruel people can be," she began as they led the horses from the barn.

**A** breeze wafted across the veranda, palm trees swaying, pleated green fronds clicking and clacking like castanets.

At an umbrella table beside the pool, Jason peered at his father around an edge of the newspaper. "More coffee, Dad?"

"Half a cup, please." Andre folded the *Tucson Examiner*, the newspaper he still owned, but no longer managed, and swiveled his chair toward the house. "I thought your mother intended to join us."

"No, she and Lauren are having breakfast on the balcony." Jason poured his father's coffee and handed the cream pitcher across the table.

"When I stopped by the nursery, mother was telling Lauren about the big ship that brought you to America, how she felt the first time she saw the Statue of Liberty. We've talked about this before, but it bears repeating." Jason met his father's eyes. "It was difficult for you to give up your desert retreat, the house you'd lived in for almost forty years, but you've blessed our lives by being here."

Andre reached across the table and gripped his son's arm. "It was a difficult decision to make. We're a couple of aging dinosaurs, and I wondered if your young family and your mother and I could bridge the generation gap. And I was sure the newspaper couldn't survive without me. Ego talking. It's done very well as you know."

"Have you given any thought to selling?"

"Several newspapers have made offers, the most tempting from *The Arizona Republic*. No, I cling to the hope that, eventually, one of your children may take it over. I'd like the paper to stay in the family."

Andre took a sip of coffee and added more cream. "That's beside the point. Your mother and I have never been happier. I'll never forget how excited Camille was the day you showed us the plans for our suite."

"Thank god, she doesn't visit the baby's grave every day as she did before. It wasn't easy for me to disinter Theresa Marie, and bury her here." Jason nodded toward the family cemetery, in the farthest corner of the estate. "I couldn't bear to think of Kathryn and mother on their knees, rosaries in hand, mumbling Hail Marys over our daughter's grave. Thank god, our three live wires keep them too busy for that. And now, we have another baby on the way." He glanced over his father's shoulder. "Well, I'll be. Look at that."

Andre frowned. "What are you—?"

"Kathryn and Carl Grayson are riding together. How did she manage that?"

Andre chuckled. "My daughter-in-law is an amazing woman."

"Isn't she though," Jason said, grinning at his father.

"Son, do you have any idea why Christian was attacked?"

"Not a clue," Jason said. "By now, maybe Shef does. He said he'd call. Since he hasn't, I'm sure he's too busy. Anyway, he ordered me to back off and let the law do its job. He thinks the kidnappers assumed Christian was investigating something for me."

"Don't tell me Christian struck out on his own."

"No, I just didn't press him for specific details."

Nodding, Andre said, "So, you may be in danger?"

Jason shrugged. "That's how Shef sees it."

Cyrus Tidwell strolled across the veranda, and plugged the telephone into the receptacle. "Mr. Sheffield for you, Mr. Borseau."

"Thank you, Cy. Speak of the devil," Jason said as he put the receiver to his ear. "What's happening?"

"I'd like to come by and run something by you, a personal matter."

"Sure, come on out. Sooner or later I knew you'd need my sage advice."

Sheffield didn't take the bait. "How come you're not at the station?"

"Because you told me to lie low, an expression you cops use to scare people."

"Okay, I'm on my way," Sheffield said and hung up.

Jason frowned at the receiver before he set it down. "Shef will be here shortly."

Andre peered at his son over the rim of his cup. "I'll make myself scarce."

"Guess what?" Jason winked at his father. "The unlikely pair of equestrians just drew up."

Kathryn and Carl tethered their mounts and pressed through the wrought iron gate. With a jaunty stride, Kathryn snapped a crop against her leg as they walked side by side to the veranda.

"Good-morning, Dad," Kathryn said brightly. She skirted the table, slipped her arms around Jason's neck, and hugged her chin to the top of his head. He brought her fingers to his lips.

"Good-morning, Kathryn," Andre said. "Mr. Grayson."

"Good-morning." Carl's massive frame cast a shadow over his host.

Jason smiled. "Carl, how about some breakfast?"

"Thank you, but Sarah will be wondering what happened to me."

"I know!" Kathryn said. "I'll stable the horses and bring her back with me."

"Oh, I don't know," Carl stammered.

"Carl," Jason said, laughing, "the sooner you learn this, the better. When Kathryn appears to offer a suggestion, it's actually a command, as subtle as it may seem to be."

Whirling around, Kathryn planted her hands on her hips. "Jason!"

Carl rubbed his chin. "She surely set me straight this morning."

"Gave you hell, did she?" Jason handed a cup of coffee to Carl. "Help yourself to the sugar and cream. I've been at the whip-end of my wife's wrath a few times," he said, with a good-natured grin at her retreating figure.

"Wrath for heaven's sake," Kathryn muttered as she mounted Pride, snatched Sizzle's reins, and cantered off.

"I sincerely hope you'll accept my apology for the way I acted." Carl looked from Jason to his father."

"Forget it, we're all on edge. Let's focus on Christian. When he's able to leave the hospital, let's bring him here. He'll need care, and together, we can give him that. I agree with Shef—Christian was *not* a random target. He must have uncovered something that put him at risk, and whoever is after him isn't going to stop. Call me paranoid, but I don't believe he'll be safe until he can tell us who nearly killed him. Shef's people and the FBI are guarding Christian around the clock." With a critical eye, Jason glanced around. "We have the wherewithal to protect him here, but I'm going to hire more men to patrol the grounds."

# Chapter Twenty-two

The door chimes resounded through the house. Cyrus Tidwell rounded the corner next to the dining room and walked with stately steps across the reception hall.

"If that's Alan Sheffield," Jason called out to him, "please take him to the library and tell him I'll be right there." As he spoke, Jason vaulted the gracefully curving staircase two steps at a time.

When he came through the door of their bedroom, Kathryn was slipping into her robe. He put his arms around her and nuzzled his nose in the curve of her neck.

"Ummm, you smell delicious," he whispered next to her ear. "You're so sexy when your hair is all wet and crazy curly like that." Rising on the tips of her toes, Kathryn kissed her husband, and moved her hands along his back.

"Don't start with me," he groaned. "I heard the chimes on the way up. I'm sure it's Shef. Can you imagine, he wants my advice about a personal matter?" Jason eyebrows lifted. "I'm just glad he's human enough to have a personal problem. Oh, I have great news: if we let Carl pay his way, he's agreed to stay with us. I told him he could work with Bill. He surely needs help."

A smile lit Kathryn's face. "And he agreed?"

Jason nodded. "I wanted them to move into the house, but Carl said Sarah loves the cottage, just goes around touching things. The upshot is that he's agreed to let us bring Christian here when he leaves the hospital. That reminds me, I'll talk to Shef about beefing up our security."

Jason closed the library doors. "Wow, you look awful," he said, seeing the dark shadows under his friend's eyes, and the anxiety in them. "What's going on?"

Sheffield tipped the cocktail glass in his host's direction. "I hope you don't mind that I helped myself."

"Hey, it's your liver." Jason glanced at his watch. "As my dad says, the sun is over a yardarm somewhere." Sheffield didn't respond. "For some reason your sense of humor has gone bye-bye," he added.

Sheffield prowled around the room. "I don't know where to begin, and you'll think I'm crazy."

"I've always thought you were crazy, so just spit it out," Jason said, dropping into a chair.

"I want to get married," Sheffield said, pacing along the windows, stopping to gaze at the golf course, whipping away to pace some more.

"Is that all? You've been dating Sandra for what—three years or so? Oh, oh, did she turn you down? Shef, sit! I hate talking to a moving target."

Sheffield collapsed into the chair next to Jason's and rolled the glass between his hands. "Not only didn't she turn me down, *she* proposed to *me*. Like an idiot, instead of flat-out saying no, I told her I'd have to think about it. It was as if she didn't hear me. Within seconds, she'd planned the wedding, with you giving her away, the reception, the honeymoon, and my diet and exercise program."

Baffled, Jason said, "Let's start again. If you want to get married, what's the problem?"

"I want to marry someone else."

Jason shot out of the chair and strode to the bar. "Now I need a drink," he said, grabbing a glass from the shelf. "So who do you want to marry? Do we know her? Hey, Shef, is she someone you know?"

"That isn't funny."

"Damn right, it isn't," Jason said, trying to keep a straight face. "Did you ask this other woman to marry you, too?" He poured a shot of brandy over ice. "Polygamy has been outlawed, old buddy."

"All right, have your little joke. That's what I get for thinking I could share my feelings with you, you pompous ass. I didn't propose to anyone. I simply said I'd like to spend time with her. My god, she tore out of my house like a wounded deer." Sheffield shook his head. "I've called her apartment a half-dozen times. Either she's not there, or she isn't answering the phone."

Jason's laugh exploded into the room. "Shef, you're so conservative, this is totally out of character for you. Who is she?"

"Jaclyn Devereaux."

"Of course, Sam's partner, and Christian's best friend. I met her a few months ago. Christian took her on a tour of the station, then they dropped by my office, and we chatted for a while." Jason returned to the chair beside Sheffield. "She's beautiful, an exotic, intangible kind of beauty. There's an aura of mystery surrounding her. She's a tortured soul. I sensed it when I met her."

"Yes, to everything you said."

Frowning, Jason leaned forward to scrutinize his friend's face. "Shef, you and Sandra were here Friday evening, and from all outward appearances, a couple. It's Monday afternoon, and between then and now, you've fallen in love with Jaclyn Devereaux? You're right this isn't funny. What happened?"

"There's no way to explain it."

"Give it a shot," Jason said.

Sheffield took a sip of his drink and set the glass on the end table next to his chair. "It started at the landing strip the other evening. It just hit me as I watched you and Kathryn. I could never feel about Sandra the way you feel about Kathryn, not even close. When that revelation struck me, Jaclyn washed over me like one of those infamous tsunamis. When I came up gasping for air, I knew I loved her, had loved her for a long time. Christ, Jace, she's probably a decade younger than I am, and she works for me. How could I pursue a relationship with her? Then, I thought, screw protocol. After all, Kathryn worked for you at your radio station in Yuma." Sheffield fretted his knuckles. "But, this is different, complicated."

Mentally kicking himself for making light of Sheffield's plight, Jason asked, "How complicated?"

"Very. Jaclyn is a holocaust survivor. She was born in the US, but she grew up in Europe, in Poland—Krakow. Her father was an investment counselor."

"Oh, my God, it's a miracle she's alive. Her family is Jewish?"

"No, they were arrested while attending a Bar mitzvah for the son of one of her father's clients. Jaclyn was eleven when they took her to the concentration camp—Trepskýa. And, as she put it, a Major laid claim to her." Sheffield pressed the palms of his hands to his eyes. "Jaclyn was fourteen when he helped her escape. I don't know what atrocities she suffered at the hands of the Major or others, but Jaclyn believes an intimate relationship with me or with any man is out of the question. Her parting remark was that she'd made a pact with the Devil, that he'd find her and come for her. I assumed she was talking about the Major, but I don't know that for sure. Whatever happened traumatized her so severely, I don't think she'll ever be able to put it behind her."

"It's the stuff nightmares are made of. Tragically, for Jaclyn, for a lot of people, the war will never be over. What about her parents?"

"According to her resume, they died at Treblinka. Jaclyn was their only child."

"Jesus, no wonder there's an aura of tragedy about her. She lived through the worst kind of hell on earth." Leaning closer to his friend, he said, "Shef, is she in love with you?"

Sheffield squinted as if he were seeing Jaclyn in his mind. "Yes, I think so." He chuckled sardonically. "Hey, buddy, you're pretty good at this." Sheffield picked up his drink and tilted it in Jason's direction. "Maybe you should've been a psychiatrist."

"Shef, if she could never have a physical relationship with you, would you still want to marry her? I mean, could you live like that?"

"If I had to." Sheffield gulped the rest of his drink. "Hell, I don't know. I've never wanted a woman as much as I want her, not even Gina, and you know how I felt about her."

Jason pushed himself out of the chair, strode to the fireplace, and gazed up at the portrait of Kathryn. The artist had captured her proud, bright spirit. "It's difficult for me to imagine how I'd feel in your situation. After ten years, if Kathryn and I are in the same room, I find some excuse to touch her. If that part of our life were over, I'd still want her more than life itself. Worse yet, I'd have the memory of loving her to haunt me. Bottom line? I'd rather be with Kathryn and have no sex life, than be with anyone else, and have one. You know how empty my life was before she came into it. I'd be destitute without her."

Sheffield nodded slowly. "Thanks, Jace, I needed to hear that."

"Have you talked to Sandra?"

"Not yet. That's where I'm going when I leave here."

"Would it help if I came with you?"

Sheffield cocked an eyebrow. "You'd do that?"

119

Jason nodded and glanced at his watch. "She'll be at the station. You can use my office, and I'll wait for you."

"Would you consider telling her for me?"

Jason laughed. "Dream on, pal. Like I'm Miles Standish, and you're John Alden. I don't think so."

# Chapter Twenty-three

"That conniving bitch," Sandra shrieked as she arched up from the sofa. "This certainly gives new meaning to the word *promotion*."

"That isn't fair, and don't call her a bitch." Sheffield's emerald eyes glittered. "This isn't about whether Jaclyn and I will be together. It isn't likely. It's that I'm not in love with you, and it wouldn't be fair to either of us, if we—"

"What happened to, 'in love' is an over-rated emotion?"

Sheffield rose and stood behind her. "I'm very fond of you, Sandra."

She whipped around, one hand flying back to strike him in the face.

Sheffield grabbed her wrist. "Don't, please," he said quietly.

Sandra jerked away from him and buried her face in her hands. "I hate you!"

His arms swept around her. If only he did love this uncomplicated woman.

"Get out." Sandra shoved him away and swiped at the tears on her cheeks. "Get out! I never want to see you again. Never!"

"I don't blame you," said he barely above a whisper.

"And don't you dare feel sorry for me!"

"Sandra, I know you'll find happiness with a man who truly deserves you. I'm just not that guy," Sheffield said softly as he left Jason's office. He closed his eyes a moment. When he opened them, Sandra's boss was leaning against the opposite wall.

"Hi, Shef."

"Hello, Caroline. Are you here to pick up the pieces in there." He nodded at the door, "or to give me a piece of your mind?"

"No, Jace is in my office driving my staff crazy, asking questions he really doesn't want the answers to. That's what he does when he's upset. I thought you might need a friend about now."

"Do I ever. I've made a colossal mess of things."

Taking Sheffield's arm, Caroline propelled him along the hall to the elevator. "Sandra's tough. Knowing her as well as I do, I think her wounds are mostly superficial. Her pride is hurt, but I'm sure her ego is intact. Take my word for it, Shef, she'll heal a whole lot faster than you will." Caroline punched the elevator button and followed him inside. "Can I get you anything—coffee, a stiff drink?"

"Thanks, but after I console Jace, who's taking my dilemma as hard as I am, I'm going to the office and try to concentrate on matters of the State."

## Chapter Twenty-four

"**M**r. Sheffield, there are a dozen messages on your desk, two from the Governor. I couldn't tell him when you'd get back to him, because I didn't know—" Moira stopped abruptly in response to Sheffield's silent warning. Eyes narrowed, index finger pointing at his secretary, he strode tight-jawed past her desk into his office and closed the door. He sat in the chair behind his desk, and swiveled around to face the windows. When he turned back, he spied the envelope marked, *Personal and Confidential*. He slit the envelope, unfolded the single page, hurriedly scanned it, and flipped the switch on the intercom.

With a self-righteous sniff, Moira responded icily, "Yes?"

"Tell Sam I'd like to see him." Sheffield dropped Jaclyn's resignation on his desk, and raked his fingers through his hair. "Come in," he said in response to the tap on the door. Sam came in, sank into a chair in front of Sheffield's desk, and raised his eyebrows.

"You know?" Sam nodded. "Where has she gone?"

Sam shook his head. "I promised not to tell you."

"I love her," Sheffield said, wiping his hands across his eyes.

Sam nodded again. "I knew that before you did."

"Why did she run away?"

"It's just a hunch, but maybe you came on too strong."

"Where is she?"

"Shef, you're asking me to break a promise."

"How can I let her throw away her livelihood, a promising career, because I'm an insensitive clod?"

"She's far from destitute." Sam hunched forward in the worn leather chair. "When her father realized what was happening in Europe, he put most of his assets in a Swiss bank, and made her memorize the account number."

"That's beside the point. I want her back, even if means it'll be like it was before—the Attorney General, who hasn't a lick of sense, and his emotionally fragile investigator."

With a shake of his head, Sam rose and strode to the windows. "Okay, but she'll have my head for this. Jaclyn has a cabin near Sedona. That's where she's gone."

"Can you handle things here for a couple of days?"

"I can, but—"

"Do a few things for me. Give me directions to her place and call Jason Borseau," Sheffield muttered, while jotting down the number. "Tell him where I'll be. When I find a place to stay, I'll call you. Also, phone George Pearson. Tell the Governor I'll be gone for a few days. He'll be upset, but he'll get over it."

"Oh, Judge Carroll called this morning," Sam said. "He's signed the court order you requested, so, officially, we're in charge of the investigations, but since he's Federal, he strongly urged you to coordinate with the FBI every step of the way, the Phoenix police, too. He added that it would've been less of a problem if Salinger had invited us to participate."

"When pigs fly," Sheffield said, chuckling.

"And Judge Carroll said to thank you for giving him two whole weeks to settle in before you laid this on him. He said your brief was compelling, and he was glad to see you hadn't lost your touch."

Sheffield laughed. "Bless his heart. Okay, if we get the order while I'm gone, have our courier deliver a copy to the Chief. I'd sure love to see his face."

"Maybe I'll deliver it personally," Sam said with a grin.

# Chapter Twenty-five

The unforgiving rays of the sun blistered the earth. The stallion strained against the bit. Nostrils flaring, sweat darkened his sorrel coat. Clumps of earth flew from the pounding hooves and pelted the boulders along the narrow ravine. Damien Santayana bent low over the saddle, savoring the rush of adrenalin flooding his system.

When at last he reined in the horse, Damien threw back his head, and laughed. The sound ricocheted along the canyon walls, echoing through the high terrain.

In the range of mountains southeast of Tucson and north of the Santa Cruz River—a waterway that separated the U.S. from Mexico—Damien Santayana owned two thousand acres of land, *Rancho de Las Patagonia's*. The estate had been in his family for three generations.

In his early forties, the wealthy cattle baron was a bachelor, though women were attracted to his gallant manner, handsome features, fiery dark eyes, and black hair. Many had tried to lure him into marriage. So far, Damien had deftly sidestepped all such efforts. As it stood now, he was the last of the Santayana line. His twin brother had joined the Air Force shortly after the Japanese had bombed Pearl Harbor in 1941. Déon still was listed as missing in action.

The sun was barely visible above the western horizon. It cast a hot pink glow along the rims of the slopes. Live Oaks lined the gully, a gentle breeze rustled the leaves. The Santayana villa lay in the heart of the canyon amid granite spires and thick stands of trees. Chaparral-covered foothills slipped away to the rugged mountains beyond.

The hamlet of Patagonia, about thirty miles northwest of the ranch, was the nearest hint of civilization. Once a thriving community, shipping Santayana's cattle created most of the current activity for the town, for the railroad as well. There were other ranchers in the high desert, but none of their operations equaled those of Santayana.

Damien gave the stallion his head, smiling when the young charger chose the shortest route to the stables.

"You are your father's son," he said, referring to The Prince of Darkness, his prize Arabian stallion. "I must come up with a suitable name for you."

Damien dismounted and handed the reins to the stable boy. In spite of the intense heat, he decided to hike up the steep hill to the cemetery where his parents were buried. Carmine Baptista Santayana had died twenty years before, Damien's mother only recently. Hunkering down, he plucked the weeds that had encroached around the headstone, as well as from the velvety blanket of moss he'd planted on his father's grave. Choking back a sob, he cast a sidelong glance at his mother's grave. Then, rising slowly, he made the sign of the cross, and left the cemetery. His hands trembled as he padlocked the gate, as if that feeble gesture could keep her restless spirit behind the wrought iron fence. Damien hurried past the massive boulders scattering the hillside.

As he strode to the rear entrance of the hacienda, he spotted a car in the driveway. Only then did he recall scheduling a meeting with two of his associates. No matter, they could discuss business during dinner. Ordinarily, he would've invited them to stay the night, but Jason Borseau was due to arrive the following morning to look over the colts that had foaled in the spring. Apparently, Kathryn was pleased with the yearling Jason had bought for her several years before.

When he'd delivered the filly, Jason had invited him to join the family for lunch. Kathryn, Damien mused, either had disliked him instantly, or, as he preferred to believe, seemed aloof because she had been as attracted to him as he'd been to her. Not only was she beautiful, her indomitable spirit was evidenced in every move she made, every word she spoke. The thought quickened his pulse. Not that he ever had trouble enticing beautiful women into his bed, but he soon tired of them, and loathed the effort it took to disentangle himself from them. He felt sure Kathryn would be a challenge both in and out of bed, and he found himself envying Jason Borseau.

Although the temperature soared to over a hundred degrees, an ancient stand of black walnut trees sheltered the villa. The rancher strode into the cool interior of his home. The heels of his black, hand-tooled boots clicked staccato like, as they struck the intricate ceramic tile he'd designed. Sun dried adobe bricks rose two stories high. True to the eminent homes in Mexico, broad balconies stretched along the upper level. Massive beams ran laterally along the ceilings, disappeared into the walls, and reappeared to extend through every room.

In the den, an antique bar, circa the late 1800's, occupied an entire wall. Damien had rescued it from a soon-to-be demolished saloon in Patagonia. He had restored it to its original splendor, the gleaming dark wood had mellowed with the passage of time. Throughout the hacienda, heirlooms brought by his parents from the *Santayana* Province in Spain, melded together gracefully with custom-made pieces from Mexico.

Damien located his houseboy and asked him retrieve an appropriate bottle of wine from the cellar, then he mounted the flowing staircase to his suite of rooms to shower and change.

# Chapter Twenty-six

Scanning the crystal clear sky, Jason followed the Peregrine Falcon's ascent. "Damien, if Kathryn knew I was even an unwilling participant in this hunt, she'd have my head. It isn't my thing, either," he added, listening to the predator's shrill whistle, cringing as it plunged toward an unsuspecting Mourning Dove, the gentle bird Kathryn considered sacrosanct. Bracing for the kill, talons bared, the falcon snatched the dove, and went to ground. As he turned away, Jason spotted a boy near the stables. Upon closer inspection, he realized it was a young man, late teens or early twenties, with immense dark eyes that instantly tugged at Jason's heart. When the lad saw Jason gazing at him, a solemn smile curved his lips.

"Forgive me, I didn't realize my favorite sport would make you squeamish," Damien said. "Enough then. Let's go to the hacienda. A bottle of gewürztraminer is cooling to pique our palettes for a luncheon of trout stuffed with crab, and a side of fresh artichokes."

Wondering what was sporting about launching a dove and throwing a falcon at it, Jason said, "As tempting as that sounds, I should get back. We're so short-handed at the station, I feel guilty about playing hooky this morning."

"Yes, I was sad to hear of Christian Grayson's misfortune. How is he doing?"

"His wounds are healing, but he's in and out of a comatose state," Jason repeated the tale Sheffield had created to keep Christian safe. "God knows if he'll ever come out of it, or if he does, what shape he'll be in."

"I can't tell you how distressed I am to hear it." The falcon returned to its master, and Santayana secured a black leather hood over its sleek blue-gray head. "Is it possible he was targeted because of his ethnicity?"

"That's one of the theories Sheffield is pursuing."

"The Attorney General is heading the investigation? Isn't that unusual?"

"Alan Sheffield isn't your everyday, garden-variety Attorney General. He's hands-on. The Feds are cooperating with him, doing the lab work, fingerprint analysis for the catastrophe at City Hall as well as the attempt on Christian's life."

"Of course, Sheffield was once an FBI agent."

"The Feds still consider him one of their own." Jason extended his hand to the rancher. "If you can bring yourself to part with that beautiful satin-black filly, I'd like to buy her for Kathryn. Her birthday's in October, if you can decide by then."

"Let me sleep on it, and I'll give you a call. Please give my regards to your beautiful wife."

Smiling, Jason said, "I'll do that. Oh, the young man I saw near the stables, is he your son?"

"*Madre de Dios*, no. I've never been married, and to my knowledge, I have no children," Damien said, with a wink. "Ah, you must've seen Peter, the orphan I took in years ago, a wetback, as you call those who cross the river to escape the poverty in Mexico. I hope you'll forget you saw him."

"Surely you don't think I'd turn him in?"

"Of course not, forgive me. However, I wonder why you're so interested in one of my hands?"

"Curiosity, I suppose, his solemn eyes."

"More vacant than solemn, I'm afraid. Peter is good with horses, but he's mentally challenged, as we say. He can't read or write. His English, though I understand him, is unintelligible to most."

"How kind of you to have taken him in, and forgive *me* for prying."

"Not at all. It would seem we're kindred spirits, you and I. We feel compassion for those less fortunate than ourselves. But I'm delaying you, and I know you're anxious to be on your way. Oh, keep a light foot on the accelerator, the road to the main highway is in terrible shape."

"I'll keep that in mind and good-bye for now, Damien," Jason called back, feeling as though he'd been summarily dismissed. It seemed he'd gone from being invited to lunch to being, however politely, kicked off the Santayana ranch. Besides, he'd already driven that lousy road and surely, it hadn't gotten worse in the past two hours. Between then and now, what had changed? They'd talked about the young man who worked in Damien's stables. As he angled through a grove of trees, Jason searched the area where he'd seen the lad, but he was gone.

He got into his car, started the engine, and backed out of the driveway. "Compassion?" he muttered, gearing down when he hit gravel, zigzagging to avoid the cavernous potholes, jazzed by the way his snazzy new Corvette handled, as if he was piloting a sleek gold bullet. He grinned, feeling like a kid with a new toy.

"No way is compassion a word I'd use to describe Damien Santayana," Jason murmured, as he exchanged gravel for pavement and sped up. "I'd sooner think he's harboring illegals in exchange for slave labor."

# Chapter Twenty-seven

Autumn was a spectacular event in Arizona's high country. The leaves on the Big-toothed Maples rustled in the breeze, a brilliant crimson and gold panorama. Towering behind the Maples, a regiment of Ponderosa Pines stood at attention, stiff and straight, long arms reaching for the heavens.

Alan Sheffield's silver Mercedes plunged northward. The scenery zipped by so fast it was little more than a beige blur. Still, it was the longest hundred miles he'd ever driven. When that thought struck him, along with a nagging sense of urgency, his foot jammed the accelerator to the floor. The only thing that mattered to him was going to evaporate if he couldn't somehow, magically, grasp it in his hands, and never let it go. Especially unbelievable was that "it" was a young woman named Jaclyn Devereaux. It was sheer lunacy for him to leave two investigations behind, something he never would've done before. Sheffield couldn't decide whether he'd gotten his priorities in order or had lapsed into second childhood.

When the landscape began to change, Sheffield's foot eased up on the throttle. It had been years since he'd been there. Over time, he'd forgotten how much the region appealed to him—the towering spires, shimmering crimson in the light, progeny of an ancient ocean—marine fossils evolving and compressing into layers of rocks, to create one of nature's treasures. The process had begun three hundred million years before, a reminder to Sheffield of how insignificant he was.

His foot eased up some more. He took a deep breath and forced himself to relax his tense muscles. What was he going to say to Jaclyn anyway? Sheffield pulled to the side of the road and turned off the engine. Leaning back, he just sat there, listening to silence so profound, it was deafening.

He got out of the car, and circled around, reaching out with both arms to embrace the crystal-clear, sapphire sky, marveling at the fiery hues that would dazzle the most jaundiced eye.

North of Sedona the landscape would change again. Volcanic activity, somewhat like a potpie, had simmered through the earth's crust, creating a crack fourteen miles long. Over a relatively short period of time, four or so million years, a stream, eventually called Oak Creek, resolutely sculpted the spectacular canyons, mesas, buttes, and spires that lay on the southern edge of the high Colorado Plateau.

A sense of peace seeped into Sheffield's soul. He reached into the pocket of his windbreaker and retrieved his pipe, moving languidly, forcing the panic away—filling, tamping, and lighting the Meerschaum. Once the soothing ritual was done, he puffed contentedly.

According to Sam, Jaclyn's cabin was ten miles north of Sedona on a gorge that joined Oak Creek Canyon, near West Fork. It was so remote, Sam advised his boss to get directions from the locals. Sheffield got back in the car, eager to finish what he'd started, one way or the other.

Within minutes, the Attorney General was in Sedona. He chose a coffee shop on the main drag, a white wooden structure with bright blue trim and ruffled, stiffly starched curtains at the windows. It reminded him of a mid-west farmhouse, where there was always room for one more at the supper table.

Once inside, Sheffield took a stool at the L-shaped counter. Directly across from him, an elderly man with white hair and rheumy blue eyes, wearing jeans and a western shirt, with a bolo tie, and a sheepskin vest, stared at him.

Cocking his head first one way and then another, he said, "Hey mister, has anyone ever told you how much you look like that feller Sheffield, the Attorney General?"

"I've been taken for him before," said Sheffield, smiling.

"But you're not him?"

"Actually, you pegged it right, I am Alan Sheffield. I don't expect to be recognized, so I'm flattered." Every head in the restaurant swiveled in his direction.

The old man slid off the stool and came around the counter to stand beside the Attorney General. "The name's Fondse, Carl Fondse, and I'm surely proud to meet you, sir. I voted for you, and I'd do it again in a heartbeat. I surely do like the way you shoot from the hip."

Sheffield thrust his hand toward the elderly fellow. "Thank you, Carl. I seldom have the privilege of talking to people, like yourself, who are the blood and bone of this state."

Carl Fondse shook the Attorney General's hand. "Say, what happened down there at City Hall? 'Not up here tracking down criminals, are you?"

With a shake of his head, Sheffield laughed. "No," he said, pausing, deciding to tell it like it was. "I'm here to talk the woman I love into letting me court her."

The old man grinned and rubbed his chin. "And who might she be?"

"Jaclyn Devereaux, and I hope you folks can tell me how to get to her place," Sheffield said, glancing around. The other patrons, visibly intrigued by the AG's personal life, leaned eagerly in his direction.

"Well, sir, her lodge is near West Fork, and I can tell you how to get there. Did you have a lover's spat?"

"Something like that," said Sheffield, now thoroughly amused.

"Well, sir, I hope you can patch it up."

"Thanks, Carl, I hope so, too."

Sheffield pulled his car behind a sandstone butte. To get to Jaclyn's lodge, he'd have to navigate a circuitous route on foot, downhill. The old gent's directions were straightforward enough, but implementing them was another equation—one butte tended to look like every other. Sheffield had relied on Carl Fondse's estimate of the miles from one dubious landmark to the next.

It took more than an hour to descend the steep, boulder-strewn slope. The sun was setting. An icy wind seeped through Sheffield's windbreaker, forcing him to wonder what he'd do if he'd taken a wrong turn.

Even before it loomed into view, Sheffield could hear what turned out to be more than a creek, but less than a river, white water roaring and plunging past moss-covered boulders, gurgling cheerfully over a bed of rocks worn smooth by time. The stream was shallow, but the flat rocks marching from one side to the other were so far apart, Sheffield felt sure he'd end up wading across. It surprised him when, although disaster seemed imminent from one rock to the next, he'd made it to the other side without getting drenched. It took a moment to regain his balance and to collect himself. Glancing around, Sheffield spotted a log cabin nestled snugly among the trees. He leaned against the trunk of a pine, talking to himself, practicing what he was going to say to Jaclyn.

"What are you doing here?" she said, peering at him through the thick branches of an ancient Piñon. The barrel of the rifle dropped as she stepped from behind the tree.

Sheffield grabbed his chest. "Damn, you scared the breath out of me. I haven't the vaguest idea what I'm doing here or anywhere else," he said, loving the way she looked. A black turtleneck caressed her graceful neck, the long sleeves almost hid her hands. She wore black tights and mid-calf hiking boots. Her hair, drawn into a ponytail left a few rebellious strands hugging her cheeks and framing her chin.

Jaclyn set the rifle against a boulder next to the graceful Piñon. "I guess you'll have to come in. It's too late to send you back. I have a tent you can pitch on the lee side of the cabin. It'll be warmer there."

"What?" Sheffield glanced from side to side. "You're going to leave me out here with—"

"Mountain lions, Cougars. They seldom bother anyone," she said offhand, as if it were a fact he'd readily accept. "They're seldom seen, very reclusive. They weigh about two hundred pounds. How much do you weigh, Shef? Beautiful creatures, with amazing yellowish-green eyes, especially at night if there's a moon." She picked up the rifle, slung the strap over one shoulder, and came toward him.

"You can't be serious! I'm here, because I can't be where you're not. I'm a pathetic excuse for a man, and you're the reason."

"Let's go in, your teeth are chattering." Jaclyn hooked her arm through his. "It's hard to believe the Attorney General is such a panty-waist."

They walked through a closet-sized entryway into the living room. "Thank god," Sheffield said, spying the stone fireplace. Hurrying across the room, he stepped on the hearth, and turned his back to the roaring blaze.

Jaclyn walked past him through the dining room toward the kitchen. "I'll fetch some coffee."

"Do you have a bottle of Scotch?"

She stuck her head around the corner. "On the rocks with two ice cubes, right? Oh, if you're hungry, I'm having spaghetti, and you're welcome to join me."

"Jaclyn, please talk to me."

She blinked back the tears pooling in her eyes. Sheffield rushed across the room and took her in his arms. "I need you," he whispered.

Her head lifted, wistful eyes drinking in his face. "That terrifies me," she said quietly. "When the war was over, I thought nothing would ever frighten me again."

Sheffield frowned. "Surely you're not afraid of *me*."

"Not afraid. It just doesn't make sense," she said, drawing in a breath and holding it.

"You mean us? Jaclyn and Alan."

"Alan Sheffield." With an impish smile, she said, "Imagine the expression on Sam's face, if I started calling you Alan."

"He knows I'm in love with you."

"How can you possibly love me?" She turned away from him. "A part of me died at Trepská, the best part, I'm afraid. The nightmares come, and there's no way to escape them. I'm in the camp again, the sights, the sounds, the smell of fear, and death."

Sheffield grasped her shoulders. "We'll work through it together."

"Oh, please." She closed her eyes a moment. "I'm already drowning in guilt. You said it yourself—everyone died but me, all those dear people I left behind. I don't want to hurt you, and I don't want to be hurt. It's an impossible leap from Sandra to me. Think about it."

"I've done all the thinking I need to do."

"I'll never have children," she said softly.

Sheffield led her to the sofa and tugged her down beside him. "I've already been down that road." Jaclyn's haunted eyes gazed into his. "My son Michael died in Korea during the *conflict*." His eyes narrowed. "Sounds reasonable, doesn't it, a little spat between two countries?"

137

She took his hand in hers and brought it to her cheek. "The pain never goes away, never gives you a moment's peace."

"Exactly, no matter where I am or what I'm doing, when Michael fills my thoughts, it knocks the pins out from under me." Sheffield touched his lips to hers. "Jaclyn, come back to Phoenix with me."

Her eyes searched his. "Running away isn't the answer, is it?"

"No," Sheffield said. "And where's the harm in spending time together. We'll take in a movie, have dinner, go dancing."

Slanting a shy glance at him, she said, "I don't know how to dance."

"I'll teach you."

"No pressure?"

"No pressure," he said, lowering his forehead to hers.

"But—"

"No buts, just say, yes."

She hesitated a moment. "All right, yes."

"Okay, where's that tent? Oh, may I borrow a nightgown?"

Jaclyn's eyes narrowed. "Don't push it."

Sheffield pulled her close, praying he would spend the rest of his life with her.

# Chapter Twenty-eight

"Sooo, as I was saying, before we were so *rudely* interrupted." With a smile, Sheffield tore up Jaclyn's resignation and let it flutter, piece by piece, into the wastebasket.

Sam laughed, and Jaclyn slanted a murderous glance at him.

"Sorry," her partner said, wiping a hand across his mouth. "Hey, I'm excited about having my partner back."

Jaclyn made a fist and jabbed it within an inch of Sam's face. "I'll show you excitement."

Making an unsuccessful effort to quash his smile, Sam said, "So much for hoping a little R & R might improve your disposition."

"All right, Sam," Sheffield interjected, "bring us up to date. Start with how it went when you delivered the court order to the Chief."

"It's hard to believe I got out of there alive. Salinger was livid, apoplectic, stroke city. But, after he talked to Sean Campbell, the City's attorney, he had his lackeys copy the files, the photos, too.

"It's as bad as it gets," Sam continued, nodding at the files on the Attorney General's desk. "We're looking for a serial killer, a psychopath. The guy gets off on torturing his victims. The medical examiner said the women were raped repeatedly, evidenced by severe trauma to their vaginal areas. No semen was found, so he must've used a condom."

Sam shook his head. "After ten years on the job, I thought I'd seen everything, but I've never seen anything like the photos of these women. We gotta get this guy, and fast. No way he's going to stop. Salinger's nowhere with the investigation, and no one seems to give a damn."

"Because they're prostitutes. Imagine the outrage if the killer moves from the brothels to the upscale neighborhoods in Scottsdale."

Sheffield opened the top file. "I see the Chief added the words *under duress* beneath his signature."

He turned the page. "What's this?" Sheffield said, recoiling. "Eyes gouged out, ears lopped off, tongue cut out? 'See no evil, hear no evil, speak no evil?' Oh, my God, he excised her nipples, either before or after he burned her breasts—make that *methodically* burned her breasts— some sort of design? Trussed her up and branded her many times over," Sheffield murmured more to himself than to his investigators, "Head drawn back, legs arched over her back, a slipknot around her neck, wrists and ankles?" Sheffield whispered, "Why you sick, satanic bastard. Is this his MO? All the women were mutilated in this manner?" Sam nodded. "Where's the ME's report?"

"Under the photos."

"This guy's a monster," Sheffield said, as he read. "The more she struggled, the tighter the rope got. She strangled herself.

"Yes."

"He took the body parts with him?"

"He did."

"Trophies, souvenirs."

Sam shrugged. "So it would seem."

140

Rising, Jaclyn skirted Sheffield's desk and leaned over his shoulder. "It can't be!" she cried, pressing the air in front of her as she backed away.

"Jaclyn?" Sheffield said, seeing how deathly pale she'd become.

She stared at him, eyes flaring, pupils dilated.

Sam scowled. "You've seen real bodies, not just photos."

Forcefully thrust back in time, Jaclyn drew in the pain the Major had inflicted on the other women, recalling the grateful tears she'd shed when they no longer struggled, when the sound of their last ragged breaths shuddered out. "He mutilates them while they're alive, while he's raping them. Young," she sobbed, "they're so young—children."

"How can you possibly know that?" Sheffield said softly.

Tears flooded from her eyes and spilled down her cheeks. "I can't work on this case."

"Have you seen this MO before?"

"What? No, I mean, it's just so horrible. It's just . . ." Jaclyn bolted to the corner window and stared through it, hands fisted at her sides.

Sheffield slid the files to one side. "Let's leave this for now. What's happening with Christian's case, Sam? Any progress?"

"Comme ci, Comme ça." Sam frowned and jerked his head toward Jaclyn.

Sheffield raised his eyebrows and shook his head.

"Okay, we checked out Joseph Anderson, the attorney who spotted the van. When I asked for a list of his clientele, he raved on and on about attorney-client confidentiality. I assured him that this was routine, and the information would be kept in-house. He said he wished he'd never come forward. 'Can't say I blame him."

"What about his clients?"

"A prestigious collection of companies. It's on your desk, along with the information about all of Shady Creek's tenants." Sam chuckled. "*Shady Creek*, without a tree in sight or a drop of water. Anyway, so far, no one else has come forward."

Sheffield mulled it over. "See if any of Anderson's clients have done business with the City."

"Without a scrap of paper, that'll be a challenge."

"Start by interviewing Paul Hewitt, Lee Crooks, and the Council, and get them on tape."

Jaclyn turned toward them. "Let me do that."

Sheffield nodded, wondering what was going on with her. "Nothing more on Christian's kidnapping?" Sam shook his head. "Okay, let's call it a day. Please stay, Jaclyn," Sheffield said as she started toward the door.

"It's after seven. I have to feed my cat, and—"

"Escape from me, so you won't have to tell me what has you by the throat. Too bad, you're coming with me."

"I'll do no such thing."

Taking her elbow, Sheffield grabbed his briefcase, and propelled her through the door into Moira's office. "Wanna bet?"

# Chapter Twenty-nine

Sheffield opened the passenger door of his Mercedes. Jaclyn crossed her arms over her chest and ignored the hand he held out to her.

"It's a long walk back to Scottsdale," he said.

"How dare you bring me here without my permission? It's—"

"Unthinkable?" Sheffield leaned down to peer in at her. "You *kidnapped* me."

He smiled. "If you press charges, I could get life in prison."

"Shut up, just shut up," Jaclyn fumed. "Let's get this over with."

He grabbed the cat carrier in one hand and helped Jaclyn out of the car with the other. "This is nasty business, but you fell apart," he said.

Fear, like a viper poised to strike, coiled inside of her.

"Sooner or later we have to talk about this." With a strangled cry, she jerked away from him. He pulled her to him again and they struggled along to the front doors. He had to set the carrier down to ring the bell.

"Missy hurt?" Sejii said, hastily locking the doors behind them.

"No, just upset. Would you take Fancy, the Siamese kitty, find a basket, line it with a blanket, and bring it up to Jaclyn's room, the one next to mine. Then brew a cup of tea and bring it there, too, please. Oh, maybe you could open a can of tuna for Jaclyn's feline."

"*Hai*, Sejii hurry, boss." Bowing, he took the carrier and rushed away toward the kitchen.

The photo of the murdered girl had terrified Jaclyn. As grotesque as it was, the worst Sheffield had ever seen, her reaction had been instant and dramatic, as if it were personal. He intended to find out why.

As Jaclyn had said, the victims were young, ranging in age from thirteen to sixteen. Most likely runaways, turning tricks to eat, to put a roof over their heads. His investigators would lean on their pimps to see what they knew or would admit to. Probably nothing. Still, since the murders compromised their livelihoods, they might be more inclined to cooperate. It was worth a shot.

Jaclyn pushed up the sleeves of the nightgown he'd packed for her, took a sip of the strong, green tea Sejii had prepared, and handed the mug to Sheffield. He set it on the nightstand. Fancy was asleep at the foot of the bed.

"I could fix you a hot toddy." She shook her head. "Would you like to be alone?" Tears swam in her eyes. "Was that a yes or a no?"

"No."

"Then I'll sit beside you until you nod off."

She pressed back against the pillows, closed her eyes a moment, then she stared at the ceiling fan, following it as it went round and round and round, whirring, whirring, whirring. "The windmills of the Gods," she murmured. Against her will, her thoughts flew back to the day the Colonel ordered the Major to shoot her.

It was late evening, the shadows deep, the silence profound, the air still. The prisoners that had survived the day had returned to their barracks. At this hour, the infirmary was officially closed. That was where the Major always brought Jaclyn, away from prying eyes. "Never again are you to put me in a situation like the one you created today. If you do, I'll be forced to execute you," the Major said. "He chopped that helpless old man to pieces—fingers and toes, arms and legs. His—" A sob lodged in her throat. "His head."

"For disobeying, for refusing to work. Instead of digging, the damned fool embraced that spade as if it were an impassioned lover, dancing around, giggling like a fool, raving like a lunatic."

"Because he'd been driven mad by all of you. Yes, he disobeyed the Colonel, and so did you. But the Colonel is afraid of you."

The Major shrugged. "If he'd lifted a hand to you, I would have shot him, not you, and he knew it."

"You saved me. Again," she added softly. Every minute of every day, Jaclyn was aware of how eager death was to consume her, or worse yet, the gaping jaws of insanity. Only her parents, her silent sentinels from the past, kept her from sinking into the hopeless condition that had dehumanized so many of the others.

Despair was the ultimate enemy. The Major was studying her so intently, Jaclyn wondered if he was seeing her, as she often saw herself—the desolate dark eyes, the purple smudges under them. Maybe he was trying to envision her with hair, with meat on her jutting bones, or maybe he was imagining, under other circumstances, the woman she might have become.

"The war will be over soon," he said. "It does not go well for the Fascists. How could it, with idiots like Berndt in command? Pomposity and arrogance will be their downfall. It is only a matter of time until their enemies invade this camp and others like it. None of the prisoners will live to tell them what has happened here. If I don't get you out, you'll die, too."

"Their enemies?" Jaclyn searched his face. "Not your enemies?"

With a grim smile, the Major said, "No."

She stared at him. "You're a spy."

"No, but if they find me out, they'll think I am."

Jaclyn took a step back. "Then, what are you doing here?"

The Major tucked in his shirt, shrugged into his jacket, then leaned against the operating table to pull on his boots. "A German officer tried to capture me. I took his life, liberated his uniform, his weapon, and his identity."

"Why are you telling me this now?"

"If we're to have a life together, you had to be told."

"A life together?" A chill spun down Jaclyn's spine, her mind raced. "I don't even know who you are."

He hesitated. "David." Seeing the question in her eyes, he added, "Santiago, I think. I really can't remember. If you don't like it, I'll pick another."

"It isn't your real name."

"Does it matter?"

She rubbed the tattoo beneath her forearm. "No, only numbers matter here. Were you in a different army?"

"From one impostor to another, the less you know, the better," he said as he strapped on his sidearm.

"What does from one impostor to another mean?"

The Major hooked his thumbs beneath his belt and circled around her. "You're not Jewish."

Her eyes locked with his. "No," she said, pivoting in tandem with him, like a miniscule cog in the center of a massive wheel.

The Major edged a hip on the operating table. "I'm guessing that your family was in the wrong place at the wrong time. The invaders made a mistake."

"We were attending a Bar mitzvah." The Major cocked his head. "For the son of a business associate of my father's."

"Prudent of you not to tell them. They bury their mistakes."

"How did you know?"

"Jews don't pray to the Virgin Mary, Jaclyn."

"I didn't know I had."

He smiled. "In the heat of passion."

Passion? He'd mistaken her pain and fear for passion. She spun away from him. "You're no better than they are. You murdered those women."

"Jaclyn," he said softly, "I didn't murder them."

She turned to him. "You tortured them, and you killed them. They're dead!"

He looked bewildered. "But they were gifts, for you."

"Gifts? For me?" Jaclyn cried.

"To prove that I only want and care about you."

Suddenly, the big black dog she'd had as a child grew large in her mind. He, too, had brought her gifts, tail wagging wildly, proudly dropping dead carcasses at her feet—rabbits, birds, cats. Then he'd gaze up at her, eagerly waiting for her to reward him with a pat on the head. She'd never had the heart to scold him. He wouldn't have understood. The Major wouldn't either. Who or what had created this monster?

As much as she despised him, she'd learned to subjugate her feelings. "Promise me something." He took her hands in his, waiting, scrutinizing her face. "If you want to give me another gift—"

"Yes, tell me what you want."

"Your promise that you'll never take the life of another innocent person."

The Major still studied her intently. "Then you must promise me something."

Jaclyn drew a breath and held it. "What?"

"That you'll never leave me." She hesitated. "Give me your word, Jaclyn."

"You have my word," she said. As she spoke, she turned away, knowing that if he could see her eyes, he would know she was lying.

The Major drew her into his arms. "I'll never forget the first time we were together. In that moment of passion, I marked you for my own. Remember?"

"Yes." The scars on my body, and those on my soul, are grim reminders. She wanted to lash out at him, to tell him how much she despised him, how fervently she wished he were dead. Instead, in a quiet voice, she said, "I was eleven years old."

He shrugged. "It didn't matter."

It didn't matter to you, her mind raged. It was a struggle to keep the intense loathing she felt for him from showing on her face. "If they catch you trying to help me escape, they'll execute you, too." If by some miracle he gets me out, how will I escape from him?

"Then we'll die together." The Major lifted her face to his. "You belong to me, Jaclyn. Forever."

His words churned in her mind. You belong to me. As if anyone else would want her, could bear to look at her. Forever? Until his death, or hers. Easily done if she taunted him, if she told him she'd never be his, he'd end her life, and take pleasure in doing so.

Suicide, the unforgivable sin, was an option she'd considered, then rejected. If she goaded the major into killing her, she might be able to slip into purgatory. Under false pretenses, of course.

Peace, that elusive spirit, nudged her sense of self. Contemplating the end of this life no longer terrorized her. It would be the beginning of forever—an altogether different forever than the Major envisioned for her. She'd soar with the angels. She'd be reunited with her mother and father.

Or would she? The Major had defiled her, stolen her innocence. Six women had died because of her. The Major was right. His mark was on her. She wondered if it was the mark of Satan or simply that of a lunatic.

Jaclyn stared glassy-eyed at the fan. Her skin was ghostly pale, perspiration glistened on her face, her breath shuddered in and out.

Sheffield touched his fingers to her cheek. "Come back to me now."

She cringed away from him, staring at him as if she didn't know who he was.

"Jaclyn, it's all right. Look at me."

She blinked, glanced around, and blinked again. "It's him," she said.

"Who?"

"The Major."

"What Major?"

"From the Camp."

"Oh, Jaclyn, no. How could a German officer from World War II, be here?"

"I don't know how, but it's him. Alan, he wasn't a German officer. He said a German Officer tried to capture him, so he took his life, his uniform, his weapon, and his identity. I asked him if he'd been in another army, but he wouldn't tell me." Jaclyn closed her eyes and shivered, as if she had seen something vile. It was the first time since she had left Trepskýa that she had relived those horrifying memories.

"He was smart and educated. He spoke impeccable German. The soldiers, even the Commandant, were terrified of him. He was tall, with a massive build, but it was more than that. It's impossible to explain the power he had over them."

Sheffield lifted her face to his. "Over you as well, it would seem. What was his name?"

"David Santiago. It wasn't his real name. He said if I didn't like it, he'd pick another. At the time, it didn't matter. Now it does."

"So he picked David Santiago, an English, American, or Spanish name. Or, for that matter, Mexican. Jaclyn, could he have followed you here?"

"How? After we escaped from Trepskýa, we literally bumped into the British Army. Along with hundreds of other refugees, they took us to a relocation camp in England. That's how I got away from him. I'm an American citizen. After the officials verified my status, I came to the States. It was years before I came to Arizona. But, I *know* he's torturing and killing those girls."

"I believe you *think* it's him, because the Major tortured and murdered young women in a manner similar to what you saw in those photos."

"Not similar, exactly the same." Jaclyn buried her face against him. "Alan, the burns on their breasts, the pattern?"

"Yes."

"The scars on my breasts are identical." She lifted her head and began unbuttoning the pajama top.

He grabbed her hands. "I believe you.

"He will never let me go."

"But he did, for many years. The baffling thing is: why didn't he kill you?" She turned away. "Jaclyn?"

The rage she'd repressed for years exploded like a bomb in the room. "Alan Sheffield, ever the prosecutor. I didn't conspire with him against the others, if that's what you think."

Sheffield smiled. "It isn't what I think, nor would I ever believe it."

Falling back on the pillows, she said, "He said he was in love with me, as if he could love anyone."

Sheffield laced his fingers with hers. "That's what set you apart from the others, isn't it?"

With a shrug, she said, "He saved my life—more than once."

Her eyes flew open. "He said he killed the others for me, to prove how much he cared about me. He said they were *gifts*. Gifts! Six young women tortured, mutilated." Tears seeped from her eyes. "Now there are four more."

"And, you're blaming yourself."

"Yes, because I made a pact with the Devil."

Sheffield frowned. "What was the deal?"

"That he'd never hurt another innocent person."

Sheffield studied her face. "And your promise to *him*?"

Jaclyn bit her lip and looked away. "That I'd never leave him."

"A pledge you couldn't possibly keep. If it's him—"

"Not, *if*, it's him!"

"All right, let's say it is. You describe him as smart, educated, powerful, intimidating, a psychopath, who raped and mutilated his victims." Sheffield looked into the distance. "You're describing a serial killer. Did he stop killing, and then start again six months ago? That's approximately when the kidnappings and the murders began. If you're right that the current murderer and the Major are the same man that seems atypical of serial killers."

"If, if, if! What will it take to convince you?" Jaclyn cried.

"It may be a colossal coincidence."

"No!"

"Being defensive isn't the answer. We have to pursue this logically. What else can you tell me about him?"

"Only that the night we left the camp, he said we'd have to hurry before 'he' figured out what we were doing. When I asked him who *he* was, he told me to stop asking questions, or he'd get rid of me the same way *he* had gotten rid of the others. After that, if I asked about 'him', the Major seemed visibly confused, as if he didn't know what I was talking about."

151

"All right." Sheffield closed his eyes and blew out a breath. "Tomorrow, we'll get whatever else you need from your apartment. Until we apprehend this maniac, whoever he is, you're staying here. On the job, you'll be with Sam or me, never alone. We'll do everything we can to protect you, but you have to cooperate. You can't go off by yourself, thinking it's okay. Is that clear?"

"Yes, but—"

"Just listen. Let's say that the Major is our killer. If he'd known where you were, he would have silenced you. Jaclyn, you're the only person alive, at least in this country who knows what he looks like. With your help, our sketch artist will put a face to this maniac. As for this unnamed person. Maybe he's a figment of the Major's imagination, his alter ego." Sheffield shrugged. "I've always pooh-poohed split personality as a defense, but who knows?"

Sheffield's mind teemed with what would happen if the Major were the serial killer they were seeking. Could there be two killers with the same MO thousands of miles and nearly two decades apart? It wasn't likely, although he wasn't convinced the Ladies of the Night killer was the Major. Right or wrong, Jaclyn thought he was the lunatic kidnapping and mutilating the young women in Phoenix.

If she was right, and if they found enough evidence to apprehend and charge him, would Jaclyn have to testify against him? His mind raged at the injustice, if that scenario were to occur. Had Jaclyn survived a living hell, only to have Satan's progeny rise up from the netherworld to torture her anew? Sheffield knew he would have to come up with a strategy to spare her that denigrating ordeal

"Jaclyn, I don't like surprises. Is there anything else you need to tell me?"

She shook her head.

"You're positive?"

"Yes!"

Sheffield felt sure she was holding something back—something so crushing, so humiliating she couldn't force herself to put it into words. He pulled her close. "Try to sleep." She nodded against him. "I'll be right here when you wake up." He leaned down to study her face, grateful to see the terror in her eyes begin to recede.

# Chapter Thirty

The maddening sound of water pinged when it struck, a doomsday clock ticking off the minutes she had left to live. Instinct told her she was underground in a cellar or cave. It was damp, the air stagnant with a musty odor. Even the coppery smell of her own blood couldn't overcome it. It didn't matter, nothing mattered now.

"Help me, please help me," she sobbed, knowing no one could hear her. Only him. Sooner or later, he'd come. He'd blindfolded her, trussed her up like a pig for slaughter. He'd raped her, burned her, cut her. The slightest movement tightened the noose around her neck, the ropes cut deeper into her wrists and ankles. Pain lanced through her body, her breath shuddered in and out.

She was lying on her stomach with her head cinched up, legs bent at the knees, the rope taut between her neck and ankles. The muscles in her calves and thighs trembled. When she could no longer keep her legs in that position, the ropes would strangle her.

For months, the killer skulked in the shadows on the Phoenix Westside. Chantelle warned all of the girls to stop turning tricks. None of them paid any attention to her advice. Hikers and spelunkers discovered the remains of the four kidnapped girls in the desert.

Seeking adventure, "Moonglow" had run away from home a month shy of her fourteenth birthday. That first winter, after she'd nearly frozen to death in Colorado, she'd hitched to Phoenix.

Moonglow wasn't her real name. She was Susan Walsh, a farm girl from Iowa. Now, as her life ebbed away, she thought about home—the heady scent of new mown hay, the strident voices of the roosters crowing at dawn, cicadas breaching the silence at night. Hot, bitter tears scalded her eyes and rolled down her cheeks.

Footsteps echoed in the distance, growing louder with each passing moment. Her heart thudded wildly as terror flooded through her. "Nooo," she whimpered. "Please don't hurt me any more."

# Chapter Thirty-one

Searching for a pattern, Sheffield stepped away to get some perspective. He'd had an immense three-dimensional map installed on one wall in his office. Like the spokes of a wheel, with Phoenix as the hub, every town within a two hundred mile radius of the Capitol City was included. Moving to it again, he pinned a tiny red flag at the site where the fourth murder victim had been discovered. Jaclyn stood beside him.

Sam squinted at the sketch their artist had drawn. Jaclyn's memory had guided his hand. "If Bill had drawn a white collar around this guy's neck, he could pass for a priest. 'Sure doesn't look like a sadistic killer," he observed, "handsome devil, Joe college type."

"Devil is right," Jaclyn muttered.

"Oh, I asked Jason to come by and look at the sketch. He knows more people in Arizona than anyone else I know," Sheffield said.

"Won't he wonder why?" Sam said.

"I'm sure he'll know the guy isn't in line for the citizen of the year award."

Concentrating on the map, Jaclyn said, "Willy nilly, where's the pattern? It's as if he covers his eyes and stabs the map with his finger. Ahhh, that's where I'll drop the next body."

"Let's talk about what we know, see where it takes us. No blood has been found at any of the dumpsites, so we know he doesn't kill his victims where they're found. They bled out somewhere else.

"Jaclyn, you described the Major as a giant." She nodded. "Even so, all of the sites are miles from the nearest road in rugged terrain—ravines, caves, steep mountainsides strewn with boulders and scrub vegetation. In every instance, seasoned hikers found the bodies. What do you make of that?"

"He didn't do it alone," she murmured.

"Exactly. Assuming he's the killer, if I've judged the Major correctly, I can see him directing the operation, but I can't see him doing the clean-up work. One other thing: if any evidence is left behind, it won't be his. Either he thought the bodies would never be found, or he believed they would be in such an advanced stage of decomposition it would be impossible to identify them and any evidence would have deteriorated.

"Think about his choice of victims. If the Major—"

"You keep saying *if*. It's him. Why don't you believe me?"

"Until we've identified the suspect and have him in our sights, we have to make assumptions. Jaclyn, if you're too emotionally involved to work this case, I'll understand."

"Maybe I'm not as objective as I should be, but don't take me off the case."

"This is all speculation, and we have to perceive it as such. Assuming it's the Major we're looking for, even if he wasn't, in reality, a German officer, he has the Nazi mentality. He's still targeting women—only now they're not Jews, they're prostitutes, worthless creatures he believes the world would be better off without. After all, it's his god-given right, his mission to rid the earth of scum. Maybe he thinks of himself as the savior of mankind, rather than what he is—a sadistic monster, satiating his appetite for violent, deviant sex. Before he kills, he mutilates his victims. It's possible we're looking for a man the world may see as exemplary. If that's the case, it won't be easy to unmask him, even after we find him."

When the intercom buzzed, Sheffield walked swiftly to his desk. "Yes, Moira."

"Mr. Borseau to see you."

"Send him in."

"Good afternoon, or is it?" Jason said as he strode through the door and glanced from one of them to the other. "Hey, I just left my legal eagles, who perpetually look like they're sucking lemons, only to join three other sour pusses. What's up?"

"We'd like you to look at the sketch our artist drew, hoping you may know who it is."

"Before I do, I'm happy to say that Christian is well enough to leave the hospital. Tell me how you're going to get him out of there, without whoever put him there in the first place, knowing."

"We'll cover him with a sheet, deliver him to the morgue in a hearse. And then, we'll do a bait and switch. We'll put Christian in another vehicle and transport him to your place in the dead of night. An escort of unmarked cars will keep Christian's vehicle in sight. They'll switch out every few miles at designated roads."

"Wow! Just like that. Good for you, Shef, I think that'll work."

"Actually, 'not just like that.' I've been ideating for a long time about how we could transport him safely to your estate. Is he conscious?"

"Yes, and Andy Kirk says Christian will make a complete recovery. His memory isn't one hundred percent yet, but in time, it should be. I can't tell you how relieved I am. I know you are, too.

"Now, back to your business. What has he, or she, done? Allegedly, of course. You're acquainted with that word, aren't you, Mr. Attorney General?"

"Just look at the sketch."

"Do I hear a pretty please with sugar on it?"

Sheffield's eyes narrowed. "Over my dead body."

"Testy, testy," Jason said, grinning at his friend. "All right, where is it?"

Sam handed the drawing to Jason.

"Hmmm." Jason tipped his head from side to side. He squinted, then shook his head. "Sorry, I'm not getting anything."

"Humor me. Take another look."

"Shef, I honestly don't have the vaguest idea who he might be."

"Jace, another girl is missing and time is running out."

Jason shrugged.

"Damn," Sheffield said, shaking his head. "Okay, I was hoping you might have an idea who this guy might be?"

Frowning, Jason studied the sketch again. "What's he supposed to've done?"

"I wish I could share that with you, but—" Sheffield said.

"Surely you're not going to hang *conflict of interest* around my neck again."

Jaclyn stepped forward. "It's from my memory of an officer at Trepskýa Concentration Camp in Poland. Only he wasn't who the SS thought he was, or so he said. He wouldn't tell me if he had been in another army. He said his name was David Santiago, but he added, 'if you don't like that name, I'll pick another.' Anyway, he told me that when a German officer tried to capture him, he killed him, and took his identity."

Jason gazed at Sheffield. "The Major you told me about?"

"Yes," Sheffield said.

159

"A lot of time has passed since you've seen him. Right, Jaclyn?" She nodded. "For instance, hardly anyone wears a crew cut anymore. Have your artist give him an up-to-date hairdo and add some years to his face. Then, I'd like to see the sketch again.

"Shef, surely you wouldn't try to prosecute him for the crimes he committed during the war."

"No, this is about something else. I'll fill you in, but it can't go any farther."

"As if I'd even respond to that," Jason fired back.

"Okay, it's about The Ladies of The Night murders," Sheffield began. "Let me show you what tipped Jaclyn off. At first, I didn't believe her, thought she was—"

"Insane," Jaclyn interjected.

"Shef, may I please have a cup of coffee?"

"You betcha, anything your heart desires, with sugar on it," Sheffield said as he headed for the bar.

# Chapter Thirty-two

The last thing Susan remembered was the sound of his footsteps. Now she was lying across his shoulder dangling like a sack of potatoes.

Is this how it feels to be dead? Or am I alive, and he thinks I'm dead? She clung to that thought without any hope that it might be true. Her heart was pounding so hard, she thought it would burst. Surely he could feel it, too. What would happen when they got to wherever he was taking her? Maybe she could fool him into believing she was dead.

The blindfold was gone, but it was dark, and she didn't dare move her head to glance around. Of course, Susan knew they were in the desert—Mesquite scented the air. That was where he'd left the bodies of the other girls.

And she knew they were climbing. He was breathing hard, leaning back, shifting her weight.

Oh, god, I can't remember if he buried the others, or left their bodies for the coyotes. He'd stopped walking, and Susan forced herself to hang limply, to draw scant breaths.

Please God, don't let him bury me alive.

# Chapter Thirty-three

Sheffield flipped the button on the intercom. "What is it, Moira?"

"Jason Borseau is on line one."

"Thanks." Sheffield massaged the bridge of his nose, wondering if he needed glasses. "Hi, Jace," he said, shifting the receiver to his left ear. "What's up?"

"Andy thinks Christian is up to answering a few questions."

"That's great news!"

"And Christian specifically asked to see Jaclyn," Jason said.

"All right, if it's okay with you, we'll come by later."

"I have a better idea, join us for dinner."

"Sold. What time?"

"Cocktails at six, dinner at seven."

Sheffield glanced at his watch. "It's after four now. I'd better get my tail moving."

Jaclyn tiptoed across the room and sank into the chair beside Christian. The odor of antiseptic mingled with the scent of potpourri. Next to the bed, an alarming array of plastic bags and tubes were attached to Christian. The nightstands had been moved aside to make room for the apparatus.

"Christian?"

He opened his eyes. "Hey, pal, I've missed you."

"I've missed you, too. You have no idea how worried I've been."

"It's a good thing I have a hard-head." With a grim smile, Christian said, "I've lost time, haven't I?

"Yes, my dearest friend, you have."

"What day is it now?"

"January fifteenth."

"What happened to August and the rest of the year?"

"You slept through them. Christian, can you describe the kidnappers?"

"Two men, one tall, one short, Lou and Ben, no last names, mid-forties, dumb as stumps, but smart enough to waylay and nearly kill me."

She brought Christian's hand to her cheek. "Do you know why?"

"They said I'd stuck my nose into something I shouldn't have, wouldn't tell me what."

"Tell me everything from the time you went to the City Manager's office, until you were nearly beaten to death."

"I went to see—"

"Wait, are you sure you're up to this?"

"You bet. I want those bastards behind bars. One of them will have a limp from the knife I stuck into his knee. As soon as I'm able, I'm going after them. Oh, did you find the tape I left in your apartment?"

"Tape? The tape! Oh, Christian, it was on floor behind the door, but I thought Fancy had knocked it off the hi-fi. I told Alan Sheffield that I would listen to it, and until this moment, I'd completely forgotten about it."

"It pretty much spelled out what I'd discovered. Nothing earth shattering about the murders, a start maybe. Chantelle, my snitch, said the murders happened four weeks apart, as if the killer was on some kind of schedule. Check that out, will you?"

"Of course. I went to the Westside, asked around, but no one would talk to me. So what about the City?"

"Their bid process is being compromised."

"More bad news, someone bombed City Hall. Four people died in the explosion. It happened the same morning you were left at the Borseau estate."

"Oh, my god, what if my sleuthing forced someone's hand? Four people died? Who?"

"Paul Hewitt's secretary and three of the City's middle management staff."

Christian shook his head. "Poor Helen. She was upset when I asked her to copy a year's worth of agendas for me. She kept glancing at the door as if she wanted to make a break for it. Jace was right. He said, with my reputation, I'd make the powers-that-be nervous."

"Christian, the blame lies with whoever set off the bomb or arranged to have it done." Jaclyn stood, leaned down and kissed him on the cheek. "I'll get the troops and a tape recorder."

Sheffield, Jaclyn, Sam, Jason, and Carl Grayson walked into the bedroom and stood beside Christian's bed.

"I think the City's bid process is being compromised," Christian said. "Make that was, I guess."

Sheffield plucked at his lips. "You mean the way companies bid on projects?"

"More to the point, the way the contracts are awarded," Christian responded. "Unless I'm way off the mark, I believe it's a shutout before the first pitch is thrown." Christian pushed himself into a sitting position. "Say I'm a general contractor and the City has a construction project in the offing. The City's engineers put the plans and specs together, then they advertise for bids. After they estimate what they believe is the actual cost, they plug in a few extra bucks. By a few, it could be thousands, or depending upon the magnitude of the project, millions. That way, if the bids are equal to or less than the estimate, the staff doesn't have to go back to the Council. If the bids come in higher than the staff estimated, the Council has to approve the additional funding.

"What I'm saying is: if a project is to estimated to cost three or four million, the actual price tag may be one or two. If a company has the inside track, they could bid up to four million, and pocket the difference. In order to do that, they'd have to know what the estimate was before they bid. And someone at the City would have to leak it. Then, to pull it off, they'd have to dummy up the invoices for materials, pad the cost of overruns, and labor."

"Did you find any real proof of that?" Sheffield asked.

"If you mean did I find the smoking gun, no. Do you know what the Consent Calendar is?"

Jason jumped in. "It's a list of actions the Council votes on en masse, primarily housekeeping issues. But the Consent Calendar wouldn't be used to authorize major projects."

"You mean *shouldn't* be used," Christian said, "but I'm sure that's what was happening. Big construction projects sandwiched in between housekeeping issues. Even so, who would kill to cover up what amounts to a case of fraud? Sure, it's illegal, but murder?" Christian tapped his forehead. "Could it be a money laundering scheme of some sort?"

"Tune in tomorrow for further developments," said Dr. Andrew Kirk, the dimples in his cheeks winking. "Time's up, folks."

Jason smiled at Christian. "Andy's right, you need to rest."

"I'm okay," Christian said. "We're just starting to get somewhere."

"Christian, the most important thing is for you to get well," Jaclyn said. "We'll listen to the tape, see if there's anything else we can follow up on until we talk again."

"I left the stack of Council meeting agendas on my desk. Did you find them?"

Jaclyn shook her head. "Your apartment was ransacked. There were no papers of any kind on your desk, even your typewriter ribbon was gone."

"I marked what I thought were three companies that were doing too much business with the City, but I can't remember their names."

"We'll ferret them out," Sheffield said. "Also, Christian, as far as the public knows, you're in the hospital, comatose. We think whoever tried to murder you may try again. By the way, I could use another first-class investigator like you. How about it?"

"Nah, Jace would be destitute without me."

"Hey, Shef, trying to steal my super sleuth is a new low, even for you."

Sheffield grinned. "All's fair in—"

"Yeah? Just remember two can play at that game." Jason winked at Jaclyn. "Get my meaning?"

Sheffield laughed. "Over my dead body!"

# Chapter Thirty-four

Susan stared at the tall, gangly fellow, wearing a grimy white T-shirt, ragged jeans, and worn boots. A sweat-stained cowboy hat rode low on his forehead.

"You're not *him*."

"No." He uncapped the canteen and handed it to her.

Susan drank greedily and gave it back to him. "Thank you."

He nodded.

Glancing around, she realized that they were inside a cave, an occasional flicker of moonlight filtered through the long, narrow tunnel. Behind her, water seeped from cracks in the boulders, creating a rivulet held captive by a trough of small rocks. Was that the sound she had heard before? No, she'd fainted, and when she came to, the strange, musty smell was gone, and this fellow was carrying her.

"What if *he* comes?"

"Not a chance. He doesn't know this place." The young man stood and handed the canteen to her.

Susan grabbed his wrist. "Please don't leave me."

"It's all right, you'll be safe here." He hunkered down and patted her hand. "You need a doctor. I bandaged your wounds, but I'm sure you need stitches. I'll call the authorities and tell them where you are."

"What if they can't find me?"

"I'll give them detailed directions."

"After you call them, will you come back?"

"No, it wouldn't be wise for me to be here when they arrive."

"Won't you tell me who you are?"

"My name isn't important," he said. "Yours is. What is your name?"

"Moonbeam. No," she said, averting her gaze, "I'm Susan Walsh."

"Susan, I'm sorry I couldn't save the other girls, the ones before you." He shook his head. "By the time I realized what was going on, it was too late."

"Why is he doing this?"

"I'm sure insanity figures into it." He reached into the backpack beside him. "I brought aspirin to ease your pain. Don't take more than three at a time, then wait at least four hours before you take more. Also, I brought a flashlight for you, and food—chicken, rolls, and fruit. Be sure to wrap the leftovers, the garbage, too. Don't throw anything away. Most of the animals around here are harmless, but a few are not. You can refill the canteen in the stream. The water is pure."

He smiled at her. "I have to go now. I promise you that I'll find a way to keep him from doing this again. The authorities would never believe me if I told them who he is. They would want proof and I don't have any. Not yet, but I will."

"Wait, I don't even know what day it is. I was held somewhere for weeks."

"It's the middle of January. God bless you, Susan." He turned away and hurried through the tunnel.

# Chapter Thirty-five

"There's a gentleman on line two who says he urgently needs to talk to you," Moira said. "He refuses to give his name."

"I'll take it." Sheffield punched the terminal. "May I help you?"

"Mr. Sheffield?"

"Yes, I'm Alan Sheffield."

"Are you investigating the Ladies of the Night Murders?"

"Yes."

"I'm calling about the most recent missing girl. She's hurt. I treated her wounds as well as I could, but she needs a doctor. I can tell you where she is."

"Go on." Sheffield said, pressing the switch to trace the call. At the same instant, an alarm, like a mini clog horn, began beeping in his investigators' office.

"Take Highway one-sixty-five east to Harper's Road where it intersects with Winding Way. Do you know where that is?"

"Yes, its sixty-odd miles northeast of here," Sheffield responded.

"Make a right turn on Winding Way, and drive exactly 11.3 miles. The road, such as it is, peters out at that point. When you get out of your vehicle, you'll see a huge boulder dead ahead. Behind it are the entrances to three caves. The girl is in the middle one. Her name is Susan Walsh, but you may know her as Moonbeam," he said and hung up.

Sheffield dashed out of his office. "Did we get the trace?"

Sam and Jaclyn stood beside Moira's desk, shaking their heads in unison. "No," Sam said, "he knew when to cut you off."

"Jaclyn, meet us out front with the Jeep. Sam, contact Kirk Williams, tell him we'll pick him up at FBI headquarters, in twenty minutes, and tell Rip Vashay what's going down and have him arrange transport for his team. Let's move!" Sheffield said.

"It's eerie out here," Sam said to Jaclyn, who sat beside him in the front seat of the Jeep. "It gives me the creeps."

"'Hard to believe we're still on planet earth." Jaclyn pressed her head against the window and peered up at the sky. "Ah, the old man in the moon is lighting our way, from time to time."

Sheffield and the FBI agent were in the back seat. Hands fisted, Sheffield said, "Can't this heap go any faster?"

"Yeah," Sam said, "if you don't care about getting there in one piece. This abomination they call a road is as bad as it gets. What's next? Quick sand?"

"All I can think about is how terrified that girl has to be," Sheffield said. "Why didn't the caller simply bring her to our office?"

"No clue," Sam said.

"The lad is afraid, he's protecting himself." Sheffield paused. "I say lad, because he sounded young. We'll get a take on his age from our speech experts, after they analyze the recording. Or possibly, the girl can tell us."

"I assume the SWAT will go in first to secure the cave," Kirk Williams said. "This could be a hoax, but you don't think so, do you, sir?"

"All I have to go on is my gut, which tells me it's on the up and up. But that's why Rip and his team will go in first."

"By now, she won't trust anyone," Jaclyn said. "Rip should call out her name, tell her who we are, and that we're here to rescue her."

"Actually, she's more apt to trust a woman. How about going in with Rip?" Sheffield said.

"You bet."

"Is it possible the caller may be the killer, and we're going to find a dead body, or walk into a trap?" Kirk asked.

"That wouldn't fit with the killer's MO," Sheffield said, "but it's a scenario I considered, therefore the SWAT." Sheffield swiveled around to look out the rear window, spotting Vashay and his men, about a hundred yards back, in their sturdy recon vehicle.

**A**gent Rip Vashay crouched at the mouth of the cave. Two members of his team had inspected the caves to the left and right of this one, and had given their leader the all-clear signal. Vashay edged into the abyss, with Jaclyn hunkered down a few steps behind him. He turned on the flashlight and swept the rock walls, ceiling, and floor. The tunnel curved to the right about twenty feet ahead. "Call her name," he whispered to Jaclyn.

"Susan, I'm Jaclyn Devereaux with the State Attorney General's office. The young man who brought you here called our office. We're here to help you."

"Thank God," Susan sobbed.

"Are you alone?"

"Yes. Are you coming to get me?"

"Susan, can you come to us?"

"No, I'm hurt. *He* hurt me."

"You mean the young man who called us hurt you?"

"Oh, no, he saved my life."

"We'll be there in a jiffy. Let's go, Rip."

Moving forward, duck walking in crouched positions, Rip and Jaclyn inched their way through the winding tunnel. Thirty or so feet in, they rounded a sharp turn, and saw her. When the light flashed in her eyes, she shied away.

Jaclyn caught a glimpse of long, blond, curly hair, a mass of tangles around a babyish, heart-shaped face. She rushed to the girl, who, in the dim light, appeared to be fifteen or sixteen years young. Putting her arms around Susan's trembling body, Jaclyn asked, "Can you walk?"

"I don't think so, but I'll try."

"No need for that," Rip said. "Sam," he shouted. "Ask my men to bring the stretcher and blankets."

Susan gripped Jaclyn's hand. "Don't leave me."

"Not for a second. If it's okay with Agent Vashay, I'll ride back with you."

"Sure, my team can go back with the AG," he said.

"The AG? What's that?"

Jaclyn smiled and hugged Susan to her. "It's Arizona's top cop, the Attorney General, Alan Sheffield."

"He's here?"

"Yes, he certainly is. I'm Jaclyn Devereaux."

"What a pretty name."

"Thank you."

"Will I have to go to the hospital?"

"Yes, but I'll stay with you. When you're well enough to leave the hospital, you can stay with me for as long you'd like. Okay with you?"

Tears streamed down Susan's face. "I don't know how to thank you, all of you."

"Finding you alive is all the thanks we need," Jaclyn said.

# Chapter Thirty-six

It had been an anxiety-ridden night. As physically exhausted and emotionally drained as Jaclyn felt, she rallied enough strength to balk at leaving Susan's side. She adamantly defied the night nurse in charge at St. Vincent's Hospital.

"I'm sorry, but I cannot allow you to access the treatment rooms. You'll have to stay in the waiting room. It's the hospital's policy."

Jaclyn flashed her badge. "I'm Jaclyn Devereaux, an investigator for State Attorney General Alan Sheffield. That girl is the victim of a horrendous crime. She's terrified, and I promised her that I would not leave her. I intend to keep my word. Hospital policy be damned."

"Miss Devereaux, the treatment rooms are off-limits to everyone, except authorized personnel."

"Then authorize me. Right now!"

Sheffield stepped between them. "Nurse Austen," Sheffield said, lifting her name from the tag on her uniform, "I'm Attorney General Alan Sheffield. My investigator has to stay with that girl. She needs protection from the monster that tortured her and nearly ended her life. This isn't a run of the mill situation."

"All right, Mr. Sheffield. I don't like bending the rules, but I see how it is."

"Thank you for your understanding."

"Go ahead, Miss Devereaux," Nurse Austen said.

Dr. Harrison Sprague, a ruddy-faced, blonde-haired, third-year intern, was on duty in the ER. After assessing the girl's wounds, he took Sheffield aside to discuss the legal authorization he'd require, before he could treat a minor. The Attorney General signed the document, wondering how people without clout waded through the red tape incumbent to the glut of bureaucracies that were springing up throughout the country.

After Susan told Jaclyn where her parents lived, Sheffield and Sam went to the office to try to locate them.

Jaclyn held Susan's hand, while Dr. Sprague inserted a stint in the vein in her arm. He started the intravenous feeding, propelling pain medication through the girl's system. He stitched the cuts that were too deep to heal if he didn't. When he had dealt with the less serious cuts, he treated the cigarette burns on Susan's breasts.

"We're done, young lady," he said as he peeled off his rubber gloves.

Tears trickled from the corners of Susan's eyes. "Will I be okay?"

"Absolutely, you're going to be fine."

"Thank you, doctor."

"You're welcome."

Dr. Sprague jerked his head toward the far corner of the room. Jaclyn followed him there.

"I know you're anxious to question my patient," he said quietly, "but it'll have to wait. Her blood pressure is elevated, heart rate, too. I've given her a sedative to help her relax. This child has been through hell. I assume she's the latest victim in The Ladies of the Night Murders."

"Yes, but by the grace of God, *she's* alive," Jaclyn said.

"If you plan to stay with her, I'll have an orderly set up a cot in here. You look as if you could use some down time. Is there anything I can get for you? Coffee, coke, a sandwich?"

"A cup of coffee would be appreciated."

"Sugar or Cream or both?"

"No, I take it straight."

Dr. Sprague patted Jaclyn's shoulder and left the room

Jaclyn waited until Susan had fallen asleep before she stretched out on the cot next to the girl's bed. The moment her head hit the pillow, it was lights out for her.

Sheffield tiptoed into the room. It was after nine, but he didn't want to awaken Jaclyn or Susan. He sat in the Captain's chair beside the windows and stared through it. He'd been unable to contact Susan's parents. The operator told him the phone number was no longer in service. He'd contacted the Sheriff's office in, Ames, Iowa. The news he'd gotten was tragic. Susan's parents had died in an automobile accident, many months ago. Destiny wasn't cutting this girl any slack. It was *déjà vu* for Sheffield. His parents had died in a car accident during a snowstorm, shortly after his son was killed in Korea.

Jaclyn stirred and opened her eyes. She yawned and stretched. When she spotted Sheffield, she sat up, and whispered, "How long have you been here?"

"Not long. I didn't mean to disturb you."

"Did you talk to Susan's parents?"

"Let's step outside."

"What's going on? Oh, Shef, don't her parents want her to come home?"

"They were killed in a car accident."

"What? No!" Jaclyn burst into tears and collapsed against Sheffield.

"Sadly, we weren't able to locate any relatives in or near Ames, Iowa. We'll keep searching for aunts, uncles, grandparents, whoever, as will the Sheriff, Eldon Tinsley. For now, she'll be our responsibility."

"It's not fair." Jaclyn swiped at the tears on her cheeks. "She's been through so much. How are we going to tell her?"

"That would be: How are *you* going to tell her? Susan trusts you. You'll find a way to help her through this latest tragedy. Of course, she's welcome to stay with us, until a better option comes along. She needs to go to school, but the way things are, it would be prudent to hire a tutor."

"Will we be able to protect her?"

"Yes, but to be on the safe side, I'll add more security at the estate. Of course, Sejii will dote on her, as he dotes on you. You can't be here twenty-four hours a day. Until she's well enough to leave the hospital, I'll ask Rip to assign members of his team to guard her. When Dr. Sprague gives the go-ahead, you can interview her, I hope she can give us a description of her abductor. Perhaps she can offer a clue as to where the torture took place. It's likely that she'll be able to describe the young man who saved her."

"Let's not tell her about her parents until she's strong enough to deal with the guilt she's bound to feel."

"The timing will be entirely up to you, Jaclyn."

## Chapter Thirty-seven

**M**itchell Price pushed the food cart along the first floor corridor at St. Vincent's Hospital. With a furtive glance, he pressed the arrow next to the elevator. The white jacket and pants had come from an employee's locker. The nametag with a blurry photo was pinned to the lapel.

When the elevator doors opened on the fourth floor, two of Sheffield's agents boarded the lift. One of the officers keyed a two-way radio. The other searched Price, then checked the trays on the cart.

The agent clicked the two-way radio again. "Give me a description," he said, concentrating on the face in front of him. "Approximate height and weight?"

Price thought the responses to the agent's queries were close enough, but sweat coursed down his forehead.

"Go ahead," the officer waived him on.

He turned left at the first corner.

"Wait a minute," one of the officers called out.

Price froze.

"You dropped this." The officer swept a bar towel from the floor.

"Thank you." Price said, using the delay to glance around again. Two agents stood near the elevator, two more were stationed at each end of the hall. Another officer sat beside room 412. It was break time. No one was supposed to be there, but if he left now, it would look suspicious. Price reached under a stack of napkins, grasped his weapon, and slipped it under his jacket. The brass plate on the door across the hall read 411. Price picked up a tray and went in. A young woman with her head swathed in bandages looked up.

He'd been told only Grayson would be in this wing. Price forced a smile, placed the tray on the server attached to the bed, and swiveled it toward her.

"Thank you," she said, returning his smile. "You must be new here. At least, I don't think I've seen you before. I've been pretty much out of it until today. My doctor says the bandages will come off tomorrow. If everything's okay, I'll get to go home. I won't have hair for a while. It's brown," she rambled on.

"Let me fix this for you." Price removed a pillow from behind her head and pressed his gun into it.

"My husband and two chil . . ." With a spit of air, feathers exploded over the bed and filtered down around her. She slumped forward. Within seconds, blood oozed onto the sheets.

Price tiptoed across the room, flipped the light switch, and cracked the door.

Agent Christopher Caulfield sat in a folding chair across the hall. He glanced up from the paperback he was reading, frowning as he scanned the area from one end of the hall to the other. He closed the book and laid it on the floor. His frown deepened, as he stared at the cart across the hall. His hand slid to the shoulder holster.

Price hunkered down, slid the silencer through the crack in the door, and pulled the trigger. With a dull thud, the bullet pierced the officer's neck. But, as Caulfield toppled to the floor, the chair crashed into the wall behind him. Sheffield's men spun toward the sound.

The executioner raced across the corridor into room 412, slammed the door, and stared at the bed.

"It's a trap!" he bellowed as he staggered to the window, opened it, and climbed onto the fire escape. As he came to the first landing, he glanced up at the cop gripping a 3.57 Magnum, leveled at Price's head.

"Stop where you are, and drop your weapon! Put your hands behind your head and lie down, face down. Do it now!" Agent Tom Mallory took a cautious step down the fire escape. "Now, or I'll blow you into kingdom come. Drop your weapon. Drop it!"

Price hesitated a moment. It was better to die now than to wait for his employer to kill him. He slid the silencer into his mouth and pulled the trigger. Bone, blood, and brains splattered the iron stairwell.

Mallory sped back up the fire escape. "Call Erikson," he yelled to the other agents. "The shooter just blew his brains out."

With long strides, Sam and Sheffield crossed the lobby. Jaclyn had to run to keep up with them. Sheffield nodded to the two officers who stood on either side of the elevator. Sam slapped the button to close the doors and punched the number. The elevator gathered speed as it moved up the shaft.

When the door slid open, Agent Mallory was waiting for them.

"We lost a man," he said, shaking his head. "A patient, too, and the shooter blew his brains out. I'm sorry, Mr. Sheffield," he said, apologizing and acknowledging the Attorney General in the same breath.

Sheffield's hands plunged into the front pockets of his jeans. "Who did we lose?"

"Chris Caulfield, sir." Mallory wiped trembling hands across his eyes.

Sheffield studied the young officer. He wondered how old Mallory was, twenty-five—thirty at the most. Curly light brown hair fell across his forehead, he had a pug nose and freckles, a trim, athletic body. The All-American Boy. Sheffield was reminded of himself at that age. He'd attended Mallory's wedding this past June. His wife was expecting their first child. But Sheffield knew he wasn't supposed to care.

"Where's the shooter?" Jaclyn said.

Mallory hooked his thumb over his shoulder. "On the fire escape, room 412. We're waiting for a photographer and the FBI crime scene guys."

"And the patient?" she said. He pointed to room 411. "If you need me, Shef, I'll be in one of those two places." The AG waved her off.

Sam lit a cigarette. "How did we lose a civilian?"

"Sam, we went through the drill, called the kitchen, had the chef describe the waiter," Mallory said. "He had a food cart, no different than the others who've been coming up here. We searched him, searched the trays before we let him off the elevator. He went into 411, and shot the woman. The gun had a silencer—"

"Shit." Sam nodded toward the young man in the waiting room who sat with his face buried in his hands. "Is that her husband?"

"Yeah," Tom mumbled as he whipped away from them. "They have a couple of little kids."

"Go on," Sheffield said quietly.

"Well, I think Chris was going for his weapon. He'd unsnapped his holster."

"We specifically ordered the hospital administrator to keep these rooms vacant," Sam said.

"That's true, but last evening, the head nurse told us they were desperate for a room." He nodded toward 411. "The patient was going home this morning. It was my call, I made a mistake."

Sheffield raked his fingers through his hair. "What about Chris's family?"

"Mike Harris has gone to talk to Jean and the kids. Chris and Mike are good friends. Were," he whispered.

Sam's mouth drew into a hard line. "Any identification on the shooter?"

Mallory reached into his pocket, took the driver's license from a plastic bag, and handed it to Sam. "His name's Mitchell Price."

"Unless it's phony. Run him through the system and do it fast," Sheffield said to Sam. "And, Tom, I'm going to need a detailed report from you, and statements from the kitchen staff, from everyone who was on duty. The Feds, too, if any were involved."

"There were two on duty, but it was their break time. They'd gone to the cafeteria minutes before the guy got off the elevator."

"The shooter was counting on that. All right, I don't worry much about taking heat, but we're going to get a lot of it on this one. And we deserve it. I'll ask Moira to schedule a press conference for tomorrow morning. Be there and make sure Mike Harris is there too. Ten o'clock," Sheffield said.

"My report will be on your desk before I go home."

Sheffield grasped the officer's shoulder. "I know it won't be easy, but try to get some rest."

"Sam, call Kirk Williams, I want him at the press conference. We need to keep the FBI informed about everything we do. I'll find Jaclyn." The Attorney General headed for number 412. "Thank god, we got Christian out of here," he muttered to himself.

# Chapter Thirty-eight

Sheffield's agents and FBI agent, Kirk Williams, sat elbow to elbow at the rectangular table in the conference room. He studied them carefully, trying to assess how they'd handle the stress of facing the press. Sam and Jaclyn seemed at ease, but they had had considerable experience in fielding the media's questions. Tom Mallory and Mike Harris were nervous, but they were on the pan, so to speak. Kirk Williams shot a reassuring thumbs-up Jaclyn's way. She acknowledged the gesture with a small smile and a nod of her head.

"The reporters are here," Sheffield said. "Give them straight answers. Don't speculate. I'll do most of the talking, but if they ask you a question, respond as briefly and as honestly as you can. I'm not going to feed answers to you. The tape recorders are running, so everything will be documented. Any questions?" Sheffield's agents glanced at one another and shook their heads.

"All right, let's do it then." Sheffield flipped the button on the intercom. "Let them in, Moira, and bring your steno pad." He flipped the switch again. "Insurance," he said, smiling at his people. "I don't mind being quoted, but I hate to be misquoted.

"Come in gentlemen, ladies," Sheffield said, when he spotted Susan Milhouse from KTOP-TV. "Ted," he said, acknowledging Theodore Brown from KSOL-TV. "I think there's room for everyone. We'll give you a few minutes to set up your equipment."

A few steps behind the press, Jason and Carl Grayson came through the double doors.

"Jace, Carl. Mort," the Attorney General said, acknowledging the Chief of Police as he walked in. Salinger didn't respond.

"What's going on, Shef?" Susan Milhouse called from the back of the house.

"All right," Sheffield said. "Let's back up a ways. As you know, several weeks ago, Christian Grayson disappeared. Later, he was left for dead in front of Jason Borseau's estate. As enlightened as we believe Arizona to be, we needed to rule out the possibility that it was a racially motivated crime.

"Mr. Grayson was bound, blindfolded, and held captive, until he managed to free himself from his restraints. We have located the abandoned warehouse where he was imprisoned. Padlocks and chains secured the truck doors on the ground floor, the windows covered with steel bars. Fingerprints and other evidence indicated that Christian smashed a window on the second floor, and virtually flew to the fire escape, an unbelievable distance away. A trail of blood led us to a truck ramp at a neighboring warehouse. There we found two blood types, one consistent with Christian's, the other we assume belonged to the kidnapper, although we believe there was more than one.

Susan Millhouse stood. "How is Christian doing?"

"He's out of danger and recuperating in a safe place."

Ted Brown raised his hand. "Shef, how does this tie in with what happened at St. Vincent's?"

"Almost there, Ted," Sheffield said. "Disguised as a hospital employee, a hit man made his way past my agents and those of the FBI. He was there to end Christian's life.

Fortunately, we had removed him from the hospital last week. Unfortunately, two people lost their lives, including one of my officers, Christopher Caulfield."

"Jules Carson from the *Arizona Republic*. Who was the shooter?"

"I'll give you everything I can, but not that. We've tentatively identified him, but we're still tracking him through the system. We're sure he wasn't acting alone. When he realized his capture was imminent, he shot himself. His death was instantaneous."

"It's rumored that a female patient died," Susan Milhouse said.

"Yes, I'm sad to say that's true." Sheffield cringed inwardly, but his gaze didn't waver.

"Can you tell us who she was?" Susan said.

"For now, we're honoring the family's request to withhold her identity. There are children involved."

"Richard Lawrence from the *Yuma Daily Sun*. Are the Phoenix police working with you?"

"I'll answer that." Mort Salinger stood. "For those of you who don't know me, I'm the Chief of Police. The Attorney General is playing a lone hand in this investigation. If we'd been involved, maybe that woman would still be alive."

"The Chief is partly right," Sheffield admitted. "The police department isn't involved, nor will it be in the foreseeable future. As I said before, for the time being, only the FBI will assist us. In a few minutes, you'll understand why." He tapped his chest. "What occurred at the hospital last night rests here."

Ted Brown asked, "Do you know why Christian was kidnapped?"

"It's likely that Christian's kidnapping and the attempt on his life are connected to the explosion at City Hall."

Sheffield's bombshell drew gasps and shocked silence.

"Shef," Ted Brown was the first to break the spell, "has Christian been able to tell you what he'd discovered?"

"Yes," Sheffield said, "Christian Grayson, a Pulitzer Prize recipient, uncovered a conspiracy involving City employees, a cover-up of gigantic proportions. Due to that revelation, to include any city employee in this investigation, including the Phoenix Police, would be unwise.

"We're working round-the-clock to find the two men who kidnapped Christian. We have their descriptions and sketches of them are being drawn as we speak. We'll share them with the media as soon as possible. Now, another attempt has been made on Christian's life. Add to that, we have the murder of six others—four City employees, the young woman recovering from surgery at St. Vincent's, and Agent Chris Caulfield. When we get them, and we will, they'll be tried for mass murder, and we'll ask for the death penalty."

"May we question your people?" Susan Milhouse said.

"Of course. Sam Erikson and Jaclyn Devereaux are in charge of the investigations," he said, turning in their direction. "Agents Thomas Mallory and Michael Harris were on duty at the hospital last night. Kirk Williams is the FBI agent who has been working with my team is also here."

"This question is for the duty officers. If you searched the shooter, how did he get a weapon past you?" Susan Milhouse said.

"I'll take it," Tom Mallory said, laying a hand on Mike Harris's arm.

Sheffield took the chair beside Moira. When he saw the stricken expression on her face, he whispered, "Are you all right?"

"Why wouldn't I be?" she hissed. "I'm just a stick of furniture with a pencil in my hand."

Sheffield stared at her. "What did you say?"

Moira hurtled out of the chair and stumbled from the conference room.

# Chapter Thirty-nine

Sheffield loosened his tie and undid the top button of his shirt. He focused on his chief investigator: tall, with dark hair and eyes, physically strong and raw-boned, handsome, rugged features. Beyond what was visible to the eye, Sam Erikson was intelligent, his integrity without peer. He was straight as an arrow all the way.

Sheffield was relieved that Jaclyn, who was very fond of Moira, had opted to pass on this meeting with his secretary. Interrogating Moira would be tough for him, too.

She'd worked for the state for twenty-three years, a permanent fixture in the Attorney Generals' offices. Efficient, organized, and tireless, the venerable Miss Fleming intimidated the agency's budding young attorneys, both male and female. Out of earshot, they'd nicknamed her the Axe, short for battle-axe. Of course, no one was suicidal enough to call her that to her face. Even Sheffield found himself analyzing her current mood as he strode past her desk each morning.

With her face buried in her hands, Moira rocked back and forth.

"How are you involved in this, Moira?" Sheffield said in a comforting voice. She sobbed and rocked harder. The Attorney General caught Sam's eye, lifted his thumb, and pointed to himself. He'd play the good cop, Sam the bad cop. They waited.

Sam's deep voice boomed across the office. "Do you want to have your attorney present?"

Moira shook her head.

Sheffield leaned toward her. "We can call him or her for you."

"Nooo," she sobbed.

"Do you object to having our conversation recorded?" Sheffield said. Moira shook her head.

"Answer the question, you know how this works," Sam said impatiently.

She wiped her eyes with a crumpled handkerchief. "My name is Moira Fleming. I reside at twenty-three twenty-one Indian School Road. The information I'm about to give is of my own free will. I was asked if I wanted an attorney present, and I declined. Did I forget anything?"

Sheffield closed his mind to the twist of her mouth, the anguish in her eyes. No way could he have played the bad cop this time. "No, you did fine. Would you like a few minutes to collect your thoughts?" She shook her head. "Sam, read Moira her rights."

Sam walked to Sheffield's desk. "Moira Fleming, you have the right to remain silent. Anything you say may be used against you in a court of law . . ."

Sheffield walked behind the bar, took a glass from the shelf, poured two fingers of scotch, and added a few ice cubes. Stirring the drink with his finger, he returned to his desk, and waited for Sam to finish the Miranda routine.

"Sam, when we're through here, pull our surveillance team together. Have them go over everything in all of our offices, and clean them up, if there's anything to clean up."

"I'm being blackmailed," Moira said.

Taken aback, Sam's expression was one of disbelief. "Blackmailed?"

"Yes. For ten years," she added.

"Why would anyone blackmail *you*?" Sam said.

"Why, Moira?" Sheffield said softly.

"I wasn't always old," she cried, glaring at Sam who glared back.

Sheffield smiled. "None of us looks the way we did when we were young."

"Years ago, I had an affair. There was a child, a boy," she stammered. "His father was married. He was and is an important man. He and his wife adopted my son. She doesn't know the boy is her husband's biological child."

Slowly, Sheffield sank into the chair behind his desk. "Who have you been paying?" Moira paused and looked away. "Tell us who you have been paying?" he said again.

"Mitchell Price," she sobbed.

Sheffield left his desk and took the chair beside her. "You don't make enough money to keep a blackmailer happy. How did you pay him?" He suspected that he knew the answer, but she had to say it for the record.

She lowered her eyes and whispered, "Information."

Sam thundered, "About our investigations?"

"Moira, listen to me carefully," Sheffield said. "We don't believe Price was in this alone. Do you know who he was working with?"

She nodded. "Tercel. That's what Mr. Price called him. I doubt that it's his real name, but it could be, I guess.

"Mr. Sheffield, I can't bear it that Chris was murdered and that poor woman with a husband and children." Another flood of tears cascaded from her eyes and streamed down her face. "Oh, god, Chris's family. Am I an accessory to murder?"

Sheffield didn't know if he was hearing the grandfather clock ticking on the wall behind him or the sound of his heart hammering out of control. "No, you didn't believe anyone would die, did you?"

"Not unless my son and his father were hurt or killed."

"We'll get to that. The thing is: you've been leaking sensitive information to a blackmailer for ten years. How many investigations have you compromised, how many people have suffered losses because of the information you passed on?"

"I had to protect my son and his father."

"Weren't you also protecting yourself?" Her answer would be critical when the time came for a judge to sentence her.

Moira wiped her eyes. "No, I don't think so."

"So you believed harm would come to your son and his father?" Sheffield studied her face. "Did Price threaten their lives, or yours?"

She stared at him. "He said accidents could be arranged for all of us."

"Does your son's father know you're being blackmailed?" Sheffield said.

"Until now, no one knew. I don't care what happens to me, but what about my son?"

"Think about it. If something unforeseen happened to your boy, the hold on you ceases to exist."

Blinking her eyes, his secretary said, "I'm so frightened for him."

Sheffield coaxed a pale lock of hair from his forehead. "Who is your son? Tell us his name, Moira."

"No!"

"If you don't, we can't protect him or his father. Sam, turn off the recorders," Sheffield said.

"They're not the only recorders," Moira said quietly.

Sam advanced toward her. "You mean everything that's said in this office is handed off to someone called Tercel?"

"Not everything, I—"

"Jesus, Shef, they probably know where Christian is."

"Calm down, Sam. We've read Moira her rights, and we'll put her in protective custody. Right now, we have to figure out who and what she's compromised. She's going to help us." Sheffield turned to her. "Do you understand what I'm saying?"

Moira looked from Sheffield to Sam. "I'll do whatever it takes to put things right."

Sam's fingers raked through his hair. "After compromising the AG's office for ten years, how can you possibly fix that? I'd like to cuff you, haul you off to prison, and throw away the key."

Sheffield shot a warning glance at his investigator.

Sam caught the look. "All right, who shall I assign to protect our very own Mata Hari?"

"Tom Mallory. He's needs redemption," Sheffield said. "Moira, do you live in an apartment?"

"No, when my mother died, I inherited her house."

Sheffield concentrated on her face. "Is anyone else in this office involved? Take your time, because if there is, and you don't tell us, I'll throw the book at you when this unravels, and it will unravel."

"Not as far as I know."

Sheffield continued to study her. He was convinced she was telling the truth. "Sam, ask Jaclyn to use the pay phone in the lobby to call Tom, and tell her what I want Tom to do. Also, tell him that I don't want any slip-ups. Officially, until we figure out where we're at, as far as anyone else knows, Moira is ill. At least temporarily, Shannon Pearce will take over the secretarial duties," he said, referring to Miss Fleming's assistant. "Now, I'd like a few minutes alone with Moira."

"Okay, Shef." With a hot glance at Sheffield's secretary, Sam stalked out of the office.

"I need your son's name."

She covered her face with her hands and shook her head.

"Now, Moira."

Her hands fell away revealing new wrinkles in her aging skin. "Alexander Payton."

Astonished, Sheffield whispered, "Your son is Senator Payton's boy?"

Moira lifted her head. "Yes."

"My god, Maxwell Payton's son."

With a solemn glance at Sam, Sheffield said, "I could *not* have played the bad cop this time."

"Then you called it right, because I couldn't have been the good cop."

"Love, fear, and guilt—powerful weapons, devastatingly effective when sandwiched together. I'm not making excuses for her, but Moira was the perfect mark."

"Think about it," Jaclyn said quietly. "She's lived in fear for years and years. She couldn't let anyone get close to her. I knew something terrible had happened to her."

"Of course, you did." Sheffield drew her to him. "Sam, I'll let you in on a secret: Jaclyn has agreed to marry me."

Sam's giant frame shot up. "Well, that's the only good news I've heard all day. Oh, oh, will I lose my partner?"

"Only if politics force the issue." Smiling into Jaclyn's eyes, Sheffield framed her face with his hands and kissed her.

"When's the wedding?"

"We haven't set the date yet," Sheffield said. "We wanted to be married without fanfare, but Kathryn Borseau made a big fuss about that. She wants us to tie the knot at their place. It's hard to say no to her.

"Before I forget, just to be on the side of prudence, have our surveillance team go over my house," Sheffield said.

"I'll assign more agents to your place, too," Sam said.

"So, what am I? Chopped liver?" Jaclyn said. "I still have my badge."

A thoughtful smile lifted the corners of Sheffield's mouth. "While you're at it, assign a couple of people to your family, Sam."

"I'll do that," he said.

"Come on, let's get out of here," Sheffield said. "We've had more than enough for one day."

# Chapter Forty

Sheffield spotted Max Payton at a booth in the farthest corner of the remote Mexican restaurant the AG had chosen for their chat. Looks-wise, Sheffield mused, the passage of time had been kind to the Senator. He was a strikingly handsome man, tall and well built. Only the light sprinkling of gray in his perfectly coifed dark hair hinted at his age, a few years shy of fifty.

Smiling as the AG approached, the Senator stood and extended his hand. "Hey, Shef, we could have gone to my Club, although I surely do like south of the border cuisine. This hole in the wall probably serves the best. They usually do."

Sheffield avoided Payton's outstretched hand and slid into the booth.

The Senator's smile faded as he took in the Attorney General's grim expression. "Imagine my surprise when I got your call inviting me to join you for lunch."

"Well, Max, you couldn't possibly have been as surprised as I was when I learned that my secretary, Moira Fleming, is your son's mother."

The Senator's eyes narrowed. "So after all this time, Moira decided to rat me out."

"Not willingly. A situation came to light that affects the integrity of my office. I forced her to tell me why she's had to deal with a blackmailer for the past ten years."

"Moira is being blackmailed? Come on, Shef, cut to the chase. What does she want?"

"Nothing."

"Then, what do *you* want? Hush money?"

"You wish. No, Max, I'm not for sale." With a sardonic smile, Sheffield shook his head. "Just when I think I can't get any more cynical than I already am, I have to deal with the likes of you."

A waiter stopped at the table and handed each of them a menu. "May I get you something to drink?" Sheffield ordered iced tea, the Senator asked for vodka on the rocks.

"You're the GOP's rising star, Max. Rumor has it that you have aspirations to run for President."

"There is a faction in my party encouraging me to do so, but I haven't made a decision. Small talk aside, if you don't want money, what do you want?"

"For myself? Nothing. I wanted to give you a heads-up that Moira's blackmailer knows about you and Alex. If he finds out that I know, it could cost Moira her life. Technically, she's under house arrest so we can protect her. Also, to keep you and young Alex safe, Moira has been feeding information about our investigations to the people responsible for the explosion at City Hall that killed four staff people. In a separate incident, one of my agents, and a patient at St. Vincent's were murdered. The perpetrators of those crimes have made two attempts on Christian Grayson's life. Grayson, as you know, is Jason Borseau's investigative reporter.

"Again, to keep you and her son safe, Moira has lost everything—her integrity, her career, and any hope for a normal life. She did this for the love of a son she's never held in her arms, a son she's never spent time with, a son she didn't get to see grow from babyhood to manhood.

And she did it for you, too. The blackmailer threatened to arrange accidents for you and Alex, if she didn't accede to his demands. She's an amazing woman, and I'm going to do everything I can to help her."

"My god, if this gets out, the scandal will cost me everything—my political career, my wife, and probably Alex."

"For your son's sake, I'll do everything I can to keep it under wraps. Only Moira and I, and two of my agents know about this. None of us will ever breathe a word of it to anyone."

The waiter returned with their drinks. "Are you ready to order?"

"Not just yet," Sheffield said.

"I'll check with you later," the waiter said as he hurried away.

The Senator tossed back his drink. "So are we done here?"

"No, this is what you're going to do: You *will* put together a photo album of Alex from the time he became a part of your life until now. Then, every time you or anyone photographs him, you'll have copies made and send them to me. I'll see that Moira gets the album, and the subsequent pictures. Make the album impressive. It will mean the world to her."

"Shef, my wife will wonder why I'm removing Alex's photos from our albums."

"That's your problem. Maybe you should tell her the truth. Think about this: once the blackmailer realizes he can't squeeze Moira any longer, he could become *your* worst nightmare.

"The other thing is, I want you to provide regular updates about Alex to Moira—what courses he's taking at Harvard, any activities in which he's involved, every aspect of his life, his dreams and aspirations for the future. You'll share everything there is to know about Alex with Moira.

I'll be the go-between. I doubt that you'll want to deal with her directly."

The Senator's face had gone from dead white to beet red. "I'm not the first married man to have a fling. I could've turned my back on the whole damned thing. Instead, I chose to adopt Alex."

"Yeah, you're a bona fide hero. Either you agree to do what I'm asking, or as her attorney, I'll petition the court to grant Moira visitation rights with Alex. I'm deadly serious about this, Max."

"Well, hell, you've backed me into a corner. I don't seem to have a choice."

"That's right, you don't."

"Shef, do realize you're blackmailing *me* now?"

Sheffield smiled. "You'd better hope I'm the only one who does. I'm getting married this weekend, but I'll expect the album and Alex's biography to be on my desk when I return from my honeymoon. We'll be back in two weeks. Have the package delivered to Sam Erikson, my chief investigator, marked Personal and Confidential. He'll let me know when it arrives."

"I'll do my best to comply with your demands."

"Then we understand one another?"

"Yes, you sonofabitch."

"'Sticks and stones,' Senator." Sheffield stood, dropped a twenty-dollar bill on the table, and left the restaurant.

## Chapter Forty-one

Damien Santayana drove through the gates at the Borseau estate. It had surprised him to be invited to Alan Sheffield's wedding since he'd never met the groom or the bride.

After he got out of his car, as the valet was driving away, he realized he'd left the couple's wedding present in the car. He turned and walked toward the sea of automobiles.

"Damien."

Santayana spun around and smiled when he saw Jason.

"I left the happy couple's gift in my car."

"No problem, I'll send someone to get it." Jason shook Damien's hand. "What are you driving?"

"A cherry red Jaguar convertible."

"That should be easy to find." He took Santayana's elbow and steered him toward the house. "Let's go in the back way to avoid the crowd. Kathryn offered her private garden for the ceremony.

"So, Damien, how goes the cattle business?"

"Good, right now. Like any business, it has its ups and downs. Surely you experience them too."

"Our markets are pretty much seasonal—Christmas, Easter, back to school, sports related—football, basketball, baseball, golf has become a big draw. Advertisers vie for the spots in and around our newscasts, and Kathryn's Good News program."

"News wise, I especially like Christian Grayson. I hope he's recovering from his ordeal," Santayana said.

"He's conscious, but he doesn't remember what happened to him."

"A temporary affliction?"

"His long-range memory is intact." Jason recited Sheffield's scripted response to anyone asking about Christian. "Apparently, the part of the brain where short-term memory is stored is permanently damaged or so the doctor thinks."

"Then he won't be able to help Sheffield catch the bad guys."

Jason opened the gate to Kathryn's retreat. With a sweeping glance, Santayana took in the waterfall cascading into the bubbling brook, the Arizona Sycamores, Live Oaks, and Acacias that provided shade for the fragile weeping Japanese Cherry and Maple trees. Broad flowerbeds, lush with flowering shrubs defined the pathway. Long-stemmed coral-bells spiked through the ground cover. The soothing sound of the water softened and cooled the air.

"This is lovely, Jason."

"Kathryn designed it and planted the flowers and shrubs," Jason said. "Damien, what may I get you to drink?"

"Tequila on the rocks, with a lemon twist."

"I'll be right back." Jason started toward the sliding glass doors as his parents were coming through them. He turned back. "Have you met my parents?"

"Yes, when I delivered the filly you bought for Kathryn, I joined you for lunch. They're European," Damien added.

Jason nodded. "They came to the US from Alsace Lorraine shortly before I was born. I imagine you've been to Europe."

"Many times. My family emigrated from Spain to Mexico, later to Arizona. The Santayana Province is in Spain. I own property there."

"If I remember correctly, you were in the Air Force."

"No, a bum knee kept me out of the service. You must be thinking of my twin brother, Déon. Sadly, he's still listed as missing in action."

"Forgive me, I didn't know. I was a B-17 pilot. My squadron was stationed in England. On the return flight after a daylight-bombing mission over Germany, I was forced to crash-land in occupied Holland. Luckily, with the help of the Dutch underground, we got back, but some of my crew didn't make it. I've never gotten over it."

"A year after the war ended, my father died of a broken heart. He couldn't bear not knowing what had happened to Déon."

"Your father was one of the walking wounded, even though he wasn't actively involved in the war, he never recovered from the loss of a son."

"Not just any son, his favorite son," Santayana said.

The fierce expression in Damien Santayana's eyes took Jason by surprise. "If you'll excuse me, I'll fetch our drinks."

The Borseaus' master bedroom had a king-sized four-poster and several high boys and chests of drawers. A small library angled off in one direction, a kitchenette in another. There were easy chairs and end tables, walk-in closets, a bathroom with two shower stalls, and a square tub, equipped with a Jacuzzi.

Jaclyn stared at her reflection in the full-length mirror. "This is the most beautiful dress I've ever seen, Kathryn. It's so kind of you to lend it to me."

"I'm delighted that you agreed to wear it. There it was languishing in a box on the top shelf of my closet. I knew it would complement your exotic beauty."

Jaclyn blushed. "I've never thought of myself as exotic or beautiful."

"Oh, but you are," Kathryn said as she lifted the bouffant organza skirt and let it float to the floor. "There is an aura of mystery about you, and with your classic Mediterranean features, beautiful dark hair and eyes, and your rosy olive skin, you're a knock out."

"I, uh, don't know what to say. Are you sure we're looking in the same mirror?"

"Absolutely," Kathryn said, fluffing the gathered lace around the sweetheart neckline, then tugging the Basque-waist into place.

"Now, for the finishing touch." Kathryn lifted the elegant lace mantilla, positioned it over Jaclyn's hair, and let it fall into place. The delicate scalloped edges framed the bride's face.

"I can't wait to see the expression on Alan's face when he catches sight of you. He'll be bowled over."

"Kathryn, we're so beholden to you and Jason for everything you've done for us. And you have no idea how grateful we are that you invited Susan and Sejii to stay here while we're away. Sejii will see to all of Susan's needs." She laughed. "In fact, just try to keep him from it. From the instant Susan came home from the hospital, Sejii has been fussing over her like an old mother hen.

"We were afraid to leave them at home alone, even with two State Police officers on duty around the clock. As unlikely as it might seem, what if the person who kidnapped and nearly killed Susan found out where she was? Without question, Sejii would sacrifice his life to protect her, but we could never put him in that precarious position. We had decided to postpone our honeymoon, when you and Jason solved our dilemma."

Kathryn smiled. "I can't tell you how excited we are to have them."

Jaclyn pursed her lips and hesitated a moment. "Kathryn, I want to ask you something, and I hope you'll level with me."

"What is it?"

"Did Alan tell you and Jason about my problem?"

"No, he didn't say anything to me, but early-on he talked to Jason. The crux of their conversation was that Alan wanted to share the rest of his life with you. Jaclyn, it's obvious how much you love and need one another. I mean, both of you have been alone for such a long time."

"What about Sandra?"

"Don't worry about her. Alan never loved her, and in my opinion, Sandra primarily loves herself. Case closed."

"Even so, the thought that I'll fail him terrifies me."

Kathryn took Jaclyn's hands in hers. "But, it's so simple—trust him."

"I do trust him, and I want to be his wife in every sense of the word."

"In a few minutes, you're going to take the first step toward fulfilling your dreams and his. Believe me, you and Alan are going be happier than either of you ever dreamed was possible. Now, as my sainted grandmother used to say, 'Put a smile on your face, pull up your socks, and get on with life'."

Jaclyn laughed. "No wonder you're such a positive person."

"My grandmother Whittaker was a no-nonsense woman. She came from sturdy, pioneer stock. I adored her and I miss her every day."

Kathryn tipped her head from side to side. "We forgot about something borrowed. I know! The pearls I wore at my wedding." She opened the wall safe and retrieved the velvet sapphire blue case. "This was my great grandfather's wedding present to my great grandmother. She gave them to my grandmother, and my grandee, as I called her, gave them to me."

"They're absolutely beautiful," Jaclyn said. "Kathryn, I've never had a real friend before. Of course, Sam and Christian are my friends."

"But this is different. When we met, our sister-spirits bonded. I believe our friendship is a rare and precious gift from God, and I'll treasure it always."

Kathryn clasped the pearls around Jaclyn's neck. "Oh, one of the station's photographers is going to film the ceremony and the reception. Christian will be able to share the happiest day of your life. I wish he could be there in person, but it's too dangerous. He'll surely be there in spirit."

Kathryn hugged Jaclyn. "Okay, let's get this show on the road."

They left the suite and walked along the hall toward the stairs. "Look at Sam," Kathryn whispered. "He's nervous about giving you away. It's amazing how uptight men get, even if it isn't their own wedding."

"Hey, I was about to break down the door and take you into custody," Sam said, mopping his brow with a handkerchief. "Partner, you're absolutely gorgeous!"

She took his arm. "Thank you, Sam."

"Be careful, don't trip and fall down the stairs," he said.

Kathryn and Jaclyn glanced at one another and giggled.

"What's so funny?"

"Nothing," Jaclyn chirped.

They left the house and walked along the pathway to the garden. When Kathryn saw Jason, she relived the memories of their wedding day and the wonderful years since. Sam placed Jaclyn's hand in Sheffield's, then stepped back and took the aisle seat beside his wife.

"Dearly beloved," Father Jerome Wilkins began, "we are gathered here in the sight of God and before this company to join Alan Sheffield and Jaclyn Devereaux in the holy bonds of matrimony. Marriage is a sacred sacrament and should not be entered into unadvisedly or lightly, but reverently, discreetly, advisedly, soberly, and in the fear of God. Who gives this woman to be wedded to this man?"

Sam stood and stepped into the aisle. "I do."

"If any man can show just cause why this man and this woman may not lawfully be joined together, let him now speak, or else hereafter forever hold his peace," the minister said, gazing out across the congregation.

"Alan, do you take Jaclyn to be your lawfully wedded wife, to have and to hold from this day forward, for better or worse . . ."

The plane's engines caught, and roared to life. Beau Meredith, Jason's resident co-pilot, would fly the Sheffields to Carmel, where they would honeymoon at the Borseaus' seaside home.

"You're going to love Carmel," Kathryn said as she hugged Jaclyn one last time. "The house was my wedding present from Jason. It's incredible the way it sprawls along the cliffs overlooking the ocean." Laughing, she said, "I was such a Hill Billy. I had never seen a gull, a seal, or a whale. I had never seen or heard the ocean, or smelled the salt air."

Kathryn handed Jaclyn a gift-wrapped package. "This is for you. Open it when you're alone, then you can decide whether to share it with Alan or not."

"I love a mystery." Jaclyn kissed Kathryn on the cheek. "Thank you, for everything."

Jason frowned. "Jaclyn, is my wife giving you advice?"

"Not really." She winked at Kathryn. "Well, maybe a little."

"Your chariot awaits," Kathryn said. "When you get there, call us, please."

"Okay, Mom," Sheffield said. "Thanks, you two." He gripped Jason's hand. "We'll see you in two weeks."

At the top of the ramp, the newlyweds waved, before joining two of Sheffield's agents who were already aboard. Through the windscreen, Beau elevated his thumb. Jason returned the familiar World War II salute. The plane sped down the runway, lifted off, circled once, and headed west.

"Sweetheart, please tell me you didn't give marital advice to Jaclyn."

She slanted a glance at him and turned away.

"Kathryn?" Jason said as he helped her into the limo.

Sighing, she said, "Jaclyn is in love with Alan, he's in love with her. I gave her a little advice. After all, she doesn't have a mother."

Jason settled back and took Kathryn's hand in his. "And, you've elected yourself to fill that role. You didn't have much of a mother, either."

"You were my mother."

Jason took her in his arms. "Among other things."

# Chapter Forty-two

To Sheffield, the Borseau's chauffeur looked more like a businessperson, rather than a man who made a living by driving a limousine. Nattily dressed, Michael O'Reilly wore a black, well-cut suit, a white dress shirt, with a black and red striped tie. Typically Irish in appearance, Sheffield figured the chauffeur was fifty-odd years old. He was handsome, with dark hair, blue eyes, and fair skin. He exuded an air of confidence, flashing an easy, infectious smile. The lilt of Eire was reflected in his speech.

"Sure'n I'll be happy to take your suitcases upstairs," he said.

"Thanks, but I need the exercise," Sheffield responded.

"All right then, sir. Just so's you'll know, my wife and I occupy the northernmost cottage, and our extension is marked on the house phone. Mr. Borseau said I'm to take you and Mrs. Sheffield anywhere you'd like to go, day or night. Wendy, that's my wife, takes care of the cooking and cleaning, the laundry as well. There's a cold supper for you in the fridge, and a table set for two in the gathering room, next to the kitchen. Oh, yes, the missus wondered what time you'd like breakfast."

"Coffee, at what time, Jaclyn?"

"Would seven thirty be too early?"

"Not at all. Would you like it served in your rooms?"

"Rooms?" Jaclyn mouthed.

Seeing the hurt in her eyes, Sheffield drew her to him. "No, we'll wend our way down by then, and thank you. It's O'Reilly, isn't it?"

"Michael O'Reilly. And congratulations to you and Mrs. Sheffield on your marriage."

Sheffield extended his hand. "This business of getting married is exhausting." He laughed and hugged Jaclyn. "I'm sure we won't need you this evening, so we'll say good-night."

"And a very good night to you." O'Reilly nodded to Jaclyn and left.

"Take a gander at this place." Sheffield, said, pointing at the waterfall cascading down a mountain of rock to the Koi pond below. "It's amazing, isn't it?"

Massive beams topped the rough-hewn paneled walls and floor to ceiling windows. Immense, decorative pots held countless tropical plants and trees. Walls had been used for the outside perimeter only. Inside, flagstone, sandwiched into pillars, separated the rooms.

Jaclyn leaned her head against him. "This house was Jason's wedding present to Kathryn."

Sheffield chuckled. "True to form, Jace didn't tell her about it, just brought her here, and surprised her with that news."

Glancing around, Sheffield said, "Jace wanted to situate the house along the cliff to give every room an ocean view. He described it as a challenge. I guess so."

"You have tremendous respect for him, don't you?"

"Yes, and deep, abiding affection. We're as close as brothers are. 'Know what, Mrs. Sheffield?"

"Mrs. Sheffield. I can't believe it." She twisted the rings on her finger. "Alan, why did you tell them to give us separate rooms?"

Sheffield touched his lips to hers. "Jaclyn, I made a promise to you. I thought you'd be more comfortable."

"But—"

"Shhh." Sheffield touched an index finger to her lips. "Let's take a walk on the beach."

"Kathryn said I'd love the ocean, but how fierce it sounds."

Sheffield grinned at her. "I'm glad you and Kathryn are friends. She's a wonderful person."

Jaclyn cocked her head. "That's what she said about you."

"Great!" Sheffield kissed the tip of his bride's nose. "I hope you believed everything she said about me."

"I took everything she said to heart."

"Besides my being wonderful, what would that be?"

"The things women talk about. I've never had a woman to talk to before."

A solemn expression clouded Sheffield's eyes. "I'm glad you do now. Oh, don't let me forget to call our self-appointed mother."

They walked hand in hand along the water's edge. In the distance, the sun shimmered along the horizon, the surf lapped against the shore, a soft breeze whispered across the sea.

The private beach encircled the cliffs, Monterey Pines dotted the hillsides, wildflowers sprang from the heart of the rocks above the glittering white sand.

From time to time, Sheffield stopped to pick up shells and hand them to Jaclyn. She turned each one over and over in her hands, before tucking it in the pocket of her windbreaker.

"You look cute in shorts, Mrs. Sheffield. Your legs are beautiful."

"They are?" Jaclyn bent over to look at them. "I've never noticed."

"I've never seen them before, either," he teased her.

Jaclyn wrapped her arms around his waist. "I don't know about you, but I'm wearing down a little."

"And the wind is picking up. It's too chilly for a couple of desert rats, like us. We should've worn warmer clothes. On second thought, neither of us would've seen your gorgeous legs, for the first time."

Jaclyn laughed. "Jason was right, you're a frustrated comedian."

They strolled to the pathway at the foot of the cliffs. "As fearful as Kathryn is of heights, I can't imagine how she gets from the house to the beach and back again," Sheffield said.

"Maybe Jason forces her to face her fears," Jaclyn said softly.

Sheffield turned her toward him. "I know what you're trying to tell me, but I'm not Jason, you're not Kathryn, and I'll never force you to do anything. If you want me to help you face your fears, you'll have to tell me or give me a sign."

Jaclyn pressed her head against him. "I know."

Sheffield climbed onto the first boulder and reached down for her. Jaclyn put her hands in his and scaled the rock. Moving ahead of him up the steep incline, she called back over her shoulder, "Kathryn gave me a present. She wasn't sure I'd want to share it with you."

"What is it?"

"I don't know, I haven't opened it yet."

Jaclyn peered around the corner of the dressing room. "Close your eyes."

Sheffield was relaxing in a chair beside the fireplace, watching the flames, savoring the warmth radiating into the room. "Maybe we should have brought Kathryn with us."

"All right, open your eyes."

Sheffield opened his eyes and drew a sharp breath. In the flickering light, Jaclyn twirled around, an angel in the filmy white nightgown and negligee. Ringlets of dark hair framed her face.

Jaclyn gazed at him anxiously. "Do you like it?"

Sheffield rose and crushed her to him. "It's almost lovely enough to touch you."

Her hands framed his face. "Alan, you're crying."

"So it would seem," he said, brushing the tears from his cheeks. Sheffield felt his muscles bunch as his mind raced. Suddenly, he was aware of the fire crackling and hissing behind them, the sea crashing against the rocks below, the heady breeze wafting across the balcony through the open French doors. He took her in his arms, carried her to the bed, and sat beside her. "There is so much more to marriage than love-making."

She turned away from him.

"Jaclyn, who am I?"

Tears overflowed her eyes and streamed down her face. She turned to him and studied his face. "Alan, who loves me."

"Yes, your *husband* who loves you."

Jaclyn pressed back against the pillow. "If I'd known how to do it, I would have killed myself."

Sheffield smoothed the silky strands of hair away from her face. "If you had, I'd still be alone. Time, my darling, give us time. For now, just hold on to me."

Her eyes gazed wistfully into his. "But I want to be your real wife."

Sheffield smiled. "You're very real to me."

"Don't you understand how much I want to be yours? I'm just so afraid I'll fail you," she said softly.

"And, I'm equally afraid I may fail you." He hesitated a long moment before untying the satin ribbon at her throat, then he slipped the sleeves of the negligee and the straps of

209

the nightgown from her shoulders. Sheffield gasped when he saw the scars on her breasts. Cigarette burns, too many to count.

"I promise you, my beloved, I *will* send the bastard to hell."

"How can you bear to look at me?"

"If only you knew how beautiful you are," Sheffield said, as his lips moved from scar to scar. "I love you, and I want you more than I've ever loved or wanted any other woman." He gazed into her eyes. "May I have you?"

Jaclyn lifted her lips to his. "Yes," she whispered.

As he loved her, Jaclyn trembled at his touch. Agonizing breaths. Were they his or hers? The wild sounds of the surf crashed on the rocks below, a clock ticked, her passion answering his, her damp hair sliding along his skin, electrifying him, passion rising, peaking, and hurling them, as one, over the precipice.

"Jaclyn," Sheffield moaned.

"Alan," she whispered, gazing up at him. "I'm your *real* wife now."

He pressed her to him. "Without question, my love."


Sheffield stroked Jaclyn's hair as she slept, listening to her slow, measured breathing. His hand was as gentle, as his thoughts were fierce. The Attorney General's mind had gone to war. He had carried a gun for years, but other than the target practice required by the FBI, he'd never pulled the trigger. That was then. Now, he wanted to kill a man he didn't know, had never seen.

Sheffield smiled to himself. Jason was an expert marksman. He could hit the bastard from hundreds of yards away. No, the maniac who'd done this had to be tried in a court of law and judged by his peers.

He agonized over what that would do to Jaclyn. If it ever came to pass, and Sheffield prayed it would, he'd have to find a way to distance her from any involvement. The investigation had to be about the murders in Phoenix, nothing else.

Instinctively, Sheffield knew a piece of the puzzle was missing. Too many times, he'd seen Jaclyn gazing at him, gnawing on her bottom lip, on the verge of telling him something. Whatever it was, she couldn't bring herself to do it. What could be more horrifying than what he already knew?

But, tonight everything had changed. They were man and wife. They had made love, passionate love. Maybe now Jaclyn could put her tragic past behind her. Could he? An unbridled fire raged within him.

At last, Sheffield fell into a troubled sleep, his mind still churning, drifting to another time, another place. He saw the razor wire fence, the gaunt faces with dead eyes, the emaciated bodies and shaved heads, the strutting, uniformed officers, with their polished boots and shiny brass buttons, their black-billed caps, with decorative gray braid, their weapons and dogs.

Then he saw Jaclyn, pressed against a wall in a filthy, dimly lit cell, dark, haunted eyes dwarfing her tiny face, staring at him wistfully. Suddenly, a fierce wind arose, and Sheffield felt himself flung into the air, held captive there by some otherworldly force. In the distance, Jaclyn floated toward him, writhing in agony, a soul in exquisite torment, features twisted grotesquely, her mouth frozen in a scream. Her anguish radiated in waves to him, striking him with such force he couldn't bear the pain. As Jaclyn's arms reached out and drew him to her, her screams dissolved into mournful, wailing cries.

Bolting upright, Sheffield grabbed his chest to still the pounding of his heart. The fire had gone out, the room was cold, yet he was drenched with sweat. Peaceful in sleep, Jaclyn nestled close to him. Sheffield touched his lips to her forehead, then he slid out of the bed, grabbed his pipe, tobacco pouch, and lighter from the nightstand. After fumbling around at the end of the bed, he slipped into his robe and slippers and tiptoed out of the room, soundlessly closing the door behind him. If only it was a coincidence. It couldn't be, of course. The design etched into Jaclyn's breasts exactly matched those on the murdered prostitutes. He'd studied the photographs again and again. So far, he hadn't been able to figure out what it meant, or perhaps what it stood for.

The Major had tortured, mutilated, and murdered all of his victims, except Jaclyn. He'd helped her escape. A final act of contrition? No, there was no vindication for what he'd done to her. Then it hit him. Could she have been the major's ticket to freedom? When they'd reached the allied forces, had she, out of fear, remained silent about the major's activities at the camp? He hoped that wasn't the case. At some point, it could become an issue. He might have to question her. He winced, recalling what she'd once said. "Alan Sheffield, ever the prosecutor."

Sheffield went through the sliding glass doors to the lanai, and stopped abruptly. A figure moved out of the shadows. "Who's there?"

"Carl Pettigrew, sir."

"Is everything all right?" Sheffield said.

"Yes, sir, except, with all this fog, I can't see beyond my nose."

"Eerie, isn't it? Not a bit like our desert."

"For sure," the bodyguard replied. "Sir, I'd better make one last round before Carey relieves me," he said, turning to leave.

"Wait, do you have the time?"

The agent pressed the stem of his watch. "Eleven minutes past four."

"Thanks." Sheffield sat down on a chaise lounge and leaned back. He filled his pipe and lighted it, aware that the ritual was more therapeutic than smoking it.

It was almost dawn, before exhaustion silenced Sheffield's mind. He was sleeping so soundly, he didn't hear the sliding glass door open.

Kneeling on the deck beside him, Jaclyn touched his face. She didn't want to wake him, but she desperately needed to make sure he was real.

Who am I? he'd asked. Not him—not him. She stifled a scream as the Major's image overwhelmed her. How she'd hated him, his hands, his body, what he'd done to her. At times she'd fainted, spinning down and down until the blessed blackness blotted out the agony. It was years before she realized that inflicting pain was the only way he could reach a climax. He'd light a cigarette, watching her face intently, waiting for terror to fill her eyes.

Covering her head with her arms, she whimpered, "No, no, no, no."

"Jaclyn!" Sheffield sat up and pulled her into his lap.

She buried her face against him. "When I woke up, you were gone."

"Sweetheart, did you think I'd vanished, never to return?" He kissed her, cuddled her close. "I was restless, and I didn't want to disturb you."

"I like the fog," Jaclyn said, glancing at the sky. "In the camp, if it was foggy, the Major's falcons couldn't find the doves."

"He was a falconer?"

"Yes. Poor wee birds, they were prisoners, too, destined to die."

Sheffield shot up, almost dumping Jaclyn onto the deck. She stared at him. "What is it?"

213

He shook his head as an elusive memory flickered and died in his mind.

"What is it?"

"I don't know."

"We never forget about the Major, do we?" Jaclyn said.

"Is he ever far from your mind?"

"I feel him. I think he knows where I am."

The fog was lifting. Jaclyn raised her head, catching fleeting glimpses of bright blue sky. "When he hunted, he'd make me watch. I'd say, fly faster, faster, hide quickly. It infuriated him, but I didn't care; living or dying had ceased to matter. It matters now. I want to grow old with you."

Sheffield hugged her to him. "Trust me, my beloved, he'll never hurt you again."

"Oh, there ye be," said a cheerful voice. "Merciful heavens, you must be froze solid. The door to your suite was open, so I took it upon myself to start a fire."

Sheffield glanced over his shoulder at the florid cheeked, jolly looking woman, short in stature, with an ample bosom, bright blue Irish eyes, and curly black hair, sprinkled with silver. "Thank you, Mrs. O'Reilly."

"Just call me Wendy. I'll take coffee up for you right away. Now get you out of this cold and into the house. And a good morning to the Missus." Frowning, she leaned down to peer at Jaclyn. "My stars, you've been crying then. A hearty breakfast will fix you up. A good hot meal cures just about everything."

Sheffield laughed. "Our emotions are running a little wild."

"Of course they are, newlyweds and all. Sooo, get along with you."

Rising, Sheffield winked at Jaclyn as he gave her a hands-up from the lounge.

Wendy scurried ahead of them. "A nice hot bath is what you need." With a lift of her eyebrows, she gazed sternly at Sheffield. "See that she gets it."

Stifling a smile, he said, "I certainly will."

"Thank you, Wendy," Jaclyn said, smiling at her. "Desert rats like us aren't used to this damp air."

"Of course you're not, and you're ever so welcome, darlin'."

As they climbed the stairs, Sheffield said, "For a second, I thought we'd brought Sejii with us."

# Chapter Forty-three

The office was on the lower floor of the split-level. Sheffield picked up the receiver, dialed the number, while keeping an eye on the stairway. He didn't want Jaclyn to hear his conversation with Sam.

"Good morning, the Attorney General's office," Shannon Pearce announced. "May I help you?"

"It's Sheffield. Is Sam in?"

"I think so, sir. Please hold."

Sam's greeting boomed across the miles. "Shef, how goes the honeymoon?"

"There's something I want you to check out with Jason."

"Sure, is there a problem?"

"Inadvertently, Jaclyn said the Major hunted with Falcons. Ask Jason if he knows any falconers. Either he can call me, or you can call me after you talk to him. It finally dawned on me that Tercel is the name for the male Peregrine Falcon."

"Okay, I'll give him a call."

"I should get back there, but I hate giving up this time with Jaclyn."

"Stay there, boss. I'll talk to Borseau about this Tercel business. Oh, I've been working with Moira to figure out what she'd passed on to her blackmailer. So far, it doesn't amount to much. If she's telling the truth, and I think she is, I'm surprised they let her get away with it."

"You have no idea how relieved I am to hear it. Let's plead her out, quietly Sam, community service, whatever it takes. I want her back in the office as soon as possible. I'm sure Max Payton is still sweating after my chat with him. Has the package arrived from him yet?"

"Yes, it's on your desk."

"Open it, Sam. If it's the album we talked about, and Alex's biography, take them to Moira. I don't think I told you that several years ago, the Senator asked me write a letter to Harvard, my Alma Mater, on his son's behalf. Before I agreed to do it, I had lunch with Max and young Alex. He seemed like a nice kid, an earnest student. Let's keep an eye on them, but with Price dead, Moira may be the only person in danger. We'll keep her covered, Sam."

"By the way, the safe at her house is crammed with tapes she considered too sensitive to turn over. One of them, dated several years ago, is a conversation between you and Kathryn Borseau. It seems she shot and killed a guy."

"Angelo Carlotti, a classic case of self-defense. However, with her celebrity, Jace was afraid the media would crucify her. I agreed with him, sooo I took the heat for Carlotti's demise. Ironically, as it turned out, that case probably got me elected to this office." Sheffield chuckled. "If so, I'm the Attorney General under false pretenses, and Kathryn should be sitting at my desk. Anyway, Sam, if you decide to take it higher, it's okay."

"Shef, you're the most honest person I know."

"Obviously not, and I don't want you to worry about me."

"I destroyed the tape."

"You didn't. Sam, the last thing I want is to compromise you."

"A large part of our job is protecting the innocent, isn't it? Kathryn Borseau among them?"

"We'll talk about it when I get back. But, hey, is it okay to tell another guy that you love him?"

"Same-same, big brother. Just don't start hugging me. You're a hugger, Shef," Sam said, laughing.

"Hold on, Mrs. Sheffield is coming down the stairs. I'm talking to a pal of yours, wanna say hi?" he called out to her.

"If it's Sam, I do," said Jaclyn, beaming.

"Call me later." Sheffield handed the receiver to her.

"Sam, you should see the ocean, the seals and whales . . ."

Sheffield left the office, and slowly climbed the stairs, wondering what he would've done if he'd been in Sam's position. At the time, it seemed like an innocent deception, if any deception could be considered innocent, or without consequences, serious or otherwise. Certainly, there had been no intent to circumvent the law. Alan Sheffield, who held himself up as a harbinger of justice. Now, if he went public with the truth about Angelo Carlotti's death, what might the fallout be? Oh, not for himself, but for Kathryn and Jason, their children. Even more unsettling, what about the actions he'd taken while in office, the legal liability the State might incur? Resigning was the only viable option he'd have.

# Chapter Forty-four

Jason and Kathryn stood on the lanai watching the newlyweds build a sandcastle on the beach below. Their laughter mingled with the sound of the surf and sailed on the breeze to the Borseaus.

Kathryn smiled.

"Shef," Jason called out.

Sheffield's head spun around as he searched for the face that went with the voice. Jaclyn waved enthusiastically when she spotted them.

"Jace! What are you doing here? Oh, oh, I meant to call you, Mom, honest," Sheffield shouted. Rising, he brushed the sand from his legs, and reached for Jaclyn.

"We need to talk, Shef," Jason yelled.

"Look how happy they are," Kathryn said. "Couldn't this have waited until they got back."

"No, it could not."

"Okay," Sheffield called back, his smile vanishing when he focused on Jason's grim face.

"And you won't tell me what this is about?" Kathryn said. "You must think I'm a mushroom."

"Kathryn, I will tell you, but not until I've talked to Shef. It may be a tempest in a teapot."

"It sounds very serious. I hope it isn't going to ruin their honeymoon." With a toss of her head, she walked to the bar on the lanai, and poured a glass of iced tea.

The newlyweds scrambled up the hillside. When they reached the lanai, Sheffield threw his arms around a beam and hung on. "Boy, oh, boy, do I ever need to get in shape. Kathryn, as much as you hate heights, I can't imagine how you get up and down this mountain."

Jaclyn threw her arms around Kathryn. "I'm so glad to see you."

"How happy you look." Kathryn whispered next to her friend's ear.

Jaclyn drew away and smiled. "We loved your present."

Laughing, Kathryn winked at Sheffield.

"What present?" Jason said. "Never mind, I'm sure Kathryn intruded herself into your private affairs. Shef, please, we really need to talk."

Sheffield lifted his pipe from the table. "Okay, just a second. Where did I put my tobacco?"

Jaclyn slipped her fingers into her husband's shirt pocket. "Here's your tobacco and your lighter."

Jason shook his head. "Forget the damned pipe."

"All right." Sheffield took Jason's arm. "How did you get here? Your plane is at the MacDuff's," he said, referring to the rancher in Monterey, who was Jason's navigator, during World War II.

"I chartered a plane. I've been thinking about buying a jet, but I'd have to keep it at Sky Harbor, to say nothing about learning to fly it. Shef, let's go down to the office." He strode across the living room and down the stairs. Sheffield barely made it through the door, before Jason closed it.

"Christ, Shef."

"What?"

"Why do you want to know about falconers?"

Sheffield searched Jason's face. "The Major hunted with falcons."

"Well, here's your answer. A few weeks ago, when I was at Damien Santayana's ranch, he was hunting with a Peregrine Falcon. If you can call launching a dove and unleashing a falcon *hunting*."

Sheffield paced around the office. "I need to tell you about Moira."

"Your secretary?"

Sheffield nodded. "You were at the press conference. Remember how she bolted from the room?"

"Yes. I thought she was ill."

"Sick at heart would be more like it. Later, when Sam and I questioned her, she admitted that Mitchell Price, the hit man who died at St. Vincent's, had been blackmailing her for years."

"Why would anyone blackmail Moira?"

"Years ago, she had an affair with now US Senator, Max Payton. Subsequently, Moira had his child, and Max and his wife adopted the boy. She, his wife, doesn't know Alex is Max's son. Mitchell Price told Moira that if she didn't provide information about the Attorney Generals' investigations, an accident would be arranged for her son and his father. Since Alex's birth, Max has refused to allow Moira to see her son, or to know anything about his life. I recently met with Max and laid down the law. He's going to send copies of all the photos there are of Alex. Also, a biography about him, and he'll continue to do so, ad infinitum. The first installment arrived at my office yesterday. Sam took it to Moira."

"Shef, I supported that s.o.b during his last campaign," Jason said.

"I did, too. So, for the past ten years, Moira has been providing Price's boss with mostly unimportant information from the Attorney Generals' offices. At some point, Price told Moira he worked for someone he referred to as *Tercel*. It's another name for the male Peregrine Falcon."

"What are you? The Encyclopedia Britannica?"

221

"Hardly, I took a course in Ornithology. Until now, it was a complete waste of time. I couldn't find Tercel in the phone book. Finally, it dawned on me, although I admit it took me a while to connect the dots."

"Well, I'm dumbstruck." Jason grasped Sheffield's shoulders. "What you're inferring is that Santayana could be behind the bombing at City Hall, the attacks on Christian, and other atrocities."

"It may be a coincidence. However, Santayana hunts with a falcon, and Mitchell Price worked for someone he called Tercel. It may be improbable, but we should look at it.

"The other thing is: when Jaclyn saw the photos of the first victim in the Ladies of the Night murders, she immediately thought the Major had tortured and murdered that girl. The cigarette burns on her breasts, the other victims as well, exactly match the scars on Jaclyn's breasts, a pattern I have yet to figure out. I'm going to need your exquisite brain to help me with that."

"Shef, you're describing a monster, a psychopath, a serial killer. Damien Santayana is a wealthy, world-class do-gooder. Why would he do this?"

"Since when does a psychopathic serial killer have a logical reason to kill?" Sheffield's fingers raked through his hair.

Jason blew out a breath. "Does Jaclyn know?"

"Only that Moira was being blackmailed. She bowed out of the interrogation, and I didn't go into detail about Mitchell Price's boss. I didn't intentionally leave anything out, but we were all beat. It had been a long, terrible day. If it turns out that Damien Santayana is the Major, I swear I'm going to shoot the bastard."

"What happened to, 'Let the law take care of it'?"

"I am the law!"

"Like hell. Don't play that card with me. Besides, if you want him dead, I'm the one who'd have to shoot him."

A sardonic smile lifted the corners of Sheffield's mouth. "Ain't it the truth?"

Jason went behind the bar, whipped two glasses from the shelf, poured scotch into one, brandy in the other, and dropped an ice cube in each. Handing the scotch to his friend, he said, "When all else fails."

"Thanks," Sheffield murmured. "Jace, I never dreamed I could love anyone as much as I love Jaclyn. No wonder Gina left me. She knew what I didn't. Our relationship was little more than habit, childhood sweethearts and friends, never really lovers. Michael was the glue that held us together. When he died, our marriage disintegrated. As much as I hate myself for it, Sandra was someone who looked good that I could squire around, and occasionally take to bed. And you have no idea how much Kathryn has helped Jaclyn, so stop telling her that she's interfering."

Jason threw back his head and laughed. "'Got a little gravel for your duck, eh?"

Sheffield rolled his eyes. "You're an ass."

"Yeah, yeah." Jason laughed, then sobered instantly, "Shef, you have to tell Jaclyn about this."

Sheffield rubbed his forehead. "I'm afraid it might devastate her to find out that Christian may be one of the Major's victims. She'll feel responsible. After the allies picked them up, she could have, and should have, turned him in. I have a hunch she just wanted to get away from him, sans any red tape."

"Shef, do you want Kathryn and me to stay?"

"Yes, I assume Kathryn knows what's going on."

"No, I didn't want to tell her anything, until after I'd talked to you. If you keep this from Jaclyn, one way or another, she'll find out. Trust me, I learned that lesson the hard way."

"Let me think about it."

Jason grasped Sheffield's arm as they walked up the stairs. "Okay, take a deep breath and put a smile on your face."

When they walked into the living room, Wendy said, "Mr. Borseau! I didn't know you were to be here." Carrying an armful of folded towels, she stopped mid-way up the stairs. "Where's me darlin' girl." She glanced around. "Where's Kathryn?"

"That darling girl is out on the lanai with Mrs. Sheffield."

"Oh, I can't wait to see her." Wendy set the towels on the landing and hurried down the steps.

Jason and Sheffield stepped aside as she swept past them. "My wife is everybody's darling. I used to be popular," Jason said, "especially with women."

"Yeah, every woman who laid eyes on you was ready to hop into your bed and a good many of them did." Sheffield grinned at Jason. "Kathryn sure clipped your wings, Colonel Borseau. By the way, when Kathryn was shot, you said if anyone harmed another hair on her head, you'd strangle them with your bare hands. Remember that?"

Jason gazed poignantly into Sheffield's eyes. "Of course I do. Shef, have I ever let you down?" He grinned. "You want Santayana wiped out, and I'd like to get him for the way he leers at Kathryn."

"As much as I hate it, I know you're right, I have to tell Jaclyn what we suspect. We were planning to have dinner in Monterey. Let's do that. We can have a few drinks to take the edge off, and we'll talk to Jaclyn when we get back."

"Merciful heavens, you've got me darlin' girl with child again." Wendy glared at Jason as she hurried into the living room from the lanai. "Three babies in five years," she said, shaking her head.

"Six years," Jason said as he sat down on the sofa.

"Five, six, it's too many babies," Wendy scoffed. "Old before her time, she'll be. Men can't keep their hands to themselves or their zippers up." She stormed past them toward the gathering room.

Jason's eyes swung to Kathryn. "Now isn't that just dandy? Did you tell Wendy that it's you who insist upon playing—"

"Vatican Roulette." With an impish grin, Kathryn plunked down on an easy chair opposite him. "Of course not."

Sheffield winked at Jaclyn.

Jason frowned as he glanced from one of them to the other. "Oh, sure, you think this is funny, but I'm the one who'll get the cold coffee and burned eggs, not you."

"**H**ow can it be after midnight?" Kathryn said, glancing at the grandfather clock in the entryway.

"Well, who wanted to browse through every shop along the pier?" Jason said.

Jaclyn grinned. "It was wonderful."

Sheffield lifted her chin and gazed into her eyes. "It's late, I know, but there is something Jace and I need to talk to you about."

"What is it?"

"It's about the Major. We may know who he is. The emphasis is on the words *may know*," Sheffield added.

Jaclyn's eyes few open. "Who do you think he is and where is he? Surely you know it won't surprise me if he lives right here in Phoenix."

"His name is Damien Santayana. I don't know him, but Jason does. He's a wealthy rancher who owns thousands of acres of property, South of Tucson."

"Is it just a coincidence that his initials are DS? Do you remember my telling you that the Major said his name was David Santiago, DS. Why do you suspect him?"

"Damien Santayana hunts with a Peregrine Falcon. In a conversation with Moira, Mitchell Price called his boss

"Tercel." That's techno-speak for a male falcon. It may be a coincidence, but it may not."

Jaclyn's eyes glittered. "Do you have any other evidence? I mean, how do we proceed?"

"Very carefully," Sheffield said. "As Jason told me this morning, Santayana is a world-class do-gooder."

"Jason," Kathryn moaned, "We invited him to the wedding."

"I've been beating myself up about that, but we had no reason to believe that Damien wasn't what he appeared to be."

"Amazing," Jaclyn said. "I thought I saw the Major mingling with our guests, but when I looked again, he wasn't there." Jaclyn paused, frowning. "I often think I see him, but I always chalk it up to paranoia."

"I chatted with him before the ceremony," Jason said. "Someone had told me that he'd been in the Air Force. Having been in the Air Force myself, I asked him about it. He said I had him mixed up with his twin brother, Déon, still listed as missing in action."

"He has a twin?" Jaclyn said. "You mean there are two of them. Are we sure his brother is really missing in action? Dear god, is it possible they're working together? We know that one person, by himself, could not have taken those girls into the desert. We figured the killer had to have help."

"That's something we can and should look into," Jason said. "Shef, in your capacity as the Attorney General, you could call the Pentagon, and check to see if Damien's brother is, indeed, missing in action."

"Sheffield pulled Jaclyn close. "I'll do that as soon as we get back to Phoenix. For now, I'm ready to call it a night."

"I wholeheartedly agree, so we'll see you in the morning." Taking Kathryn's arm, Jason propelled her through the door and along the hallway to the guest bedroom.

"**W**e're going home tomorrow, Kathryn," he said, as he turned down the spread. "This intrigue is not good for you."

Shrugging out of her chenille robe, Kathryn climbed into bed. "I'm not leaving her."

"Do I have to remind you that you've gone into premature labor with all three pregnancies?"

"That's a low blow. You know I can't bear the thought of losing another baby."

"It's settled then. Jaclyn has Shef, they're husband and wife."

"Hold me, Jason." He drew her close. "After all the horror that Jaclyn has gone through, what has kept her from going mad?"

"She's strong, a survivor, and I believe she's well on her way to a complete recovery."


"**A**t the moment, Damien Santayana is nothing more than a person of interest," Sheffield said. "This is the United States of America. A person is innocent, unless a jury of his peers tries him, and returns a verdict of guilty."

The muscles in Sheffield's jaws worked. "The crimes the Major committed during the war have no bearing on the crimes we're investigating. I know it would be very difficult, maybe traumatic, but I wish you'd tell me how you escaped from Trepskýa."

She closed her eyes a moment and took a deep, cleansing breath before she began: "It was the middle of the night. The Major was on the cot next to mine. I could hear his breath shudder in and out. It surprised me to realize that he was afraid.

"The other prisoners huddled together as far away from us as they could get. We all knew the end was near—salvation or damnation. It had ceased to matter a long time ago. Uppermost in our minds was that, one way or another, the torture would stop.

"For days, we'd scanned the western sky, tuned in to the sound of tanks and guns coming ever closer, at last only a short distance away. The earth trembled beneath them.

"For weeks our captors hadn't strutted as arrogantly as they had before, they whispered furtively among themselves, their faces grim as they burned documents, poured gasoline on the bodies in the pits, torched them, then covered the bone fragments and ashes with dirt. The whine of giant earthmovers lamented round the clock. The naked souls destined for the showers shambled along, silently, hopelessly.

"The Major waited until the noise and chaos rose to a crescendo before he sneaked us out of the camp. He'd been planning the escape for a long time, and he pulled it off without a hitch. I begged him to help the others, but he put his gun to my head and literally dragged me out of the camp.

"We walked for four days and nights, the Major used his compass to keep us on track." Her hands fell to her sides. "When the British soldiers picked us up in Holland, he told them he was my cousin, and I didn't dispute it. There were so many people desperately needing medical attention, food and clothing, shelter. They took those of us who were ambulatory to a relocation center in England."

By virtue of her inability to look at him, Sheffield said, "Why didn't you tell the authorities who and what he was?"

"I was afraid, I just wanted to get away from him."

"Oh, Jaclyn." Sheffield enclosed her in his arms.

"Before we left the camp, he shaved his head, put on the filthy, ragged clothes like the rest of us wore. He wasn't the only one, there were other officers that escaped."

"Where was he when you last saw him?"

Jaclyn sat up and frowned. "Standing in a line with the other men, waiting to be processed. They'd segregated us— women in one area, men in another, children in another. A few little ones still had mothers, and they kept them together.

Before I went through the door into another room, I glanced at him. He was staring at me, warning me with his eyes. I was afraid they might bring us together again."

"And you never saw him again?" She shook her head. "What else? I know this is painful, but you need to tell me everything," Sheffield said. "Jaclyn, look at me."

"I can't—won't—tell you about some of the horrific things that were done to me."

"Because you can't bear to talk about them or because you're afraid I might feel differently about you?"

"They were vile—depraved. I don't want you to think of me that way."

"Come here," Sheffield said. She snuggled against him. "Nothing will ever change the way I feel about you."

"I truly believe that, but it's so painful for me to relive that period of my life."

"I understand, but one day, I hope you'll trust me enough to tell me everything. I get the feeling that something so traumatic happened to you that you can't bear to put it into words."

"It isn't about trust. I trust you implicitly. If and when I'm able to tell anyone, it will be you."

"Right now, we need to get some sleep. I love you, Jaclyn."

"I love you, too, more than you can possibly know."

# Chapter Forty-five

The four of them sat on the lanai, staring at the sea. Wendy set the silver coffee service on the table, put her hands on her hips, and glanced from one to the other. "Well, if you're not the sorriest looking bunch I've ever laid me eyes on."

"Chalk it up to a late night in Monterey," Jason said.

"Well, you should've known better, Mr. Borseau. Kathryn needs her rest."

Jason sent a warning glance Kathryn's way.

"Don't worry about me, Wendy, I'm fine. In fact, I'd like to climb down that old cliff and dabble my toes in the ocean for a while."

"We'll be starting back to Phoenix soon," Jason said.

"Today?" Jaclyn reached out to Kathryn. "I thought we were flying back together."

Taking Jaclyn's hand in hers, Kathryn said, "If I promise to stay calm, cool, and collected, surely one day more won't matter."

Jason studied her face. "You know what I'm worried about, don't you, Shef?"

"Yes, Kathryn has a tough time carrying her babies to term."

With a toss of her head, Kathryn said, "Why are you talking about me as if I weren't here? Let's have one last pleasant day together. Oh, I know!"

Jason gazed at her. With long, thick braids, no makeup, and her awesome gray eyes, she looked just as she had the first time he'd seen her. "Here it comes, my wife has an agenda."

Kathryn's hands flew to her cheeks. "Let's build a sandcastle. It looked like so much fun."

Jason stood and pulled her to her feet. "If Shef and Jaclyn are game, I am, Mrs. Exuberance of 1962."

Sheffield smiled at Jaclyn. "How a bout it, Mrs. Sheffield?"

A tiny pucker appeared between her brows. "This time, we'll build the castle farther from the sea, so the tide won't take it away so quickly."

"Okay, I'll be the architect," Jason said, throwing himself in the spirit of the thing.

Sheffield's eyes rolled to him. "Why do you always get to decide who does what?"

"All right, cry baby, you can design the cannons and decide where they should go." Jason laughed. "Hey, Shef, maybe you could hit something with a cannon."

"Ha, ha. Very funny," Sheffield said.

"From this distance, they look like children," Kathryn mused as she and Jaclyn sat on the beach at the edge of the sea. It was a warm day, the languid surf crested and fell, lapping lazily around their feet and legs. Jason and Sheffield had immersed themselves in building the sandcastle.

Jaclyn's laughter bubbled up. "They're so funny together."

"They love one another, as close as brothers." Kathryn gazed at her friend. "Jaclyn, I know how difficult this revelation about Damien Santayana is for you. Do you want to talk about it?"

"Alan made me promise not to do or say anything that might upset you. Of course, he didn't have to remind me. If anything happened to you or your baby—"

"Then, may I share something with *you*?"

"Of course."

"Three years ago, during the opening number at the music competition, I went into labor with Lauren. I used to get so uptight about playing, now I don't. She was due in a few weeks, so I don't consider that abnormal. The night Jason's son, Anthony, was kidnapped, our first baby was born too prematurely to survive. Jason didn't know I was pregnant. Legally, he was still married to Ellen. And, Josh was born at my lodge in Idaho the night—"

"You shot Angelo Carlotti."

"How did you know it was I who—?"

"Alan told me. Do you recall discussing it with him in his office quite some time ago? Because of another matter, Sam listened to the tapes. All of the conversations in the Attorney General's office are recorded. Usually, it's Alan who screens them."

Kathryn grabbed Jaclyn's arm. "Oh, no, what will Sam do? Alan was protecting me."

"And Sam knew that, so he destroyed the tape. It doesn't affect the job Alan does as the Attorney General. He doesn't puff himself up, but he's amazing—analytical, intuitive, honest. He's a stickler for the law, knows it backwards and forwards. And you know what a wonderful, caring person he is."

"It sounds like you sort of like the guy." Kathryn smiled at Jaclyn. "I was right, wasn't I? I knew it the moment I saw you on the beach."

"I've never felt so loved or so safe."

Kathryn squeezed Jaclyn's hand.

"And, I don't want to let him down."

"What could you possibly do that would let him down?" Kathryn said.

"When I saw the forensic photo of one of the victims, I knew the Major was kidnapping and killing those girls. The wounds on her breasts were identical to the scars on mine. They were from the cigarette burns I received in the camp."

"My god, I didn't know. I'm so sorry."

"Oh, Kathryn, I'm not telling you this to upset you. The thing is, when we talk about evidence, my breasts are living proof that the Major did the dirty deeds. I don't know if it has occurred to Alan that I may have to testify. Maybe I'll need to be the *coup d'état*"

"Of course, it isn't about what Alan perceives. It's about you," Kathryn said. "Faced with the choice, you'll do whatever it takes to bring the killer to justice. I know."

"That was the choice you had to make."

"Yes, but I meted out what we hill billys call, mountain justice. To make sure that Angelo Carlotti could never hurt anyone again, I killed him twice."

Letting a handful of sand sift through her fingers, Jaclyn frowned as she studied Kathryn's face.

"Alan knows. I knew the first shot mortally wounded Angelo, but I fired again. If he hadn't fallen down the flue, I probably would have driven a stake through his heart, just to make sure he was dead."

"But, Kathryn, unless you're an expert marksman—"

"Well, as my granddad used to say, I'm a dead-on shot. Maybe Jason doesn't understand that," Kathryn said, shrugging her shoulders. "I told him I could shoot, but maybe he thought I knew which end of the gun to point, and how to pull the trigger. The truth is: I knew exactly what I was doing. I wanted Angelo to feel the first shot. At the time, I thought he had murdered Jason's son, and I wanted him to know how Anthony must've felt. The second bullet took him under the chin, exactly where I intended it to go."

Closing her eyes, Kathryn lifted her face to the breeze wafting ashore from the sea. "It's interesting. Jason thinks if we don't talk about something it'll go away." She laughed. "I guess I'm a little like that myself."

"I'm not as brave as you are," Jaclyn said, brushing the sand from her feet and legs.

"Not brave? Jaclyn, I'm even too chicken to get a tattoo like the one you have on your ankle."

"Oh, you mean my butterfly?" She smiled and ran her fingers across the image. "It isn't a tattoo, it's a birthmark. My mother had one just like it."

"It's beautiful, amazing. The aqua blue and soft burgundy shades make it look like an oil painting."

"Whenever I look at it, I feel closer to my mother."

"I'm sure you think about your parents often."

"Yes, I do."

"Right now, my stomach thinks it's time for lunch. Let's go see how the Hardy boys are doing."

"The Hardy Boys?"

"A pair of fictional teenage sleuths."

They looked at one another and giggled.


Sheffield sat back on his haunches and shaded his eyes with one hand. "Look at them, Jace, like a couple of teenagers when they get together."

"So I've noticed. It's a good thing they have us." Turning his attention back to the sandcastle, Jason said, "Shef, how do you think four measly cannons are going to protect my castle?"

"Where do you get off with this, *my castle* crap?"

"Look at the draw bridge, you haven't protected it."

"You're supposed to be the architect, not me."

"You're the law man, and you should know how to cover your flanks."

Sheffield stared at his friend's face, then doubled over laughing.

Jason frowned and lifted his brows. "What's so funny?"

"Oh, I was just thinking how great it is that Jaclyn and Kathryn have a couple of grown-ups like us," he said, falling over backwards on the sand.

Jason looked down the beach. "Are they laughing at us?"

"Oh, yeah, absolutely."

# Chapter Forty-six

"Shef, if you're wrong, Santayana will sue the State for millions," Governor George Pearson said. "Drug smuggling? Let the Feds handle it and cooperate with them. Jesus, Damien Santayana contributed to my last campaign—heavily, I might add. How do you think it's going to look if it turns out he's everything you think he is—a drug lord, a mass murderer, a war criminal?" The governor focused frustrated eyes on Sheffield. "Did I miss anything?"

"The Feds *are* working with us, George. Listen, we could go to court right now and convict him for drug smuggling. The contraband is coming across the Mexican border to the Santayana ranch, but they're clever. They water the cattle in the Santa Cruz and cross it to retrieve the strays. That's where the exchange takes place, and the Feds have it on videotape. Then they drive the cattle deep into the mountains and hide the drugs in one of the abandoned mines. One man stays with the herd, but there's no activity as far as the stash is concerned until Santayana's cowhands round up a herd to ship them to market. Though we're sure the drugs are leaving the ranch in the cattle trucks, the Feds haven't witnessed the transfer. They don't want to arrest Santayana until they're certain how the drugs are leaving the ranch and where they're going. It's possible he's moving all the narcotics across state lines, in which case he's violating FIC laws." Sheffield reached into his jacket pocket and retrieved his Meerschaum. "Do you mind?" he said, tipping the bowl in the Governor's direction.

"Not at all, it's your signature." A grudging smile nudged the Governor's lips. "If I looked as professorial as you do, I'd take up the habit myself."

Sheffield laughed as he triggered his lighter, and drew on the pipe. "George, let's put this into perspective: if we go after Santayana and get him, you'll be a hero. I'm not asking you to authorize anything. If things go wrong, you can deny any knowledge of the Attorney General's activities and hang me out to dry. Surely you know I wouldn't take you down with me."

Pearson studied Sheffield's face. "Yes, I know that." Hesitating again, he said, "Still, I can't help wondering what makes you tick? Do you think of yourself as the last honest man? Is it possible that you *are* the last honest man?"

"Come on, you know I don't see myself that way. It's just that I don't want to be the Attorney General enough to compromise my integrity. Sure, I could sit back and tackle the easy ones, but I'd have a hard time living with myself."

A small smile flirted with Pearson's generous mouth. "And, you think, I want to be the Governor so badly, I'd be willing to compromise my integrity."

"Don't put words in my mouth." Sheffield hunched forward and caressed his pipe. "Being misquoted and second-guessed really pisses me off."

Pearson got up from his desk, walked to the windows, took a wide stance, and clasped his hands behind him. The Governor lifted a hand to his bald head, then patted the fringe of iron-gray hair encircling his collar. In his fifties, Pearson was six-feet-tall and slightly rotund. His face was full, but not fleshy. He fit the mold, Sheffield mused, always impeccably dressed, as neatly put together at five in the afternoon, as he was now, at eleven o'clock in the morning.

Sheffield liked him, though the governor typified the astute politician that mostly said the right things to the right people at the right time in the right places.

The Governor turned to face Sheffield. "All right, Shef, do what you feel you have to do, but this had better be about crimes against the State and not about what Santayana may have done to your wife. Jesus, if he's a war criminal and behind the bombing of City Hall, what kind of a monster is he?"

Sheffield's eyes, as hard as the emeralds they personified, narrowed. "How many types of monsters are there? Regardless of what he did to Jaclyn or to those young girls that nobody gives a damn about, what do you think dealing drugs is about? Let me assure you, where Santayana is concerned, it's not about money. It's about power, one man's insatiable obsession for absolute power. His father left him millions. He's made millions more in the cattle business. And, George, if I told you everything we know about him, it would make you physically ill."

Pressing his hands toward Sheffield, the Governor said, "Spare me the gory details. Just promise me you'll personally oversee every operation that has anything to do with Santayana." Pearson scrutinized the Attorney General's face. "I don't want to hear you tell the media that you didn't tie the noose tight enough. If you go after him, you'd better get him, or I'll distance myself so far from you, you'll think we occupy separate planets on opposite sides of the solar system. Is that clear?"

Sheffield pushed his long, lean frame up from the chair. Meeting Pearson's eyes, he chuckled and said, "Well, I'd say that's as clear as it gets."

The Governor looked at his watch. "How about joining me for lunch?"

Sheffield tapped the meerschaum against the ashtray and returned the pipe to his pocket. "Maybe you should start distancing yourself from me now."

"Shef, no matter what happens," Pearson said, "I have the utmost respect for you, and that will never change. Who knows? One day, you may be the governor."

Sheffield could see how uncomfortable Pearson was with that idea. "I don't want your job. I'm not sure why I agreed to take the job I have."

"Shall I tell you what I think?"

Sheffield shrugged. "Shoot."

"You're a Boy Scout, Shef. You've always been a Boy Scout, and you'll always be a Boy Scout."

# Chapter Forty-seven

Agent Robert "Rip" Vashay lowered the starlight scope, then raised his arm. With a forward motion of his hand, the SWAT leader signaled his team to advance. In turn, the frontrunners passed the signal along to those in the rear. They began the maneuver through sagebrush, blackthorn, and chemise toward the Santayana hacienda. When Vashay deemed it was prudent, he raised a fisted hand, signaling his team to take cover behind the forest of thick, gnarled trees along the steep ravine.

Vashay's war, which he took very personally, was the Korean Conflict, where, as a Lt. Colonel, he'd earned a chest full of medals, including two purple hearts, and two distinguished service crosses, for exceptional courage under fire. Only to himself did he speculate that his bravery might have been more external than internal, wondering if fear had numbed his good sense.

The desert had surrounded him his entire life. The freezing winters in Korea had been one of the forces that kept him attacking, even when faced with insurmountable odds. As he slogged through hip-deep snow in minus zero temperatures, the idea of spending another winter in Asia was unthinkable. Rip knew the surest way to get out of there was to win. He *led* his men. Colonel Vashay was appalled by the officers that stayed in the rear, and sent their troops ahead to die, or to suffer an even worse fate, to be captured.

"If you want to rip the enemy's ass, send Vashay," was so often repeated, the nickname—Rip—stuck.

On this day, in addition to the team commander, there were four other agents, part of Sam's Special Weapons Attack Team. In all, the force was comprised of thirteen men, although no one seemed superstitious about that unlucky number. Like Vashay, they were all veterans of one war or another and highly trained in the art of guerrilla warfare. Three of the agents were electronic wizards, specializing in the installation of surveillance equipment. Vashay and Jim Ryan, the other team member would back them up. For proprietary reasons, there were two Federal agents on site, but they wouldn't be involved, unless something went awry.

The electronic gurus would have to breach the security system, install the transmitters, tap the phones, and get out in five minutes or less.

Glued to their scopes, Sheffield and Sam watched from an adjacent slope east of the estate. The team was approaching from the south.

Sam lowered his glasses, adjusted his earpiece, and triggered the transceiver. "All clear on this side."

Checking his watch, he added, "twelve minutes, twenty seconds to first light."

"Ten-four," Agent Vashay responded. "Move out, men."

For several weeks, they had observed the activity at the ranch before deciding how to infiltrate the Santayana ranch without being detected. There was little latitude. Lights flashed on and off at irregular intervals during the night. The only consistent exception was the last half-hour before daylight. Sheffield had been nervous about cutting it so close, but the team had taken it in stride.

An icy trickle of sweat coursed down Sheffield's back. His chest tightened. He glanced at his watch, raised the scope and sighted it in again.

241

"They're inside," Sam whispered.

Get in, get out, no more than five minutes, Sheffield had impressed upon the agents. Bug the phones first and any room that looks like an office or den. If there's anything in the office that looks suspicious—files, papers, pictures—photograph them, but only if there's time.

"Two minutes to go," Sam said.

Sheffield grabbed Sam's arm and pointed to a light in the bunkhouse near the stables.

Peering through his glasses, Sam triggered the transceiver, "Heads up, get out now." Muscles tensing beneath his boss's grip, he swore under his breath as a ranch hand closed the door and sauntered toward the house. "The stable's alive, heading your way."

"How much time do they have?"

"Less than a minute; with a little luck, they may have finished what they came to do," Sam said.

Sheffield focused on the back window they'd used to gain access. "Where are they?"

"There's one, two. I see three. They're scaling the wall. Where are the other two? I told Vashay not to pick any *hot dogs*. He'd better not have, or I'll have his badge," Sam said fiercely, relinquishing his normally steady nerves to the stress of the moment.

"There they are, but Santayana's man is going through the gate. Do they see him?"

"They do now," Sam said. The two agents had glued themselves to the ground behind the massive trunk of a Mediterranean Palm. "Damn, someone's coming out of the house."

"It's someone all right. It's Santayana. He's about twenty feet away from them. Can you tell who they are?"

"Yeah, it's Jim Ryan and the team commander, Rip Vashay. Something must've held them up."

"We have to divert Santayana's attention," Sheffield said.

"A rock slide would do it, if we can get this boulder moving, but he may spot us."

"It's a chance we have to take."

"Let's go," Sam said, scooting away from the edge of the bluff.

"Remind me to get in shape," Sheffield muttered, retreating belly and elbows over the rough terrain.

"Grab that limb, and when I give you the signal, slip it under," Sam whispered, taking a stance with his broad hands pressed up against the rock. "On three," he grunted as his arms and legs constricted against the three-foot mass. "Did you get it?"

"Take a look."

Nodding, Sam cocked his head. "Push or pry?"

Sheffield hesitated, considering the alternatives. "I'll push."

"Let's do it then." Sam squatted and knit his fingers under the limb. "On three," Sam said, counting. "Push."

The boulder teetered on the edge of the bluff, then gathered momentum, shattering the silence as it careened through a grove of trees.

"Get down," Sam said, flattening himself to the ground.

Santayana whipped around, but at that moment, dawn spilled across the Patagonias. Shying away from the light, he turned away.

Agents Vashay and Ryan scaled the wall and were within a few feet of the underbrush on the south side of the hacienda.

# Chapter Forty-eight

**W**hile Sheffield dialed the Governor's private number, Sam dropped into a chair in front of his boss's desk, and took a battered pack of cigarettes and the lighter from his jacket pocket.

"I'm almost too tired to smoke," he said.

"Tell me about it. Every muscle in my body is screaming Uncle, and we're planning to attend the annual music competition tonight."

"Katie and I are going, too. We keep our seats from year to year. Once you give 'em up, you never get 'em back."

"That's true, and I feel guilty, because Jason invited us to sit with him and his parents, in which case, I should've given our tickets away. Do you know anyone who'd like to have them?"

"You bet. Katie's sister, Lisa Ann, and her husband."

"Okay, I'll contact the ticket office and arrange for you to pick them up." Sheffield replaced the receiver. "The Governor doesn't answer. He's probably where we should be—getting dolled up for an evening at the concert hall."

Sam blew out a breath and wiped his eyes. "I'll pick up the photos from the lab in the morning, and come by your place. I'll call first. Oh, I didn't have time to talk at length with Rip, but apparently there was a file about you. He saw it as he was leaving Santayana's office. I jerked his and Ryan's strings for jeopardizing the operation, but Vashay said either they had to photograph it, or steal it."

With a look of amazement, Sheffield studied Sam's face. "Where do we find these men who're willing to risk their lives for us?"

Sam took a long drag on his cigarette and stubbed it out in the ashtray. "Part of it is that we all know you're there for us, not just in spirit as was the previous Attorney General. You put yourself on the line." His cheeks flushed beneath his tanned skin, his eyes straying from Sheffield's face. "I want you to know how much we all respect and appreciate that."

Deeply touched, Sheffield grinned. "You're not going to hug me, are you?"

Sam threw back his head and laughed.

Punching the air with his fist, Sheffield shouted, "Gotcha."


Sheffield unlocked the front door. If they were going to make it to the concert on time, he'd barely have time to shower and jump into his tux.

Sejii was waiting for him in the entryway. "Boss," he whispered, beckoning Sheffield to follow him.

"What's wrong?" Frowning, Sheffield glanced up the stairwell and back at Sejii. "Where's Jaclyn."

"Misses sick. She not want Sejii to tell you," he said wagging his head. "Sejii very upset."

With another glance at the stairs, Sheffield patted Sejii's shoulder. "All right, my friend, I'll see to her, and thank you." He raced across the entryway and bolted up the stairs.

"Jaclyn," Sheffield shouted as he reached the landing. "Jaclyn," he shouted again as he hurried along the hall to their bedroom and burst through the door.

"What is it? What's wrong?"

245

"Jesus," he said, grabbing his chest and slumping on the edge of the bed. "Sejii said you were ill, and it scared me."

Jaclyn sat at her dressing table, watching him in the mirror. She put down the hairbrush, and stood. "You're as white as a ghost. You know how Sejii fusses over me." Jaclyn sat on her husband's lap and slipped her arms around his neck. "You're the one we need to worry about. Look at you—your jacket is torn, your clothes are covered with stickers and dirt." She touched his face. "Alan, you look exhausted. Where have you been? And why wasn't I with you. I'm sure Sam was there. You're cutting me out, and I want you to stop it."

He hugged her to him. "Jaclyn, let's talk about you. If there's the slightest chance that you're not well, we're not going tonight. And that reminds me, I want you to have a thorough physical exam. I've been thinking about it for some time."

Jaclyn put her lips to his and whispered, "I'm not made of glass, my love. Besides, I don't need a doctor, I just need you."

Sheffield smiled. "Let's skip the competition."

"No, I want to hear Kathryn play, and we have to hurry."

"You're so beautiful," Sheffield said quietly, thinking how the low cut, teal gown was a perfect compliment to her dark beauty. Taking her in his arms, Sheffield nuzzled her neck. "Ummm, you smell good." He grinned. "What's a haggard old man like me doing with a young, gorgeous chick like you?"

"Making all my dreams come true," Jaclyn said softly.

"I can't believe how much I love you, or how much I want you."

Her eyes flew open. "Alan Sheffield, you have to shower and get dressed."

"Married six weeks, and the honeymoon is over."

Laughing, Jaclyn pointed to the dressing room. "Go!"

246

**W**hen they arrived at the concert hall, Sheffield's limousine drew alongside the curb. An attendant opened the door nearest him. He got out and reached back for Jaclyn. Cheeks flushed, dark eyes sparkling, she smiled at the crowd that pressed against the barricades on either side of the red-carpeted entrance.

A female reporter thrust a microphone in Sheffield's face. "Attorney General Alan Sheffield and his beautiful wife have arrived. "Looking forward to the evening, sir?"

He wondered how she'd react if he said, *No?*

"Yes, absolutely." He smiled at the new recruit from Jason's station. Waving to the crowd, Sheffield propelled Jaclyn through the double doors into the Hall and merged with the crowd as it drifted toward the aisles that spun off in several directions.

Holding court on either side of the hall, busts of famous composers sat on antique gold stands, while paintings, by recognized masters, ensconced in heavy gold frames, hung between the statuary. The Oriental carpeting, in rich shades of burgundy and blue, cushioned their steps.

"Hello, Shef."

Sheffield turned in response to the all-too familiar voice. "Hello, Sandra, nice to see you. It's been awhile." She ignored his greeting. Her attention was fixated on Jaclyn. Sheffield winced at the hate smoldering in her eyes.

It was one surprise after another, he thought as Damien Santayana joined them and handed a flute of champagne to Sandra, then shook Sheffield's hand.

"It's Alan Sheffield, isn't it?"

"Yes, we meet at last, Mr. Santayana. Damien, right?"

"How kind of you to remember."

"I had looked forward to meeting you at our wedding, but Jason said you left before the ceremony began. I hope you weren't ill."

For a moment, the champagne danced in Santayana's glass. He stared at Sheffield, but quickly recovered. "Oh, yes, there was a matter I'd forgotten to take care at the ranch. Once I remembered it, I—"

"No matter." A wry smile nudged the corners of Sheffield's mouth. His emerald green eyes glittered.

"And, this must be Mrs. Sheffield," Santayana said.

Jaclyn's eyes rose slowly to meet his. "Yes, I'm Jaclyn."

"Is that short for Jacqueline?"

"No, it isn't," she responded.

"How does one spell it?"

As if you don't know, she thought, as she recoiled in abject terror at the sound of the Major's voice. It was he. God in heaven, the maniac who had tortured her for three years was standing less than a foot away from her. He'd changed very little. Of course, his black SS uniform had been replaced by a black tuxedo.

It was hard for her to breathe, but she had to pull herself together. She could not give him the satisfaction of knowing he'd upset her.

Her voice was steady when she spoke. "J-a-c-l-y-n," she said. "Just like it sounds."

"Ah, in France, it would be pronounced *Zhaclean*. Perhaps your parents were French."

"On my mother's side of the family," Jaclyn said as she studied his face. The Major's eyes—piercing, luminous, and so dark they were almost opaque.

Alan and Jason had been convinced for some time that the Major and Santayana were the same man. How could she have doubted them? They were seldom, if ever, wrong about anything. She simply hadn't been able to force herself to believe it.

Sheffield's arm tightened around his wife's waist. When he gazed at her, it hurt him to see how pale she'd become, her expression one of desperation, while fear clouded her eyes.

Sheffield knew Santayana had made a mistake when he referred to Jaclyn's parents: "Perhaps your parents *were* French," *were* as in dead, not *are*, as in alive. The Major had access to all of the intelligence about Jaclyn's heritage. That included the information that her parents had died at Treblinka.

"Shef," Jason called out as he made his way through the crowd. "Hello, Damien—Sandra."

Jason, the master of calm, cool, and collected, Sheffield mused.

"Forgive me for interrupting, but we need to take our seats." With cavalier nod at Santayana, he said. "Excuse us, will you?"

Santayana bowed. "Of course, none of us wants to miss a note of Kathryn's performance."

Jason led the Sheffields up the ramp that led to the Borseaus' box. "What is Sandra doing with him?"

"I have no idea," Sheffield said.

Frowning, Jason said, "Does Sandra know anything that might compromise you?"

"Are you kidding? I'm as pure as the driven snow."

"Thank god for that." Jason held the crimson velvet curtain aside, and they greeted his parents.

"Sit here, Jaclyn," he said, directing her to the seat in front of his father. "Shef," he said, pointing to the chair beside Jaclyn. He sat next to Sheffield. "Santayana is trying to bluff his way through this, isn't he?"

"That's how it looks," Sheffield said. "He's also trying to intimidate Jaclyn, and I'm not going to let him." He took her hand in his. "Are you okay?"

"No, I've suddenly been transported back to that alternate universe . . . Trepskýa."

"I know you're frightened, and from this moment on, you've got to be more careful. You have to be aware of your surroundings at all times, and you need to keep your weapon loaded and within reach. We both know there's no longer any doubt that he's the Major. And there's no doubt that he knows who you are. I had hoped that our suspicions would be proven wrong, but that didn't happen, so we're going to face the Major's challenge head-on. And, it was a challenge. We have the power to protect you, but, I'll say it again, you have to be alert to everyone and everything around you. He's a wealthy man. He can hire any number of thugs to do his dirty work. Keep that uppermost in your mind at all times."

Tears welled up in Jaclyn's eyes and spilled over.

"Sweetheart, do you want to go home?"

She shook her head and swiped at the tears on her cheeks. "No, I want to hear Kathryn play."

The house lights dimmed, raised, and dimmed again.

"There's Kathryn," Jason said, as she entered, hand in hand with Jon Fitzgerald. They walked with jaunty steps to center stage. She wore a knee-length, black chiffon dress with a sweetheart neckline and an empire waist. The circular skirt flared out beneath her breasts and almost obscured her advancing pregnancy. Her hair was braided and wrapped like a crown around her head. Kathryn and Jon smiled at one another, bowed to the audience, and turned toward their pianos. The crowd applauded enthusiastically.

A group of students from Arizona State College chanted, "Kathryn—Jon." The pianists stopped and turned back, eyes lifted to the balcony, as they waved to the choir of young people. The two were well-known and popular figures on campus—Kathryn being the chair, and Jon, the vice chair of the board that oversaw the Borseaus' grant program. Every year, Kathryn reserved the balcony for ASC's music majors, free gratis. Jon seated Kathryn, kissed her hand, and strode to his piano.

Jason and Jon were friends now, but at one time, they were rivals, each vying for Kathryn's affection.

Sheffield tapped Jason's arm. "What are they playing?"

"Rachmaninov's *Third Piano Concerto*. It's very difficult. Of course, they've been playing together for a long time, and they've developed some hot showmanship techniques, but it takes split second timing to pull them off."

The symphony conductor, Alexander Kleindeinst, appeared, and the applause swelled to a crescendo. Stroking his white goatee, smiling and nodding to the audience, he strode toward the podium. He bent down to say a few words to Kathryn, walked the few steps to Jon, and shook his hand. Then stepping up on the dais, he looked from side to side, a sweeping glance that took in the entire orchestra. The Maestro turned toward Jon, who nodded, and Kathryn, who smiled. He raised the baton.

An expectant hush fell over the audience as the mellow sounds of the horns, bassoons, and violins filled the hall. Kathryn touched the keys to introduce the haunting melody that hinted at the surrealistic sounds to come. With power and precision, Jon increased the tempo, expanding and elaborating on the theme. Perfectly synchronized, their hands flew across the keyboards. Wild and passionate at times, psychedelic, melancholy, serene, and capricious, the intricate and swiftly changing moods of Rachmaninov's composition captured and held the audience's rapt attention.

The pianos and the orchestra advanced the theme, retreating, advancing again, reaching with one voice toward the imperious climax. As the pianists' fingers lifted from the keys, the audience came to its feet, shouting, "Bravo." Applause thundered through the concert hall.

Jon congratulated the conductor and the concertmaster before walking to Kathryn and taking her hand in his. She slid across the piano bench and rose to stand beside him. They took the few steps to center stage, bowed to one another, and then to the audience.

The chant from the gallery began again. Jon took Kathryn's hand and they walked off stage. The audience brought them back several times before letting them go.

Jaclyn said, "They were wonderful. Will they play again?"

"Ordinarily, they do, but not this year. It's too much for Kathryn right now." Tilting his head to one side, Jason said, "I wonder if she'll stay back stage or join us while her protégés play—violinists this year. Anyway, when the competition is over, Shef, I'd like you to join us for a reception to honor Kathryn and Jon and the contest winners. In fact, let's go down and send your limousine along. I'll see that you get home."

Staring at Sheffield's face, Jason whispered, "Hey, how'd you get that cut on your chin? Have you been playing cops and robbers without me?"

Sheffield chuckled. "I'll tell you all about it later."

# Chapter Forty-nine

**S**heffield awakened to the sound of Jaclyn retching. He got out of bed and hurried through the dressing room. "Jaclyn, I'm coming in."

"No, don't," she said, gasping for breath. "It's nothing, a touch of the flu. I'll be out in a minute."

Hearing the faucet running, he said, "Jaclyn, I'm coming in."

"No, I'm coming out." Seconds later, she walked into the dressing room, swallowing to force the nausea away, smiling wanly.

"Well, now I know what green around the gills looks like. Sweetheart, you're so pale. Come here." He reached out to her and enfolded her in his arms. "I'm worried about you, and don't play this, it's a touch of the flu game with me. No wonder Sejii was upset."

"I'm all right. Truly."

"How long has this been going on?"

Shaking her head and sighing, Jaclyn lifted her eyes to his. "A while."

"And you didn't tell me?"

"It goes away. In fact, I'm starving."

Sheffield jerked to attention. "Do you know what I think?"

She closed her eyes and leaned against him.

"You're pregnant."

"What?" she cried, pushing him away. "That's impossible."

"You were told you'd never have children, but you haven't been checked by a doctor."

"Don't do this. You want a child so badly, you're willing to fool yourself. Nothing will replace your son." Jaclyn covered her face with her hands. "You said you'd been that route."

"I'd love to have another child, but it certainly isn't a priority. Loving you, being married to you, is the important thing. Jaclyn, look at me."

She lifted her eyes to his. His heart ached for her. "This is easily resolved. Let me ask Dr. Shafner to come by. In any case, we need to know why you're ill." He hugged her to him. "Tell me I'm right."

"This is fool hardy. I'll be embarrassed." Drawing away, knowing he wouldn't let this go, she sighed. "All right."

He touched his lips to her forehead. "I'll call Dr. Shafner while you shower, and thank you for humoring me."

# Chapter Fifty

**D**r. Shafner, a comforting archetype of what a family physician should be, slowly descended the stairs. He was in his late sixties, short and compactly built, kindly blue eyes crinkled up at the corners when he smiled. His thick white hair served to offset a nose that was a tad too large for his face.

Sheffield was pacing in the living room. Spotting the physician as he descended the stairs, Sheffield hurried to him. "How is she, Henry?"

He smiled and patted Sheffield's shoulder. "You were right, Jaclyn is pregnant, about six weeks," he said, with a glance toward the living room. "We need to talk."

Sheffield grinned. "Imagine that! I'm going to be a father. Oh, Henry, Jaclyn must be ecstatic."

"I didn't tell her," the doctor said as he set his bag down beside the front doors. It would remind him not to leave without it, which he'd done more than once during the past few years. Henry Shafner thought he'd seen everything. Now, he knew that wasn't true.

"Bless your heart, Henry, I can't wait to tell her!"

"Shef, please, we really *must* talk."

Sheffield propelled the doctor into the living room. "Is something wrong?"

"What happened to her?" Dr. Shafner said grimly. "Your wife, what happened to her?"

Sheffield stared at him and wilted into a chair. "I'm afraid to imagine what you mean. Jaclyn is a holocaust survivor. She was incarcerated in a concentration camp. In Poland," he added, responding to the question in the doctor's eyes. "When she was eleven, the Nazi's arrested her and her parents." His grief-stricken eyes met the doctor's. "Three years of unimaginable hell, rape, and torture."

Henry Shafner sank into a chair opposite Sheffield. "The baby will have to be delivered by cesarean section. The birth canal is severely scarred."

Sheffield clenched his hands to still the trembling. "Will carrying the baby harm her?"

Dr. Shafner hesitated, knowing by the anguish in Sheffield's eyes how important his answer would be. With a shake of his head, he said, "Not as far as I can tell. She seems healthy otherwise, although we need to schedule her for a complete examination right away."

Sheffield wiped his eyes and gazed at the ceiling. "The monster that did that to her lives here, in Arizona."

"You said it happened in Poland."

"It did, but he's here. If you have time, I'd like to tell you as much as I know. Even as close as we are, Jaclyn hasn't told me everything. She's holding something back—something she can't deal with, something she's buried." The palms of Sheffield's hands pressed against his eyes. "It's beyond agony for her to talk about what happened to her, to her family, to the others in the camp, the children, the old people. She didn't think of herself as a child, for reasons you'll soon understand," he said quietly. "At some point, you may be called upon to testify about Jaclyn's physical condition. How would you feel about that?"

Henry Shafner's mouth drew into a hard line. He studied Sheffield's face. "I'll be willing to do whatever it takes to put the maniac who did this to your wife behind bars or in hell," he said savagely.

"Sejii," Sheffield called out. "Fetch some coffee for us, please."

Sheffield walked with Dr. Shafner to his car. "Tomorrow, I'll make an appointment for Jaclyn's physical."

"Congratulations, my boy. I'm sure everything will be fine."

When the car disappeared, Sheffield walked slowly to the house. When he closed the door behind him, Jaclyn was coming down the stairs.

She smiled at him. "See, I told you, I'm fine."

"You were right." He put his arm around her waist. "It's such a beautiful morning, let's enjoy it on the veranda," he said, aware that he was looking at this extraordinary woman who was carrying their child. Surely she could hear his heart pounding.

"Do you remember the first time we walked out here together?"

"How could I ever forget?"

A warm breeze touched her hair, shiny chestnut strands caressed his cheek. "I have something to ask you." Barely able to contain his elation that bordered on euphoria, Sheffield knew he would never forget this moment.

Smiling, she turned to face him. "You look as though you're going to burst."

Overwhelmed with emotion, Sheffield said, "If you had your druthers, which would you prefer, a boy or a girl?"

Jaclyn stared at him. "What?"

Sheffield grinned and patted her tummy.

With the cry like that of a wounded animal, she collapsed against him.

"Hey, wife, you didn't realize how virile your forty-six-year-old husband is, did you?"

"There's no mistake?"

Sheffield shook his head. "No, Henry said you're about six weeks along."

Tears streamed down her face. "Oh, my beloved, thank you for giving me a baby."

"You're very welcome," he whispered next to her ear.

# Chapter Fifty-one

Sheffield was working at his desk, when Sejii ushered Jason into the den.

"Jace, my friend," Sheffield said as he stood. "You're looking at the happiest man who ever lived."

"The happiest man?" Jason walked to Sheffield and shook his hand. "Congratulations, I'm happy for you. I couldn't wait to tell you so."

"How do you know what I'm—?"

"How long do you think it took Jaclyn to call Kathryn?"

"But I wanted to tell you myself." Sheffield shook his head. "I thought Jaclyn was taking a nap."

"Dream on. Those two women have already divined whether it's a boy or a girl, figured out when and where they're going to shop for the layette, and picked the colors for the nursery. In fact, when I left, Kathryn was tearing through her maternity clothes to see what she'd outgrown that Jaclyn might like to wear when her clothes no longer fit."

"But I'm the father," Sheffield said. "I want to be involved."

"No way that's going to happen," Jason said, laughing. "This is how it goes: We get to deposit those little guys in the right place at the right time. After that, I'm grateful that they don't banish us from the playground until they want to have another baby."

Sheffield glowered at him. "That is the most cynical thing I've ever heard."

Jason clapped his friend on the back. "You're a great teacher. Surely you recall telling me I still had time to get as cynical as you?"

"Yeah, well, the student has surpassed the master." Sheffield rubbed his forehead. "Jace, I used to spend eighty or more hours a week at my desk. Would you believe sixty now? It should be okay for me to have a life beyond the Attorney General's office, but I feel like I'm shirking my duty."

"You have options. Since I've been investing your money, you've become a relatively wealthy man. You could resign if you wanted to."

Sheffield's brows lifted. "How relatively wealthy am I?"

"Don't you look at the statements my accountant sends to you?"

"No, I just tuck them into a drawer."

"Shef!"

"How wealthy am I?"

"The last time I checked, you were worth about three million."

Disbelief flooded Sheffield's face. "Dollars—three million dollars?"

"And change."

"Enough to take Jaclyn away from this nightmare."

"Jon Fitzgerald once said, he didn't think Kathryn was ever tempted to rage against the angels. I don't think you are either, Shef, unless Santayana pushes you across that line."

"You believe I'm not tempted to rage against the angels," Sheffield whispered. He opened the sliding glass doors, drew a breath of heady desert air into his lungs, and squinted against the blazing light.

Memories roiled about in his mind. He could see his mother's golden hair, a little frazzled, bright in the sunshine. She reached down into the worn wicker basket, took a mound of dazzling white cloth into her hands, and laid it across the clothesline, far too high for him to reach. Grabbing clothespins from the pocket of her apron, she clipped each sheet into place. The corners had to match perfectly. He could still hear the linen snapping in the wind. He could see himself scrambling into bed and burying his face in the pillow, savoring the fresh, sweet scent, the stuff his precious memories were made of.

Although Sheffield was an only child, he never felt lonely. Their home was full of love and laughter, lively conversations and debates. Friends and shirttail relatives, as his mother called them, regularly dropped by. All were huggers. He'd never forget how stunned his parents were when they learned that he had received a scholarship to Harvard. They seemed in awe of him after that. He heard them whispering late at night, wondering how they had they produced such a brilliant child. From that day on, his mother referred to him as, *"My son, Alan, the one who got the scholarship to Harvard."* As if there were another son that didn't get one.

Sheffield smiled, blinking away tears. "From the moment I learned about what that monster had done to Jaclyn, I've been raging against God and his angels."

Jason frowned. "Okay, then, I'll go to the Santayana ranch and execute the arrogant SOB."

"Or maybe Kathryn could do it," Sheffield said.

Jason stopped on his way to the bar and swiveled around. "What are you talking about?"

"Jace, you have to know that Kathryn meant to end Angelo Carlotti's life, not merely to disable him, as you'd like to believe. It haunts her. Surely you know that."

"Shef, you're mistaken." Jason waved him off. "I know how methodical her actions seemed to be—pulling the bolt, shoving it forward, snapping it into place, but Angelo terrified her. She fired out of fear, a couple of lucky shots." Jason's hands skimmed across his hair. "What brought this up?"

Sheffield let out a long breath. "I've wanted to talk to you about this for a long time. Kathryn told Jaclyn she wanted Angelo to feel the first shot, the pain, when she told him you were alive. The second shot caught him under the chin, exactly where she intended it to."

Shocked, Jason stared at Sheffield. "My God, no wonder she has nightmares. I know growing up in a wilderness, side by side with an assortment of predatory animals, she had to learn to protect herself." He closed his eyes for a moment, then muttered, "I thought she'd be safe at the Aerie, and it almost got her killed."

Sheffield leaned his elbows on the bar. "Tell me what happened between you and Crystal Gormann."

Jason shrugged and grabbed two glasses from the back-bar. "I need a drink. Crystal and I dated for a short time in college."

Sheffield stood elbow to elbow beside his friend. "No, I mean, after you and Kathryn were married. Did you have an affair with Crystal?"

"No, absolutely not." Jason set the glasses on the bar and stared into them. "Why are you asking about this?"

"It came up the night Josh was born, remember?"

Jason's hands white-knuckled the edge of the bar. "Crystal called me, sobbing hysterically, said she needed help. I told her to call her father. She said she couldn't do that. I believed her, until she opened the door without a stitch on. She jerked me inside, began tearing at my clothes. Somehow, without realizing it, my watch came off in the tussle. I got out of there as quickly as I could, but she still had the watch Kathryn had given me. There was an inscription inside, and I couldn't remember exactly what it was. Then, if you can believe it, Crystal called Jon, told him she was lying naked on the bed I'd just left. Jon called me. We met. Of course, Jon raked me over the coals, but he finally believed me. It was Jon's idea to replace the watch, which I did. What I didn't know was that Crystal also called Kathryn to tell her that I'd left my watch in her hotel room. Kathryn didn't tell me about the call, just suffered in silence. When the truth came out, she didn't believe me when I said nothing had happened. And why would she? How could I have gone there in the first place? And why am I telling you this?"

"Because we're brothers," Sheffield said.

Jason poured their drinks. "Yeah, I guess we are."

Sheffield smiled thoughtfully. Over the years, he'd seen Jason impale himself on a variety of crosses. He'd probably bring the nails to his own crucifixion. It was time to change the subject. "Three million, plus change, huh?" Sheffield said. "You really have it, don't you?"

Jason's jaws worked. "What?"

"The Midas touch, everything you touch turns to gold."

Jason met Sheffield's eyes. "Sometimes what I touch turns to shit," he growled.

"Well, Sam would get on my case, but I have to hug you," Sheffield said, throwing his arms around Jason.

"Jesus," Jason muttered.

# Chapter Fifty-two

Jason, Sam, and Sheffield were in the AG's office.

"It's beginning to make sense," Sam said. "Mitchell Price and Ricardo Montez worked as engineering consultants for three construction companies. Montez *is* a structural engineer, a Stanford graduate, but we know Price was nothing more than a thug. These are photographs of Montez, arriving and leaving the Santayana estate, on three separate occasions this past month."

He stood and handed them to Sheffield. "He wasn't hard to trace, drives a car that's licensed to him. Of course, there's a certain amount of arrogance in that. Price's driver's license was in his pocket when he tried to execute Christian." Sam flipped through the pages of his notebook. "The three construction companies in question are Talbot, Grewald, and Wallace. Now get this, they only bid on certain projects—the big ones. There are other companies that consistently bid, but more often than not, the City rejects their bids, based on one technicality or another. It's legal, though, remember that," he added. "Another interesting thing is—none of the construction companies in question bid on the reconstruction of City Hall. The Council awarded that contract two weeks ago. Normally the big three would've bid on a project of that magnitude. Something put them off, probably Montez, acting on Santayana's behalf."

"Have you talked to the big three, as you call them?" Sheffield said.

"Oh, yeah, the purported presidents. I say *purported*, because it's obvious they're not in charge."

"And," Sheffield said.

"Without exception, they were visibly nervous. After I left each of their offices, I popped back in to retrieve my briefcase. To a man, they were on the telephone, with, *I'll have to get back to you*. It gets better. About ten years ago, these companies got financial assistance from some foreign investors, in Switzerland, Spain, and France. On the face of it, that isn't unusual, Phoenix being one of the fastest growing cities in the country."

"Of course the investors are nebulous," Sheffield said.

"You got it. No corporate headquarters of record, multi-millions of dollars funneled through numbered bank accounts, wired from dozens of other numbered accounts, and so on. The three companies have to be fronts, but we can't tie our rancher to any of them yet. The FBI is following the money, so maybe in time—."

"That's how Santayana is laundering drug money and the millions he's raked off of the City. It looks as though we're at a dead end with the bombing at City Hall," Sheffield said. "We can't tie any of the survivors to that dirty deed, including Paul Hewitt and Lee Crooks."

Sam shook his head. "No, in fact, we can't link Hewitt or Crooks to anything other than questionable management practices. I don't think they knew what was going on. Their financial records are straightforward. They don't appear to be living beyond their means. Paul Hewitt's had a couple of affairs, short-lived, and seemingly harmless enough. A couple of Councilmen had been padding their expense accounts, a few bucks here, a few bucks there." Sam laughed. "Of course, once we started poking around, they're squeaky clean now. As far as the bombing victims are concerned, if they were paid off, it was in cash, and the amounts relatively insignificant. But, you know, to folks who earn twelve to fifteen thousand a year, an extra few thousand bucks might seem like a fortune. Still, I have to believe terror and blackmail were key to their entanglements, if any."

"Getting back to Montez. Let's bring him in and question him."

"On what grounds?"

"We suspect he's involved in the holocaust at City Hall, and we know he worked on many City projects. Without the benefit of records, we need to find out what the projects entailed. Jesus, he worked with Price. That alone is enough to bring him in."

"Wait a minute, Shef," Jason interjected. "If you can't charge Montez, what's to keep Santayana from making him disappear? You could be setting the guy up to be executed."

"And Montez needs to know that," Sheffield shot back. "Maybe we'll have to play our trump ace—tell him what we suspect. We know Santayana is dealing drugs, and we know Montez is doing business with him. We can pursue that angle first, then hit him with a connection to mass murder. I'd be willing to offer him protection and immunity. It's Santayana I want to get."

Sam scowled. "What happens if Montez doesn't fold?"

"Then we lock him in our sights until he makes a mistake." Seeing the reservation in Sam's eyes, Sheffield said, "You don't agree with me."

Sam leaned toward his boss. "No, I think we should get a search and seize warrant and go over every inch of the Santayana ranch. And, I think we need to do it right away. We can't give Santayana time to get rid of evidence, if he hasn't already."

"He doesn't know we suspect him of orchestrating the bombing, or drug smuggling, or The Ladies of the Night

Murders. He suspects that I've connected him to the war crimes at Trepskýa, that's all."

Sam shook his head. "We need to arrest him and charge him with the crimes we can prove he's committed. Once we've done that, we can bring Montez in with some expectation that he'll crack. If we bring him in now and we can't hold him, I agree with Jace, Montez is a dead man. Then where would we be?"

"We still have the company presidents," Sheffield said, frowning at Sam.

"What if, like Moira, they have no idea who's calling the shots? We know Montez is directly tied to Santayana. With Price dead, he may be the only one."

Sheffield glanced from Sam to Jason. "Have I lost my perspective?"

Sam shrugged.

Sheffield wiped a hand across his mouth and hunched forward in his chair. "Oh, what was in the file Rip Vashay felt he had to photograph."

"I was hoping you'd never ask. It's a complete dossier on Jaclyn," Sam said quietly. "Without a doubt, Santayana knows who she is."

Sheffield's head pressed back against the chair. He looked from one of them to the other, grabbed his pipe from the side of his desk, opened the leather pouch, and began the stuffing-tamping ritual. He snapped the lighter and drew fiercely on the stem. "What's happening with the Feds?" He was mixing up the investigations again. "Yes, I'm talking about Jaclyn."

"The investigation is being coordinated through Interpol. Weisman and a group of Nazi head hunters are working with them," Sam said

"That's why I came by, Shef. I talked with Irv this morning," Jason said. "Though it isn't much, they've pulled the films and documents they recovered from Trepskýa, and they're reviewing them. He wondered . . ." Jason paused as he studied Sheffield's face.

Sheffield cringed, knowing what was coming next. "When Jaclyn will be able to look at them."

Jason nodded.

Sheffield shot out of his chair and walked to the windows. "Where?"

"Warsaw."

"In my opinion? Never." Sheffield shook his head and stuffed his hands into his pockets. "Until now, I've never, in my entire life, felt so overwhelmed, even when Michael died." Hesitating a long moment, he said, "That isn't true. When Michael was killed and Gina left me, I pretty much shut down. But now, I have Jaclyn, we're going to have a baby, and I can't seem to get my priorities in order. It was easy to be objective before."

Jason frowned and walked to the windows to stand beside his friend. "For what it's worth, I think Sam's right. Your first priority is to get Santayana behind bars. The rest can wait. I'll call Irv to remind him that Jaclyn is pregnant. He'll understand. You need to address the Major's crimes on this continent first. Frankly, in my opinion, Jaclyn can't deal with it right now, and I know you agree. And this should be a joyous time for you. Hey, I get so involved when Kathryn's pregnant, it drives her crazy." Jason grinned. "She says I cluck around her like an old mother hen."

Laughing, Sheffield grasped Jason's arm, and turned to Sam. "If you thought we should move in, why did we install the surveillance equipment at the ranch? Everything we've collected so far is ho-hum."

"Hey, boss, it still may be useful. After we charge Santayana, he'll be out on bail and back at the ranch within hours. No judge in this State is going to hold him until he goes to trial. Am I right?"

Sheffield turned a wry smile on his right-hand man. "All right, I'll have the warrant issued. Put all of our agents on alert. Contact the FBI, and get our transportation in order. Three helicopters. Let Chuck Olsen decide who he wants flying wing. We'll rendezvous at midnight, brief our people, and roll by one o'clock. You'd better get Vashay and Olsen on-board as soon as possible. Oh, we'll have to search every abandoned mine on Santayana's property. We'll need to study the aerial maps again. And, Sam, this has to be by the book, no hot dogs, as you call them."

"Gotcha, boss!"

"I'm going with you," Jason said quietly.

Laying his pipe on the desk, Sheffield shook his head. "You know I can't let you do that. If something happened to you, the State couldn't afford the liability. Believe me, I'd be glad to have you along, but it's too risky."

"I'll sign a hold harmless agreement, whatever it takes to get the State off the hook," Jason said.

Frowning, Sheffield shook his head. "No."

"What's the problem? If I were wounded, I wouldn't sue the State."

"It's—"

"Why would I? I probably have more money than it does," Jason said.

Sam took hold of Jason's arm. "Can't we deputize him? I really would like to have another sharpshooter along. There are a lot of men on that ranch, and they're all armed."

Sheffield shook his head and turned his back on them. "Because it would upset Kathryn."

"What if I just stick with you and cover your backside?" Jason said.

Sheffield was quiet for a time. "Only with your wife's blessing. She's very pregnant, and directly or indirectly, because of you, she's had more than her share of traumatic experiences."

Jason sighed and slanted a glance at Sheffield. "Jaclyn's pregnant, too."

"This is my job. That's the deal. Take it or leave it," Sheffield said.

"All right, we'll expect you at six, and you can ask Kathryn yourself."

"Oh no, my friend, you'll ask her. All I want is her answer. You're like a kid, Jace. This isn't cowboys and Indians or cops and robbers. We aren't the Hardy Boys."

"Oh, yeah, the Hardy Boys." Jason grinned at Sheffield. "Does Kathryn still call us that?"

Sheffield nodded, but he wasn't smiling.

# Chapter Fifty-three

**D**riving home, Sheffield thought about what they'd face in a few hours. He could sidestep the operation, sweat it out at the office or at home with Jaclyn. That's what the previous Attorney Generals would've done. It was tearing him up to put his life on the line. It was hard for him to believe how everything had changed. His life was now a precious commodity that he couldn't bear to jeopardize.

Jaclyn was joyous, radiant. When he got home from the office, he could barely get through the door before she and Sejii rushed him, both talking at once, describing in detail how the day had gone. Sejii hovered over Jaclyn while his boss was at work, and Sheffield hovered over her when he was at home. Her sentinels, she called them.

Sejii's culinary talents had gone beyond anything Sheffield could've imagined—Japanese cuisine to produce a strong baby and keep Jaclyn healthy. The Attorney General chuckled to himself. Seaweed! He'd lost eleven pounds in the past six weeks. Maybe some of the pounds he'd shed could be attributed to their morning walks. It was impossible to believe he'd begun looking forward to them.

Sheffield made a right turn onto the winding gravel road to their house. Scared, he'd never been so scared. What if something happened to their baby? What if something happened to Jaclyn? And what would she do if something happened to him?

He waved at his agents as he drove through the gate to the carport, turned off the engine, and sat there thinking. Santayana wouldn't take this invasion lying down. He'd fight. Sheffield was sure of it. Of course, he wanted Jason with him, but it wouldn't be fair to Kathryn or their children. "Oh God," he said, aloud.

Sheffield opened the door of his Mercedes and moseyed to the front door. While he fumbled for the key, the door opened, and the bright faces of Jaclyn and Sejii greeted him. He forced a smile. "Well, how is my love and her faithful keeper, and how is our son or daughter today?"

Tears gathered in Jaclyn's eyes. "Alan, the baby moved. Sejii felt it, too," she said, turning to him for concurrence.

"Hai, strong baby, big kicks," Sejii said with a broad smile as he nodded his head exuberantly.

Sheffield pulled Jaclyn to him. "So, while I slave behind a desk all day, the two of you stay home and play with my baby."

Jaclyn stepped back and searched his face. "What is it?"

"What? I just wish we didn't have to go to the Borseaus. I want to stay home with my hand on your tummy until the baby says hello to me."

"No, it's the way you looked when Sam and I had to tackle a dangerous assignment. What's going on?"

Sheffield loosened his tie and undid the top button of his shirt. Trying to sidestep the issue wouldn't work. Jaclyn would know.

"We're going to invade the Santayana ranch tomorrow, but before we go to the Borseaus, I'd like to change into something more comfortable." He took Jaclyn's hand and led her to the stairs. "Sejii, how about going to the Borseaus' with us?"

Sejii shook his head and hurried away toward the back of the house.

Sheffield frowned. It was the first time Sejii had cast aside his bowing ritual.

**W**hile he changed into jeans and a western shirt, Jaclyn watched him with solemn eyes. He sat on the edge of the bed, pulled on his boots and tugged the legs of his jeans down over them. He glanced at her over his shoulder. "Jason wants to go with us, but unless Kathryn agrees, it ain't gonna happen. Sam wants me to deputize him," he said, grinning at her. "You know Jace. He thinks I need him." Seeing how pale she'd become, he said, "Jaclyn, I've never asked my folks to face anything I'm not willing to face. It's part of the reason you love me, isn't it?"

"Yes," she said. "But it's the smallest part."

"All of my agents have families."

"As if you need to tell me that," she said, closing her eyes and shaking her head. "It doesn't matter who does or doesn't have families. All right, I'm being selfish, but I can't help it. Don't go!" she cried, collapsing face down on the bed.

"Don't, please, I have to do this. Surely you understand that."

"He'll kill you, Alan."

"Sam will keep me so far from the action—"

"We can hide from him," Jaclyn cried. "We can go away."

Sheffield stroked her back and tried, without success, to swallow the lump in his throat. "No, we can't, but I've considered doing just that. More than once," he said softly.

# Chapter Fifty-four

How had the years gone by so quickly? Kathryn pondered, as she concentrated on Jason's face. For the past ten years, only he had been in true focus, everything else, hazy bits and pieces, shadows floating around the fringe of her life. Their children, of course, each a subtle brew—Jason's nose, her mouth, his eyes, her hair, created at the peak of passion. Anthony, the beloved child of her heart, a mirror image of his father.

Ten years before, she'd applied for a job at Jason's radio station. After earning a degree in Communications at the University of Nebraska, she'd entered a convent. A year short of her final vows, she'd left the convent and returned to Idaho to spend a few weeks with her paternal grandparents, Ben and Sarah Whittaker, before striking out for Yuma, Arizona. Why Yuma? Was it fate as Jason thought? When she'd called the dean at the U of N, he'd just received a flyer from KCOY. Then, miracle of miracles, she'd met Jason before, on a train, the Super Chief, on her way to Nebraska. The war had ended shortly before. He was still in uniform. She'd been fourteen, well, almost. And she'd never forgotten him. For years, she'd fantasized about the handsome air force officer, who'd been kind to her. Fantasized, until destiny stepped in and sent her to him, to Jason, to love him, forever after.

That day at the station. Her first glimpse of him—eyes that met and couldn't look away, hands that touched and couldn't let go. He was married, though separated. He had a son, who'd been abused by his mother.

Maybe she could survive without him now, hating every agonizing breath she took. Destiny, the force that had brought them together, could as easily shred the fragile fabric it had woven.

Suddenly, she was twelve years old, leaning back to gaze up at Eagle Mountain in Idaho's Bitterroot Wilderness. Her parents' embittered marriage had ended in an equally bitter divorce, and Kathryn hadn't been able to choose between them, nor could she bear the cruel treatment her friends were heaping on her, the humiliation and abuse. Her grandparents had agreed to let her live with them. But her parents never forgave her for rejecting them. It struck again—the anguish of telling them good-bye. She'd been a mere child, too young to know it would be forever. Then her grandfather's arms, tight around her as they made their way on horseback from the foot of the mountain to the top of it, where the lodge at the Aerie, a pale granite monolith, rose as a magnificent tribute to her grandfather's skill as a stone mason. She'd found peace there.

From her balcony, Kathryn could hear the River of No Return thundering through the gorge thousands of feet below. With the slightest turn of her head, she could gaze across a ravine to the Continental Divide's serpentine ridges in the distance. Her spirit had become one with the mountain— the frozen stillness of winter, the tranquil awakening of spring, buds bursting from the ancient marrow of the trees, the wildflowers, carpets of purple crocus, braving the last vestiges of winter, the merry buttercups, thimbleberry fringe. And then, her soul had become one with Jason's.

Reacting to the fear in Jaclyn's eyes, Kathryn blinked away the past. Looking from Jason to Sheffield, she said, "Alan, do you *need* Jason, or is this something he wants to do, because he's never going to grow up?"

Sheffield concentrated on Jason's eager face. "I'm not going to answer that, because I don't think it has any bearing on your decision."

"You just answered it." Kathryn turned to study her friend's face, Jaclyn who had become so dear to her. "If Jason goes with Alan, you'll feel better."

"Oh yes, but I wouldn't think of asking you," Jaclyn said, wringing her hands.

"Why do either of you have to go?" Kathryn demanded. "You don't have to do this, Alan. I know you don't!" They flinched in unison.

Sheffield glanced from Jaclyn to her. "You're wrong, I do have to do this."

As she scrutinized Sheffield's solemn face, Kathryn's anger vanished. "All right, Jason, I couldn't bear it if anything to happened to Alan, and you weren't there to back him up. But you knew that. So, Jaclyn." She turned to look at her. "Shall we sit this out together? Would you mind coming here. It's a little hard for me to get around these days."

Jaclyn rushed to hug her friend. "Thank you," She whispered next to Kathryn's ear. "He can't shoot straight, you know."

Sighing, Kathryn smiled at Jason. "If we weren't pregnant, we'd go with you, two extra weapons, two more crack shots."

# Chapter Fifty-five

Sheffield and Jason crouched behind a massive boulder. Jason looked through the telescopic lens of his rifle. Sheffield had deputized him a few hours earlier. The Attorney General's agents, fourteen in all, surrounded the hacienda.

The utter stillness was unnerving. Sheffield glanced at his watch, then closed his eyes a moment to get his emotions under control. The beat of his heart escalated, thundering in his chest when Sam's baritone, magnified by an electronic bullhorn cut like a sword through the silence.

"Damien Santayana, this is Sam Erikson. I'm an agent with the State Attorney General. We have a warrant to search your premises. Lay down your arms, if any, and come out."

They waited.

"Damien Santayana, we have a warrant to search your premises," Sam said again.

"Oh, Jesus," Sheffield said when he saw the rows of rifles slide through the windows of the hacienda. "He's going to fight."

"You knew that," Jason said as he brought his rifle up and sighted it in.

Sheffield raised the twin to Sam's electronic device to his mouth. "Damien Santayana, this is Attorney General

Alan Sheffield. Don't expose your people or mine to danger. Lay down your arms and move out. Do it now. You can't win this."

"Señors," a man shouted from the open hacienda door. "Señor Santayana isn't here. We did not know who you were. Don't shoot, por favõr."

"Where is he?" Sheffield said to Jason. "He was there last night. We saw him go in, and he didn't leave." The Attorney General stood and edged around the far side of the hillock. "Come out where we can see you with your hands up, all of you," he shouted, inching forward until he could see the front doors.

Jason lowered his rifle and turned his head. "Oh, Jesus, where'd you go? Shef," he yelled, moving in his friend's direction. "What are you—?"

A shot rang out. The impact of the bullet lifted Sheffield into the air and threw him against a boulder behind the ridge.

"Oh, God!" Jason yelled as he rushed to his friend's side. "How could you be so stupid?"

Sheffield clutched his chest, blood oozed through his fingers. "Jace, take care of Jaclyn and the baby."

"The hell I will. You're going to take care of them yourself," Jason said as he tore Sheffield's shirt open. The bullet had entered above his right lung and below his shoulder. On closer inspection, Jason didn't think it had struck any vital organs. "Shef, if you live, I'm going to kill you." Bowing his head, he let out a long sigh. Sheffield had lapsed into unconsciousness. Jason shredded the tail of his shirt, packed the wound, and pressed the palm of his hand against it.

Activating Sheffield's transceiver, he shouted, "This is Borseau. Sheffield's wounded. I need medical assistance on the East Ridge." Jason waited, then said "Shef is wounded, and I need help!" He turned the device over and groaned. It had been smashed when Sheffield fell. He took off his leather flight jacket and covered Sheffield with it. Then picking up the rifle, Jason moved to the giant boulder and began firing through stands of Manzanita.

"If it's the only way I can get Shef out of here, I'll kill every one of you," he shouted. As Jason fired on the Santayana army, one by one the rifles disappeared from the windows.

Sheffield's agents hunkered down behind the wall that encircled the hacienda. Sam's eyes moved to the ridge. He'd seen his boss at the edge of a rugged crag, but when he looked again, the Attorney General had disappeared.

"Take them out, if you have to kill every damned one of them," Sam hollered to Rip Vashay, as he retreated through the thick stand of trees. He raced up the hill. His heart pounded so stridently, he expected it to fly out of his chest. Bullets ricocheted off the trees and rocks, whining as they spun at crazy angles into the wilderness. Using the larger trees as shields, Sam sped from one to another. He was within a hundred feet of the ridge.

"Shef—Jace, are you all right?"

"Shef's been hit," Jason shouted. "Pull a helicopter down. We have to get him out of here."

Still racing from tree to tree, Sam activated his transceiver. "Condor, this is Tonto. Do you copy? Condor, do you copy?" he shouted again. "Set down behind the ridge, about a hundred yards east of the hacienda. Lone Ranger is wounded." As he mounted the crest of the hill, he recalled how amused Sheffield had been when Sam suggested their code names. Laughing, he'd said, "I hope we never have to use the Lone Ranger and Tonto? We'd be the laughing stock of the State."

"Set one of those birds down now," Sam ordered. He squatted down and lifted the leather jacket from Sheffield's chest. Rising to his feet, he shouted, "Where are you, Condor? Talk to me, you Johnny-come-lately."

At last he heard the giant rotors beating the air as the helicopters rose above the Patagonias southeast of them.

"Condor here, Tonto. It took a minute to key in your frequency," the pilot advised calmly.

Waving his arms as the helicopters flew over their position, Sam turned to Jason. "What does it take to get you fly boys excited?" He triggered the transceiver again. "We're directly below you."

"Roger, we've got you," the pilot responded evenly.

The helicopters hovered above the plateau. First one and then another landed. The third helicopter stayed aloft and circled the area. Two men flew out of the open cockpit, grabbed a stretcher, and rushed to Sheffield. Two others left the second helicopter and patrolled the area.

"Get the Attorney General to St. Vincent's," Sam shouted as they laid his boss on the stretcher. "Radio ahead so they're ready for him. He took a bullet in his right chest just below the shoulder. Go with him," Sam yelled next to Jason's ear. "I'm going down there and kill every one of those bastards, and I hope Santayana is one of them."

Jason walked beside Sheffield to the nearest helicopter. "Don't you dare die," he said, taking one of Sheffield's hands in his. "If you do, Kathryn will have my hide."

"Rip, pass the word, we're going over the wall, and rush the house," Sam said into his transceiver. "Are your people in place?" It was a question he didn't have to ask. Rip Vashay was always way ahead of everyone else, quick to assess the best strategy in any situation and take advantage of it. A native son, in his late thirties, Vashay's keen dark eyes seemed to take in everything at once. He was a born leader. His compact, hard-edged body set a grueling pace for the rest of the team.

"Roger," Vashay said, falling back under pressure into military jargon. "Count down ten seconds from *now*, then begin firing."

Sam slung the rifle over his shoulder, grasped the top of the wall, hoisted himself up and rolled over. He flattened himself against the ground, laid the rifle beside him and pulled his forty-five. Vashay's team rapid-fired from six high ground positions around the hacienda.

"Hold your fire," Sam shouted into the transceiver. "We're moving in. Rip, I can't see any weapons from here. They're not returning your fire, but you're in a better position to—"

"Sam, hold up where you are. Let us go first. It could be a trap," he said, moving the binoculars from window to window. "Report to me, laddies, what do you see?" One by one, Vashay's team responded, "All clear."

"John, Adam, Ben, hit the gates. "Ty, back up John, Harrison, back Adam. I'll take Ben. Let me know when you're in position," Vashay said, crouching low and moving toward his man.

"We're set," Ty Morgan said.

"I'm holding Adam's trembling hand," Winston Harrison muttered.

Vashay chuckled. "It's a go for Ben and me. Soften up the locks. Sight them in on your scopes, laddies, and commence firing."

Sam listened to the verbal exchange between his agents followed by a barrage of gunfire. He glanced from the north windows of the house to the only gate he could see from his position, breathing a sigh of relief when it swung free.

"Good shooting," Vashay said calmly. "Move in, ten seconds from now."

Sam watched Ben McFay bolt through the gate with Vashay right behind him. They zigzagged toward the hacienda and threw themselves against the house between double panels of windows.

"Sam, have your men soften up the doors," Vashay said. "Then, we'll rush them, and you can come in behind us."

Sam eased the pistol down in front of him and picked up his rifle. "I hope you copied that, men," he said. "Commence firing."

Bullets riddled the doors, reducing them to jagged splinters of wood.

"Hold your fire," Sam shouted, laying down his rifle, grabbing his familiar hand gun. "Let's hit it," he shouted, leaping to his feet and zigzagging toward the house.

Sam flew through the rear door and rolled across the floor, gripping his gun with both hands, swinging it from one side of the room to the other, until he spotted Rip Vashay. The team leader stood at one end of the reception hall. His rifle hung by his side. He was staring down at the bodies of six men. He bent down and rolled two of them over. "Jesus Christ, they were executed," he said, "shot in the back of the head."

"After you check the rooms, search the cellar." Sam got to his feet and holstered his weapon. "I'll bring the helicopters down in case we find anyone alive. How did Santayana get out of here?" He walked through the rear door. "Condor, this is Erikson. The hacienda is secure, but we may need transport for wounded. Land as close as you can and send a couple of medics our way." Sam sank to the ground and leaned his back against the wall of the house.

"Roger, copy that," the pilot responded.

Within minutes, the birds had landed on the south side of the hacienda.

Sam pulled a pack of Winston's from his pocket, shook it, and put his lips around the cigarette that popped up. After searching for his lighter, he realized he must've lost it when he scaled the wall.

Rip Vashay came through the door and stood looking down at him.

"Got a light?"

Reaching into his pocket, Vashay handed his lighter to Sam. "Win thinks his mother named him for that brand of cigarettes. She denies it, of course," he said, watching Sam tuck the pack back in his pocket. "The team is checking out the cellar."

Sam torched the cigarette, and squinted up at Vashay through a haze of smoke. "Did anyone survive this massacre?"

Rip shook his head. "Not unless they're down there," he said, nodding toward the cellar. "It looks as though we took out five, possibly six of the eleven dead we've found so far."

The flashlight beam cast eerie shadows along the walls, splaying out across the narrow corridor as Winston Harrison made his way back through the narrow tunnel. The light expanded when the corridor opened into a large, musty-smelling room. Harrison shot the light from side to side. Floor to ceiling racks held hundreds of bottles of wine. He bolted up the steep stairs, raced across the ceramic tiled hall through the door. "There's a tunnel, Rip."

In a single motion, Sam flipped the butt of his cigarette and leapt to his feet. Rip was already through the door. The three of them groped their way down the dark cellar stairs.

Sam shouted over his shoulder, "Aren't there any lights down here?"

"Shot out, the flashlight is it," Harrison said. "The rest of the team is trying to find out where the tunnel comes out."

"Jesus," Sam bellowed as he turned and raced back to the stairs. "What's the matter with me? We have to get the helicopters back in the air. God knows how much of a head start Santayana has on us. He could be across the river and in Mexico by now."

The blades were idling when Sam and Rip raced to the helicopters. Sam hoisted himself into the cockpit and reached back to give his team leader a hand. "Fire up this sucker and get it back in the sky. Santayana has escaped."

Charles Crash Olsen, his square jaw set, blue eyes hot, put on his earphones and triggered the mike. "Condor here, Phoenix. Heads up, we're going on a man hunt." The sound from the rotors swelled to a shriek. As he lifted off, Olsen kept his partner's bird in view to maintain a safe distance between them.

"He'll try to cross the river into Mexico," Sam shouted.

"Phoenix, Condor here, as if you didn't know who it is. Rendezvous at the North Fork of the Santa Cruz and sweep south along the east bank. I'll take the west bank," Olsen said.

"If he's more than half-way across, we'll have to let him go," Vashay shouted next to Sam's ear.

Sam turned raging dark eyes on his team leader. "Never was any good at geography, so I won't know where that is."

"Don't play dumb with me!"

Erikson shot a warning glance at Rip, raised the binoculars, and scanned the landscape below. Indecision gnawed at him. Maybe Santayana had gone north instead of south. The other helicopter could tackle that area.

"Crash," Major Zachary Frazier's voice crackled through Olsen's headset. "There's a horse and rider, fording this ole river at the narrowest point. I'll just buzz that old boy and turn him back."

"No, keep your distance. If it's Sam's guy, he's armed."

Colonel Charles Olsen and Major Zachary Frazier had flown together in Korea. Near the end of the conflict, Olsen had spotted an enemy helicopter strafing a road teeming with civilians. They'd expended all their ammunition and were headed back to base. "Hey, Zach, shall we give that bird a nudge."

Zach grinned and raised his thumb. Several minutes later, as they crawled away from the burning rubble, no longer bearing any resemblance to a helicopter, he'd wisecracked, "Well, if it ain't Colonel Crash Olsen in the flesh." And the nickname stuck.

Olsen swung his bird to the east. "Major, did you copy *armed*? Add dangerous to that, Zach. We're on the way," he added. "My partner's trying to turn a cowboy in the river," Olsen shouted over his shoulder to Sam. "Could your man be on horseback?"

Sam shrugged and lifted his hands palms up.

"There he is," Olsen said. Quickly assessing the situation, he shouted, "Zach, you're cutting it too close. Back off, get some altitude. Copy that? He's armed. Repeat, armed, and you're too low. Phoenix, do you read? Back off and pull up. That's an order, Major."

"I hear you bro', but that ole scoundrel looks like he's turning his steed," Zach said.

"Listen up, you bull-headed Carolina Kraut, I said to put some altitude between you and the suspect. That's an order, Major."

"Roger, Condor. I thought he was convinced, but that ole boy is shooting," Zach shouted. "Hit, I'm hit, Crash!"

Olsen activated his throat mike and screamed into it, "Get out, Zach, you're over the river. Get out! If you don't get your men out, I'll fire your ass! Oh, no!" Olsen cried as the helicopter roller-coasted crazily, slammed into a tree, dropped like a rock, and exploded on impact. "Zach, you crazy bastard." Tears flooded the Colonel's eyes.

"Zach's team made it into the river. Drop me in, Crash," Sam shouted.

"The men are swimming to shore."

Sam swiveled around. "Disable Santayana, Rip."

"He's in Mexican waters," Vashay shouted back.

"Disable him!"

Seeing the rage in Sam's eyes, Vashay spread-eagled next to the cockpit opening, shoved the rifle against his shoulder, and moved his right eye to the scope. Santayana dove from his horse and swam underwater. He was within a few feet of the opposite shore.

"When he comes up for air," Rip said to himself. Taking a deep breath, he squeezed the trigger.

"If you missed on purpose, I'll retire your badge," Sam bellowed.

Ignoring him, the team leader concentrated, sighted in the rifle again. Santayana was scrambling onto the beach. Rip froze and squeezed the trigger. Santayana' reared back and grabbed his thigh. Then dragging his injured leg, he disappeared into the underbrush.

"Set this crate down," Sam shouted next to Olsen's ear. "Set it down now! There's a wounded man down there who needs our help!"

Olsen's eyes locked with Sam's. "Is that how you're going to play this? You'll never get away with it."

"Maybe not, but that's how I'm going to play it," Sam said through clenched teeth.

Olsen stared at him, shook his head, and searched for a place to land.

Sam tried to shove the Attorney General's words, *by the book*, to the back of his mind.

"I'll have to go inland," Olsen shouted over the roar of the engines. "We can't land down there."

"Go back to the beach and set her down." Sam shouted.

Rip grabbed Sam's arm. "Sam, let's go back to Phoenix and contact the Mexican authorities. That's what Shef would do."

Sam's massive hands passed across his hair. "We're pursuing a murderer."

Vashay's grip tightened on Sam's arm. "Legally, we're on shaky ground. What's with you? I've never seen you like this. Let's get our men out of there and do this right."

Sam slumped against the bulwark. "You don't know what I know," he said, aware that his feelings were colored by what Santayana had allegedly done to Jaclyn. He wiped his eyes and shouted, "Crash, do we have enough fuel to make it back to Phoenix, or do we head for Tucson?"

Olsen checked the fuel gauge. "We can make it."

"All right, let's get our folks off the beach—our beach," Sam said, shaking his head.

Olsen nodded and circled back toward the river.

# Chapter Fifty-six

"I'm so damned tired of this hospital," Jason muttered.

He turned to see Dr. Shafner striding toward him. "Shef will be fine," he said, looking past Jason to Jaclyn who was running toward them. Jason's father and Kathryn were steps behind her.

Jaclyn searched the doctor's face. "Will he be all right?"

Taking her hands in his, Henry was quick to say, "Yes. I'd release him, but he lost some blood, so to be on the side of prudence, we'll keep him overnight." He smiled at her. "But you, young lady, need to go home, and rest."

Jaclyn shook her head. "No, I'm fine. Please, may I see him?"

Dr. Shafner took her elbow and led her toward the recovery room. "I suppose you'll be better off here than worrying about him at home."

"Henry," Jason called out, "don't lose that slug. It has to go to Shef's lab."

The doctor waved over his shoulder.

Kathryn waddled up, took Jason's hand, and leaned her head against him. "Thank God, Alan will be okay."

Andre gripped his son's arm. "Son," he said, peering at Jason over his glasses, "I don't think—"

"You don't have to say it, Dad, and neither do you," Jason said looking at Kathryn. "This Hardy Boy is swearing off, and if the other one has any sense, he'll swear off, too. I should've put a leash on him."

Jason put his arms around Kathryn and laughed. "Whoa, baby, it's getting mighty hard to get close to you. Is this what we can expect with each succeeding pregnancy, bigger and bigger? But, then," he said, teasing her, "maybe bigger's better?"

With an impish smile, Kathryn said, "What do you think, Dad? Would he survive the shock? Of course, he's such a smart ass, do we care?"

Jason put a hand on her tummy and stared at her. "No, we're not."

"Twins!" she said, throwing her arms around her husband's neck.

# Chapter Fifty-seven

## January, 1962

With her storm-tossed eyes flashing ominously, Kathryn clutched the arms of a chair and lowered herself into it. "Jason, you're not going back there."

"Beau and I thought we'd just fly over the area. What? Do you think I'm going to jump into the middle of that mess?"

"Mother, Dad, talk to your son."

Camille put her hand on Jason's arm. "Forget it, you're not going."

"Let it go, son," his father said.

"The first thing Shef is going to ask is—"

"Then let his people tell him," Kathryn said.

"Dammit, I feel like I'm letting him down."

Suddenly grabbing the arms of the chair, Kathryn cried out, "Jason, see if Henry is still at the hospital."

Jason stared at her. "Is it the baby?" he stammered.

"Babies, Jason! I'm doing it again. It's too soon," she cried, clutching her belly.

Jason sprinted toward the phone. "Dad, have a car brought to the house. I'll call the hospital."

Andre rushed to the house phone, Camille rushed to Kathryn.

Christian came through the door. "Is it Kathryn?" he said anxiously.

Camille nodded. "Christian, please find Cy, tell him what's happening? When I came down, Lauren was asleep, Anthony and Josh were watching television. Ask Cy to keep them upstairs," she said.

"Actually, I'd like to keep an eye on them. Of course, Anthony doesn't need a sitter." Christian turned toward the door. "Kathryn, I know you'll be fine," he called to her over his shoulder.

"Henry, is Jaclyn still there?" Jason listened and said, "Tell her what's going on." He paused and turned toward Kathryn. "What do I know? I'm just the father. Mother, has Kathryn's membrane ruptured?"

"No!" Kathryn cried, panting as another contraction struck. "We have to go. Why aren't we?"

Jason hung up and rushed to her. "Put your arms around my neck." Bending down, he put one arm under her knees. "Oh, Jesus," he groaned, as he lifted her from the chair.

"That isn't funny, Jason!"

"It sure isn't," he said, struggling to the door. "Sweetheart, forgive me for upsetting you."

Kathryn pressed her nose into the curve of his neck, loving his scent. Having the insane urge to lick him, she laughed.

"Why do you think it's funny when I'm so remorseful?"

"Oh, Jason, it isn't that. No, I was laughing at myself," she said, stifling another giggle. "And stop fretting. Josh was six weeks early and the twins are due in five weeks. And Henry didn't think I'd carry them this long." Panting for breath she cried, "Hurry, Jason. The pains are so close together."

**J**ason brought Kathryn's fingers to his lips. "Hi, wife, mother of my many children."

"Jason?"

Seeing tears swimming in her eyes, Jason's fingers trailed down her cheek. "Are you in pain?"

"Only a little. No, it's just that I love you so much. Are the babies all right?"

"They're perfect. They weigh four pounds eight ounces and four pounds ten ounces respectively."

Kathryn's hands groped her forehead. "Boys or girls?"

"Oh, sweetheart, don't you remember?" She shook her head. "Boys, and they're beautiful."

"Poor Lauren, four brothers. Do they have hair? Are they identical?"

"Don't tell me you're worried about Lauren. She may look like me, but she's you through and through. Four boys or a dozen, she'll hold her own. And let's see, they have strawberry blonde fuzz, like Josh's was, and yes, they're identical. If we don't put name bracelets on them, we won't know who's who. But have you thought about names? I can't believe we haven't talked about names."

"Alan and Christian, but you have to pick the middle names."

Jason grinned and kissed the tips of her fingers again. "What if Jaclyn has a boy, and she wants to name him Alan."

Biting her lip, Kathryn frowned. "Oh, I hadn't thought about that. What if Christian—?"

"Christian will be tickled pink," Jason interjected.

"Is that supposed to be funny?"

Jason laughed. "Shall I ask the nurse to bring our sons to meet their mother?" Seeing more tears seep from Kathryn's eyes, he pulled her to him.

Her arms slipped around his neck. "Two at a time. I didn't know if I could pull it off."

Feeling the beat of his heart begin to race, Jason drew away, and studied her face. "Kathryn, do you have any idea how much I love you, how much I need you? This production line has to stop. Henry had to do a cesarean section. The first baby was breech, and he couldn't turn him."

"Please get our sons, I need to hold them."

Jason coaxed a ringlet from her forehead and touched his lips to hers. "Sweetheart, we have all of the time in the world." But seeing the distress in her eyes, he said, "I'll be right back."

"What time is it?"

He looked at his watch. "Almost midnight." He started toward the door and stopped as fear washed over him.

"Jason, Jason," Kathryn gasped.

He rushed to her side. "What is it? Oh, god," he cried, feeling for the pulse in her throat. "Oh, God, please, God!"

How strange it was to hear Jason from some distant place, his voice rippling the water's smooth surface, echoing, eddying, flowing. What was Jason doing in a rain barrel? She'd always loved them, dark and deep and mysterious. Try as she might, she couldn't focus on Jason's face. Loving him so, she tried to reach out to touch him, but her arms were too heavy, yet she was floating, a feather drifting away. Lights, like shooting stars, flew through her brain. Her hands fell limply to her sides, her lips parted, her eyes closed.

Bolting out of the room, Jason spotted Dr. Shafner coming toward him. "Henry, it's Kathryn! Something's happened to her!"

The doctor raced into the room. With one hand, he slapped the panic button above the bed and pressed the stethoscope to Kathryn's chest with the other. Within seconds, a nurse charged into the room, pulling a crash cart behind her.

"Is she breathing?" Jason burst into tears. "Henry!"

"You're in the way!"

"Don't make me leave her," he sobbed.

293

Dr. Shafner's gaze snapped to the nurse. He jerked his head toward Jason as he bent over Kathryn, lifting her eyelids, pressing the stethoscope to her chest again.

The nurse took Jason's arm and led him from the room.

"Get your hands off me," he shouted, shoving her away.

Jaclyn rushed to him. "What's wrong?"

"God, please don't take her away from me," Jason cried.

Disinfectant and talcum powder. Suddenly, Jason was aware of the weird concoction of scents surrounding him. The nursery was utterly silent, the babies slept. He sat in a rocking chair, holding his sons, staring at nothing, moving the chair with the touch of one foot to the floor.

He hadn't prayed since the war. Why should God listen to him now? His thoughts slipped back to Yuma, to the first time he'd seen Kathryn. She'd come through the door at his radio station, twenty-two years old, with impish eyes, and a mischievous smile. He didn't believe in love at first sight, but there it was. His gaze swung to the door as Dr. Shafner pressed through it.

"We're not out of the woods yet, but God willing Kathryn will recover. She had an aneurysm in her brain. Dr. Kirk thought he'd dealt with it once and for all, some years ago. It's a good thing you were with her. If she'd been alone—"

Jason burst into tears and clutched his tiny sons closer to his chest.

"Now, Jason, pull yourself together. I want to speak frankly with you. Andrew thinks carrying the twins created additional pressure on the blood vessel that ruptured."

"Oh god, Henry, oh god, god."

"Yes, I know."

"Brain damage?" Jason whispered.

"Without tests, Kirk can't be sure, but when I left the ICU, Kathryn was asking for you, asking about the children. She seemed perfectly lucid to me."

"Henry, I've been in the darkest place. Trust me, there won't be more children."

"Let me be the first to applaud that decision. Whether Kathryn will agree is another matter," Dr. Shafner said, smiling wryly.

"She'll agree or the next baby will be heralded by a star in the East," Jason said. "Take one of my sons, would you?" He rose from the rocker. "Where is she? And don't tell me I can't see her or that she needs rest and quiet. That goes without saying." After laying the twins in their bassinets, Jason stood looking down at his sons. "Have you ever seen two more perfect faces? So like Kathryn's. Our first baby looked like her, too, a girl, too premature to survive. We've never gotten over it."

Nodding, Dr. Shafner patted Jason's shoulder. "By the way, Kathryn's determined to breast feed. It's out of the question, and you'll have to convince her of that."

Tears slid down Jason's cheeks.

"I won't let you see her until you've gotten yourself under control."

With a quick nod, Jason wiped his eyes. "Kathryn is the breath of life to me. I won't do anything to upset her."

# Chapter Fifty-eight

Sheffield stopped by the reception desk. "Good morning, Moira. Welcome back! We've missed you. And you look wonderful."

Moira beamed at the Attorney General. "I'm very happy to be back, Sir, and I can't tell you how much I appreciate everything you've done for me. Truly, your kindness and compassion have changed my life. Thank you, thank you, from the bottom of my heart."

"You're welcome." Sheffield leaned down and gave his secretary a hug. "Jaclyn asked me to give you that hug. Moira, you have no idea how much I've been looking forward to a cup of your marvelous coffee. Please tell me you've brewed a pot."

"I certainly have and I'll bring you a cup right away. Oh, Mr. Sheffield, I want you to know how thrilled I am that you and Jaclyn are married, and that you're going to have a child. Jaclyn is wonderful, but I don't have to tell you that."

"She's the best thing that has ever happened to me. I'm so blessed," Sheffield said. He went into his office and closed the door."

Minutes later, Moira rushed into his office. "Mr. Sheffield, I'm positive that the young man who called, the one who told you where to find Susan Walsh, is on the line.

I've started the tape recorder and Sam is tracing the call. Oh, enjoy your coffee," she said, hurriedly putting the mug down. "I'll put the call through," Moira said as she dashed back to her desk.

Sheffield let the phone ring twice before picking up the receiver. "This is Alan Sheffield."

"We haven't met in person, but I've talked to you before. I'm the guy who called you about Susan Walsh, and I'm calling to find out how she's doing."

"You're the young man who saved her life. She's doing very well. Actually she's living with my wife and me. Unfortunately, her parents were killed in a car accident, and the authorities in Iowa, where Susan is from, have been unable to locate any of the family's relatives. Susan doesn't remember ever meeting any relatives, either. Happily, we've been awarded custody of her, and we have petitioned the court to allow us to adopt her."

"Thank God. I've been worried. She was so severely injured, I didn't know if she'd make it."

"She spent a week or so in the hospital, but other than the scars that will never go away, she's in excellent health. We're hoping that she'll be able to attend school in the fall. Right now, she has a tutor. Tell me, since you have no culpability for the vicious attack on her, wouldn't you like to meet her, and us? You're a hero, and we're grateful to you."

"If only I could have helped the other victims. I just didn't know what was going on until it was too late."

After a long pause, Sheffield said, "Are you there?"

"Yes, but have you caught the monster that committed those murders and tortured Susan?"

"No, but we will. We know who he is and we know he's in Mexico. No matter where he is, we can and will protect you. Actually, you can live with us. Our motto is: 'the more the merrier'."

Sam opened the door and gave Sheffield a thumbs up. They had successfully traced the call.

"Mr. Sheffield, I'll have to think about it. I'm terrified of him and I always have been. He likes to hurt animals, people, too."

"Remember, once we arrest him and he goes on trial, you may be the only witness who can testify to his crimes. So, while you're thinking about whether or not to come forward, think about that."

"I will, I promise you. Goodbye."

Sheffield dropped the receiver and hurried to Sam's office. "Where is he?"

"He's calling from the office we bugged at Santayana's ranch."

"So he's the young man Jason told us about—the one that Santayana said was mentally challenged. I'm going to call Jason. He said the boy smiled at him when he was at the ranch."

"**L**et me go alone, Shef. I think in that moment when our eyes met, that boy and I connected. As I've told you before, I knew there was intelligence behind his somber smile. He reminded me of someone, but I've never been able to come up with who it is."

"Jace, what if he rabbits? He's scared, and I don't blame him. Only God knows what he's been through. I wonder where he came from and how long he's worked for Santayana."

"Well, Damien said he was a *wetback* that crossed the Santa Cruz River from Mexico. He didn't say how old 'Peter' was when he got to the ranch. Damien said he felt compassion for the boy. It went through my mind as I was leaving the ranch that the word *compassion* is the last word I'd use to describe Santayana."

"Well, I think the boy and I have developed a rapport, too, and I want to go with you, Jace."

"Okay, but I need to drive my Corvette. He'll remember it."

# Chapter Fifty-nine

**W**hen they arrived at the ranch, Jason parked the Corvette in front of the hacienda. He and Sheffield sat there for a minute before they got out and cautiously approached the front doors. Sheffield had positioned Sam and Rip at the tunnel's exit, just in case the boy decided to "rabbit," as he'd said.

"Jesus, Jace," Sheffield muttered. "That wreath on the door has been there since Christmas. The SOB celebrated the birth of Christ?"

Before they could access the door, the young man they were seeking opened it. He smiled at them. "What kept you? I thought you'd be here an hour ago. I would have come to you, but I didn't have a ride."

Jason and Sheffield looked at one another and burst out laughing. Jason stepped forward and threw his arms around Peter.

"Do you want to hug me, too, Mr. Sheffield?"

"You bet I do." Sheffield hugged the boy to his chest, then held him at arms length. "By the way, what is your last name?"

"I don't have one. Mr. Santayana said I waded across the river when I was three or four. It must've been a really dry year, or I would've drowned. I remember teaching myself to swim, and to read, when I was maybe six or seven. He said I wasn't an American citizen, so, if I left the ranch, I could be arrested and sent back to Mexico. Anyway, he didn't give me a last name. Do you want to give me one."

"Yes, I do. How about Sheffield?"

"Great, I accept," Peter said, beaming.

"Do you remember anything before you forged the river?' Jason said.

Peter laughed. "I don't remember doing that, but I have hazy recollections of grown-ups, but they didn't speak Spanish, some other language, but I don't think it was English, either. Maybe my mind made up a family, so I would have people that cared about me, instead of being an orphan."

"Trust me," Sheffield said, "you have a family that cares about you now."

"Two families, in fact," Jason said.

"Okay by me." Peter grinned as he held up a plastic bag. "I packed my stuff, but I'm worried about the horses. There's no one else to take care of 'em. All of the other hands are dead, but you know that."

"I'll send our foreman to retrieve them and take them to our place," Jason said. "We have a stable and there's plenty of room for them. How many do you have?"

"Twelve, but two of the mares will foal any day. Can you shelter and feed that many?"

"Absolutely!"

"Oh, you'd better take the wreath. It's gruesome, but it's evidence."

Sheffield scrutinized the decoration. "Oh, my God," he muttered.

Jason staggered back and turned away.

"I have a gunny sack you can put it in. Oh, and thank you so much for coming for me. I never want to see this ranch again."

"Neither do I," Sheffield said. "Let's get out of here."

# Chapter Sixty

"They have him," Sam shouted as he burst into Sheffield's office. "The Mexican authorities picked up Santayana a few hours ago."

Gripping the edge of his desk, Sheffield rose to his feet. "Where?"

"San Luis, in a bar."

"The documents are in order?"

"You bet. All we have to do is sign the extradition papers."

Sheffield's eyes bored into Sam's. "Where is he now?"

"En route. They're driving him to the point of entry at San Luis. We'll take him there."

"Well, let's go get him," Sheffield snapped. "Talk to Olsen, have him arrange for two helicopters, and tell Vashay to get his best men to go with us."

"Four should do it, Shef, two in each bird."

"How soon can we put it together?"

Sam glanced at his watch. "It's eleven hundred. I'll call the border patrol and tell them to expect us mid-afternoon, around fifteen hundred." He hesitated and studied the Attorney General's face. "Shef, you should sit this one out. Let me handle it."

"Why? He can't take a shot at me this time." Sheffield massaged the shoulder that still gave him trouble. Residual nerve damage the doctors said. If he used his right hand for any length of time, pain radiated down his right arm through the tips of his fingers.

When Sheffield graduated from law school, his parents gave him a gold fountain pen they could ill afford. Since then, he'd used it to put his thoughts on paper. He never picked it up without thinking about his mother and father and the many sacrifices they'd made for him. Initially, talking into a tape recorder had been difficult, but little by little, he was getting better at it. Still, while he dictated, the pen was in his hand, as if it had to be there for his thoughts to flow.

"That isn't the point, Boss. It's personal with you, and you need to keep some distance." Sam picked up the Meerschaum from the corner of Sheffield's desk and handed it to him. "Here, why don't you and your friend think it over?"

A rueful smile touched Sheffield's mouth. "Don't mistake this for a peace pipe," he said, tipping the Meerschaum in Sam's direction. "Oh, have the agents who are tailing Ricardo Montez pick him up."

Sam nodded and left the office.

The helicopters landed in a barren field adjacent to the shack that served as a checkpoint between Arizona and Mexico. A dust-covered van stopped a few feet short of the border. Four Mexican police officers, with Santayana in tow, got out and headed for the gatehouse. A beard covered the bottom half of the rancher's face, but his dark eyes narrowed when he spotted the FBI agents and the Attorney General's men.

Sam jumped from the cockpit with Rip Vashay right behind him. When he caught sight of Santayana, Erikson shoved his jacket aside, unsnapped his holster, and fingered his forty-five. "If he'd just make a run for it," Sam murmured to his team leader.

"It's not likely," Vashay said. "There must be a hundred pounds of chain on him."

Sam reached for a cigarette. "I'd like to string him up right here."

Rip Vashay studied his chief's face. "This is personal, isn't it?"

Dark eyes burning into Vashay's, Sam muttered, "If you knew everything I know, we'd have to flip a coin to decide who'd put a bullet between his eyes." He torched the cigarette. "Let's go get him."

With a steely grip on Sam's arm, Rip said, "Take care of the paperwork." He turned toward the helicopters. "Win, Ty, Ben." Vashay pointed to the gatehouse. The three agents shouldered their rifles and jogged the short distance to the shack.

"You're going to ride back in the other helicopter, Sam, and don't give me any shit about it. Then when we get back to Phoenix, we're going to talk. No way you're keeping me in the dark any longer."

"He's a war criminal," Sam said, blurting it out with a rush of air. "One of his victims is the Attorney General's wife."

"Jaclyn?" Vashay stared at Sam. "The prison camp in Poland?"

"Trepskýa. She was a child, eleven years old when Santayana began raping her. Think about it, Rip."

Looking over Vashay's shoulder, Sam focused on Santayana. "He may try to jump for it on the flight back to Phoenix. What do you think?"

Vashay jerked off his fatigue cap and raked his fingers through his curly dark hair glistening with sweat. Turning away, he stared at the ground. It was minutes before he turned to face Sam again. "I'll have to think about it."

"Listen, Rip, we'll take him in Olsen's helicopter, just the two of us."

"Give me some time!"

"What's to think about? He's a murderer many times over."

"Murder is murder, no matter who commits it. The law, Sam, remember the oath we took? It's important to me. I thought it was important to you."

"All you have to do is turn your head for a split second."

Vashay jammed the cap back on his head and strode to the three members of his team, who stood in a meager strip of shade near the shack. They pulled their handguns, rounded a corner of the building, and headed toward Santayana. Sam pulled the extradition papers from his pocket and followed them.

# Chapter Sixty-one

**O**n an isolated stretch of desert south of Phoenix, the grim cement block walls of the State prison blistered in the sun. There wasn't a tree or shrub in sight. Even cactus seemed loath to grow there. Sheffield pressed through the revolving door and glanced around. The warden was supposed to meet him in the waiting room. Turning full circle, he spotted Sam in an interrogation room.

"To hell with the warden," he murmured to himself as he flashed his badge. The guard, who stood at attention beside the door to the prison's intersanctum, saluted, then motioned Sheffield through.

"May I help you?" The young, raven-haired receptionist lifted her fingers from the typewriter. Her eyes widened. "Oh, Mr. Sheffield. The warden should be—"

The Attorney General pointed to the interrogation room. "That's where I'll be."

"But, sir—"

Sheffield pressed the palm of his hand toward her. "It's all right." His emerald green eyes were as hard as the gems themselves. The young woman shrugged and began typing again.

Sam sat at the conference table. Two Federal agents Sheffield didn't recognize sat on either side of him. As he looked from face to face, Sheffield was stunned to see Jason's attorney and close friend, Raul Rodriguez, leaning toward Damien Santayana. Sheffield hadn't seen the attorney for years, not since he'd resigned his job as the district attorney for Yuma County. As far as he knew, Raul was still practicing law in Yuma. They'd been colleagues. Jason and Raul had been close friends.

Smiling broadly, Raul thrust his hand toward the Attorney General. "It's been a long time, Shef." The years had been kind to Raul, Sheffield decided. He was easy to look at, over six feet tall, raw-boned, without an ounce of fat. His skin was a mellow shade of bronze, his dark eyes sizzled, his once black hair sprinkled with silver. A perfectly manicured mustache outlined his upper lip.

Sheffield grasped Raul's hand, then moved cold eyes from him to Santayana. "Don't tell me you've agreed to represent this piece of slime?"

The attorney's genial expression disappeared. He studied Sheffield's face. "Mr. Santayana has asked me to represent him," he said quietly.

Santayana brought his fingers together in front of his face. The chains shackling his wrists grated noisily along the edge of the conference table. His fierce eyes didn't waver as they gazed into Sheffield's.

"Santayana didn't single you out by a throw of the dice," the Attorney General said nodding toward the prisoner.

"Regardless, it's appropriate for me to make that judgment."

Sam stood and drew Sheffield aside. "Before this goes any further, I need to talk to you, in private," he whispered to the Attorney General.

"Excuse us a minute," Sheffield said as he followed Sam into the hallway. "Raul Rodriguez. With all of the attorneys in this state, Santayana had to go after him."

"I was going to kill him, Shef. On the flight back, I was going to pitch his evil ass off the helicopter. If it weren't for Rip Vashay, he'd be dead."

"What?" Sheffield staggered under the weight of Sam's revelation.

"I hope you'll let me resign instead of firing me."

"Christ all mighty, Sam, what were you thinking?"

"Jaclyn." He shook his head. His gaze fell under Sheffield's intense scrutiny. "I was thinking about Jaclyn."

Sheffield frowned at his investigator. "Obviously, I know you better than you know yourself. You wouldn't have done it. You can't begin to imagine how many times I've dreamed of killing him."

Sheffield gripped his chief investigator's arm. "I'm not going to fire you. I'm not going to let you resign. After we're done here." He nodded toward the interrogation room. "We'll go to my place and sort this out. What about Rip?"

"I ordered him to write the report. He just shook his head and walked away shouting, 'After what you told me, I came close to doing him myself, with or without your help'."

"You told him about Jaclyn?"

"What else?"

Sheffield nodded slowly. He took Sam's arm and propelled him to the door of the interrogation room. "If Raul takes Santayana's case, he'll do whatever it takes to get his client off. Trust me, Jason will go ballistic when he hears about this."

# Chapter Sixty-two

**D**imly lit, the Flame, touted as the classiest restaurant in downtown Phoenix, had the usual crowd of important people—as well as the pretenders that struggled from obscurity to lofty heights. To accomplish their goals, it was essential for them to be in the company of, or in the same room with, the elegant elite—smartly dressed and coifed, tanned, and polished. Some were famous—movie stars, who frequented the desert for rest, relaxation, and an occasional stint with off-season theatre productions, national and international businessmen, baseball players on hand for spring training. Even the infamous, crime bosses, who were gaining a toehold in the Phoenix business and industry, dined at The Flame. To a man or woman, they seemed nonchalant about ordering from a menu that didn't list its prices.

Full length behind the bar was a huge glass terrarium replete with miniature trees, grasses and flowering creepers, waterfalls, and streams. A variety of exotic birds strutted, perched on limbs, or dipped their beaks into the cascading waters. Other creatures—harmless snakes, frogs and toads, and lizards indigenous to Arizona scurried across moss-covered boulders, hid in the ground covers, or swam in the pools. Waiters, with flaming entrees, appeared to move at an unhurried pace, yet the service at The Flame was without equal.

"Help me to understand, Raul. After everything you've heard about Santayana, how can you consider defending him?"

The attorney shrugged. "Would you believe money?"

"No."

"Two million, Jace, up front."

"Turn your back on him, and I'll give you whatever it takes."

"It amazes me that you and Sheffield, the Attorney General, mind you, don't believe in due process. Surely you know me well enough—"

"To know that money isn't the object."

"That's right. It's a high profile case, and Yuma, being what it is, there are few legal challenges." He laughed. "And without you and Shef to stir things up, it's deadly dull."

"You'll lose."

"Maybe so, but regardless of what Santayana has been accused of doing, under the law—"

"Don't spout legalese bullshit to me. For starters, when Sheffield's wife was a child, he raped and tortured her—"

"Allegedly, Jace. See if you can add that word to your vocabulary. Besides, he isn't charged with the war crimes you *allege* he committed."

"So that's it, you're going to defend that monster."

"Yes."

Jason threw the napkin on his plate and stood. "Then we have nothing more to say to one another."

"Except this, Jace. Tell Shef, if everyone in Phoenix is as prejudiced against Santayana as you two are, and if it becomes clear that selecting an impartial jury will be impossible, I'll ask the judge for a change of venue."

"Tell him yourself, Counselor," Jason spat through gritted teeth. "I'm not your carrier pigeon." Heads turned as he stormed out of the restaurant.

# Chapter Sixty-three

"**S**hef, Warden Miller here. Damien Santayana insists upon talking to you, face to face, one on one. I know how irregular this is, but I had to pass it along to you."

"I won't talk to him alone, Charley. The trial is set to begin—" Sheffield glanced at his calendar. "One week from today. I will *not* let him compromise it. I'll agree to see him, if Sam Erikson, my chief investigator, is with me. Otherwise, no deal. And Charley, tell Santayana our conversation will be taped."

"Okay, Shef, I'll let him know, and if he won't agree to those terms, I'll call you back. Otherwise, would two o'clock work for you?"

"Two it is." Sheffield hung up and tapped the button on the intercom. "Moira, is Sam Erikson in the building?"

"He's walking past my desk as we speak."

"Please ask him to step into my office."

Sam knocked once and opened the door. "You wanted to see me?"

"I just had a call from Charley Miller. Santayana wants to talk to me. Alone. Of course, I wouldn't agree to that. How's your afternoon shaping up?"

"Nothing I can't reschedule."

"Good, the meeting's at two. Have you had lunch?"

"No, Moira caught me as I was heading for the elevator."

"Let's leave now and grab a bite on the way."

"I'll get the car and meet you in front of the building. In five?"

"Fine." As the door closed behind Sam, the AG shrugged into his jacket. "What card is Santayana trying to play now?" he muttered to himself.

As he was walking past Moira's desk to the elevator, she said, "Wait, Mr. Sheffield, Jaclyn is on the line. She urgently needs to talk to you, and I'm quoting."

Sheffield raced back to his office and grabbed the phone. "Jaclyn, are you all right."

"I've never been better. Truly, I'm wonderful, excited. I've had a few twinges, so—"

"Oh, my God, it'll take me at least twenty minutes to get home."

"No, no, don't come here. I'm going to drive to St. Vincent's. Susan and Peter are going with me. Dr. Shafner is expecting me, and he's contacted Dr. Jenner," she said, referring to the surgeon who would perform the Caesarean section. "Everything is under control. We'll meet you there."

"I'm leaving right now."

Jaclyn laughed. "Is that panic I hear in your voice?"

"I love you with all my heart, but puleeze stop talking, and get going."

"Alan, I can't wait to meet our baby."

"Me, too. I'm hanging up now. Drive carefully!"

Sheffield hurried to Moira's desk. "Jaclyn has gone into labor. Please call Warden Miller, tell him that I can't meet with Damien Santayana, not now, not ever. I'll clue Sam in. He's probably wondering what's keeping me."

"Oh, Mr. Sheffield, will you keep me posted?"

"Yes, absolutely."

Traffic-wise, everything had conspired against him as he drove to St. Vincent's: A minor accident held him up for twenty minutes. The lights were red at most of the intersections. It even took ten minutes to find a parking space once he got to the hospital.

Sheffield glanced around anxiously as he waited his turn at the information desk.

The young, smiling clerk asked, "May I help you?"

"Yes, thank you. I'm Alan Sheffield, Miss Williams," he said lifting her name from the tag pinned to her uniform. "My wife, Jaclyn Sheffield is in labor, and Dr. Jenner is going to perform a Caesarean Section. Our family physician is Henry Shafner. I'd like to know when she's scheduled for surgery. For obvious reasons, I want to be with her."

"Of course, let me check." She picked up the phone, dialed a number and waited. "Hi, could you update me on Mrs. Sheffield's condition, also what time she's scheduled for surgery. I'll hold," she said.

Sheffield blew out a breath, glanced at his watch, and paced back and forth.

"Thanks, I'll let her husband know."

"Mr. Sheffield, your wife is in surgery now. Take the elevator to the third floor. When you get off the lift, turn left and check in with the nurse at the desk.

"Our teenage son and daughter were with her."

She smiled. "They're probably in the waiting room on three."

"Thank you," Sheffield raced to the elevator and pressed the lighted arrow. "Come on, come on," he murmured until the doors opened.

Peter breathed a sigh of relief when he saw Sheffield. "Thank goodness you're here," he said. "We were getting worried."

Sheffield hugged them. "Do we know anything more than that Mom is in surgery?"

"We know nothing, Dad," Susan said. Mom and Dad sounded wonderful to Sheffield. "We were hoping you could ask the nurse at the desk."

Sheffield smiled. "Tag along with me."

As they turned, the big double doors at the end of the hall opened and Dr. Shafner came through them. When he saw Sheffield, he beamed.

"Congratulations, Shef, you have a beautiful baby girl. And it looks like you have two built-in baby sitters."

"How is Jaclyn?

"Amazing, truly amazing. She wanted a spinal so she'd be awake and have a front row seat when the baby was born. She's a real champ!"

"Can we see her and the baby?" Peter asked

Henry Shafner winked at Sheffield. "I think that can be arranged. Follow me."

Sheffield rushed to the bed and took Jaclyn in his arms. "Good job, Mommy. She looks just like you, but with blonde hair even lighter than mine."

"I'm so happy." Jaclyn said as tears overflowed her eyes and streamed down her face.

"Weeping on such a joyful occasion?"

"Tears of happiness" Jaclyn said, "Where are Susan and Peter?"

"They're at the nursery window, watching their baby sister sleep. They spotted her right away. By the way, did we decide on a girl's name?"

"We both like Amy and Megan. It will take a few days to see which one fits our little angel," Jaclyn said. "We may even come up with a name we like better."

Dr. Shafner came into the room. "I hate to kick you out, Shef, but Jaclyn needs to rest. We also need to get her on her feet for a few minutes so clots don't form. Unfortunately, it would be better if we could keep her flat on her back for a few days, because the spinal may have a side effect, namely headaches. Jaclyn, since you won't be nursing, if you need it, we can give you something for pain."

"Okay, Henry, when can I come back?" Sheffield said.

"How about dinner time around six o'clock?"

"Would it be okay if Susan and Peter see their Mom before we go?"

"For fifteen minutes or less."

"I'll tell them on my way out." He blew a kiss to Jaclyn and backed through the door.

# Chapter Sixty-four

## September, 1962

Christian propelled himself out of the pool, toweling off as he joined the others: Jason and Kathryn, their three older children—Anthony, Josh, and Lauren—along with Jason's parents, Andre and Camille, and Christian's parents, Carl and Sarah. They were on the patio, relaxing around a glass-topped table, grateful for the shade cast by the huge umbrella.

Kathryn peered at the twins through the netting covering their playpen. Naming them had been a challenge, because everyone wanted a say in the matter. Finally, Christopher and Paul were the hands-down favorites. Jason had been right. The boys still wore identification bracelets. Without them, only Kathryn could tell the twins apart.

"It looks to me as though you're in great shape, Christian," Jason said. "Are you anxious to get back to work?"

"Am I ever."

Jason grinned. "Surely not as anxious as I am to have you back."

Cyrus Tidwell strode to Jason and plugged the phone into the receptacle on the deck. "Mr. Sheffield for you, Sir."

"Thanks, Cy. Hi, Shef, what's up?"

"Last night, Damien Santayana hanged himself in his cell. He used a bed sheet, attached it to the light fixture, tied it around his neck, and stepped off his cot. He left a letter for me, and I desperately need your advice. Jaclyn doesn't know anything about this, but the letter has everything to do with her. Would it be okay if I grabbed her and the kids and we dropped by for a visit?"

"We'd love to see you, Shef. Plan to stay for dinner, and tell Susan and Peter to bring their swimsuits. Sejii is welcome, too, of course."

He replaced the receiver. "Shef and Jaclyn, and their family are joining us for dinner. I'll let Cy know."

"Wonderful," Kathryn said. "Jaclyn has been staying close to home, and I've really missed her." Kathryn cocked her head as she gazed at her husband. "What's going on, Jason? You have *that* look."

He laughed. "What look would that be?"

"Hmmm, the Hardy Boys are up to something look."

"In due time, Shef will share some information with all of us."

"It's serious, then."

"Yes, it is."

# Chapter Sixty-five

In the den, Jason and Sheffield sat in easy chairs in front of the floor-to-ceiling windows. In the distance, the gardener was mowing the last tee of the Borseau's three-hole golf course. The muffled sound filtered into the room.

Jason stood, handed Santayana's letter back to Sheffield, and strode to the bar. "Well, I sure could use a drink. How about you?"

"A tall scotch and soda."

"Shef, did you know that Jaclyn gave birth to a son while she was in the camp?"

Sheffield shook his head. "No, I just knew pieces of the puzzle were missing. I suspected that something so traumatic, so horrifying had happened to her that she couldn't bear to share it, not even with me. My god, Jace, she was a mere child herself."

Jason handed Sheffield's cocktail to him, and returned to his chair. "I think you told me that Jaclyn was incarcerated when she was eleven and escaped when she was fourteen."

"Right."

"According to his letter, Santayana told her the baby died." Jason shook his head. "It doesn't surprise me that Damien couldn't allow *his* flesh and blood, *his* son, to be used for experiments or outright murdered, as the other babies born at the camp were. He describes how he spirited the boy away, and left him with a family, not far from the camp. Of course, he doesn't say who they were."

"It could be a lie," Sheffield said.

"Yes, if his primary motive is to make Jaclyn suffer, and you. He wants you to tell her that she may have a son out there somewhere, but you have no clue where."

"What he doesn't mention is that they made a bargain she didn't keep. He promised Jaclyn that he'd never kill another innocent person, if she would never leave him."

"How naïve of him to think she could keep such a promise. Shef, the prostitute murders began about a year and a half ago. Are we to assume that Santayana hadn't killed from the time he left Trepskýa, until then? Once serial killers start killing, they usually don't stop. Although, apparently, he did. Maybe, just maybe, he saw Jaclyn somewhere, recognized her, and it pushed him over the edge. The other possibility is that he *has* been killing all these years. How difficult would it be to cross the Santa Cruz and commit the foul deeds in Mexico?" Jason shrugged. "I guess it doesn't matter now that he'll never kill again."

"Jace, he really was a monster. I mean, decorating that Christmas wreath with the body parts he took from those young girls, spraying it with gold leaf, adding holly berries and displaying it on the hacienda's front door. My god, I've never seen anything like it."

"Neither have I. And, how *thoughtful* of him to finger his co-conspirators, spelling out their specific involvement— drugs, prostitution, money laundering, murder, and God knows what else the FBI will uncover. They'll be busy for months rounding up that unholy gang, to say nothing about the time they'll spend prosecuting them. Years, probably."

"I forgot to bring the map he drew that pinpoints where he buried Mutt and Jeff, the names Christian gave to the two men who assaulted him. When Christian was well enough to describe them, Santayana took care of those loose ends. We shot six of Santayana's hired guns. He executed the rest."

"Thank God, he didn't kill Peter," Jason said.

Sheffield smiled. "He probably couldn't find him. There are plenty of hidey-holes on that ranch, in the stable, the barns, the mines, or the vast acreage surrounding them."

"Have you decided to tell Jaclyn about her son?" Jason asked.

"No, you'll have to help me make that decision," Sheffield said.

"Both of us should sleep on that, if we're able to sleep." Jason drank the last of his brandy, and went to the bar. "The very first thing we need to do, before it leaks to the press, is to tell our families about Damien's suicide. Like every other station in Arizona, I'm sure, by now, KSOL has been tipped off. I'm going to contact our news director to see what they've heard, if anything. They won't run the story without my approval."

Sheffield rose, joined Jason at the bar, and set his glass down. "Right now, we need to join the others. I'm sure everyone's wondering what we're doing in here."

"After I got your call, Kathryn said I had *that look.* She knew something was up."

# Chapter Sixty-six

**A**s the sun was setting, a rainbow of brilliant colors streaked across the horizon. A hefty breeze kicked in, rippling the water in the pool and cooling the air. Jason had surprised the children with a floating basketball hoop. He'd tethered it to a ring at the deep end of the pool. The children had chosen sides and were playing their version of the game. Anthony and Josh made up one team. Peter and Susan, the other.

Lauren, wearing water wings, was sitting on the steps at the shallow end of the pool, kibitzing. She was learning to swim, but hadn't achieved her brothers' acumen for the sport.

"Josh missed the basket. Nanner, nanner, nanner." she yelled in a sing-song voice.

"Lauren, that isn't kind. Josh is younger than the other players," Kathryn said as she slathered sunscreen on her skin.

Lauren rolled her eyes. "I'm sorry, Josh."

"Good girl, that's much better. Daddy and Mr. Sheffield have asked the grown-ups to have a chat with them in the den."

"Can I come with you?"

"No, but you'll be happy to know that Nana is going to join you on the patio."

"Where's Granddad?"

"He's in the nursery, taking care of the twins, and little Megan. And Lauren, either stay on the steps or get out of the pool."

"I'll get out and sit with Nana. Maybe we could have ice cream."

"I'll ask Cy to bring you some: Chocolate, strawberry, or vanilla?"

"Strawberry."

Kathryn smiled. "That's Nana's favorite, too."

"I know," Lauren said, pertly angling her chin.

"Have fun," Kathryn said as Jason's Mother came through the sliding glass doors.

"Lauren thought you and she should have strawberry ice cream. I'll ask Cy to bring it to you," Kathryn said.

"Goody, goody! I love strawberry ice cream," Camille said, clapping her hands.

"Thanks, Mother." Kathryn winked at her mother-in-law. "If you need me I'll be in the den."

**J**aclyn's eyes flew open. "Damien Santayana is dead? But, but . . . how? He's in prison, his trial begins next week."

Sheffield sat beside her on the sofa. He took her hands in his. "Damien Santayana, aka the Major, committed suicide. I don't think he liked the idea of being judged by his peers."

"It's over, it's truly over," Jaclyn said. "Thank God."

Kathryn burst through the door and rushed into the den. "Peter fell and . . .and . . ." She covered her face with her hands. "I was putting an ace bandage on his ankle. Oh, God, I need to sit down. Jason, I'm so dizzy. I must be dreaming. I mean, how could it be?"

"How could what be? Sweetheart, you're not making sense," Jason said as he hurried to her, and took her in his arms.

"Oh, dear, what happened to Peter's ankle?" Jaclyn exclaimed. "Is it broken or what? Where is he?"

"On the patio. His ankle is probably just sprained, but there's something you have to see."

"Like what?" Jaclyn said. "Did something bite him?"

"No! Jaclyn, he has what looks like a tattoo."

Jaclyn stared at her. "A tattoo? On his ankle? Oh, my god, on his ankle!" She backed away, turned, and raced out of the room.

Sheffield stared after her. "Kathryn, what's going on? Why are you and Jaclyn upset about a tattoo?"

"It's not a tattoo, Alan. It's a miracle." Tears flooded Kathryn's eyes and streamed down her cheeks. "It's a butterfly. A beautiful aqua blue and burgundy butterfly. Exactly like the one on Jaclyn's ankle, on Megan's ankle, and on Peter's ankle, too."

# *Epilogue*

"**P**eter, the first time I saw you, I knew you reminded me of someone. Do you remember my telling you that, Shef?"

"Yes, I remember."

"I just could *not* put it together," Jason said. "Of course, now that I know, it's so obvious."

"It's ironic," Sheffield said. "As evil as Damien was, he saved your life, Peter. Probably not for any altruistic reason."

"I was so naïve," Jaclyn said. "They told me my baby was still born, and I believed them."

"Well, here I am, Mother, alive and happy to be with you," Peter said.

"Jason, if it's okay with you, Susan and I are going to walk to the stables. I'd like to visit my old friends."

"Actually, that's a good idea. The horses we brought from the ranch are skittish. Two of the mares are going to foal any day now. I think it would be a good idea for you to be on hand for those blessed events. How about staying with us for a few days, Peter. You, too, Susan if you'd like to and your folks think it's okay."

"Of course she can stay," Sheffield said. "Susan grew up on a farm, so she can help you deliver the colts."

It was a beautiful evening for a stroll. The brick path to the stables was shaded by a bower of trees.

"I keep pinching myself, Susan. Surely I must be dreaming. We have families that love and support us. Do you feel that way, too?" Peter said.

"Yes, but it's different for me. I have a lot of guilt to live with."

"I have a hunch you're blaming yourself, at least in part, for things other people may have done to you."

"Peter, after all of the terrible things that have happened to you, you risked your life to save me. I'll never forget that as long as I live."

"Well, I certainly hope not," Peter said, laughing. "Come on, Susan, I'll race you to the stables."

"You're on, brother dear!"

# *About the Author*

**P**atricia Huff has always had a passion for reading mysteries, and now she writes them. Silent Sentinels is the sequel to her first novel: The Mourning Doves. She's already plotting her next novel in the Doves series.

Ms. Huff's career began in radio. After a brief stint in television, she accepted a public relations position at the Port of Stockton in California. The job included writing and editing a four-color bimonthly magazine distributed around the world. It literally put the Port on the international map. Ms. Huff also wrote speeches, editorials, newspaper articles, brochures, and articles for magazines such as the Journal of Commerce and Bulk Materials Handling and Shipping.

Year after year, the Stockton Port was the recipient of the American Association of Port Authorities' highest award of excellence for the promotional brochures Ms. Huff produced. She was also instrumental in the realization of two projects vital to the future viability of the Port.

Printed in the United States
By Bookmasters